PAROUSIA

PAROUSIA

GARY K. PRANGER

Pleasant W rd

A Division of WINEPRESS PUBLISHING

ISBN 1.4141.0041.8
Library of Congress Catalog Card Number: 2003112744

DEDICATION

I wish to acknowledge the many people who helped in the writing of this novel. This is unusual, I suppose, because fiction is mainly a work of the heart, whereas non-fiction is mainly a work of the mind. However, I need to honor those whom God has utilized to work on this heart over many years. Hence, this novel is dedicated to all the following: an electrician in Wheaton, Illinois, an aging group of InterVarsity pals, a host of students, faculty, friends, pastors, and fellow church members in Normal, Illinois, Chicago, Singapore, Beijing, Changchun, and in Tulsa— whether they ever have the opportunity to read these pages or not. Some of these patiently put up with me and read this story and gave me their comments and encouragement. A few have received the ultimate honor of having fictional characters modeled after them in this story.

Finally, this story is dedicated to my wife Michele, my daughter Leah, and my son Mark. They have put up with their own tribulation in allowing me to write this book. It is my prayer that their lives will be hidden always in Jesus Christ's abiding love—no matter what happens.

CONTENTS

PREFACE

This story is about the growing spiritual lives and adventures of four individuals and the issues that confront every young Christian. All true Christians face the antichrist or his spirit, whether they ever meet him in his most organized form at the end of the age or are simply seduced, deceived or confronted by him in the meantime.

This story is not intended to foretell the future. The author claims no prophetic gift. It is not speculation about the identity or coming of the antichrist, nor does the author claim to know what Jesus Christ's Second Coming or life afterward will be like. This is simply the author's love letter to Jesus Christ and it is meant to honor all those earnest believers who have had to suffer persecution and/or their "tribulation" in this world, either in the past or in the present without ever seeing the Rapture. This story utilizes an historical post-tribulation view of Scripture and the Lord's

Second Coming for several reasons. First, the author believes this line of interpretation. Secondly, in order to let the Hero of all time rescue those who love Him more than their lives in this story. And lastly, the tensions of a second coming story line were utilized because I am simply not sufficiently gifted to think of a better plot. This is the plot that is inherent in all of history and the Bible.

The title, *Parousia*, from the New Testament, means *His coming, His presence* or *His arrival* and was used in the Hellenistic Greek to designate the visit of a ruler. "The same Jesus Christ who ascended into heaven will once again visit the earth in his personal presence at the end of the age in power and glory to destroy antichrist and evil, to raise the righteous dead and to gather the redeemed" (Acts 1:11; Matthew 24, 2 Thessalonians 2, 1 Corinthians 15:23). Christ's return, or parousia, is usually associated with two other words and so will also be an *apokalypsis*, an unveiling or disclosure of His power and glory (1 Corinthians 1:7; 2 Thessalonians 1:7; 1 Peter 1:7, 13). *Epiphaneia* means His appearing and the visibility of His return (2 Thessalonians 2:8; 1 Timothy 6:14; 2 Timothy 4:1, 8; Titus 2:13).*

---

* J. D. Douglas, Editor, *The New Bible Dictionary* (Grand Rapids, Michigan: Wm B. Eerdmans Publishing Co. (1962) 1973), p. 387.

Chapter 1

ROSEDALE

Rosedale is a small middle-class and industrial suburb on the southern border of Chicago. It is only two-and-half square miles and it occupies nobody's thoughts except for those who live and work there. The town has never changed geographically, being bordered on three sides by other bigger suburbs and the river on the north. The river, a steel mill and two rail yards break up the pattern of rectangular blocks of neat rows of brick houses and apartment buildings. A railroad, the Illinois Northern, cuts across from north to south on a high, wide embankment. There are two commuter stations that serve the office workers as the I & N shuttles them to their jobs eighteen miles away in downtown Chicago.

There are little green parks on either side of the "I & N" hill as it is known. A small school, called Park School, is at the edge of the eastern side, almost up against the hill. On the main street are numerous stores and a library that used to be a grocery store. An older part of town exists in memories that once comprised an old city hall, brewery, and a theatre but these have long since been demolished. Only a bank and a tavern are there today.

Crime is not a major factor except when it boils over from Chicago or one of the larger suburbs. There are only three grade schools; high school students must be bused to the neighboring suburbs east and south.

The town has seen its share of changes, but its stability has contributed to the feeling of a "nothing special" place in the midst of more important places. The weatherman on television would never use Rosedale as part of his report. If anything great happened in Rosedale it has been forgotten. If anyone really important ever came out of it, few knew it. The feeling one gets when living there is that history is made somewhere else and nothing ever has or ever will happen in Rosedale except the everyday proceedings of life: the dog barking next door, the children playing, and people streaming to the train on cold mornings and returning in the evening rush hour. The evening news is ignored for the latest weather report and two-and-a-half centuries of reruns of *Leave it to Beaver*.

Kings and presidents frequently visit Chicago, but never Rosedale. It seems safe and snug from dangerous or unpleasant matters. Inflation and unemployment have had effects on the populace, but nobody knows the serious effects of broken homes, divorces, or suicides except by some grapevine over the backyard fence. One only sees these problems somewhere else. Grumbles and complaints are a way of life.

There are churches in Rosedale, but unless one is a devout Christian it is hard to ever dream of religion really affecting life. Just as politics, war, terrorism, crime, and poverty exist somewhere else, so too is God above and beyond the reach or desirability of the people. Even the Christian tends toward a serene complacency. Church and Sunday school are well attended but are anachronistic and remembered only for unpleasant feelings and abject daydreaming. At the time of this story there is an unprecedented revival and persecution that is taking place in many nations and in remote corners of the world, but few people including Christians in this nation had any organized understanding or knowledge of it. There were no newspapers anymore and even if there had been they would have said nothing about it. Magazines and books that helped one to think were becoming relics or relegated to edited and manipulated versions on the computer. Life was becoming simpler and most people in Rosedale liked that.

To most citizens of Rosedale things really do not change. The humdrum of life seems to drag out and deflate all of the devout and noble beliefs and desires. Adventure is associated with movie micro-discs, computer games, and the yearly family vacation. Few understood that this was the last oasis of freedom. Most believed that this kind of life would go on just as it had and would never stop.

As in average lower middle class suburbs, the more successful the bread winner becomes, the higher the promotion, the more a temptation it is to move to the higher class suburbs or into the very heart of the city. It is some day in the future. The more things change, the more they stay the same.

Chapter 2

. . . .

A NORMAL DAY

Mark awoke from a deep, dreamless sleep. Pushing off the covers, he stretched until he felt his body would break. Bright sunlight made a stream through a slit in the curtains onto his face, blinding him for an instant. He stretched again, yawned, and sat up rubbing the sleep from his eyes. While he cupped his face in his hands, a thin naked arm clasped him around the neck in a tight embrace. He whirled around and began wrestling fiercely on the bed. Tumbling onto the floor, his attacker pursued him, jumping down on him.

"Ow, not so rough," yelled Mark.

The commotion stopped for a moment, then with renewed struggling, prolonged giggling, he pinned his adversary.

"Breakfast is ready dumb-dumb and you're late," said his sister, muffled below him.

Mark released Joanne and she left the room as stealthily as she had come. Sitting on the floor for some time unperturbed by his sister's actions or words, he thought about how she had made a morning ritual out of waking him with a wrestling and tickling match. She did it without fail ever since he started high school. Only on Saturdays did she not dare come in as she did not want to incur his wrath for not letting him sleep late. Occasionally, he became angry or irritated by her constant presence especially when he was preoccupied with problems. His sister's presence usually made him forget worries and made the drudgery of getting ready for school more pleasant.

"Mark, are you up? Breakfast is on the table!" sang the melodious voice of mother.

"Yes, I'm up!" he shouted. Slowly he got up off the floor, changed, and walked a few steps to the bathroom. He knocked persistently on the door. "Please be done in there," he yelled. The door opened slightly and he walked right in. He stood before the sink and began wiping the moisture on the mirror off with his hand, ignoring Dianne, his other sister and Joanne's identical twin. She was in her bathrobe, drying and combing her hair out after her shower. He washed his face with cold water to awaken himself further and picked up the razor his father had just given him for his seventeenth birthday, shook the can of lather and let a small amount onto his hand, dabbing it gently on his chin and cheeks. He really had almost nothing to shave.

"Don't cut yourself—ugly!" snipped Dianne as she hung up her towel to leave.

As soon as she left he flexed his muscles in the mirror and admired himself. At breakfast mother yelled at Joanne for leaving her dirty clothes of the day before strewn about her room, made sure Dianne did not forget to pack her gym suit and interrogated Mark about the homework he was up late trying to finish the night before. Mark assured her that advanced algebra was getting easier.

Dianne gave him a curious glance from across the table, her eyes penetrating his mind, and the ends of her mouth curved up in a slight smile. Mark felt her stare but ignored it. Secretly he had been getting up courage to tell his parents he might have to drop it since Dianne actually did the homework. This being the early weeks of school, he could still do so and pick up another class. Physics was another thorn in his side. If only he could have all history and English; he was good at those subjects. He made up his mind that today he would talk to his counselor and if all went well, to his parents this very night. He hated to have heavy things on his heart that made a lot of fuss and bother and hoped to have the whole situation cleared up quickly. Mother doled out three vitamins and each took them and drank their juice.

Mother kissed the three on the cheek as she always did while they filed out the door. The three of them walked down their front stairs and then to the right for half a block and then turned left at Miller's for a block to the familiar mailbox that seemed to have always marked the corner of 142nd and Wabash. It was only four blocks from there to the tiny Park School where all three had served their kindergarten through their third grade years. Mark remembered it best for those sleepy late afternoon hours when the teacher let the children rest their heads on their desks until the bell. The trains would rattle by one after another and he was always wondering where they came from and where they were going.

The mailbox was where the three parted company. The two girls walked another eight blocks to Roosevelt School. They could take the bus if they wanted, but they loved to walk instead. In the eighth grade, they were pretty for their age when most kids become gangly and grow in all sorts of ways. The twins had a delicate feminine appearance and yet they possessed a wildness that expressed itself in their interest in boyish physical activities. Climbing trees, wrestling, playing soccer and basketball had given them slim wiry forms. All of this seemed to enhance their beauty instead of detracting from it. To the person outside the family they were identical, without flaw, and had the same long golden brown hair that was parted down the middle. They had the same green eyes and features as their father. Father and Mother needed tags for the early months of their lives, but Mark was rarely fooled, even from the beginning. Mark enjoyed his family and sisters and loved them very much. He found it surprising that his sisters liked him even though all three had very different personalities.

Mark was not tall or short, fat or skinny and in every aspect, average, with his mother's brown eyes and brown hair, average grades and silent, sometimes slow, personality. Having been born in the summer he was always the youngest in his class.

Dianne had a cool, silent, and calculating mind that made her snappish and cold at times. Her genius for mathematics was recognized very early. Her aptitude went far beyond anyone else in her junior high or the neighboring high schools and she was featured in educational news and awards events. Early on her parents and teachers were slow in realizing her gifted nature but when they did they encouraged her to go to different schools. She received mail from every college and university. However, she was reluctant to leave her friends. She could play the piano expertly and do almost everything that required a high technical ability and learned at a phenomenal speed. All this embarrassed and made Mark jealous.

Practical jokes were a favorite pass time and kept the whole family on the alert. Mark was a most amusing target and the least vengeful. He found his bed short sheeted, crackers at the foot of his bed, his room re-arranged, or toads in his boots. Joanne, Dianne, and sometimes Mother teamed up to pull some trick on Father and Mark and the latter two then devised a scheme in revenge. Mark was the big brother, but Dianne was really like a big sister and Joanne like the youngest of both.

Dianne became an embarrassment to her father who sometimes could not comprehend his daughter's fantastic abilities, especially when she corrected him when he was trying his hardest to help Mark out on a math problem. Despite this she remained humble and rarely used her gifts as a way to be overbearing. Papa had to make sure he balanced his love for both daughters equally.

Joanne tended to be more like her mother, emotional and a talker. Her abilities were more average except when it came to sports. She took them very seriously and the more physical the better. She was extremely good with her hands, learning to sew and knit easily. Where Dianne tended to be silent and a careful listener, Joanne asked about everything but often missed the point of an answer given in return. She had a sensitive heart and was easily hurt when truly offended. Like Mark she became jealous of Dianne's extraordinary abilities but really did not know why. She hated math and had no interest in the piano.

The twins had become far more popular among their peers and teachers than Mark had ever been among his. Despite the differences the three siblings had a love for each other and their parents that went farther than most families. Yet it was hard for all of them to express it.

Mark watched them go for almost a minute then he turned and was greeted by the gruff presence of Andrew, a teenager who loved to antagonize others into quarrels and arguments.

"Still babysitting your sisters?" he asked sarcastically as he stared up and down at the two figures walking in the distance and then at Mark's face. He gave a few sharp swear words as an emphasis and then asked, "When are you gonna stop walking with them?"

Andrew knew this was a tender spot for Mark and was surprised at this silence. Andy was much heavier and a bit taller than Mark and liked to use his size in his bullying.

"Come on Andy let's go," said Mark softly.

"What do you see in those stupid sisters, been sleeping with them or something?"

Mark would have taken a swing at him like he did in a similar incident in his freshman year, but now Mark knew Andy better. This was what he was looking for. That fight had ended in a draw with both suffering bloody noses and black eyes. Mark did not talk back, but remained silent.

Andy and Mark joined a group at the corner of 142nd and Indiana waiting for Thorngate bus number twelve. The group laughed and joked sometimes mildly, sometimes savagely, making lewd or sarcastic remarks at anyone who seemed a good target. Mark had grown used to all of this. His quiet nature made him a target only occasionally and he used his silence as a buffer or weapon that neutralized destructive jokes or slander. Those who tried to retort only made the insults worse and he tried to stay away from fights at all costs. He believed that if his family were ever attacked he would fight without thought, but this had never happened and he really never thought it would.

The group of bus riders was composed of other quiet "mind your own business" kids, as well as distinct groups that Mark identified simply as the rabble. One group was the "neo-greasers." They took their image from those who were teenagers over a hundred years ago with long, slicked-back oily hair and black leather jackets though they thought they were being original. They felt high school was a stage for their personal war against boredom or whatever issue was current fare to start a fight or cause a scene. They vied for their turf with *Goths* and *Wraiths*. Another group sported extremely long hair and fuzzy beards.

The bus traveled the two and a half miles to Thorngate High School. It was one of the largest and oldest in the area. Mark's father had gone to school here and his father before him. The electro buses lined up among many others along one side of the long yellow brick three-story building. It was a two-minute walk to his locker after he got through the metal detectors and computerized scanners.

The hustle and bustle of kids always seemed so disorganized. But once the bell rang at 7:55 the halls emptied out like the students were rats running into cracks at the fear of being caught in the light. With the crowds jostling and swirling, Mark made a sort of game out of getting to class without touching anyone. If he did, it was as if it had been the loss of a down and he would try again.

His first class was P.E. where he was a class leader in basketball. This was the one place where Mark came out of his shell. Mark had been proud of his making the third string as a guard last year considering the size of the school and the competition. He sat on the bench almost always and usually saw action in the waning minutes of a one-sided game. To his embarrassment the ones who would cheer the loudest at those moments would be his parents and sisters. He was forever proud of the fact that he scored the last basket that gave Thorngate a hundred points in their victory over its toughest rival. This year he would be the backup to the first string guards and he was looking forward to it. He went to class to clear himself and get a pass from Mr. Hendricks the coach, who was also his physics teacher. Hendricks knew immediately what Mark was after.

"Getting out of my class I'll bet."

"Yes, sir. It's just too much. I've tried hard but I can't even comprehend the first chapter," said Mark sadly.

"You don't have to explain—get out of here. Get something you can pass, I may need you this year," the coach replied, leaning heavily on Mark's shoulder and putting his arm tightly around him, bringing his face so close to his he could feel his breath. Mark smiled and quickly walked away, extremely happy at this last statement. The coach was very tall and muscular with graying silvery hair. He peered after Mark brightly as he said under his breath, "I wish you were like your smart sister."

Mark walked back through hall after hall of tiled surfaces. He approached a tall muscular kid sitting at a monitor's desk in the hall by the statue of Lincoln. His dour face turned into a smile on seeing Mark.

"Brogen, whatcha doin' outta class! Lemme see that pass." Jerome Gates, probably Mark's best friend in school, was also the current star of the basketball team. Mark enjoyed basking in his shadow of fame as the sleek six foot seven inch forward-center always gave his team much of the credit for his success.

Jerome booted Mark playfully in the seat of his pants and told him to move on. Mark moved on thinking about his jealousy of Jerome. This was one kid who had it all; he was extremely intelligent in his studies as well as a superb athlete. Like Mark, he came from a close-knit home with Christian parents who had become friends with the Brogen family. Jerome was an outspoken Christian who had influenced Mark in his decision to accept Christ into his life.

Mark was also jealous of his outgoing nature as he himself was reserved and felt embarrassed sometimes about his faith especially at school among *school people*. He hated crowds and in a way was glad that he was not in the limelight like Jerome. Except for his few neighborhood friends, he knew only those on the basketball team and three or four others in his classes and he was happy this way.

He did not like dating and was too embarrassed and shy to ask girls out. Except for practices and games he had very little social life outside of his family's friends. Many girls had shown an interest in him though they were too shy too. A pudgy school computer news editor once wrote him a love letter but he was not at all interested. At one time he had a crush on a pretty cheerleader in his history class and worked himself up to a nervous frazzle in order to ask her for a date over a period of months. At last he stammered and strained at her locker one day with his heart palpitating, but she said no. A strange sense of relief came as if a burden had been lifted from his shoulders. He really did not know what he would have done if she had said yes. Then he would have had to worry about a successful date; a movie, a place to eat, and then what? After that he made a personal vow that he would not ask any more girls for dates until someday in the future.

At the counselor's office Mark hesitated before he opened the door. He walked into a large tiled outer office with a secretary's desk to one side and another joining it at an angle where a student office girl was busy at a computer. Mark then confronted the secretary. In a low voice, Mark inquired about seeing his counselor, Mr. Drummond. Mrs. Winsley reminded him of a Sunday school teacher he had once. She had a hawkish nose and cool brown eyes. Her grayish brown hair was a perfect bowl and her lipstick was heavy and she wore a perfume that could be detected long after one was with her. She looked as if Mark had committed a horrible offense by interrupting her and asked him if he had an appointment.

"Ah, not really," he replied, feeling as if it would be better for him to turn into a puddle and be swept away.

"You should have an appointment! We are very busy people around here. This school is far too big for informality. What is your I.D. number and last name?"

She then punched a few keys on her computer in a way that seemed like it took some extra effort. As he stood facing her he could see her eyes narrow and widen and after some time she told Mark to take a seat. The room was empty and he immediately thought of how the situation was so absurd. No sooner had he sat down than the portly Mr. Drummond shuffled into the room with a cup of coffee in one hand and a small brief case in the other. Drummond took the situation in and motioned to Mark to follow him to his office. "Oh, how I wish I still had my morning newspaper," he said to anyone who could hear.

"Sit down, please. I'll only be a minute to get your file," he said. Mark saw his flat-screened computer with what used to be a morning paper but was now the morning report site. The last newspapers had just ceased operations the month before. Drummond punched a few keys and looked with the same narrowing and widening eyes like the secretary.

"Here is the Brogan file. Now let's see, wait one moment," said Drummond. He turned his chair and took a sip of coffee as he looked at his administrative computer board.

There was always a disconcerting period of silence at these times and Mark stared about the sterile room and at the artistic calendar on the wall, trying to escape the embarrassing silence. It was the same with the doctor and dentist. The silence was fairly tolerable when one was alone waiting for the doctor to come in, but it was worse when sitting with him in the same room. Suddenly Drummond swung around in his chair, sat back, stretching his arms high over his head and clasping his hands behind his head.

"What is it you want?"

"I . . . I would like to . . . transfer from f-f-f-physics and advanced algebra to some other classes, b-b-but I still want to be in the college preparatory curriculum," he said.

Moisture formed on his brow as he said this.

Sitting up with his arms on the desk, Drummond replied in an authoritarian way that revealed more of the desire to advise than to help. "Brogen, you came to me just in time for the change. But glancing over your file I remember telling you last year to get some vocational training. You'll never make it through college. Your abilities are in vocational work. Your aptitude test scores indicate this."

Mark remembered, and like the last time, this came as a blow to his hopes. He wanted so much to go to college. More nervous than ever he said, "but . . . I, well . . . I like history, sir, and I like to read history . . . and well I thought I could . . ."

"That is not going to help you at all in the future. The future is in technical, scientific, and mathematical fields. History and all that goes with it, philosophy, literature . . . and religion. They're just not important anymore. Even in the past those subjects were only for the unfit and lazy who wanted to play games. These are dying subjects and even history is a lot of made up nonsense. Like dinosaurs, they are dying out. There is no money there. Language is a tool and that is all it is. What other kids do you know who are really ever interested in history? Look at our department here. It has dwindled. All kids want today are interesting things to read; they want a good story and a safe future, not to dig around in some miserable past."

Mark did not look at Drummond as he gave his oration, but looked at his shoes and a slug hole in the front of his desk and wondered how it got there.

"In fact, I'm going to help you out. There is a new computer math class I would like you to take—and as I understand it, it doesn't take much effort at all."

Mark cringed inwardly but acquiesced because he wanted this to be settled. He nodded in agreement but did not say anything until Drummond got a form and started filling it out. He then argued in a deprecating manner for another history class. He already had a world history class. In the end, after conceding to Mark's interests, he put him in a world geography class because there were no other history classes.

"Will this hurt my college prep at all?"

"No, because the computer math will still give you four years of math and you are all set in the other requirements. But my advice would be to go to a good technical college and forget the old myth of a broad liberal education. It is being replaced by the needs of the future. History is bunk and whoever said that was right."

"Henry Ford," interjected Mark.

"Yes, that's right, but who really cares who said it? It's all just facts, names, dates, and prying into useless controversies. Nobody really knows what happened when or even why. The past, like the present, is relative. Well, I hope I've helped you."

Drummond tapped at some keys on his computer for some time. He looked at the date and said, "I can't believe how time flies." Then he produced a flat computerized screen with a document emboldened on it. It looked like a modern version of a slate and he gave Mark the computerized pen that would have been the chalk centuries earlier and he signed it. Mark then filled out a few computerized forms that appeared on the same screen thereafter. Then he inserted his I.D. card in a slot on the side.

"There, all verified. Ok, you're free to go Brogen," said Drummond as he ushered Mark out with a pat on the back. Then he added, "Tell your sister, Dianne, we're all behind her here. She is something else."

He was tremendously relieved as he left, but disturbed by all that Drummond had said. He vowed to himself that he would prove Drummond wrong and that he would go to college as his father and grandfather had before him and he would find out the truth about the past. He daydreamed of an awed Drummond when he came back to see him some day as a professor having written books about the truth and not the rubbish they made him read in his classes.

He woke to the realization that he still had to explain to his parents the change and to reconcile the lie he made to his mother about the easy time in algebra. But he pushed all this out of his mind and the rest of the day went smoothly.

No homework was assigned all day and he looked forward to practice. When it came he seemed to play better and felt more confident. As they worked on plays Mark went up the center of the lane challenging Jerome who lazily blocked his shot, slapping it away and being nearly knocked over by Mark's body.

"That would've been goal tending and a foul Gates. You're slow today," said the coach.

Gates gave Mark a sidelong glance and proceeded to turn on the finesse for the rest of the day. It was his habit to let up on Mark because they played alley ball together when their families got together or in their free time.

On the late school bus he thought about what he would say to his parents. His mind wandered as he gazed out the window as the bus approached the G&O overpass. He looked down at the long sleek boxcars and container cars in the dusk as the bus rattled over the long bridge. He noticed policemen searching the boxcars of one train. This did not seem strange as policemen often searched for vandals or bums. But what made the difference were the uniforms of a third group of policemen. Usually local police and railroad guards were the only two present. The third Mark had never seen before. What helped Mark to see this better was the long backup of traffic from the stop light at the bottom of the overpass that forced his bus to stop. He assumed they were state or county police, as he could not see them clearly in the dimming light of day. The third group of police seemed to not want the other police to see what was inside, but it was only for a moment and he could not be sure. There was probably a plausible explanation. Then as the bus started moving, Mark thought he saw people in those cars but because it was a momentary glimpse he dismissed it as imagination. He knew he had a vivid imagination. Besides, he had other thoughts which now drifted back into his head.

Chapter 3

FAMILY AND THE TRIANGLE

It was five thirty when he reached the front steps of his house. Few lights were on. The living room was dark and made eerie by the light of the television. Only the kitchen light was on and immediately the homey smells of food and home came to him as he closed the door and took off his shoes. Joanne was lying on the floor on her stomach, her arms and hands holding her head up as she watched the TV. Dianne sat in the corner in the old chair, legs scrunched up under her. One sock on, and one sock off, she watched the TV while picking a scab from her foot. His mother's image came between the light and dark living room.

"Sssshhhh, be quiet. Your father had a long and rough day."

"I'll say, he must have left home at 4:30," said Mark.

"Try four, dear, they had a deadline to meet. He only got home at five," she said as she mixed some batter in a bowl.

"Will he be eating supper?" Mark asked.

"Yes, though it'll be a little late. You do some algebra homework. Maybe your sister will help . . ."

"I don't have any homework tonight and besides, I have something to tell you when Dad gets up."

Mom hurried back into the kitchen. "Oh, those green peas, I forgot about a vegetable for tonight," she said as she went. "Joanne, it's your turn to set the table! Please do it at once." Her voice carried like a song in the air.

Dianne's eyes had moved from the TV screen to Mark's eyes and when he looked at her in that eerie light she frightened him.

Joanne rose without question as if she were a heavy sack lifting slowly. She hesitated as her show finished.

"Did you do it?" Dianne asked.

"Yeah."

"Boy, are you going to get the interrogation treatment tonight."

Dianne spoke these words as Mark lay down on the couch near to her and changed the channel.

"Yeah, I know. Don't rub it in," Mark said, as he tried to get absorbed in the sports report. Dianne inquired about his day and Mark told her of the class changes.

In a few minutes there were five assembled for dinner at the kitchen table. The dining room table was only used on Sundays and special occasions when guests came.

The old kitchen table was the real center of family life and business. The kitchen counters were lined with pots and dishes that mother had left for Dianne to do that night. The refrigerator was decorated to excess with notes and pictures. Father sat yawning at one end of the rectangular table which was full of plates, bottles, bowls, and food;

Mother sat at the other end, Mark on one side and the twins on the other. The kitchen light defused the light so evenly that if the cabinets, food, and people were not all there it would have been a dreary light. Instead it was a homey light to the inhabitants.

As in most lived-in homes, the occupants were oblivious to the smells and the look of things. There was a feeling present that it had always been this way even while day-by-day life was changing in natural ways; the kids getting bigger, the new brand of hot dog. The humanness—the family—made the atmosphere comfortable and livable. Mark had occasionally thought about what it would be like to live without these people around. They had always been here and it seemed inconceivable that this companionship and togetherness and this life would ever be threatened by anything except petty arguments and misunderstandings.

Dan Brogen sat at the head of the table, his eyes puffy with weariness and the remnants of a sinus cold from the late summer weather, his brown hair disheveled. He wore an old white T-shirt, old trousers which he always wore around the house, and the worn slippers Joanne had given him two years ago for Christmas. Dianne was the neatest, dressed with slacks, matching top and light blue socks. Gwen Brogen had her apron on over an old shirt and a pair of household slacks. Mark was still in his school clothes with his shoes off. Joanne wore a monogrammed T-shirt with an old pair of jeans with holes in the knees and was forever barefoot.

By habit all bowed their heads at an unspoken look from Father and then he prayed, "We praise You our Savior and

Lord for all Your love and Your saving grace. Thank You for our food and our lives, amen."

Dan Brogen worked for one of the last independent publishing houses that printed Bibles and Christian literature as well as textbooks for Christian schools and for libraries in the nation. His job as a supervisor crossed the lines of an editor and technical supervisor in the printing process.

He often worked late because of deadlines and business was booming lately. He took great interest in his job, not only as a printer but as an intense reader. His habitual reading had rubbed off on all of them, but especially Mark and Dianne. They took an interest in historical subjects, theology, and prophetic literature. Having gone to college and then seminary for a while, to get his family to be readers had been one of his family goals. However, Joanne, like her mother, read serious things only occasionally and enjoyed fiction. She would listen to discussions.

As soon as prayer was over and dinner began, Joanne shared her view of her new science teacher, Mr. Wilkie.

Then Dianne had the floor.

"Dad, I've been given permission or rather urged to attend classes at the University of Chicago," said Dianne looking into his eyes as she spoke and then away.

"Wow, that's a big step, think you can handle it, punkin?" Father looked at mother, both thinking the same thing. Perhaps she would really go.

Dianne smiled and blushed, "I don't know," she said still looking down. Then she looked up again, "Mr. Anders and Dr. Jacobs from the university want to have a conference with you and me," she said, trying to look at both parents at the same time.

Mom and Dad agreed together at once and set a date. Then Mom asked, "Don't you think you'll be scared going down there alone and with no friends?"

"Oh, Mom, it's perfectly safe, and the neighborhood is one of the restored ones and they say I'll be in classes with other gifted kids my age. Anyway, Mr. Anders says I'm too advanced for high school and should go right on to the university."

Dad whistled and looked at Mark and said, "I'm sorry, but she's beaten you to it."

Mark looked at Dianne in a wicked face for a moment, his mouth full of food, then put his thumb to his nose and wriggled his fingers at her.

"What about me? We were supposed to grow up together," said Joanne.

"Nobody takes hillbillies like you anyway—naked knees!" said Mark to her in a ridiculing response.

Mother scolded Mark for his insensitivity and turned the conversation to food and clothing sales. Father ate silently, patiently listening and nodding while his mouth worked. As this went on Mark ate very little and played with his peas. Mark thought of how unsuitable a time this was to talk about his bad news. He waited for silence.

"Dad, Hendricks may use me as a starter for a couple of games to see how I do."

Father's eyes widened slightly and smiled. "Great, but don't get a ballooned head over it. Try your best."

Mark was too frightened and nervous to tell them the important news.

"Jerome might come over Saturday. Can he stay for supper?"

"As long as his parents don't mind. By the way Gwen, we haven't seen Joel and Martha for a long time. Why don't we invite them over," said Dad, referring to Jerome's parents.

Mother chewed and looked at the calendar on the bulletin board once again and they agreed to try for a week from Saturday. Then just as dinner was almost over, with Mark intending to let his important announcement wait until later, Dianne spoke out. She had been looking at Mark inquiringly all through dinner.

"Dad, Mark has something to tell you about algebra and trig," she said.

Mark gave a scowl at Dianne. Father looked at Mark and he felt that sinking feeling.

"Well, I . . . I . . ."

"He canned algebra and physics," exclaimed Dianne.

"Dianne, let him tell it. You what?" Father gave a serious look at him and then at mother and mother returned a fierce stare at Mark.

"I . . . I switched . . . algebra two and physics for a computer math class and a world geography class," said Mark, looking at the salad bottle on the table and waiting for an ax to fall.

Father looked seriously at the bones on his plate. Mother looked at him, her eyes blazing.

"What did you tell me this morning, mister? You told me it was getting easier and you said nothing about wanting to change. You lied to me! Don't you ever lie to me again!" Her voice raised at every syllable. The twins sat bone-still, looking down and trying hard to suppress any movement or expression that would draw them into the turbulence.

"Say you're sorry to your mother and ask her forgiveness," said Dad.

In a low voice, eyes downcast, his head throbbing and all hunger gone, he said, "I'm sorry, Mom."

Mother was still too angry to feel forgiveness immediately. She was devoted to her children and had always loved to hug, hold, kiss, and forgive them. She worked long and hard to bring them up right and at times it was hard to keep her feelings in control. To the children their mother was an over-sensitive and moralistic person who sometimes sounded petty and frivolous. She was from a very traditional Christian family that went far beyond the frivolous to a deep relationship with a personal God, but she found it hard not to seem petty to the changing lifestyles that swirled around her in the neighborhood and the wider world. She was a throwback to the older times when mothers were in the home all day and the little things seemed terribly important, which made her life deep without being profound.

The discussion turned to algebra and physics and to questions surrounding the change. Then it progressed to a debate on the requirements for college. Father seemed satisfied, but mother remained skeptical. Both parents warned him to study hard. Mark felt it was unnecessary and wondered why his parents always found such things so important and told him things he already knew. Plus, he had to go without dessert for the lie he told. He went to his bedroom bitter and meditative.

Why are my parents like this and my mother? I am old enough not to have to be scolded and deprived of desert because of a lie. What a little thing.

However, he thought about Andy. He had discovered how Andy's parents didn't bother him about anything. Then he was told how Andy's parents fought each other, many times physically. Andy simply went home and watched movies and had a sister serve him his meals while his parents went out in different directions.

Soon Dad came and talked to him for a short time, consoling him, and telling him it all came as a shock since they thought he was doing so well. Dad made sure his son understood that they were behind him and did not want him to hide his feelings or troubles. Mom soon brought him his desert and kissed him.

A little while later Mark heard a voice through the crack in the door.

"I suppose you don't want this now," said the voice of Dianne. She put her hand and arm through the widening crack with a piece of paper held out and waved like a white flag. Mark looked up from the book he was reading while he lay on his bed. He ignored her at first, after what she did to him at dinner, but he eventually took the paper and looked at the neat figuring written on it.

"Is this the problem I gave you?"

"Yeah, it took me a minute."

"What? You mean about two seconds." He wadded it up and made a high arcing shot to his waste paper basket.

"I'm sorry, but it was for your own good. Please don't be mad," she said. Mark said nothing and she left.

Dianne played the piano from 8:00 to 9:30 in the family room. Mother watched old classics. Tonight it was part of a really old series called The Walton's. Joanne did her homework. Father called out for his newspaper, but was reminded of its demise. So he slept in front of the television with a reprinted computer news report covering his face. However, it was just not the same.

At a quarter to ten the five assembled slowly for the nightly ritual of family worship. Almost every night in the same pattern Dad read a passage from the Bible, left a few moments for discussion and then they took turns praying. Some nights they studied methodically and sometimes they simply discussed interesting points. Sometimes lengthy discussions ensued, especially on weekend nights and vacation time. The favorite topic was about Christ's Second Coming.

Father believed in a pre-tribulation rapture that was imminent, but he felt it necessary to teach all sides to a question. Mother went along with Father but could not really say why. She really did not like to argue about it. Dianne poured through the Bible with intense interest. She thought Christ would return in one post-tribulation coming, as she could never find any evidence to suit her about a separate rapture before the time of a worldwide persecution. She argued that Christ would in effect come back twice and instead, argued that it probably would be one huge event. Joanne only read enough of the Bible to satisfy herself but she lined up with Dianne only because she loved to be part of an argument where she could see Dad get flustered. In the middle of long arguments about this she would say things like. "Oh, I just love Jesus. Someday I want to wrestle with Him."

Mark sat most of the time between Dianne and Dad, not sure what he believed. Mother and Joanne added seriously to discussions only occasionally.

Church was Father's biggest problem. The twins, mother and Mark tried hard not to talk about it, because when the subject came up he would get furious. They remembered their days at the Rosedale Community Church, when Dad was a deacon and mother had been involved in Sunday school and women's guilds. Mark and the twins remembered their Sunday school days with distaste. Mark remembered being given verses to memorize and how he never got them right. The Sunday School class made up of sixteen boys and twenty-one girls formed cliques; he found himself an outsider and the butt of many jokes and pranks.

Church had been fun when Mark and his sisters were much smaller. He remembered in the middle of a sermon how Dianne had gotten away unnoticed from the nursery and crawled up the stairs all the way from the back to the front in the center aisle when she was only one year old. She had investigated most of the church before her third birthday as she had the habit of escaping from the distraught old women who watched them. Joanne always tried to follow and was caught first. When the twins were older they discovered the fun of switching places and acting as the other to fool people. When he was smaller, Mark used to think it was fun to stare at the people in the pew behind when he got to sit with his parents. He would stand, turn around in the pew and stare until the people behind squirmed or tried to humor him. He remembered how by his freshman year in high school he never went to church without a pocket full of hard candy or some gum.

Time moved slowly in church and was comfortable and tiring all at the same time. The thought that church was for worship never entered his head. Reverend Tully was a smiling, rotund man and Dad seemed to like him. He had christened Mark, Joanne, and Dianne and he came over for coffee. Mom was a good friend of Mrs. Tully. Then Reverend Cheshire, a bachelor, came when Mark was in seventh grade. He was a vibrant, charismatic man who preached about evangelism with dramatic fervor. Mark remembered how Dad had liked him at first, and he even helped the new reverend to publish a book. But on the whole, church bored Mark and where Reverend Tully sent Mark to sleep, Reverend Cheshire irritated him. Dianne and Joanne thought the latter funny, but most of the congregation seemed mesmerized by him and fell into line behind him. However, when Mark filed out of a service he deliberately tried to go out a different way. To shake the reverend's hand was like being in the grip and stare of something overpowering and uncomfortable. A number of families felt uneasy about him, mostly friends of his parents, especially when he talked about perfection on earth. Mark viewed Christ in two ways; one comforting and warm at home, and one intolerable and ritualistic at church.

His sisters and he came to believe in Christ outside of church from the family Bible studies. Dianne had expressed belief in Christ when she had been seven. Joanne followed her sister as she did in most things; Dad and Mom thought this was rather superficial. Mark held out until his fourteenth birthday when he met Jerome at a Teenagers for

Christ rally. He then told his father on one of their evening walks that he wanted to be with Christ.

When Dad's irritation over things at church grew, it fueled Mark's own apathy toward it. Reverend Cheshire had supposedly had a "third experience" during this time and preached about giving money incessantly in a subtle message that said that if enough money did not come in, the work of the Lord would be stunted and the church would be liable to Christ Himself. Dad and Mom were bothered about this but it did not seem a bad idea. The church had always been given far too little, and besides the church was growing, and it became increasingly charismatic with more lively worship and a more energetic demeanor.

One day, father's suspicions were confirmed after an extensive fund raising campaign had been completed for a new building. Reverend Cheshire had disappeared along with an elder's wife and all of the money. Father came home in a boiling rage and the family watched him go through a state of furor over the following days, to depression, to doubt, to resolution. Father had prided himself on being a man who was hard to fool. He had given hundreds of the family's money to Cheshire. The worst part about it was Grandpa Brogen had gone through a similar experience many years before. The family quit going to church and found a number of other families who were bitter too. Together they resolved never to go back. The Danforths, Bass's, Templetons, Burnshaws and Dudleys banded together with the Brogens and formed a house church. Mr. Templeton had been in something like it before. Soon the six families began to study about worship and the church, among other things, all on their own. A warm bond was forged as the families became so close that they were almost like an extended family.

Mark did not know why, but he often thought of these events as he got ready for bed. Sometimes he started thinking too much and could not sleep. They had been in the house church for almost three years now. He secretly had a crush on the Dudley's eldest daughter, but she was two years older and already had a boyfriend. His mind turned to the policemen in the train yard that afternoon and for some reason could not get them out of his mind. He prayed for a while, thought about basketball, but his mind drifted back to those railroad cars. He had not talked to Dianne during worship and he felt he ought to be reconciled, plus he wanted to talk. So he resorted to the outlet and institution that the children had created for all purposes, their inner sanctum—the Triangle.

As soon as the whole house was silent, he thought of going to the twins to see if they were awake. Dad and Mom had set a strict curfew and did not like them up late but it was a rule the three could not abide by at times, especially since they liked to sit up in the dark and talk about everything and anything. It so happened the twins met him on his way to their rooms. They made their way back to his room and as quickly as possible. They all sat on Mark's bed and formed a triangle as they sat with legs bent and crossed under them with their knees touching. They sat silently for a moment until someone wished to talk.

The triangle represented many things for them. They could open up in a way that they could with nobody else. It did not make their love and respect for their parents any less, but it provided an opening that only they could enjoy.

Even more important, there was a mutual understanding of problems and ideas that might simply be shrugged off by adults. It represented a place for comfort and acceptance that was increasingly hard to find in day-to-day relationships at school or in the neighborhood, because they were Christians. The three understood better than their parents thought they did about the hazards and distance between Christian and non-Christian peers.

As the triangle evolved it became more self-contained. When cousin Cassie from Atlanta stayed over for a week and joined the folded knee meetings it was just not the same. As there are family jokes that outsiders cannot understand or appreciate, so too the ways of the triangle could not be understood by outsiders. As they came to understand God and Christianity in their lives and as their father succeeded, many times unwittingly, in teaching them, they pledged to go on together. No matter what happened to one the other two would be there to help. Often the triangle became mere animated fun, a place to laugh and blow off steam, but as life began to invade and press on them, they began to study the Bible together, talk about personal problems and pray.

"I'm really sorry for getting you in trouble tonight," said Dianne starting off.

"Oh, it's Ok, it would have happened anyway, but don't get mushy about it," said Mark.

"Hey, guess what I saw today at the principal's office?" Joanne broke in going from a whisper to a normal voice.

"Sssssssshhhhh," hissed the other two, trying to keep her to a whisper.

"I saw a funny-looking policeman with a purple uniform talking to Mr. Onyet," said Joanne in an airy whisper.

"I suppose he looked like the one we saw last week in that old movie Dad liked," joked Dianne. "Did he have SS on his shoulders? Or you must have mistaken him for the new gym teacher," she said with sarcasm.

Mark was trying to follow Joanne but Joanne lost her thought and began pushing on Dianne. While they struggled, Dianne gave a retort to her own answer, "Yeah, isn't that new guy a mean one?"

"No, but Di, I really did see this guy," said Joanne while she wrestled Dianne and poked her in the ribs. She knew her sister was in one of her silly moods. Both began to wrestle harder.

"Cut it out Di!" Mark interrupted and he tried to break up the match and said, "I saw some fellows like that in the train yard today. Or at least I thought I did," he said. Dianne started laughing.

Suddenly the lights went on and Mother stood in the doorway with a tight-lipped expression, her eyes dilating in the sudden light and her night-capped hair frightening them more than anything.

"What is the meaning of this! Your father is sleeping and I thought we had told you. No more parleys on weeknights! Now scat!"

She gave each girl a spank as they left the room.

"And as for you—young man—you have been in enough trouble today without this. Good night!" And the lights went out.

Chapter 4

....

A RETREAT

The fall was a long and unusually warm one. The leaves seemed slow in turning and for everyone who shuffled through the piles, there was a hope that the sun would shine a little longer. Perhaps winter would not come after all. Surely there had been some unusual winters the past few years.

There was time, time to wrestle in the crisp, dry leaves. The birds that remained seemed perplexed, but enjoyed feasting on worms pushed up by late thunderstorms. The smells of leaves, trees, and mown grass and soil were thick in the air. There were sounds of children playing around the neighborhood in the late afternoon.

An old man walked block after block, occasionally stopping in front of a house or at a corner. His eyes observed everything as he recollected the past. To his old eyes the neighborhood had changed subtly; a tree missing here, a new curb, a new paint job on that house over there. Like Father Time he knew every crack and cranny of the town. He remembered the old city hall that had gone down thirty years ago and when the old Jewel Food Store moved into the new one. It would have surprised him even more to know just how many times it had moved all these years. He had seen every brick go up in the building of a newly expanded police station.

His gray head revolved slowly and his eyes alighted on Joanne walking up to him quickly, her golden brown hair tousled over her shoulders and parted in the middle of her head. Her slim figure jogged up to him and she did not hesitate to put her hand into his. His head bent to one side, she glanced up into his face and smiled warmly. He smiled back. She had greeted him, but as always had nothing to say to him but still wanted very much to talk. Then, as if some cue were given, he launched out on a familiar conversation that she had heard numerous times. He made it a point to tell her that kids were just not the same as they used to be and in fact many adults were so strange. He explained how he had watched numerous people grow up, none of whom she knew, and how they had all come to such miserable ends. Then as if concluding a lesson, he told her to stay good. His hand slowly searched in his pocket for something. "I want to show you something," he said. A small coin lay in his palm.

"What is it?" she stared at it in amazement.

"It's a penny," he said, watching her gawk.

"A what?"

"Read the date. I can't read without my glasses."

"1963. Wow!" she said, studying it with fascination.

"It's yours, keep it," he said, enjoying her reaction.

"Oh, no I couldn't. I've never seen anything like it."

"They don't have them around anymore. People bought things with them, when some things only cost one cent."

"Like what?"

"Gum, candy."

"Oh, maybe it's like our pennick note [which was worth 10 cents]," she said as she continued to study it.

"Keep it. I have a date with my maker soon and I won't be needing it." He had said this many times before; usually after they had talked he had given her odd things like rare marbles and other relics of the past. But he said it with such profound simplicity that the penny seemed to be a fortune.

Meanwhile, Dianne fought her way to the door of the train. She pushed her way through those who stood thickly packed and knotted in the aisles by the doors. Like a salmon trying to fight its way up stream. Dianne seemed to be caught in the rocks, her small, slim frame pushing against the weight of thick, tall dark-suited bodies with little success. The train glided to a stop sooner than she expected and she yelled and squirmed. She did get the computerized conductor's attention. Like obstinate forces, the men and women around her only gave her complacent stares as she wrenched through to freedom and the platform.

As she stood for a moment, she made a disturbing discovery. Her package of new books was missing from among her things. She immediately gazed in the direction of the train, now a spot on the horizon. When she made it to the ticket machine that ate up used tickets and opened a gate that resembled a toothless alligator on its side, it ate her ticket but it did not open its mouth. She fought back tears. The eye of the camera in the corner seemed to study her with interest and she turned to it and was about to scream when the computerized gate gave a clucking sound but did not open. Then she put her hands on her hips and looked at the camera again. Suddenly a worker appeared and apologized and explained he had been working on it. He inserted a key and it opened.

All would have been better had she not snagged her pants suit trousers on a bent link in a chain link fence a block from home. Then the whole of the day's proceedings engulfed her in a wave of emotion. The professor who seemed so rude and demanding, the spilled drink at lunchtime, the first week of riding the train alone, inconvenience, crowds, losing her new books, the gate, the trousers all came to a crescendo. "Why me!?" she shouted to the air as she kicked the leaves on the sidewalk. She walked on in tears, her mind spinning at all of the problems. When she neared home she saw the familiar cement step of the walkway that led to the porch. The trunk of an immense elm tree was nearby. Its high, mature branches reached over most of the front yard and the street in front of the house. She sat down there with no thoughts, just sitting in silence, feeling the breeze, watching the waning of day. She bowed her head to her knees and closed her eyes.

Joanne bounced up and tugged at her in a familiar gesture for wrestling in the grass, but Dianne fought her off and Jo ran off. Dianne remained on the step for some time. When she did go in the house she went straight to her room to be embraced by her bed.

At dinner that night, mother talked about her pleasant day with Mrs. Densler, sewing a new dress. She had also found more sales then she anticipated at the Super-Town Food Mall. Mark had had an agreeable day at school and basketball practice. Joanne told about old Mr. Woodcock and showed her penny with glee. The whole family became fascinated and that made mother reminisce. Mark thought it might be worth a lot of money since it was so old. As usual Dad was eating silently, meditatively, and listening to anyone who would talk. He noticed Dianne's sullen disposition, but was hesitant to ask her how her day was at the university. Mark noticed Dad's look at Dianne.

"What's wrong, mastermind, your screws too tight?" said Mark, grinning sarcastically.

"Oh shut up!" Her face turned red and tears approached once more. She left the table in a hurry.

"What'd ya go and say something like that for?" Mom and Dad said almost in unison. At any other time there would have been a round of name calling that was more brother and sister fun, but this time something was wrong.

Dad left the table and spent a long time alone with Dianne in her room.

Later he sat down next to Mother on the couch. Joanne and Mark watched Wednesday night football from the floor.

Dad sighed and then spoke quietly to Mother. However, they were still audible to Mark and Joanne.

"I thought sending her downtown to the university would be easy for her," said Dad.

"We all did when we signed those papers last month sending her. Her teachers, the heads of the math, physics, and computer departments, and the representative from the university could not praise her enough. We all thought she was enthusiastic about it," said Mother.

"Yeah, she was so thrilled," said Dad. "Well, it has only been the first week and she's never gone so far away from home alone."

"Perhaps she's scared," said Mother. "Maybe we're pushing her too fast, for her maturity, I mean. She was happy all last year when Mr. Dillard tutored her. And she was so perfect in her studies. Remember they really wanted her to go last year but we didn't think she wanted to leave her friends? Perhaps she's just satisfying us."

"No, she genuinely wants to go, she told me, and anyway, other child prodigies much younger seem to adjust, even to college classes. Her counselor told us. Anyway she's too smart, she should go on. She's just had a bad day, that's all," said Dad.

"But even they have to take time to have friends and for playing," said Mom.

"What about me? I may never get to see her anymore," exclaimed Joanne suddenly. She had been listening to the conversation along with Mark. Mark remembered the family arguments over home-schooling versus public schooling, and how they argued they would never get out into the world and be on their own and how Dad had changed his mind and let them do the latter.

"Well, how would you like to go from Roosevelt Junior High to the University of Chicago within a week, stopping at high school for a two-hour conference?" said Mark.

Dad looked at them for a moment while he thought and said, "I think we need some time together, perhaps with the Dudleys up at the cottage."

"Yeah! And they have that neat paddleboat. Or if it freezes and snows we can do other things! Let's please!" exclaimed Joanne.

"They don't have the paddleboat anymore, it's a pontoon boat and it won't freeze fast enough to skate—dough head," said Mark sarcastically as he threw his floor pillow at her.

"I'll call Frank tomorrow, and see if we can go up this next weekend," said Dad.

It was not until the weekend before Christmas that they could get away and at first there was no sign of snow, though it was cold. They drove the three hours in a festive mood. The Dudleys could not come, but let the Brogens go up by themselves. The family car was a bit cramped with five. Mark sat in the front with Father. Mother was pitted in between what seemed to be twin speakers as they sang loud and boisterous little travel ditties and hymns. One consolation was that her presence stopped them from bickering. The countryside was pretty but bland. Then as the billboards got fewer and they drove through the flat terrain of northern Indiana, the farms cheered them up and they welcomed the subtle hills and dunes of Michigan even more. It was dark when they finally reached the turn off at the place where there had once been a small town.

"Welcome to Dopeyville, one bar, one gas station and of all things a furniture store," narrated Dianne. Joanne yawned.

"How ya doing back there Mother. Mother?" called Dad.

"She's asleep," said Mark in a whisper.

"Are we almost there?" groaned Joanne.

"This is Hicksville," said Dianne.

They passed innumerable farmhouses and they were going fairly fast, but another car caught up with them and zoomed by.

"Hey, that's an old pick-up truck," said Dad, "That company went out of business years ago."

Up hills and down hills the car hit and missed potholes. Bright lights got in their eyes as a car came from the other direction.

Then father slowed down almost to a crawl and they looked for the mailbox along the road. The illuminated letters of Dudley popped up and father almost went past it and had to back up a little. Mother woke as they drove up the bumpy dirt driveway.

Years earlier the Dudleys had bought this old farm from its impoverished owner. For years they were laughed at as the place had piles of garbage strewn over the landscape and many useless shacks and buildings. Mrs. Dudley kept saying that Frank had made a big mistake but he persevered. Like the tip of an iceberg there was much more garbage buried under the ground. The jokes persisted as they lived in a trailer at first. Slowly the rancid and dilapidated buildings were torn down. Frank and his son Jeff, a year younger than Mark, and a number of uncles and friends, including the Brogens, worked weekend after weekend, summer after summer and cleaned it up. The uncultivated fields were rented out and were made usable again.

Frank had a house built and then he worked devotedly putting in a garden and restoring lush green lawns until it was picture perfect. Soon other family and friends could not be there enough. The lake was a quarter of a mile down the main road and a golf course the same distance the other way made it a great place for the families of the house church who could not afford a big vacation. It became the retreat place for the house church families. It retained the name of "the cottage" to the exasperation of the Dudleys who wanted it to be known as "the farm."

The Brogens had been there before as helpers and company but never alone and it proved refreshing as the family hiked around together, spent time talking, getting frustrations out, forgetting them as they walked. They went to the lake but all the boats had been taken out of the water. Snow began late Saturday morning as the words of a storekeeper told them of the impending snowstorm. Dad became frantic at the thought of being stuck. They drove back to the farm and were about to embark but for the protests of the girls.

"Who cares about the snow! We were supposed to get away together and from everything," said Dianne.

"Yeah, like our own retreat and what's the hurry, we're off school for two weeks," said Joanne.

"But, I'll miss work if this goes on till Monday," said Dad.

"Dan, we need it, remember? Besides, it would be nice to be a little helpless, it might even be cozy," said Mom.

"And we can play in the snow!" the girls said in unison.

"And shovel out of the snow!" persisted Dad.

"So what!" interjected Mark.

"Ok, Ok," said Dad, shrugging his shoulders. "I'll try to relax."

The snow fell heavily with no sign of a let up. The kids went out in it as it got deeper. Dad built a fire. Mom cooked a late supper and made hot cocoa. Soon the snow people walked in and shook it off.

Joanne remarked, "This is what heaven will be like. It's like a Narnia tale.

Dad sighed and laughed.

As soon as they finished dinner they noticed how the snow had grown even deeper.

Sleds were discovered and off the three went. Mom and Dad went out some time after them to watch and try a few runs down a small slope thirty yards behind the house. They laughed and shouted, made snowmen and threw snowballs. Then at one point they all stopped and ended up sitting silently in the snow at the top of the hill. They looked around as far as they could see, at farmhouses a little distant, their yellow squares of light representing the warmth within. The winter white and dark made the scene soft like that of a heavenly downy frost. Barn owls could be heard in the distance behind the wall of darkness.

Joanne repeated herself, "This is what heaven will be like. It's like we're in Narnia for a moment."

"Winter is not miserable at all when one has the health and life to enjoy it. It's we, the busy bees, who can't stop to look around at who is miserable," said Dad meditatively.

"Sssssshhhhh, Jesus is here with us," whispered Joanne.

"Well, of course He is," said Mom.

"No, I mean, I can feel His presence at certain times more than others."

"Where two or three are gathered in His name, there He is in the midst of them," said Dianne.

They were silent again. Mark was within himself, wishing that this time would never stop. He looked at his family in the dark and thought how he loved them. He did not know why, but he wanted to say it as if there was no more time and he had to. Shyly, hesitantly, he said, "Mom, Dad, Jo, Di . . . I love you." He immediately felt embarrassed and blushed, but they could not see his face. The others were silent, all to their own thoughts. But as if awakened from a sleep, this statement made them tell each other that they loved each other and then back to Mark. An awkward silence followed.

"What if something happened and we could never see each other again?" said Dianne, breaking the silence in a soft voice.

"We would have God to comfort us," said Mother.

"At school we saw some men with strange uniforms once or twice, and we've noticed other strange things. What if the antichrist is for real and something terrible happens? It's supposed to isn't it?" said Joanne.

"Christ will come back and take us all away," said Mother.

Dianne cut her off and said, "What if He doesn't, what if He waits and the church goes through the time of tribulation and Christ comes back in the midst or after it has started, or at the end? That end seems so close. We've heard so many strange things this year," said Dianne. "And these policemen that Mark and Joanne have seen. What if this is the beginning of some conspiracy against . . . against Christians right here in mid-America? I've read your whole library and the evidence seems so clear. Dad . . . I'm scared."

"Me, too," said Joanne. "I'd rather go to heaven and wrestle with Jesus."

"Me too," said Mark.

"Well, it's time we went in," said Dad, as if he were avoiding the subject.

"Yes, I think we've been out in the cold long enough," said Mom.

Everyone except Mark went in. He lingered on the hill, thinking and praying that they could remain together as long as possible. He did not know why because he wanted them to have a normal life but there was uncertainty.

By the fire Dianne persisted in her unanswerable questions. Dad stared at the fire, visibly thinking. "Ok, I want to clear the air. We have had many debates and I think we are old enough and intelligent enough. I admit of having avoided this talk only because I felt you three were not mature enough as Christians. I've been waiting for the right moment. Rumors started around the plant four months ago, strange rumors, that Brinker was merging the company with another that publishes computer magazines, then another; that Kaufman the oldest vice president was having an affair with another woman. Still another a few weeks ago said the company was to be sold pending legal action against Brinker and from a lawyer whom we've always thought to be a Christian, but who works for a government agency that we've never heard of before. All of the rumors, or plots, from where ever they started are completely erroneous, but they seem to have a purpose of discrediting us or driving us out of business.

"I don't know what this all means, but it could be the beginning of something—perhaps an organized anti-Christian movement. We have heard from another source that other publishers are facing new difficulties with government agencies. Together, these publishers still produce two thirds of

the Bibles and Christian literature for the world. But now—
hold on Dianne—let me finish before you get lots of ideas. It
may be nothing, but it may be the start of something that has
frightened me. I don't know anything about those new policemen. There are lots of different police these days, state,
county, city . . ."

"And many private security firms," interrupted Dianne.

Father held his hand up, and said, "But the way world
affairs have been over the last few years has frightened me
into thinking it may begin. All of you have to remember that
many other Christians have felt the same persecution and
the same antichrist spirit down through the centuries. What
is hard for me to understand is that we may be in for some
kind of suffering or persecution in our lifetime, right here in
our own home. All I'm asking is that each of you think out
your own faith and we as a family must agree that no matter
what happens we will be true to God, because He will save
us . . . sooner or later . . . but He will come through. Death
has no hold on us. I believe that before long all Christians
everywhere will have to think these things out if they haven't
already. I do not want you three going and blabbing about all
of this beyond our family church members. You all know
how I hate Christian conspiracy mongering. None of it is for
sure. Let us go on with our lives, but let us be ready. If something happens to me I want you all to remember that God
will provide for you."

"Oh, Dan, don't talk like that," said Mother, rising to go
and make some coffee. But Father put a hand on her arm to
keep her down.

"I cannot promise any of you," here he looked at Mark,
Dianne and Joanne, "what your lives will be like in the fu-

ture but if you have any questions about your faith let me know. I have hoped that all of you would lead normal, free lives, but that cannot be assured. There are things that are happening in the upper echelons of this country and the world that the middle and lower class person knows nothing about, nor have we the power to stop it. We only have our faith in God and each other."

They all sat silently looking at the fire as it hissed and sputtered.

"Come on, that doesn't mean we cannot be happy and enjoy ourselves. Let's play some pool, Mark," said Dad.

"Some ping-pong, Mom?" said Joanne.

"No, you and Di go ahead."

Mom made some coffee and hot chocolate and hummed quietly. The rest played for some time.

"Will there be ping pong tables in heaven?" asked Joanne as she swatted the ball and made it fly into Dianne's face.

"Yeah! And a wrestling ring for you, monkey," retorted Dianne. They rushed together in grim embrace and tumbled into a bean bag chair.

As they slept snugly in their beds with two or three blankets, the snow fell heavily once again. The heat was kept low as they wanted to conserve the Dudley's fuel oil that was now an even more expensive substance. All slept well in the still, absolute silence, complete darkness and crisp coolness for the first two nights.

Sleep always comes easy after such days of traveling, thinking, and playing. But lying in bed looking and thinking in the darkness is comfortable too, that is most of the time. On the third night Joanne stared into the absolute darkness, wondering what it would be like to live in such blackness. She felt this was unusual as in her urban home there was always a light on somewhere, whether it was the streetlight at the corner that made it easy to walk about her own house. She thought about the kind of darkness at church camps. There even the moon showed on summer evenings and there were fires and flashlights. Here the darkness hung like a shroud, suffocating if one allowed it to be. She thwarted the darkness by closing her eyes and pulling the blanket over her head. But she knew it was still out there. Sometimes in the darkness of her own bedroom at home her imagination played with the objects around her. A lamp became a man, a stack of clothes in the corner became a body which frightened her. Joanne thought of this and with a dreadful fascination tried to see in the black. She waved her hand. She put it close to her face but it was still invisible. She reached as far out as she could with her arm extended and her hand struck a closet door with a thud. Frightened, she scrunched down in bed and pulled the covers over her head. A car passed along the road. She peeped out, her imagination still playing with her. She saw what she thought was a person in the corner of her room, a demon or a monster. She scurried and switched on the light in a second. She sat breathing hard. It was only a large plant on a table.

How did she get into these grotesque moods? She turned out the light, got in bed and prayed softly. Her mind relaxed, sensing nothing upsetting about the room but her own fears.

She prayed that Jesus would cover her and watch over her and keep the others safe. She fell asleep trying to think of a particular missionary's name that the family supported in Africa.

Mother slept soundly in a ball on her right side with few thoughts to bother her, none more deep than tomorrow's meals and the laundry. She never had a problem sleeping anywhere.

Father and Mark were deep thinkers and because of it spent many a night awake or restless. They were retrospective, remembering things they thought and said right or wrong the day before. Mark was this way though he had few real worries in his young life. Father had over the years slept less and become more restless and prayerful. His job was not oppressive, but his conscience was soft and pliable and he was conscious always of his work, worship, and family. Mark worried like his father, and prayed for everything and all things. Prayer did not always have a calming effect, especially when he really did not give his thoughts and problems over to God but kept them to chew on some more. He knew God was listening and interested and felt that it was always best to get things out in the open in the presence of his best friend. This is what brought him peace.

The fresh air did much to make Dad and Mark's sleep heavy and deep. This is the kind of sleep one would like not to end because the dreams are of a kind and the sleep so complete that the outside world is strange when one wakes in the morning.

Dianne, like her sister, was uneasy and was unfortunate on this night in sinking into a deep sleep and into the deep of a dream. In her dream, as in real life, she had the ability to perceive her sister's feelings and even her thoughts in times of trouble. And Joanne, though not her sister's equal in intellect, had the uncanny ability of feeling for her sister and thinking like her in ordinary circumstances even when they were separated by distance.

This was the subject of the dream. Joanne was close to her. They were walking on a sidewalk through a neighborhood remotely resembling Rosedale homes, except all of the houses were enlarged and grotesque. There seemed to be a depressing yellowish atmosphere that made her uneasy. A tall man in a light blue three-piece suit walked up from a distance. He was in his late fifties with gray hair and glazed blue eyes and he wore a light blue bowler hat. He walked up to them and his eyes turned into lights like those of a car. Dianne felt the lights penetrating into her mind, searching as if with hands—searching for something. He looked to where Joanne was and she turned to look at her sister. Her head was turning like a mannequin's and was being lifted from her neck, and then her head opened into halves. Dianne screamed in terror as they were progressively separated by an infinite gulf and she could still feel the outrageous act—the poking around in Joanne's brain. She could not stop screaming.

Joanne felt an inner unexplainable restlessness and she also had the dreaded burden of going to the bathroom on a night when she had had enough adventures with the darkness. She heard a muffled scream and turned on the light while Dianne was still convulsing from the dream and shook her until she woke. Dianne grabbed hold of Joanne and asked her if she was all right. Her eyes dilated in the light. After a few minutes of sitting up and catching her breath, she said,

"I had a nightmare."

"I thought something was wrong but I thought it was just me. Can you go back to sleep?" Jo did not need an answer as she studied her sister's face. "Do you want to talk about it?"

Dianne nodded, but told her to get Mark. She did as she was told and woke Mark. He was led along wearily and weak in the head, then stubbed his toe on the foot of Dianne's bed making him almost fall on her when he woke completely from the pain. Dianne proceeded to tell about the dream. Joanne was impressed and frightened. Mark looked at Di as interestingly as he could, but was still bleary-eyed.

"Shouldn't we tell Dad?" said Mark. "You look upset."

Jo swallowed and felt her head and said, "It's, it's a remonition or whatever they call it."

"That's *premonition*," said Mark. And then he studied Dianne's face and said, "And don't be goofy, it's probably nothing of the kind. It may only mean that . . . that somebody's going to test you both. It probably has nothing to do with the future."

"But I never saw this man before—never! Can our minds make someone up? I've never had a dream like this before," said Dianne.

"How about subconsciously, from TV or a magazine? Maybe you're just thinking too much about our talk tonight?"

"Yeah, I suppose so," said Dianne, confused but thinking. It frightened her to think of even having a nightmare.

Then she said, "Joanne, didn't you say you dreamed one time of walking through gothic type buildings with engravings on the outside and then into a room which you saw a short stocky man with a white coat? He was partly bald, with a big nose and thick glasses."

Joanne stared at her and said, "Yeah. And he turned out to be one of your new physics teachers at the university whom you had never seen before last month and whom I have never seen except in the picture you brought home."

Mark stared blankly trying to recall this. They were all silent. Then Dianne looked at Mark with that knowing look and she said, "Well? Don't you get it? This is something Jo and I will see, or something like it."

"Oh—go to sleep you guys, you give me the creeps. And maybe monsters will come out of the walls," said Mark cryptically to get a laugh out of them. But they did not laugh. Mark got up to go.

"Don't go, let's pray," said Dianne insistently.

Mark could see that she desired their company and just now realized how much the dream had shaken her.

They prayed for a long time and then started a word game until all became exhausted. Next morning mother and father saw nothing unusual in the three sleeping almost until noon. By a secret pact that Mark was reluctant to keep, they never told them about the dream.

Chapter 5

CHRISTMAS AND WINTER

As hopes of a mild winter faded and the wind whipped like the cutting edge of a knife around the desolate street corners, the families of Rosedale struggled through one of the worst winters on record. After working hard to get home before the storm really broke out, the Brogens tried to maintain the routine of work and shopping.

All of their plans to have family in were ruined. However, some of the house church families created an impromptu Christmas gathering that became a small, comfortable time despite the weather. Even the Dudleys, Burnshaws, and Danforths had trouble getting across town. The snow had turned to sleet, which then froze on impact and the streets became skating rinks as all surfaces were covered with three inches of slippery enamel.

"I'm glad we don't have to go to their house," said Joanne, grinning as she looked out of the living room window. The

Danforth's small kids, Timmy and Jimmy, were tugging at Mrs. Danforth from different directions and ironically keeping her up as they trudged delicately over the frozen hills that seemed to make a new permanent lunar landscape in the front yard. Mr. Danforth caught Mrs. Danforth as she slipped on the front steps.

"Joanne, what are you standing there for—help them in for goodness sake!" yelled Mother as she came up behind her. "Dianne, get out of the bathroom! Mark, wake up Father!" The orders were given and everybody hopped about. Joanne opened the door. A gust of cold air came through the house. Joanne gripped unseen arms and her own slight weight was pulled out. Getting a good grip on the door she struggled and finally the Danforths stood disbelieving they made it. They were hesitant to unwrap and disengage from their heavily bundled and booted bodies.

Soon the house was filled with people with runny noses and red unfeeling cheeks. Mother passed out hot cocoa and cider. The Danforth children, knowing the Brogen home, soon had all of the old toys and games out. The Dudleys, with Jeff and their daughters Mindy and Emma who were around the same age as the twins, arrived last with Mr. Dudley very angry and trying to keep from swearing. One side of his car had been scratched by another. They had narrowly missed a more serious collision.

"This is some night. If the good Lord don't kill us tonight we'll do it ourselves before this weather turns. Can you believe it?" said Mr. Dudley.

No one wanted to say it, but before dinner the prayer came out with more thanks and praise for life than anyone expected. It seemed the grim weather brought out everyone's feelings. Everyone there seemed to feel God's presence ever more and there seemed to be more joy and rejoicing than usual. The dinner came with more thanksgiving as they ate the turkey and dressing, mashed potatoes and gravy and hot steaming home-baked rolls. Warm pumpkin and minced pies with whipped cream were served. Nobody spoke and the only noise was from the clanking of knives and forks.

With dinner over, the women and girls cleared the table, the men pushed themselves back from the table and sighed with relief. The children ran off to play. Mark and Jeff played a computer game.

"Isn't this winter something?" said Mr. Dudley looking at nobody in particular. "Hasn't the whole year been some-thing?" said Mr. Burnshaw with a toothpick in his mouth. This started a round of jokes and pleasantries. As the laugh-ter died there was a silence as the men stared at the empty plates being gathered and taken away. Then Mr. Dudley's grey eyes looked toward Dan's.

"How are things in the publishing business these days?"

"In our place it's still the same, but in others it's chang-ing, new books presenting a new twist in the theology are being introduced," said Dan.

"I wonder if that has anything to do with this neo-christology that is coming into vogue?" said Mr. Burnshaw. But before anyone could answer he continued. "I've been meaning to tell you Dan that we, that is the Bass's and us . . ." here he looked at Danforth, "have been thinking it over and we think we should be with the organized church again— neo-christology or not. We think He would want it that way. Maybe we could help out if this is in error."

"In error!" said father. "It's not only in error, don't you see what it is?"

"Now Dan, don't get so exited," said Mr. Dudley. "Besides there are a lot of good churches left. We also have been thinking of attending a Baptist church that seems very stable still. Mary's at a young people's worship tonight. She says she likes it and the pastor seems like the right sort."

Mark's spirits went down as he heard this last part about Mary and from then on he didn't listen well.

Mr. Dudley continued, "The Templetons have also been hedging at rejoining a church too. We seem to be heading in slightly different directions, but our thoughts are the same. We feel, historically, Christ wanted His people in the Church, not only in the past but now too. And it is in these organized churches that we feel we can still help."

"Or go down with the ship in some bog of compromise. It was Bonhoeffer who told orthodox Christians in Nazi Germany to stay away from compromising churches to the effect that true Christians, no matter how noble, cannot run in the opposite direction on a speeding train that is bound for hell," said Dan.

Mr. Danforth sat up and lay his folded arms on the table, ready to speak at the first crack. "Dan, you don't know what you are talking about—and how can you say things like that? We all sympathize with your feelings. We've all had a bad time and the house church was a good idea, but this is still a free country. The church in general is still sound and we have an obligation to try to be true to Christ or die for it there. After all, this still is the church age. If we really were being tyrannized, and free worship really was in jeopardy, we would be the first ones to savor this house church as long as we could, but . . ."

Mark had heard this argument before, but not with the emotion that was being aroused this time. Mark never understood this kind of arguing; nor could he decide what he believed about the church. For the last year the family church had been occasionally discussing the possibility of joining a church again, but nothing was ever done about it, and Father refused to think about it.

Dad began again, "Bob, don't you see the church is not in free worship now? Don't you see the subtle change that has taken place over the past forty years? We may have had troubles with Reverend Cheshire, but the problems he caused were nothing compared to what he represented. Addictions, greed, deceit, and hypocrisy have co-mingled with free worship. What's worse is the cloud of antichrist behind the doings of Cheshire."

"Are you saying Cheshire's simple case of stealing and adultery was a portent of the antichrist?" asked Danforth.

"Not a portent, but the calm before the storm. A scavenger picking at the body before the predator arrives. This neo-christology with its heaven and Christ perfecting the present earth—saving all mankind and becoming our political, social, and religious leader is just the beginning. This is the antichrist's theology if there ever was one. It is an attempt to counterfeit everything the Bible has promised, but without the true Christ and Creator. The machinery has been here for many years; a one-world economy, the advocacy of a one-world society, computers being refined to create the one-world communication system, and now the one-world religion. It's a hole for the antichrist to fill in, whoever or whatever he maybe in the future. I don't know if it will be today or tomorrow. All I am saying is that neo-christology is setting the stage. Don't you see Dudley, Danforth, Burnshaw? The real church, you and I, we now represent a church that makes up a body of believers, as far as we can now determine, from every nation, tribe, and tongue or close to it. But most people who don't know the true Savior will eat up this eternity on earth; hell doesn't exist except in the imagination theology. Our joining the church is going to signal our joining them! And if you do, there will come a time when you will be watched or monitored or something."

"Dan," said Mr. Dudley, "this Baptist church or the Methodist one with the revival down the street—both preach Christ, second coming and judgment and all that we want. You're right but there are still a few bastions—there has to be. That's all we are saying, Dan. We would like to fellowship more widely. We are starting to feel too confined here and we feel as if we are blowing the whistle too early, before any persecution comes. Besides, we've been in the house church nearly three years now and we think it would be good to have a little change. And anyway, the Rapture will spare us from any antichrist or persecution, so why worry about it?"

"Ok, I see your point, but what I am saying is . . ."

Mark noticed Dianne listening while she put away the dishes in the buffet. They stared at each other as the men argued on and on. They knew Father was hard headed and that the house church had been heading toward this for some time. Perhaps they had all blown the whistle too early. Perhaps the world was not as bad as they all thought.

Mother cleared the air by announcing that the ladies were done in the kitchen. With a smile, and not a whit or care about the men's arguments, she herded people away for she was pleased with the success of her meal and the complements it drew.

Soon the families were singing Christmas carols as Dianne played the piano. Father began to relax as he always did when she played. Mr. Danforth gave the Christmas message, reading the account of Christ's birth from Luke and trying in a slow plodding way to make some special message from it. Everyone listened seriously, considerately, no one caring if the aging shoe store manager with his cherubic face lost his main point occasionally. Everyone's thoughts seemed to run into the same stream; happy to be alive, being under God's protective grace, the warmth of being together, and enthralled with the simplicity, knowing that there were many miserable souls who might never know such moments.

Each heart was touched by the thought of at least one person they wished could be saved by Christ while each prayed aloud at the end of the sermon. Mark thought with sorrow about Andy; Dianne about her prodigy friends at the university who seemed so snobbish; Joanne about Ricky, the Burnshaw's eldest son who rebelled against his parents and joined a fraternity at college and now had a drug problem. Mother thought of Mrs. Miller, the next-door neighbor, whom she had talked to for years over the back yard fence and had been a good friend until she tried to tell her about Christ and invited her to their Sunday worship.

Father felt guilty before God and the company for possibly misleading the family church into something out of his own personal revenge against the organized church. He knew he had always had a problem here and hoped God would give him a forgiving heart to all those who had fed his hatred over the years, including Cheshire; he prayed for the latter's repentance as well.

In this way all the families prayed, even the small children with some promptings from Mrs. Danforth. Then they recited the Lord's Prayer in unison, and sang another hymn. Dianne played classical selections from Handel, Mozart, Bach, and Beethoven and took requests. Mother brought out brownies to groans and cheers. Then it was time to open presents. The children screamed with delight over various new toys and gadgets. Everyone said a polite thank you for such mundane items as socks and sweaters. There was raucous laughter at prank gifts.

The time came when the three visiting families had to think about leaving. They all got suited up, including the host family to help pick ice. Mark, Joanne, Dianne, Tim, Jim, Emma, Mindy and Jeff followed and slid over the icy sidewalks. Mrs. Danforth sat in the living room with mother to wait for the eventuality. The Dudleys were the unhappiest as their electric car, already low on power, sat cold. They had to wait until Mr. Burnshaw made it to his service station and brought out the tow truck.

Joanne, Dianne and Mark stayed outside and played in the late night long after the Dudley's left. For the next week the Brogens were happy and contented. There was no school to worry about for another week and so they stayed up late reading and talking and playing games together.

The following day they sat with mother and watched a truly ancient classic with the rest of the family, *White Christmas*.

"They sure don't make movies like they used to," said Mark.

Mother looked at him in a serious look and said with unusual sarcasm, "You don't even know what the real old days were like!"

"Oh yeah?" Mark contended, "ask me something about the twentieth and twenty-first centuries. I've been learning all about that from some of Dad's books."

Mother laughed. "That's what my mother said while watching the oldies when I was a girl."

Next they watched *A Christmas Carol* and felt more snug then ever. Joanne accidentally hit the automatic control on the couch and for a few seconds they saw the undulating bodies of a choreographic group dancing semi-naked to no digestable music but to intermittent chaotic sounds that grated against the family's ears.

"Turn it quick, Joanne! Get that garbage off there!" moaned Dad.

"What was that?" asked mother.

"That was the end of this year's Christmas special," said Dianne with a grin.

"No, but what was that? That dance or music?"

"It's a rendition of a famous composer. His name is Sage and the music was from his Chaos Series. That's one of the basics of modern music theory. Wonderful isn't it?" said Dianne sarcastically.

"What is the world coming to!" said mother as she smiled at the sight of Scrooge and sipped a hot cup of coffee.

The blizzards ceased and the temperature moderated and winter settled into a slow rhythm. The family started going occasionally to a Brethren church along with intermittent meetings of the house church. Dad still predominantly held to a family service. No more exiting dreams came and Joanne and Mark saw no more funny policemen. The routine of life seemed tame as ever. In Rosedale, life never seemed better.

However, in the outside world many things were happening. As the family read their daily computer news, Tokyo had another great quake, and Mount Fuji erupted again. Thousands upon thousands were homeless and many more were dead. Terrorists had tried to blow up the Eiffel Tower in Paris. The new United States of Europe, including Russia, elected Premier Aliadin, a Swiss citizen, as their administrative leader. The United States was joining them in a larger economic and social treaty. A unique figure in the world, Aliadin appeared in cyberspace on all computer news outlets. He was extremely handsome and vibrant. His fame rose meteorically as a powerful speaker and statesman with a most benevolent air. He had been successful in negotiating numerous peace treaties including the Middle East, for which he won the Nobel Peace Prize.

Then there was Bella Arcane, an American, who became a new prophet in the eyes of many world religionists. He taught that the next Christ or Messiah was coming from heaven a second time and indeed was already present in Aliadin. He used Christian terms easily, like creation and salvation and was ready to help all to know that all religions pointed to this teaching and that all would be accepted.

Many people believed Aliadin was a messianic figure, a Christ for the world's problems. This was the neo-christology that was being argued about between the proponents and opponents who cared. For the followers, this new Christian theology seemed to fit in with all that they taught, which included elements of every faith. Even atheists could fit in.

Orthodox Judaism refused to yield and held to its own, leaving Israel more and more precariously isolated. Evangelical Christians who now called themselves historic Christians were slow to fit the pieces together and refused to believe such notions and simply were content to wait for the Rapture. However, for Historic Christians, Jews, and minorities and for most of the public at large who had always watched political, religious, and social news closely over the years, it was disjointed and filtered because television and computerized news was edited, disjointed, and filtered. This was intended. No one saw the secret changes and deals. Some historic Christians tried to organize, some headed for the hills, but most did not know what to do and tried to live normally.

Besides, most people were busy with living and did not look or take time to listen carefully to the news that was received. Most of it went over the heads of the people in Rosedale and millions of communities like it. Most people in the Western world were in the middle and did not think in terms of good and evil forces. Besides, political, economic, social and environmental problems and catastrophes had happened before but life had never uniformly or drastically changed. They did not care about any viable future, except for the pleasures and freedoms of non-political or capitalistic enterprise imbedded in every part of the world which was normal. That they were powerless to stop any changes did not occur to them. The system that Aliadin and Arcane worked with still promised that everyone had rights and freedoms that would be protected under the law, and Americans and Europeans and many of the world's citizens could vote. Everything was legal and normal.

Chapter 6

THE TROUBLE WITH TWINS

On a late Saturday afternoon, in the last week of January, Dad, Mark and Dianne sat watching and playing with their new computervision. TVs and computers had long become one and they were always being improved. The Brogens had always been behind the times when it came to getting the latest gadgets, even for historic Christians. It was a large flat screen that took up most of one wall. It came with a standard keyboard but could also be controlled in other ways. They watched multi-channels at once for a while and then with a wave of a hand the all-news channel came on which also told the weather in the upper corner. As it had its own power source, it could wake up sleeping families in the event of a storm or disaster. As a computer of course it could be used to communicate to others. You could have two way or more conversations and see your friends while you talked if they also had the proper computer. Father was hesitant for a long time to get this kind of technology for his home because he feared Big Brother's encroachment.

As nothing good was on the regular channels, which were infinite and worldwide by now, they selected a favorite movie disk. They watched contentedly, but just as Sir Thomas More was making his last speech of defiance to the Church of England the movie disk stopped with a click as if an invisible hand had pushed a button. Instantly, the constant news channel clicked on. The familiar face of E.K. Smith, the oldest anchorman on the news, came into view. "Let me repeat. the president has been assassinated . . ."

"Wasn't this the day that Alliadin was supposed to meet with him?" asked Father, leaning forward with a dumbfounded expression. "Mark, look for the copy I made of the CP news."

"Sssssssshhhhhh," hissed Dianne who lay on the floor.

". . . also critically injured was Premier Alliadin and an unknown number in Congress and . . . I have just received word that the vice-president has also been killed. Let me repeat . . ."

Mother and Joanne came in, back from a church social, and asked what was going on. The family met before this immense TV for a long time. It took several weeks for the emergency shadow government to reassure all Americans that going back to normal was the best way to cope with the new problem. Everything would be rectified soon. There were many more family prayer times now and even more meetings of the three siblings in their triangle after midnight.

However, in the spirit of trying to remain calm and normal amongst the activities that resumed was high school basketball. In March the Brogens went off to the senior night at the high school. The national tragedy still delayed the game for a half hour of remembrance. Then they watched Mark play three minutes, score two points and make no serious blunders to threaten Thorngate's victory over its sister school, Thornhill.

For the next month the family was preoccupied with basketball as Jerome Gates led his teammates into the super-sectional before losing in overtime.

Mark was proud for getting into all of the tournament games, but was sad that the team had not turned out as well as predicted. Just four years before, Thorngate had won the state championship. After the tears had dried, Jerome led his teammates in one last assault at the team dinner. Jerome let Mark know his secret news that nobody else knew yet. He had turned down an offer from a pro scout and would be attending UCLA next fall.

Dianne was making rapid progress in the most advanced mathematics and physics courses and many professors had come to interview her more than any of the other prodigies in her class. Dianne was considered to be the most exceptional. She had produced answers to the most complicated physics problems that only a few scientists in the world had attempted to solve, some having to do with the control of nuclear power and others having to do with the disintegration or neutralizaton of nuclear fallout particles. While doing all of this she left her work at school. She tried hard to act very normal at home and even denigrated her abilities in the face of family company. She discussed less important things around the dinner table and felt it important not to discuss anything that might make her parents worry. Sometimes she shared her experiences with her brother and sister and one time she asked for their help.

In the spring, Dianne was sick for several days and the doctor and Mom refused her any activity. Joanne and Mark happened to be off because of a teacher's institute. In a midnight powwow, she persuaded her sister to fill in for her but not to tell her Mom and Dad.

"Now remember, copy everything down exactly as he puts it on the board. You can do it," said Di.

"But why can't we just pick up a disk or something with it all on there," said Mark.

"And what if they ask me some questions?" Jo said.

"He brings these problems up spontaneously, some original, some memorized and he often doesn't have them copied because they're not done yet and never before a camera, so there won't be any chance to get it on our computer. And he does not like strangers in his classroom. They won't ask questions. I simply can't miss this class."

Joanne was silent and then said, "Well . . ."

"You've been me a thousand times and we've fooled them every time, sometimes even Mark." Dianne said, looking at Jo through her feverish haze.

"But that was with friends and relatives," Jo said.

"That was the best test, these people are strangers. They'll be chumps," said Di with more fervency.

Jo sat for a while looking at her and then said as cheerfully as she could, "Ok, I'll do it." Mark promised to go with her and they could go to the Museum of Science and Industry afterward. They decided they had to get Mom's approval but they did not tell their parents the whole plan, only that Mark and Joanne were going to pick something up for Dianne.

When the request came in the morning, Mother was about to disapprove but for Dianne's protests. Then as if she had been in their night conversation, she insisted that she pull no tricks but simply pick up the material for her sister. Here she looked at Joanne and said, "Make sure you identify yourself." Joanne nodded to Mom but winked at Di as she left the room.

Joanne and Mark trudged off to the train station and twenty minutes later they had a grand view of Dianne's university from the platform. To Dianne it was a stuffy, boring place, but to Joanne it was stately and mysterious. Snow still lay on the ground in small clumps and the air was frigid though spring should have been arriving.

Joanne's stomach turned as they got closer, but as they entered the building her fear dropped away and she smiled playfully at Mark. He knew that look, that she had no intention of identifying herself. She knew how to be Dianne. Recently, she had begun to mimic her genius. She walked into class before Mark could say anything. Her appearance was that of Dianne's; the meticulously neat clothes and hair, the elfish maturity in her face, the quick purposeful walk, her green eyes cool and unperturbed with life.

The students and professor assembled, but in the back two observers had already taken their places before their arrival. Joanne ignored all the others and did not look at all to the back of the room. By luck, the door which had a window remained partly open. Dianne had been wrong about Professor Dryer's love for privacy in class at least for this day because of these men who sat in the back of the class watching. But Mark took no notice of them at first. Like Joanne, they heard the familiar gobbledygook that Dianne was heard to mutter at home in her room, usually to herself, as she banged speedily on the computer. He could see Jo and the other students. There were only six. Then as he rapidly lost track of the teacher's message, he began to study the students and then the two men in the back. One man was rather fat, with dark red hair almost like a mop. The other man was balding, in his fifties, and rather dapper Mark thought. He was very neat in a light purple three-piece suit and he was fondling a cane; sitting by him on another chair, unseen by Mark, was a bowler hat that matched the suit. He was wondering if he had seen him before but couldn't think of where. Fortunately, they could not see his stare and he soon withdrew to where he could only hear.

Meanwhile, Joanne was scribbling down everything the professor wrote on the board as Dianne had instructed her. All of a sudden the professor asked a yes and no type question for another solution that he put on the board and without a moment's hesitation called on Dianne to affirm or deny it. Mark closed his eyes feeling sure this was the end. The Dianne that Dr. Dryer thought was there took her pencil up to her nose just as Dianne would have and she smiled just as Dianne would have when stumped without any sweat. The professor, impatient for a reply, made a childish grin and Joanne, without moving or replying felt her time was up. However, he understood her smile as a yes and he

was overjoyed with the thought that he had finally convinced his favorite pupil of a problem that the real Dianne
had been questioning him on for weeks. He affirmed her
and applauded her.

The class went on in lecture but Jo did not realize he
was getting through his material faster than expected. Before she knew it he was asking for them to put problems
they had done last week on the blackboards that surrounded
the room from ceiling to floor. Mark put his hand to his
mouth and walked off to the bathroom. He did not want to
be around when Joanne could not come through. Besides,
a middle-aged woman walking down the hall looked at him
curiously and frowned.

Joanne broke into a sweat for the first time, but fortunately the bell rang before she could present her problem
and she erased it quickly. The professor smiled at her but
said nothing. She stepped out quickly and ran to Mark coming out of the men's room.

"Saved by the bell," she said like Dianne might say in
her most breathy suave voice.

"But according to Dianne's schedule I have two more
to go," she said.

"Well, I'm going for a walk. Meet you back here," said
Mark.

"Thanks, Einstein, for your support. I think I'm enjoying myself—for a day."

Mark never saw Jo quite like this before. She looked
and acted sophisticated and showed no signs of the tom-
boy she had always been. He was impressed.

They spent a long day after the classes investigating the
museum. When they got home Joanne was moaning that

she did not feel very well and she spent dinnertime lying on her bed and did not eat.

The appointment to see the doctor again had to be switched to the next day because their family doctor had an emergency operation to perform. The already sick and bedridden Dianne simply phoned in to the college that she could not attend and laughed when she heard Joanne's story edited by Mark; and they never told Mom or Dad the whole story.

Joanne's appointment was for 1 P.M. Mother and Joanne sat waiting. The diagnosis was a chest infection with an accompanying fever. She had not been to the doctor since she was nine with the measles. Dr. Smith and his protégé gave her a thorough examination that included every aspect of her head. After a shot and a trip to the pharmacy, it was off to Shopping City as a reward for her helping her sister. They did not notice the car that followed them.

As they marched around, Joanne thought she would look for the cleanser they wanted as Mom went to the grocery section. She knelt down and studied the prices, as Mom had taught her. Then she noticed a man down the aisle. He wore a light blue three-piece suit and had an ornately carved cane in one hand and a matching blue bowler hat in the other. She felt that she had seen him somewhere before, but she couldn't think where for a moment. Then it flashed in her mind that this was the man Dianne had seen in her dream. He was staring at her and he came toward her. She half expected him to fulfill the dream as he came closer with what appeared to her as hypnotic eyes. Her heart beat faster, but she had no desire to scream and remained crouched and unable to move as he approached to within three feet of her. She stared up into his eyes and she thought that they were cold and hard, like a frozen pond, but there was power in his eyes and she felt weak. He started to say something. Just then a little old lady trundled up behind pushing a noisy shopping cart and asked Joanne, "What is the price of Topsy-turvy Cleanser now, young lady?"

She turned around without hesitation to see her and said with a strange sense of relief, "Yes, yes. It is only $7.85 for the 36-ounce bottle, cheaper than the others because there is more liquid and it is more concentrated . . ."

Her mind cleared and as she turned back to see the man, he was gone. She stood up and looked around but he was nowhere to be seen. She felt stunned but her illness relaxed her, making her less frightened.

Mother walked up. "Did you find it?"

"Yes, Mom, and you were right. It is cheaper than the other brands and it's on sale."

There was a great deal to talk about that night at dinner and even more in the triangle of knees and legs on Joanne's bed, which was the farthest from Mom and Dad's hearing.

Joanne was still quite proud of her display the day before but was now shaken. She exclaimed, "Maybe we really need to tell Dad and Mom about all of this, and that man. He is real and not just in your dream."

As she described him again, Mark began thinking. "Maybe, I saw this man too. There were two men sitting in the back of your special class and one of them fit your description, though I did not see his hat. But his suit was purple."

"Those are the fashions downtown now; bright, colorful retro looking suits and clothes, especially among the rich and famous," said Dianne. "No, I know it may be wrong, but don't tell Mom and Dad. I don't want them to worry. He is really interested in me. There have been spectators before who have been interested in the prodigy class whom the faculty has told to buzz off. I will deal with it."

"But you had a dream about this one! Perhaps this is a warning from God," said Mark.

"Yes, that is true," said Dianne sitting with a perplexed look.

"Who is this guy?" Mark asked and they sat silently in the dark.

Mark loved to walk. He liked to be out in the clean fresh air looking at different houses and yards, parks, churches, and schools. When he had time he walked a couple of miles at a time. Of course walking one mile in any direction from his house would take one out of Rosedale. Though he would gladly walk with friends and family, he preferred to be alone, set his own pace, which was pretty fast. It was easy and pleasurable. As he grew up, like an explorer in a foreign land, he gradually advanced from his own block to adjoining blocks until he had the whole town in his grasp. He could roam into neighboring suburbs all the way to his high school four miles away. To the west one could go as far as Hamsted Street. Beyond it was a big wood that was a forest preserve. There was always trouble in it with drug pushers, vandals, and gangs. Though he would have loved to walk around in the woods he dared not. So a pleasant walk meant sidewalks. Wherever there was a sidewalk he would follow it. Isolated places with paths would be nice, but isolated places were also trouble spots and where bad luck was known to hang out when it was not in the woods. So it was that he associated a pleasant walk with a clean tree-lined sidewalk and curb-bound street with homes on each side and some people around, someone sprinkling a lawn, some sitting on a porch. Barking dogs were good.

This particular walk in May brought Mark onto the main street of a neighboring suburb. His objective was a Christian bookstore. Dianne wanted one more book to complete her collection of an obscure twentieth-century theologian-philosopher named Schaeffer. He was also shopping for Joanne though he did not know what he was looking for. It was the twin's birthday next week on May 11.

As he rounded the corner he was suddenly in a large throng of people on the sidewalk and some in the street with their backs toward him. As he looked over them he saw fire engines and emergency vehicles in the middle of the street. Hard streams of water were being trained on the huge flames licking out of the windows on the first and second floor of what used to be the Christian Book Center and a number of stores on either side of it. Smoke poured from the roof. The building cracked as floors and walls buckled and collapsed and firemen ran to get out of the way. He overheard one onlooker mentioning something about the building being a firetrap and that it was inevitable that someday it would happen. Mark watched until it was put out and then began walking back and forth behind the crowds and up and down the main street to get different views. He noticed a limousine among the backed up cars as he began the walk back home but he did not want to be seen as nosey and so he passed by and walked on. Perhaps it was the mayor or for a wedding party he thought.

That night in the triangle: "But no mayor in these parts has a limousine. The mayor is an ex-newspaperman," said Dianne. "Maybe he's the man in my dream. He was dressed like he should have been in a limousine."

"No, Di, the fire was just an accident. I heard some people say that it started in the bakery next door. "It could have been for a wedding," said Mark.

Dianne looked at him with her penetrating green eyes. Her face knitted in thought like a detective with problems to solve.

Mark continued, "Look at Dad's publishing company. It's still making the same books. Remember what he said at dinner the other night? All the problems they seemed to be having have all come out right."

Joanne looked on watching her brother as if he had won a point in a tennis match and then looked back at her sister waiting for a reply. When Di said nothing she added, "Anyway, Dad and Mom don't even want to talk about that stuff anymore. They say it's not good to discuss rumors and pumping up our thoughts over nothing.

"Do you believe it is all nothing—the dreams, the man in the class and the supermarket, those odd policemen?" said Dianne turning her gaze on her sister.

"I believe you. I'm just saying they don't want to talk about it. Mom told me so," said Joanne.

"How about you Mark? Do you believe me?"

"Yes, of course I do. Besides, we have all seen one thing or the other. But I haven't seen any of those funny policemen since last fall."

"Maybe they wear regular clothes now. Maybe they're using computer eyes now," said Dianne.

"Yeah, maybe—but let's talk about something else for awhile," said Mark.

Dianne did change the subject, but only in a different context. "Did you hear that they're going to computerize everyone in a few months? It's going to be a voluntary experiment; computer chips for the hand. Apparently, that will only be temporary though. I heard about it at the university. It's the beginning of various methods of computerizing everyone so they won't have to carry ID cards or charge cards. And you know what that sounds like?"

"Yeah, it does, but where is the antichrist?" asked Joanne.

"Dumb, dumb, he's recovering in a hospital, remember Aliadin? I've heard at school that the best doctors in the world and from this area are working on him. They say he has a brand new head and that he'll be out of the hospital in a few months. It's all fitting together more and more and no one is doing anything about it. It's like we're in a horror movie without the hero," said Dianne.

"Don't say that—Jesus is the hero. He will come back, any time now," said Joanne.

"But when, until we're all toast?" said Mark.

"Dad says there's nothing any of us can do about it, except maintain our faith," said Joanne.

"But why don't they say more about these things to all of us together now," said Dianne. "Mom and Dad are so dumb. You would think they would tell us about all of this instead of ignoring it, and Dad is so smart, why doesn't he . . ."

Mark put his hand to her mouth as she grew louder. "Di, they're silent because they are frightened for us and they don't want us to be."

The days seemed to be passing quickly as the final weeks of school came. All of the outward happenings of the past year seemed tragic. The Brogen family tried to maintain normal life despite the world-wide news. The family drew close to the other families they knew and closer still to each other. Father now ended every worship time with the statement, "Jesus will come for us any time now." In the triangle they began to wonder what the future really did hold for them, especially for Mark as he was graduating from school and would be entering one of the state universities. The ordinariness of life still dulled the jagged pieces of apocalyptic doom and it seemed so attractive.

Mark thought about all his reading and the history study he loved so as he lay in bed. Next year always came before.

Tomorrow and next week were still more real than illusive comic-book-like dictators, mysterious policemen and strange dreams. But then Hitler, Stalin, and Hazziz had been real. Was civilization about to make one of those dramatic shifts that might be understood if one could step back from it all? No one ever stepped over a boundary line from one era to another as one stepped over the lines of a football field and been aware of it. Nobody ever got up and said one morning, "Yesterday was the Middle Ages and today is the Reformation." On the other hand, in every century the end was anticipated and Christians looked forward to it, longed for it, dreaded it, and feared it. Were they now there? He looked into the darkness of night and put all these thoughts and questions before God.

Chapter 7

A SHATTERING BLOW

Mark awoke, yawning. A warm spring aroma drifted through the open window. One more week to graduation he thought as he lay back in his bed, thinking how the time had gone so quickly. He got up, put on his trousers and T-shirt. As he was doing his push-ups, Joanne appeared.

"What do you want, Bozo?" he said.

"To wrestle, what else."

"Don't you think it's about time we stopped this? And anyway it's Saturday, remember?"

"Never, why should I? Next year you'll be off to college and then I'll only have Di and she doesn't wrestle like you."

"She'd claw your eyes out if you tried this in the morning."

"Anyway, you going with us to Dad's special company day?"

"Naw, I was there last year and besides I have to see Jerome today," said Mark with a yawn.

"It'll be really neat and they're having a fun fair along with it. I got an idea, if I win this wrestling match you go with us, okay?"

"That's an easy bet, short stuff."

Joanne got on top of Mark who was on his hands and knees and they tussled for some time. Mark was determined to win and he didn't even horse around like usual but Joanne was determined to win and was getting stronger all the time.

"Mark, Joanne, breakfast is on the table. Please come now!" yelled mother. She always yelled when she made pancakes and they were ready.

"I can't wait until college, then I can get away from this old routine—finally!" groaned Mark as he finally put Jo's back and shoulders down on the floor and sat up.

"You're a crab," Joanne said mockingly and threw a sock in his face as she ran out of the room.

Around the breakfast table Mom and Dad were in good spirits. But Mark and Joanne quarreled over a final piece of sausage.

"Why can't you go with us today," asked Dad wanting the family to be together and to have Mark meet his boss. "You know that he's hiring summer help and it would be good if you went along," persisted father.

"But Dad, I wanted to be with Jerome and the guys today. Besides, after next week he'll be going on his vacation with his parents and then to college orientation in California. I probably won't see him again."

Mark finished breakfast and was about to leave the table.

"Before you go, could you sweep out the garage and empty the garbage?" asked Mom with a smile. Then Dad suggested, "The lawn needs mowing too, you know."

"Oh, Mom, can't I do it . . ." Mark said, completely ignoring the last suggestion.

"Mark! Do as your mother asks," said Father pointedly.

"And remember the wheel you promised to change on my bicycle," added Joanne.

"Can't you change it yourself ?"

"Mark, you promised her," said mother.

"Ok, Ok, Ok!" he moaned, as he went out the back door with a slam.

"Gee, he's in a bad mood today," said Father.

After the table was cleared and the dishwasher filled and everyone was ready, they went to the car and found Mark putting on the new wheel.

"Honey, don't forget the garbage, Ok?" said Mom as nicely as she could. "We'll be home around five." She gave him a kiss on the cheek and insisted that the twins give him a kiss too, one on each side. Mark felt embarrassed as the two sisters did as they were told. Mother made them do embarrassing things like this at unusual times, and the kids hated it.

"Tell Jerome we'll see him next week at the commencement, if it pleases the Lord," said Father as he got in the car.

"I will. See you later," he said after them.

The "if it pleases the Lord" tarried in his mind as he worked.

The day went well as Mark, Jerome, Allan Bovard, Wendell Tyler, and two of Jerome's cousins played in a back alley for more than three hours. The warm spring air felt fresh and invited them to shed the sweatshirts, play hard, and breathe deeply. They finished with a series of trick shots. Then they reminisced over soda pop while sitting on the picnic table in Jerome's back yard. For senior cut day, Monday, they decided to go downtown. Mark hoped he could square it with his parents. Jerome told him they couldn't be that old fashioned and that everyone had had a senior cut day and did not tell their parents unless they got caught.

"I bet even your mother did it," said Jerome in his most innocent manner, and then in a roaring voice he said, "Me and my girl are going on the town tonight!"

They walked around for awhile, went into Jerome's house to watch TV and at about five everyone went home. In the end Jerome gave Mark a ride home. Both were happy and boisterous. Everything was going well. The sun was low but bright. As Mark got out, Jerome's car pulled away with a screech and a roar. He laughed and shook his head and then sat down on the front step of the walkway that led up to the porch under the shade of the huge elm tree in their front yard and watched the waning of day. Then when he had sat long enough he went around the back and puttered in the backyard and garage for a long time.

He had forgotten what time it was when he went into the house and saw the kitchen clock which read 6:30. He checked the phone messages but there were none. He sat in the living room until it got dark, but he didn't turn on any lights. He started looking at a sports magazine and fell asleep. Consciousness came back to him when his stomach began to growl. He found his watch and saw it was

8:08. They should have come home by now, he thought. They should have called by now.

He wandered around the dark house, turned on the kitchen light and leaned on a counter. He got some cheese out of the refrigerator. He felt panicky. It was the first time he could remember that nobody else was around the house at this time. Mom was a fixture. Why had they not phoned him? Should he have called them? He found Dad's cellular phone in his chair but did not know who to call.

With a gnawing need for company he turned on the television and sat before it but not listening. The noise was enough. Should he call someone? But who? They should have been home by now. They definitely would not be at the plant. Many thoughts went through his mind. He ate cookies. He felt sure that everything would turn out normal in the end. After all, he had been late many times; Dianne and Joanne had been late, Mom had even been late, they all had been late corporately and individually. When they went to church they were late. They always seemed to be late when they all had to be ready and arrive somewhere at a certain time. The ticking of the miniature grandfather clock on the wall now seemed to get louder as his mind started running faster and faster to the thought, but never this late.

Suddenly, there was a knock on the door. He laughed at himself for his stupid fears. Opening the door, expecting to find four figures, there was only one and it was Mr. Danforth. It was not unusual for Mr. Danforth to come over on Saturdays to talk with father but it was the new situation that seemed different.

"May I come in Mark? I called at four and five-thirty but nobody answered. Then I decided it was better to come over to see you here. I rode by earlier but there were no lights on and I knew you were probably still out."

"Sure, come on in. Mom and Dad aren't here. They're still out, but I'm sure they'll be home soon."

The two sat down across the room from each other. The pause and silence in sitting down with a man he had never really talked to alone made him feel uncomfortable. Mark heard the ticking of the clock again. Mr. Danforth looked like he was trying to say something but he stopped and Mark noticed a tear coming down his left cheek and then one on his right. His heart beat faster and he sat up.

"What's happened? Is there something wrong?"

"It's . . . it's about your parents and Joanne. They're . . . they're dead . . . and Dianne is critical," he said as his emotion made him stop at every word. Then Danforth kept talking and improved over his halting emotion and was explaining something about an explosion and a fire. Mark was stopped at the word dead. A thunderclap; strange, terrible, and nerve twisting had struck his heart. His stomach clenched and his head reeled. It was like all the air in his lungs had gone out and he could not breathe.

Danforth was on his feet asking Mark to come with him to the hospital to see Dianne. Mark's legs moved. He even picked up a jacket and turned out the lights but he was struck dumb.

In the car he slumped down and closed his eyes. The tears came down hot and wet. The world did not matter— nothing mattered now. Time had stopped. Life had changed in a moment for him with one word. Dead. Then his mind

clung to Dianne and his heart yearned for her companionship. Danforth was talking but Mark did not hear.

The hospital emergency unit was only a mass of noise
and confusion, with people walking about all looking the
same, sounding the same. They went through many corridors, then up an elevator to a desk. All of their house church
families were there and either gave Mark a hug or spoke
reassurance to him. Mr. Danforth whispered something to
the nurse. He would be allowed only fifteen minutes.

Mark then awoke from his trance to say to Mr. Danforth,
"I want to be alone with her."

He went in and was startled at the damaged body: the
casts on her right leg and left arm, the tube, the monitors,
the extensive bruises on her chest that he could see above
her gown and the covering sheet. There were bruises on
each side of her face. Mark knew the explosion and fire had
killed and injured a great many people, but it was inconceivable that his family had been in the midst of it. He looked
at his sister who was trying to move. Her head moved slowly
and her green eyes peered at him weakly. Tears formed in
them. Mark moved around the monitors, came close to her
and found her hand and held it.

He studied her and then looked at the chart which said
Dianne, but it was Joanne, he was sure of it. The girl lying
on the bed tried to say something, inaudible at first, but it
got clearer as he put his face close to hers.

"Can't wrestle too good."

It was Joanne. A nurse came in and told him he had
only five minutes left and she was not to talk much. Mark
did not know what to say. He felt the error in names at this
point did not matter. Joanne tugged on his hand to come

closer. She whispered what seemed to be nonsense and he thought she was not herself.

"Mark, run . . . far, di . . . far . . . don't . . . let hat . . . man get . . . you."

Mark bade her not to speak and tears ran uncontrollably from his eyes and he could hardly control himself. Joanne kept speaking and eventually got clearer.

"Man in hat was . . . there at . . . the factory." Joanne closed her eyes and rested a moment. The nurse came in saying time was up. Joanne mustered her last strength.

"Mom, Dad, Di, with Jesus . . . but die."

She stopped. The monitors sounded alarms. All of a sudden people appeared and started doing things. They pulled him away and out in the corridor. The family doctor appeared and patted him on the shoulder and told him he could do nothing but leave her to the better surgeons. Soon a number of doctors appeared and Mark and the families saw them all go into her room which was adjacent to an operating room through an inner door. Mr. Dudley asked what was happening. A nurse told them she was going for more emergency surgery and explained the problems; the multiple fractures in her ribs and damaged organs.

They sat praying together occasionally and silently watching a clock round out two hours. Mark thought of Joanne's last words, but he could not think through the forest of gloom and depression which made him weep. Mr. Danforth sat close beside him, his eyes closed much of the time and his lips moved. Two different doctors came out and walked slowly toward them. They made them stay seated.

"I'm sorry son, but she didn't make it. We did all we could but . . ." The doctors continued their explanation, but Mark ceased to listen. The others asked some questions but Mark was in a nether world. The question of why went through his mind and stuck there.

Mark found himself in a car and soon at the Danforth's house lying on a double bed in a perfectly silent dimly lit room. It was very late but he would not sleep. He lay with his face down, his clothes still on, with no intention of doing anything. He sobbed hard and at regular intervals, making his chest tight, the tears soaking into the bedspread. His questions of why became vocalized into the mattress. He just could not understand it. His life, the day, everything changed in a moment.

He buried his head in a pillow and continued to sob. Every time he thought of sleep he also thought of his mother, father, and sisters. All dead! He thought of the day that had just gone before. He remembered the wrestle with Joanne and wished he had lost and gone with them. He remembered breakfast and his temper at having to do the work, how the twins were forced to kiss him, how his mother and father consoled him and how they were going to his graduation, "if it pleases the Lord." Were those the words his father said? All these things, so commonplace, suddenly became important last words and deeds that went through his mind a hundred times, that signified things he was too dumb to see.

Was God playing a cruel joke on him, leaving him alone? He tried to think about Joanne's final words and that she was trying to tell him something. It was said that his parents and Dianne were burned beyond recognition along with countless others. This sickened him and a new round of uncontrollable sobs washed out any possibility of significance. He had rarely cried before this day and he even thought about that briefly, but he did not care about anything.

Countless scenes of life with his family flitted through his mind; wrestling, the triangle, Dad's taking long walks with him, Mom's sitting on his bed and stroking his head when he was sick, her embarrassing kisses, all the games, and antics. Then the stab of the present broke in. Alone! Them gone! How can it be? It should be I who is dead, not them! Why Lord?

Margaret Danforth quietly walked in the room and sat down on the bed beside him. She did not speak but began to massage his shoulders. Mark's thoughts seemed to fall to pieces before God's feet. He felt as if Jesus were rubbing his back. He felt ashamed for all his questioning and cursing. And a heavier, heart cry came over him and he sobbed and sobbed and prayed, "I love you, Lord. I need you so much. Please . . . help me! Please . . ." He prayed this over and over. In his mind he saw a picture of Christ on the cross that hung on one of their walls, only he was looking at him and weeping. Then he wished Jesus would come and hug him. Soon he fell into a deep sleep. Mrs. Danforth removed his shoes and covered him up.

The next morning he awoke and in the next moment Mrs. Danforth broke the silence. "Would you like something to eat, Mark?" she asked. Mrs. Danforth had been close enough to the family and now to Mark she was an angel. She was a counselor by profession and Mark had always found her manner warm and accepting. She had taught the teens in the house church's version of Sunday school. He got up and she sat him at the counter. It was late morning and Mark forgot how hungry he was.

Mr. Danforth came in and sipped some coffee and began talking.

"Mark, I want you to know that we have taken care of all the funeral arrangements," he said, looking at him and then cautiously said, "They died quickly, Mark, and they're safe with God. I'm truly sorry for you and you can stay here as long as you like. Are there any relatives we can contact?"

Mark stared into his third helping of pancakes. He had not said a word to anyone since he asked to be alone with Joanne. His voice cracked and wavered with the tidal wave of emotion that seemed to well up just as he was to speak. "I have . . . an aunt in Baltimore and one in Atlanta." He swallowed and regained some composure, "And I'm supposed to have an uncle, but my mother only spoke of him once that I can remember; something about a black sheep in the family. My father was an only child. All our grandparents are dead."

"Mark, about this uncle, there's been a fellow; I've been called by him several times today. He was with the police and at the identification. He seems very concerned."

Mark only shrugged his shoulders and nibbled on a pancake.

Danforth continued, "About your house, Mr. Burnshaw said he would help and I will take care of the legal matters of liquidating . . ."

Mrs. Danforth cut him off and said, "I think Mark is too tired to talk about that now dear."

After having eaten, Mark went back to the bedroom to sleep but he lay awake most of the time crying and praying.

The only funerals Mark had ever been to were for three grandparents. Grandpa Wilshire had died five years before he was born and the others were at various stages of his childhood; important times filled with confused and uneasy feelings, but easily forgotten after they were over. Mark assumed that old people die. Only a few days ago death had been associated with news reports and war movies.

Now death had a personal meaning. It changed things, made everything ugly. The world seemed to have a new tint, a veil had been drawn; his family wiped off the stage. Where were they now? Where was he? Everything that he learned in the Bible, everything that had ever been talked about or prayed about with Dad and Mom and in the triangle was strained and put to the test. What about this depression that hung like a shroud about him? Even the promise of heaven and eternal life was difficult for him. Mark nodded in agreement with the Danforths as they consoled him and explained about them being in heaven and the assurance he had of God's continued faithfulness. But the shock of it, the loneliness that he felt was so overwhelming. Even if they had had time to say goodbye, it would have been better.

Hence he found himself sitting and looking at four closed caskets. Pictures of them were placed around and among the flowers. Two little teddy bears were placed on two of the caskets. He was astounded at the number of people who paraded by and filled the place; people his parents had known in church, friends of his, friends of the twins and many others he had never known. Employees of Dad's firm who had survived the explosion and fire congregated around like wounded war veterans. The surviving leader and spokesmen, Mr. Clancy, came to Mark and commiserated. He put his arm around Mark and spoke in his ear. He confirmed that the investigation found arson and terrorism to blame. He said, "Some Middle Eastern group dedicated to destroying Bible producing companies that supply missionaries lay claim to it. You can be proud, they died for Christ."

Jerome, his parents, his coaches, and the team appeared. Aunt Helen and Cousin Cassie came up from Atlanta and Aunt Kate from Baltimore came to be with him. Both offered to take him in, but he told them he did not know what he wanted to do yet. All of the attention made him feel better. With the crowds of people about he hoped by some bizarre mistake that his family was still around. But one more glance at the caskets and pictures brought tears to his eyes.

At the cemetery Mark stood for a long time after the others had left. The Danforths waited for him understandingly down by the car. He thought of how Mom and Dad had joked about inheriting six cemetery plots. Dad had hoped that they would never use them. He stared at the grey marble, the roses, and carnations all around. The wind blew, the leafy trees bowed and rustled about him.

He walked down the gentle hill thinking how tomorrow was graduation day and how they were to have a big party.

Chapter 8

UNCLE

Margaret Danforth persuaded Mark to attend his high school graduation as she said it would be good for him. Afterward, he was warmly received in the house church get-together for various graduates, among them Robert Bass from high school and Mindy Dudley from junior high school. The latter only made him think about his own sisters and he sat disconsolate through most of it.

The next day he sat around in the family house looking at everything, gleaning every memory. He would go from room to room, sit, think, stare. In Dianne's room he sat and looked at her math notes. He did not notice that her laptop computer was missing. He looked at the pictures and keepsakes about the walls and room and then at the stuffed dog on her immaculate bed. He wished that she would come into the room and yell at him to get out. In the kitchen he wished Mom would come around and tell him not to eat the cookies, ruining his appetite before dinner.

"There are perfectly good celery sticks and apples to eat," he could hear her say.

Silently, reverently, he sat in his father's den, fingering all his books. Then he looked through all the family photos, making him cry once again. He seemed to remember every little detail of his family's existence, from the color of toilet paper Mom preferred to Dianne's writing her own piano music as a hobby. In Joanne's room he looked at the dirty clothes still in a heap and the generally disheveled and messy appearance of everything. "A place for everything and everything in its place," he could hear her say as Mom insisted that she clean it all up. It was impossible to believe that they had just been here alive four days ago and now were . . . dead. All of the things in the house were attached to living people.

He looked at his own room, lay on the bed and thought of the triangle; all their discussions ran through his mind, all their seriousness, and silliness, laughing and Mom or Dad coming often to break them up. He remembered Joanne memorizing Bible verses and Dianne reciting whole books of the Bible, and with their commentary from the notes. Hence, in the dark they could study anything without a light on or open books. It was Joanne, however, who seemed to have the most direct and uncanny way of praying so appropriately. She was so simple and sincere that one felt God hung on every word. He cried as he thought of their wrestling matches and how she was probably wrestling with Jesus now.

In a new wave of emotion and depression he looked at the ceiling and yelled, "What about me! What's going to happen now?"

"That's simple my boy, you can have me sell all this stuff and you can come live with me."

Mark jumped up, frightened and embarrassed by the sudden voice. "Who—who are you and how did you get in?" said Mark looking at a slim man, impeccably dressed, in a black three-piece suit, with a bowler hat in one hand and a smooth plain cane in the other. His blue eyes were sharp and penetrating.

"But who are you?" questioned Mark as all past visions or sightings of this man rushed into his mind.

"Why, I'm your Uncle Theodore Wilshire. Didn't your mother ever tell you about me? Then I suppose she thought I was not very interested in the family. And she would! My sisters always did think I was a nuisance. Come boy, let me see if your mother has a picture of me."

Mark showed him where Mother's pictures were. Then Uncle Ted did find several, but one especially of four teenagers. It was funny Mark had never noticed them before.

"I'm sorry, but Mom never did tell us about you," said Mark, noticing how much like Mother's his face was, except for those eyes. His light gray hair was very short and he was almost bald.

"You don't remember but I did meet you at a family reunion. You were much younger then," his uncle said. "I was at the cemetery yesterday but stayed in the crowd and didn't want to make a scene. Please call me Uncle Ted, and don't worry, my eyes are the same brown that your mother had and you have. These are just colored contact lenses. Can't see an inch without them," he said as he studied Mark.

Mark studied his uncle as he saw him as he was described in Dianne's dream, and how Joanne had seen him in the supermarket and how he had been sitting in the back of the room the day Joanne and he went to substitute for Dianne.

"Have . . . have you been . . . around this area long?" asked Mark hoping to find out more definitely.

"Why yes, I live downtown."

"Have you tried to contact anyone in our family lately?"

Uncle Ted smiled and laughed a short laugh. "Well, yes and no. If you mean have I tried to make your sister Dianne's acquaintance, yes. But if you mean seeing your parents, no. Your mother, God rest her soul, and I have not been on speaking terms for years and I have avoided her."

"So you did see Dianne?" queried Mark.

"See her, yes. But unfortunately, I never met the departed lass. But enough of this, all that is by us now. Why don't you come with me for dinner and we can discuss you and your future."

Mark suddenly found himself being lavished upon like he had never been in his life. He continued to stay with the Danforths for another week and the matter of the house was put into Uncle's lawyer's hands, and his own belongings were moved by Uncle Ted's men.

The Danforths were not sure about any of this and queried Mark about how he would be. However, Mark could not see any harm in his uncle's interest. After all he was part of the family and he felt there was no other place to go. His uncle also enticed him by including a college education at one of the best city universities, all expenses paid.

One partly cloudy day in June Mark found himself leaving Rosedale in frosty air conditioning. The black limousine moved quietly along the main streets and highways that led toward the loop. Mark had always enjoyed seeing the many tall buildings and enjoyed the thought even more that he was going to be living in one. Uncle Ted looked on proudly as well and said, "Why people like mountains and the countryside is beyond me when really they are all more awed and proud of the creations of men." As they rode along the lakeshore, Uncle, as his name was now shortened, pointed out a very tall complex on the edge of the lake. "That's where you will live my boy." In minutes a private elevator took them to the top, the penthouse.

Mark had always wondered what it would be like to live in a place like this. The living space was immense and there was much he would enjoy exploring but the view attracted him first. The lake was a radiant blue. Sailing boats looked like tiny moths and cars looked like ants. He had to be pried away from this vista in order to be shown his room and begin an informative tour of the basic amenities and facilities that were the best and most advanced. The ultra modern décor made him feel like a bumpkin and out of place. There was the computerized housekeeper that was three-and-a-half feet tall that cleaned, made beds, dusted, and even made small conversation. The robot was the only moving part of a computerized apartment-wide system that performed its various functions automatically or by command. Televisions, computers, air conditioning, and heating all ran on their own. Air and humidity monitors made sure that just the right amounts of the elements were in the air for the healthiest atmosphere. Water and filtering for the full-sized pool in the rooftop garden, heating and the perfect control of the various hot tubs and whirlpool baths in the bedroom quarters and near the pool were all controlled automatically or by voice command.

Uncle took him on a tour of the whole building and Mark understood that he did not just own the penthouse but the whole building complex. Back in the penthouse he showed him, among other things, part of his collection of old and new gadgets and inventions. A museum on the first floor housed the rest of his collection. In the collection were things called the typewriter and the mimeograph machine. This led to an evolving line of things leading up to a series of computers of the late twentieth century, and then there was the whole line for the twenty-first century. Uncle pointed out that all of the computers were brought into line with the latest technology. Even the older ones could do most of the things of the latter but they were slower. Then he smiled and said, "Each one can communicate back of its own accord, either in audio or on the screen and best of all, each has its own personality. Try them and you will see." They played with them. One had a very intellectual bent, another was a flirt, beckoning him to caress her keys and find her secrets, another had a religious proclivity, another had a scientific personality, and on and on.

Uncle Ted was a bachelor and somewhat of a loner. Mark would learn of his parties and unusual friends only in the months to come. Uncle's business remained a mystery. His belongings seemed shabby and ancient compared with all the modernity; the housekeeping robot confirmed this. It made quite a fuss when it found the appearance of his room and clothes rather distasteful and it said so. The meals were diverse and first class being cooked by gourmet chefs who catered the food up to the penthouse at just the right times of day. However, it was obvious Uncle Ted was not used to living with anyone. He came and went willy-nilly. Thus Mark ate his gourmet meals at a round white table in the watchful company of the robot and some pets. Uncle had a parakeet and a large tank with a variety of fish living in it. Sometimes he made believe the series of computers were people and he talked to them and they communicated to him. He was given free run of the place while Uncle was gone for many hours at a time.

Then there were the hidden cameras that he observed as he studied the penthouse carefully. Some were not obvious. Others seemed to look at him with interest. He noticed one in his room, but he hung a coat in front of it. Uncle said, "These are for security reasons only; in fact they are computer run and no human is really watching. It's a nuisance I know, but it's because of those blasted terrorists. If something serious happened they would immediately notify the security force in the basement levels."

He spent most of his time roaming the penthouse and trying out the pool and hot tubs, playing pool and trying out his computers. One room was a movie theatre that had everything just like an old movie theatre. In Uncle's den he found only trivial novels, technical and diet guides, and some exercise magazines. However, one of Mark's favorite gadgets and the most curious to him was the story machine, a computer that had many parts and compartments from the rear, but in front it looked like an old coke machine. There were a number of tabs and buttons in straight rows under a sign in Latin that indicated reading was here to stay. There was a small computer board arranged in the center. The soda pop machine like buttons had the names of common subjects on each one. One only had to push a button to get the desired literature of any time or genre, poetry or prose, fiction and non-fiction. He typed in history but only got the closest related subject title—social studies. There were many titles but few that he had seen before. He chose one for fun. He entered and pressed the pop-bottle button. The publishing computer whirred and clicked and entertained him on the screen with a cartoon. Ten minutes later a book dropped out into the tray below. It was entitled, *Capitalism, the Current of Time*. It told how capitalism was prepared for and how it was the central plan of all history. Its thesis was that world capitalism was inevitable and was growing stage by stage until it reached the whole world and became the economic vehicle on which a one-world government would be established. As he studied the list and the notes alongside, he realized that there was a whole series of books on one-world government and its establishment in history.

He pressed the religion button and found a bible and many titles that he had never seen before. There were tracts on how to love one's neighbor, American civil religion, how to give money to charitable causes, the Mormon plan for health and, one entitled *Modern Christianity*. The book he received stressed that Christ was a gifted teacher who had tapped into the spirit world and understood the nature of man and how he could be saved. There had been many christs, but one would come to re-establish the world and set it straight from its evil, ignorant ways. The last chapter stressed that this Christ was in the world today and had appeared and would be established to bring the world into one harmonious system. He would lead all mankind in the scientific-religious quest to find immortality.

The bible he received was tailored and edited to correspond to the books in the list that again appeared to be a series. The last book in this modern and modified bible was called "Revelations," and it mimicked the real book of Revelation in the Bible. Here the Savior of the world would be resurrected in the near future and bring total harmony and peace. The ideas he read here were not new to him, but he had never encountered the literature before. He recalled Dianne discussing these things and Dad saying to stay away from them.

The most amazing feature of the machine was not the dispensing of books, but the writing of them. He tapped into this feature on the keyboard and then typed out an idea or a random sentence. The computer then produced a poem or story. If one became more elaborate in the instructions it would churn out novelettes, short stories, and comic books. There were key words that could produce volumes with illustrations such as romantic, racy, sexy, or perverted. Uncle understood his interest in the machine and lamented that he ordered one made for newspapers, but it was still being developed.

By the looks around Uncle's den and in the drawers kept unlocked, it appeared that Uncle Ted had a rather debauched taste in literature.

There was much in Uncle's penthouse that certainly appealed to Mark's youthful interests and libido. However, in the opening days and weeks of his life with Uncle he remained true to the Christian and family values that were instilled in him. His mother and father would have been amazed at his self-discipline. Of course the cameras, hidden and visible, did help. As he adjusted to his new home his mind was still unsettled and this made him seek the Lord. Brooding over the tragedy left him awake many a night. The robot usually woke him with a feminine voice every morning around ten thirty. Uncle explained that men needed a female presence in the morning for one's mental health. The robot could speak in such human qualities that the first time he heard the voice he looked in every direction but at it. The robot's name as he was reminded daily was Vicky.

One day when Uncle was away, Vicky woke him and proceeded to tell him about how it had been observing his troubles with relaxation and suggested he follow her. Vicky led Mark to a contraption that might have reminded one of a telephone booth or as Mark saw it a casket but it was larger. The large rectangular booth had glossy dark-tinted glass and doors. Inside was the most comfortable chair he had ever sat or lay in; it adjusted perfectly to the human shape of any size. He asked Vicky, "What is this machine?"

She whined, "It relaxes people who ask too many questions and need a little vacation."

He did not feel reassured by this answer, but thought it would be worth a try. As he lay back hesitantly many soft pliant arms gripped him and several straps were comfortably brought around his shoulders and legs so that he could not fall or move. Then a headset was placed over his ears and special goggles placed over his head and eyes. The door was closed and he felt as though he was not lying or standing or sitting. The air conditioning unit kept the temperature perfect and breathable. There was no discomfort about being snugly tied in except for a feeling of helplessness but even this was pleasant. He received a terrific massage as he listened to classical music, the kind Dianne liked to play and a three dimensional world appeared all around him. It was as if he had entered into the woods and was walking up a trail with mountains and vistas opening up before and all around him. Soon he was flying over the valleys and mountains, fertile cornfields, hills, mountains, lakes, and streams—all teaming with life. Then he flew through cloud formations and saw the sun rise and set with geese flying only a few feet away from him.

Mark was just feeling as if he was going to enjoy all of this when he felt a slight jab of pain in his left arm. Suddenly he felt dizzy and he closed his eyes. When he opened them he was flying crazily and laughing hysterically. Then he was flying through a spectrum of colors and doing cartwheels all at the same time. He closed his eyes again and when he opened them this time there were alluring girls dancing in mid-air flirting, taunting, beckoning him. Pulsating rock music came over the earphones and he felt as if he were dancing. One of the girls flirted with him. Her beauty was a combination of extraordinary sensuousness and uninhibited lustfulness. Then his whole body seemed to let go as she got closer and closer until they partook in natural and unnatural acts until he experienced a wild release of pleasure. He was laughing wildly, everything was spinning around and around as if he were a fighter plane losing control. He heard himself shouting, babbling, talking obscenities, then he felt faint and drifted into sleep.

He awoke, unaware of any time, still enclosed in the machine; it was massaging him. The same gentle music played as before, the same hills, waterfalls, and forests were around him. When the door opened and he was released, he staggered out, not sure what had happened. Every muscle and sinew in his body was definitely loose, but his head was still spinning and he felt a heart-gripping guilt that began to build as he recalled the act of debauchery. He spent the night reeling from the experience and laden with guilt before God. He had experienced nothing like this before. His high school friends used to jeer at him for not being sexually active.

"That is just the effect of the drug. It will wear off," said Vicky observing him through her large lenses. "Did you find your experience stimulating? The Somodrome is programmed to administer hundreds of different programs. One can choose one or let the machine give you what it thinks you would like. Dr. Wilshire does it regularly. He says it is important to experience total freedom in all things."

"That was a drug?" asked Mark astoundingly and looked at his left arm and saw a small bruise there. He was not sure now how relaxing and freeing this thing had been as he now had a headache. He made a personal vow never to go close to that thing again. From then on he questioned everything that Vicky introduced him to and shied away from invitations to visit the Somodrome.

Uncle Ted related to Mark with no sign of embarrassment that the Somodrome was programmed to administer stimulants and relaxing drugs without a person's will being involved. He said, "The visitor feels no guilt or tension for taking a drug. The machine monitors all bodily functions and prescribes just the right dosage. The one drawback is it cannot monitor for allergies and other bodily reactions on the first visit." Uncle was a strange man to Mark and most decidedly not a Christian, but he was attracted to him.

During the third week Mark was admitted into City University and began classes. He started to take long walks all around the city. He went to baseball games and enjoyed life as never before. He enjoyed his classes and walked across downtown every day, avoiding all efforts of his uncle and the doormen to offer him transportation. After establishing his usual route to the university he discovered various cameras at corners; he was sure there were other hidden ones. He switched his route and eventually found more along that way. Were they following him or did he see them because he looked for them? He decided he would live with it as the university had them everywhere as his high school did. He wanted to enjoy life and be normal. He forgot about reading his Bible and to pray. He watched sports and began to read Uncle's books.

One Saturday night Mark was introduced to friends and a number of business-related individuals whom Uncle was entertaining for business reasons. The empty handshakes and hellos tipped him off that he was not going to enjoy this. The music began, the drinks and food were displayed and consumed. Soon the place was filled with people in each room and in the indoor and outdoor pools and hot tubs. Tours of the penthouse led to periods of talking, dancing, and loud jokes. Young women came to these parties as well as other kinky types that his high school mates copied. A fuzzy redhead tried to seduce him right off. Uncle tried to get him to take a drink but he passed on these propositions. The Somodrome had a long line of visitors. When Mark saw his uncle against the backdrop of these friends and associates, he saw how much like them he was and how different these parties were from his family's gatherings. He now saw how the strange suits and bowler hats fit in with every flip new fashion.

As the party got louder and more loosened up, the more difficult it became for Mark. He disappeared into his room. Later, when his room was thought to be empty by a drunken man and woman who barged in and sat on the bed, he took off down the elevator rather than argue. At this moment he felt the most awkward. It was two thirty in the morning. He walked through the lobby past another indoor/outdoor swimming pool that was still active and large gaming rooms that opened out from the basement. People were everywhere, so he went past the electronic sensor doors that knew him by name, picture, voice, and code word. The door asked why he was leaving and where he was going, since it was so late and so it could record when and if the occupant came back. "I'm lonely and I want to take a walk," he said. The computer said that the first part did not compute, but gave him the temperature and the weather conditions. "Have a nice day," it concluded.

He went onto the nearly deserted beach, looking back at the gleaming buildings, then out into the dark lake where a few boat lights could be detected, then at the marvelous skyline and he thought about his past friends and family. When he came back two hours later he found Uncle asleep in the Somodrome and other people lying around, half unconscious. Someone had vomited all over the carpet. He found that his own room had definitely been used; the sheets torn off the bed and a great wet spot on the carpet that gave off the acrid odor of urine.

The party stripped away his peace of mind and the feeling of settling in nicely disappeared. Instead he now only wanted to get along and to endure these episodes with whatever patience he had. Mark found that Uncle entertained every other weekend without fail. He decided to go out on the town at these times. He allowed Uncle's chauffeur to take him to football, hockey, and basketball games, concerts and plays and to stay out as late as was possible. He enjoyed partaking in Uncle's wealth, but he desired to be a loner here. He did make some acquaintances at the university, but he felt no need to seek out friends. He enjoyed being on his own. The parties turned the penthouse upside down with no regard for anything. One night, Mark even found that one of his trophies had been used for obscene games. On the days after these parties, when Vicky was freed from her closet, she and the penthouse systems went to work until the house was perfect and immaculate once more. When Uncle recovered from his parties he acted as if none of it ever happened.

Eventually, Mark began to take long walks almost every evening and Uncle tried to dissuade him as he might be mugged. Occasionally he asked if he could stay with the Danforths or at a friend's house for a weekend. Uncle would get very silent and Mark understood this to be a negative answer. Their conversations became shorter and broke off when ever Mark tried to discuss anything theological or philosophical, and especially when he asked about his business. He only said he was at the head of an extremely diversified international company that was purely American. The only subject he did address at length and heatedly talk about without any prompting was how

Mark's mother and her sisters despised him and how his father had turned him out.

It was not until Christmas when he finally got out of the city and could stay with the Danforths. When he saw them and all of the old company he felt sure that they had changed. Or was it he who had changed? He saw the stark contrast in lifestyles and homes. It took him sometime to relax, especially when all of their attention was on him. He told them how he had started college and had no difficulties getting into the work, and how he was majoring in history and minoring in English. Mr. Burnshaw asked him why his uncle did not come and Mark replied that he was busy having guests of his own. What he did not tell them was that these guests meant days of parties and not just one night. His guess was that Uncle did not want him around to be a nuisance and this was why he was allowed to go away.

The missing family had a great effect on everyone. Mark had tucked away all thoughts of this kind for a few months. Now all of his memories came back in a flood. At dinner tears welled up in his eyes and suddenly in the worship afterwards he realized what he had missed. He saw his parents and was reminded of the triangle, the commitments, prayers, and vows they made to be true to each other and God. He felt nervous, embarrassed, and uncomfortable with this family worship now; the adults and various kids, Dudley's daughter and her boyfriend and relatives of the various families were all there. But this atmosphere of people who felt and showed their pity for him made him feel convicted to confess his forgetfulness and sin in open prayer. He had forgotten his quiet times, praying, and God; but all of a sudden he felt more comfortable and free than he had in months. He regained the conviction that he was still very much obligated to his parents and sisters to do the right thing. Throughout this whole evening he never noticed a small camera in an upper corner which was trained on him.

With this renewed faith Mark tried to confront Uncle about his religious beliefs one day after classes. To his amazement, instead of cutting him off, Uncle clamored long on the new Christianity, and the love of man.

"If we must talk of religion—the only religion is humanity, God in humanity. We are one with Him and He with us." From the philosophical to the legalistic, Uncle ranged up and down the spectrum of thought while pacing up and down the room not once looking at Mark, nor stopping to see if he understood any of it. It appeared as if Uncle was preparing for an exam.

When a crack in the one-sided conversation did come Mark threw in his only question which acted like a rock splashing into a pool and settling to the bottom.

"Do you believe in the historic Jesus Christ, who died for our sins on the cross, rose again from the dead and who now is with the Father, and who will come again?" he said.

Uncle smiled and said, "Oh, how like your mother you are when you say it like that. Of course I do, and He is now with us on earth in mankind. To get to the true Christ is to get close to our real selves . . ."

Mark could not get any satisfaction here and no longer responded. Uncle prattled on until he finished and then he moaned, "I think I need a drink."

Chapter 9

THE DECISION

Mark felt confused about his life and felt as if he were being drawn into something, but did not really know what to do about it. He had always depended on others to do the real thinking. Dad and Dianne and even Joanne at times had been so good at giving answers, seeing through things, figuring out what to do. If there was some conspiracy happening he did not detect it. He felt Uncle was not an enemy, but just a rich nut and actually, by the world's standards, normal.

Mark had only been a Christian for four years and he had grown slowly from conviction to conviction and there were moments of wavering. Though he surprised himself in asking Uncle about Christ, he was always timid when it came to talking to others about his faith.

He walked slowly down State Street and he was not really seeing the sidewalk, the store windows, and the people, but how dependent he was on other people. His prayer life had never been too active. Dianne and Joanne prayed most in the triangle and Dad at worship. However, he liked to talk to God, but did not think of it as real prayer. He pretended he was in a conversation. Usually he felt it was going only one way, but sometimes God surprised him with heart-felt answers as he read the Bible or recalled a passage. What he liked most was feeling God's presence, just being together, knowing He was there and close by, but lately with his new lifestyle he ignored his friend. But also he had this craving to just be normal and enjoy life and he thought he had reached it. More often than not, he forgot about God and praying at all. He so hoped that somehow he could get along with Uncle and that everything would turn out well. On the other hand, visions of Dianne and her conspiracy theories haunted him and ruined this normalcy by making him uneasy. He noticed a camera on a corner of a building as he waited to cross a street. They always seemed to be looking at him. Thus he lived in a perpetual tension.

He continued to eat most of his meals at the round white table being served and entertained by Vicky, the computers, and the pets. More and more his mind was now drawn to Uncle's racy novels and movies, and the endless sports channels instead of studying his Bible and talking to God. Vicky and Uncle's easy philosophy of life were having their effect on him. Day in and day out they dropped little suggestions; "get out and loosen up, live a little, it can't hurt, nobody sees and nobody cares, if it doesn't hurt anyone else, do it." Uncle created proverbs like, "We will always be young with the Somodrome. Work is a necessity, but pleasure is a must. Satisfaction from one's work is important but pleasure is all important." He knew all these ran counter to any proverb in the

Bible but then he realized Uncle read the newly created *Bible of Modern Christianity*. However the sheer repetition and the fact that all the pleasures of life were at his disposal made it now a tough choice.

However, his habit of taking walks, as he was now, became a sobering activity where if God was not talking He certainly was making Himself felt. Suddenly, Jesus, the triangle, Mom, Dad, and a host of Christian saints that he had been fond of reading, all seemed to come to mind on this particular day as he walked in the afternoon sun from class.

Suddenly, he stopped. He had forgotten an appointment that his professor had made to see him. It was one thing for a student to want to talk to a professor and being made to wait. It is an entirely different thing when the professor wants to see the student. It was 3:36. He was to be there at 3:45. He alternately walked at his fastest pace and ran back the four blocks. He moved through one campus building into another to avoid crowds on the sidewalks and he finally came to the tallest of the university's buildings. There was a long impatient wait for an elevator. It was 3:55 when he knocked on Dr. Donald Crawford's partially opened door.

"Come in, come sit down," said Dr. Crawford, coughing from an ill-timed sip of coffee. Books, journals, papers, lined the shelves all around the professor. More papers, books, a coffee mug and a paper plate with crumbs on it surrounded a small, black, laptop computer. There were more stacks of books, and old newspapers all over the floor. Mark was currently taking Dr. Crawford's large lecture class and he admired him but had never met or talked to him. Crawford had grey hair and a grizzled beard and large brown eyes that now watered as he cleared his throat. To Mark he was intimidating and the silence made him nervous. With his hands on his knees he looked Mark's way again and took some time to start.

"I called you here because of something very important."

"Is it about class?"

"No."

"About that book report, I know I could have done better but . . . ."

"It's not about that either. It's about you." Before he spoke again he got up and opened the office door and looked up and down the hall. Then he looked about his office, its walls, and ceilings. He looked at Mark's clothes carefully. "Try not to be alarmed, but have you received any injections lately?" Mark shook his head. Then as a second thought he asked, "Please, Mark could you step into the bathroom. Try not to be alarmed, but we need to have a very private talk," he said. An awkward silence followed which made both of them nervous.

"This isn't a joke is it?" asked Mark. His mouth formed into a silly smile.

"No, it is no joke. Please, step in here." He closed the door, locked it and leaned on it as he faced Mark who leaned on the tiled wall by the toilet. "You must not discuss our conversation with anyone, and I mean anyone. Do you promise?"

"Yes, sir," said Mark as he braced himself for some homosexual advance or weird demand that he might have to fight his way out of. Dr. Crawford did not look like he would do any of these things. But then no one could tell who would do what to anyone anymore, and especially as he learned about all these things in Uncle's parties.

"It has come to my attention that you are living with a Dr. Theodore Wilshire. Is that true?"

"Yes sir. He's my uncle."

"Do you know anything about him or what he does?"

"No sir. Not really. Why is this important to you?"

"I am an historic Christian. Do you believe in Jesus Christ, the historic Savior who died and rose for your sins and that only in His grace and in a believing relationship with Him you are saved and that He is coming again at a time nobody knows?"

"Yeah, yes sir," stammered Mark, "with all my heart." He was stunned at the pointed question from a professor in a secular college. No teacher in any of his time in school had ever brought up the subject. But he was encouraged that someone in this university was also a Christian, even if he had to admit it in a private bathroom.

"Let me see your hands and arms."

Mark rolled up his sleeves and held out his arms. The professor examined the tops of his hands, then his arms, and his forehead with a magnifying glass.

"Have you had any operations recently?"

"No!"

"How long have you lived with your uncle?"

"Eight months."

"Where did you live before that?"

Mark explained about his family and their death and his uncle taking him in. The professor mumbled to himself, "Just what I thought."

"Mark, I know this is going to sound strange and difficult and I don't want to frighten you, but you must run away from your uncle."

Mark looked at him agitatedly for a long moment. "Wait a minute! What is all this and what do you mean—run away?"

"It's for your own safety. I cannot tell you anything more. You will have to trust me."

"But what's wrong with my uncle?" asked Mark. It never occurred to Mark to ask how Dr. Crawford would have come to know anything about him to confront him like this.

"I cannot tell you and it's better if you did not know either. I'm sorry. I can make arrangements to pick you up this afternoon after school and get you out of town to somewhere safe."

"Is my uncle a criminal?"

Dr. Crawford forgot himself and said, "He's much worse than that . . . but I've said too much already. You'll just have to trust me, Mark. Everything will be explained to you in good time. I realize how strange all of this must seem to you. I will tell you about myself another time too."

"I don't understand. Why should I run away from an uncle who has been kind enough to give me a place to live and paid for my education? And besides, he's part of my family. I admit he's strange, perhaps eccentric, but harmless as far as I can tell. Why is any of this stuff a concern of yours?"

"Your uncle is a dangerous man and is connected with some very high powers in this land; one of many who would sell his soul to the highest bidder. And you . . . he may be using you. That is all I can say."

"But who are you and what do you represent?"

"An organization opposed to the rapidly coming one-world government. But unless you join us, I cannot tell you anymore. I've already said too much. Will you run away tonight or tomorrow? Will you trust me?"

"I don't know, let me think about it. Does it have to be tonight? Why can't it be next week, or at the end of the semester? Why should I run away from college too?"

"Because you would lose the element of surprise and it would give you more time to succeed in getting away. You risk being sucked into his work."

"I . . . let me think about it for a few days."

"That may be too late, but if you do change your mind, meet me here at 7:00 P.M. and say you are going to a seminar for the evening."

Mark shook his head in confusion and shrugged his shoulders. "I don't know," he said softly as he was allowed to walk out into the office and then out the door. The professor shook his head. Dr. Crawford thought that perhaps he had been too rash in trying to talk to him so quickly. Would he tell his uncle or anyone else about this? Should he have waited and gotten to know him better? These thoughts worried him as he put on his coat and left the office a few minutes behind Mark.

He said nothing to Uncle about his afternoon and spent the night studying and watching Monday night football. The hour that Dr. Crawford had wanted to meet him was long past. He had no intention of meeting him. Why should he? He pushed all thoughts of God and prayer away. He tried hard to forget the undesireable conversation he had with Dr. Crawford, but his thoughts came back to it and it became a sticky, unbearable shadow. In bed he spent a restless night thinking, half-sleeping but always waking. It took Vicki some time to awaken him the next morning.

When he did get up he thought about how things were going very well. But Dr. Crawford's conversation tormented him and he fought it. His uncle had not given him trouble about his own affairs and he felt happy in not troubling Uncle. Life here was not perfect, but he would get along. He liked it. Besides, in another year or two he would be on his own completely, would transfer to another college, get a job; any number of gratifying, normal, possibilities lay ahead if he stayed with Uncle.

He could not think of even one good reason to run away. Dr. Crawford seemed to talk about doing something dangerous—against the law. Distant conversations flitted through his mind from the triangle, about underground organizations fighting evil. But that had not been real to him. His father used to cringe at such thoughts and called these groups fanatical and extreme. Yesterday he had come face to face with a man who claimed to be from a real secret organization fighting a one-world government. He knew Dianne and Joanne would have been very excited and probably would have run away if they were in his place. But running away; wasn't that for little kids, fantasies, novels, and movies? If he did run away what would happen? There was no assurance of anything. He would be breaking the law and going against the society he longed to become a part of and he would not be able to return without being punished and perhaps thrown out. This was not normal and he just wanted to be normal and live as countless Americans had lived—an average, free life. If Uncle was really out to get him, perhaps running away would be one solution. But if he were not, what then? He would be making a mistake, one that could not be reconciled easily.

In the end he resolved to stay with Uncle and ignore Dr. Crawford. Forget him! He would be Ok and Uncle would be Ok.

He had worried so much about all this that he felt tired and crabby. But he felt good about making his decision, good enough to be talked into a visit to the Somodrome by Vicky. Thereafter he went to the Somodrome often and enjoyed all the facilities that were offered, which pleased Uncle. He even joined in on one of his parties.

About a month and a half later Mark was piddling with one of his favorite personality computers. He played a game for some time and decided to check his z-com. The computer made what looked to Mark like a mistake and brought him inside one of Uncle's coded areas and offered him an urgent message that he decided he would open. A three-dimensional holographic image projected from the computer's camera. Beside him on the desk was a well dressed man with red kinky hair and a fair complexion. He said, "Hi Ted, how are you, Ed here. How about that golf game Friday at three."

Mark was about to get out when he heard, "We need to talk about the kid you picked up. You'd better stop coddling and playing around, leading him on. We'll need him pretty soon, so call me and let me know when we can have him. See you Friday."

He had the message repeated and he watched and listened once more. Did the message mean him? Did Uncle have others or perhaps in one of his philanthropic enterprises he helped orphans and runaways? Did he want to test this? He looked at the man's face and asked himself if this was someone he could trust. A stab of fear went through him. There was no doubt that something was going to happen which involved him. Now the world became complicated. He looked at the computer and asked if it knew what the message meant and if it had intended to show this to him. It was silent when it was usually highly talkative. He knew that if he was the one intended, that the computer was protecting itself as any answer could be retrieved later. A cold sweat formed on his brow, his heart thumped, he felt paralyzed.

Before he got up he knew he must compose himself, especially in front of Vicky. He decided on a plan of action and looked around his room for things to take, but Vicky's presence made him drop the idea of taking anything. He ate as normally as he could with Uncle even though he was not hungry. The two said very little as was usual. The TV blared on the wall and Uncle watched the twenty-four hour news intently. Time ticked by agonizingly.

"Well, I need to go to my office and catch up on my work," said Uncle politely as ever. "Oh, I was thinking of making a basketball court for you on the activity floor."

Mark smiled at him and said, "Ok, that would be wonderful. Thank you! I think I'll go for a walk tonight.

"But it's raining miserably, I think you should stay in and not get sick. Go down to the running track," responded Uncle looking out the window. Vicky was asked for her opinion and she gave a report not only for the weather but of Mark's health and said, "A sinus cold could result from my monitorings of your bodily functions." This was something Vicky did while they slept.

Mark knew he could not go out without suspicion, so he waited and obeyed. He ran on the track in the exercise facility on the fourth floor. He then returned to his room and tried to read. Knowing that Uncle probably had heard the message made him edgy. And what if his uncle really wanted to keep him and not give him away. Perhaps he was having second thoughts. Did he want to test this? He would have to gamble;

he hated the idea of making a huge life-changing decision. He would have avoided it in any way if he could, but what if it is all true? He swore to the ceiling and at God. He did not want to make this decision. He wanted someone to make it for him.

He made plans. Tomorrow was Wednesday. He could go to college and not come home. That would be good considering Uncle always had a cocktail party on the Northside on Wednesdays and he did not come home until late. He switched on the TV and quickly bypassed the news which he ignored whenever he could. He found a basketball game, but was mindless to it. Instead, he tried to console himself. Perhaps his friend had only wanted to give him a job. Mark had wondered when Uncle would get around to asking him to work. "Yes, that must be it," he muttered under his breath.

Uncle appeared on the TV screen in one corner, and said, "Mark, would you like to go to a friend's house on Saturday for dinner? I promise you'll have a good time. Mark? Mark? Is anything the matter?" He stared at the two-way screen and said, "Oh yes! It would be fine."

"Good, do try to get some sleep. You look tired. Good night."

Did he want to wait and put his consoling thoughts to the test? He knew he had to make a decision for sure now. Could Uncle really be so dangerous? How could he face Dr. Crawford whom he had not talked to since their encounter? These conflicting thoughts made for a very restless and sleepless night. "I must sleep," he told himself. "It could be a long day tomorrow." He prayed now for the first time in a long time and found himself instead of asking God for help, confessing his ignoring Him and longing for His reassuring presence in his life. But it was the kind of night he hated and dreaded; a big decision was coming and he must act on it—alone.

The day was the coolest and rainiest of spring days. It was almost a year since his family had died and the dread of being alone hung on him once again as he left the elegant penthouse without even a toothbrush or a hand computer. He forgot his daily vitamin which he never missed and brought none with him. But he did have $12.50 and one pocket handkerchief along with a now-useless backpack of books and a notebook. He went to the university and sat through his classes not paying any attention. Then came Dr. Crawford's class. He sat through it impatiently, drawing up courage to tell him afterward. The hour crawled by.

Fear, tension, hopelessness all vied to dominate his mind. He expected Uncle to read his mind and walk through the door any second. His stomach became knotted, the palms of his hands became moist. Why could he not just melt into a puddle and evaporate from the earth forever? Why did he matter to people? Why did people want to do things to him or take him away or make him do dangerous and unpredictable things? Why did God make the world so complicated?

Why couldn't Christ just come back right now, and take him up in the Rapture or make him invisible to everyone but God and normal people? Why couldn't he simply go unnoticed and get away from the two forces squeezing him: on one side was Uncle and his mysterious friend who were going to use him. Dr. Crawford was on the other side, wanting him to run away. Why couldn't he have died with his parents and sisters? The bell rang.

People were moving to the door. He got up and his legs carried him to the front. He heard his voice say, "I need your help."

Dr. Crawford led him away back to his office and back into the washroom. He was not angry but surprised by Mark's sudden turnabout. Mark did not explain what happened but only asked, "Is it too late?"

"It's never too late, come with me," said Dr. Crawford as he took him to the history department library and made him sit and wait.

After committing himself to the act, he felt as if he had crossed some invisible border between the normal world as he had known it into a strange one of the unknown. He found that a weight had been taken from his shoulders. All routine, work, study, and play fell away. Two graduate students looked at him curiously as he sat in his coat, his backpack on the floor and no apparent interest in the library. He looked back at them. Before today he would have been envious, even jealous of their position. Now he did not care if the sun rose again. It was just as he felt when his parents and sisters died; the world ended for him. He had gone right out into oblivion and felt no concern for his own life whatsoever. He was helpless and hopeless of any future. Only one thought came shouting through his mind, "God, help me!"

Chapter 10

REPENTANCE AND HELP

The rain pitter-patted on the roof of the car. Water was suddenly everywhere as it ran down the sides of people, buildings, and cars. It got heavier. Drops plopped onto the front window of Dr. Crawford's small sedan, but just as they formed and ran down the window a wiper blade erased them. The pendulum swung to and fro, collecting and erasing everything in between. Mark was glad to be riding in a car and hoped that the ride would be a long one. He sat limply with an expression of dejection, eyes fixed complacently at passing streets and neighborhoods which were all meaningless now. He was glad that the professor did not talk to him. He was in no mood for questions or for conversation of any kind except for the yes and no variety.

"Did you tell your uncle anything about our conversation?" asked Dr. Crawford, breaking the silence all too soon for Mark's liking.

"No," said Mark, wiping the condensation on his window with his hand.

"Do you want to know where you're going?"

"No."

Dr. Crawford gave him a sidelong glance. "Do you have much money?"

"No."

"What changed your mind about coming back to see me?" asked the professor who was looking for a way to get Mark to loosen up and talk.

"Because . . . because, I overheard a conversation my uncle had with a friend."

"About you?"

Mark turned on the radio without asking, hoping that the conversation would end. "Yes," said Mark. With this he laid his head back on the head rest and closed his eyes. Dr. Crawford became silent.

About fifty minutes later the professor turned down a little alley and proceeded to the back of an old red brick church and parked on some newly laid white gravel which crunched under the tires. Mark was sorry the trip was over. He was led through a back door into a cool, spartan basement with numerous metal folding chairs and rectangular tables. Dull light came through the glazed basement windows. Told to sit and wait, Dr. Crawford disappeared through another door.

Fifteen minutes later, the professor came back in the company of a minister. They sat down at the table with him. The minister introduced himself as John Casey. Another man came through the door and brought a carton of clothes and an old sleeping bag. He introduced himself as Bob.

"I'm sorry, Mark, these things are the best we can give you for now," began Dr. Crawford. "I know how you must feel right now, but I can say this, you are a brave young man. You may not know it, but you are in the place many of the church fathers were throughout history."

Mark looked at the professor distantly as he said this.

"We will be sending you to a place far out west tonight. You will have to stay here for now. We're sorry you could not have gotten your own clothes and things, but we have to be as secret as possible. We are all in very grave danger. We have learned that the antichrist, Premier Aliadin, is now in charge of a trade confederation which includes the United States. His miraculous recovery from that head wound has made him more than a hero. The peoples of the nations are clamouring for him to be the head of a new triumverate of world leadership that has been approved by the majority of high level people. More and more companies are pledging and contributing support as a hedge against instability. That means his power will increase. We also know that your father and the company he worked for were one of many objectives listed to be subverted or wiped out."

Mark became more interested and sat up. "But what about the president and Congress?"

"You will recall the explosion in Congress and the assassination of the president and the attempt on Aliadin. The men who stepped into all the empty offices had Aliadin's backing. Your uncle is involved though we don't want to frighten you by telling you too much," said Dr. Crawford.

"But who is he? You can surely tell me now," Mark interrupted.

"Let's say he is powerful enough to have us all killed. We have reason to believe he was behind your family's murder," said Rev. Casey. Mark closed his eyes and when he opened them they were running and he looked at a distant corner of the basement. After he had digested this and swallowed he wanted to know more.

"I want to know everything! Why should you hide all of this?" Then he directed his attention to Dr. Crawford alone. "Why didn't you tell me all of this when we met months ago?"

"We were not sure of any of this a few months ago and we didn't want to scare you. He is one of Aliadin's key men in this country."

"What does he do?"

"We are not exactly sure. There have been many rumors, none of which are confirmed. We think he has something to do with scientific research as well as political scheming in business circles. But enough of this, let's get back to you. You must be taken as far away as possible because where you are Christians will be in danger," said Dr. Crawford.

"What do I have to do with it? I don't have some seal on my forehead or a microchip in my hand. I hardly know my uncle."

"No, but once your uncle knows you are gone he will put on a search and, among other things, he will suspect the historic Christians. If you are found with us or any Christians, we will die," said Rev. Casey.

Mark stared at them not quite comprehending. "Isn't that what Christians are for—to stand up courageously and be persecuted or die for Christ?" he said.

Bob broke into the conversation enthusiastically, "Yes, it is, but the task remains to keep Christians alive and organized as long as Christ tarries."

Suddenly Mark perceived the situation and was unnerved by it. "But I am a pariah to you then," he said in a loud voice.

"No, Mark," said all three men at once.

"Then why did you want me to run away? Why didn't you just let me be used or killed? Then I wouldn't be a problem to anybody. I'm confused, I'm sorry I am alive." Tears formed in his eyes. It was all he could do to keep them back, embarrassed that he should cry in front of them.

"Because, Mark, you can perform a valuable service to us," said Dr. Crawford.

"Which is?"

The three men looked at each other pensively. The minister spoke first, "To be . . . to be a sort of decoy, to see how the secret police security works so we'll know how to get around it."

"I am a fox for the hounds?"

"Don't put it like that," cried Rev. Casey.

"Mark," interrupted Dr. Crawford. "It is not like we are going to throw you to the wolves. That is why we must get you out fast and far away. We are saving your life and you know it."

Mark looked away to the corner again in silence. He could feel his heart thump.

"As far as a decoy goes, it will simply be a test for our underground to be able to observe their tactics over the city in searching for you. You will not even be around. They do not even know there is a specific underground organization for Christians. They think we are just a band of disunited churches and denominations working separately.

Remember that I told you we were an organization fighting one-world government? Many Christians don't even know, because we have been trying to make sure our secret is kept and so we are working slowly to inform them," said Dr. Crawford.

Mark hunched over in his chair putting his elbows on his knees and cradling his head in his hands as he looked at the floor. He suddenly saw Dianne in his mind as he remembered her telling him long ago that she believed there was an underground organization.

"So now you know enough. You will be leaving late tonight with some other people. I'm sorry we cannot provide you with a better place to stay, but the less you're seen the better. Tomorrow your face will be recognized by every policeman—that is if your uncle wants to find you."

Mark's stomach turned and his head throbbed as he listened to this last statement. They gave him some books and a Bible to read, showed him some old clothes and prayed together. The professor shook Mark's hand, said goodbye and left. He ate a lonely meal of hamburgers and French fries. Already he felt like a prisoner as time ticked by ever so slowly.

He knew his uncle would not be home until late. His guess was that he would not be missed until tomorrow morning at the earliest. Now that he really knew who Uncle was, he felt frightened and sorry he had not left sooner. He shook his head at his own stupidity as he suddenly remembered Joanne's puzzling words before she died. Of course, the hat man was Uncle and she had warned him to stay away from him. And because he was his uncle he had not wanted to believe Dr. Crawford either.

The basement grew darker and dreary as night came on. He had the urge to investigate the church but he didn't. Instead he paced up and down the basement. He went to the bathroom numerous times for something to do. He turned on a light and read for awhile, but he could not concentrate enough to read for any length of time. Sometimes his eyes perused the shadows for something to look at or fiddle with. At one end of the basement there was a locked closet door and the back door he had come in through. To one side was a portable black board with no chalk. Close by were some punched out biblical characters pasted to a wall. At the other end of the basement were doors leading to the toilet and the stairway and another locked one that he suspected led to a furnace. A pile of old hymnals were stacked neatly on a table in one corner. Close to the other corner was a serving counter and a barren kitchen behind it.

The absolute silence was broken by footfalls on the wooden stairs leading to the sanctuary. The door opened and a young girl about his age appeared. She wore a winter coat and carried a small suitcase and a sleeping bag. There was an awkward silence as she moved about.

She gave him a meek smile, and said, "Hello, my name is Laura Simmons, what's yours?"

"Mark. Mark Brogen."

As she turned on more lights he could only see her face because of the tight fitting knit hat that she wore. She went to a table on the far side of him. As she unzipped her coat and pulled her hat off Mark could see her blonde hair fall about her shoulders. As far as he could see in that light she was pretty and quite slim. Immediately Mark's mind began fumbling for things to say, but his desire to speak died before he could verbalize anything. Instead, the two sat silently for a long while with only the squeaking of chairs and the creaks of the tables making any noise. Laura was just going to say something when a group of older people filtered in, all carrying baggage. They looked at Mark, then Laura and said their hellos but they stayed in their own groups. In a short time there were twenty people standing or sitting in small clusters.

Reverend Casey stepped into the room. Mark had forgotten his name but was reminded of it as someone spoke up.

"Reverend Casey, when are we going?" asked a heavy woman sitting fairly close to Mark. Before the pastor could speak another voice interrupted. "Reverend Casey, is there any truth to the rumor about Dr. Crawford being arrested this evening?" I heard Bob talking about it," said a short, squinty-eyed man. Mark was shocked and he recalled that the third man he had met earlier was a Bob, and was unnerved by all the wonderful talk about secrecy earlier.

The other people gave interjections of shock. Rev. Casey came over to Mark and spoke quickly and quietly as he could, but was still overheard, unaware of the subtle shifting of the heavy woman.

"Mark, there has been some trouble. It seems your Uncle found out about your being missing and made some quick phone calls around." Mark cringed as he had forgotten about Vicky and the computerized front door to the building. Together or separately they could communicate with Uncle at any time they thought it necessary. Rev. Casey continued, "Our sources were too late in warning Dr. Crawford. The secret police are faster than we imagined. They have found out that you were last seen with Dr. Crawford, but don't worry, you'll be safe."

The heavy lady got up and motioned to the minister to talk with her privately. Mark watched as they went to a corner and as they talked she faced him while Rev. Casey's back was to him. He could see her look at him while she talked and noticed that she got louder. Her husband went over and joined in. The minister whispered and tried to calm them. They sat down agitatedly and spread their story to the others. Soon the room was buzzing with nervous conversation with Rev. Casey's voice rising above them.

"Now let's talk together. We are all Christians. We are all under a great God, and many of you came because you fear persecution is coming in some way, or you need a new home. Though the underground is new and we are badly organized, we need to be strong. Now let's pray together. You all have a long journey together."

Before the pastor could pray a voice spoke out. It was the heavy women's husband. "But do we have to go with . . ." Here his voice softened and was hardly audible and he pointed discreetly with his head toward Mark. Then his voice grew louder as he said, "We could get into more trouble."

Another older woman seconded this statement and a short, partly bald man said, "Yeah," but then asked what the problem was. A chorus of voices started up again.

Mark had the distinct feeling that a tide had turned on him and it was being circulated before his eyes as to who he was and how Dr. Crawford was arrested because of him.

Rev. Casey tried to restore order, and was embarrassed for Mark, regretting telling even one person who Mark was related to.

Mark had no idea that Uncle's name was known to other people. By some sort of grapevine it was apparent that many did and now that he was connected to him by relation, even the most inordinate fears went through the minds of the people in the basement.

Up to now persecution had meant pressure to conform. This persecution was of varying degrees of visibility from neighborhood to neighborhood, town to town, city to city. By word of mouth many knew who and where this pressure was coming from. They had heard about the new antichrist and began to feel and think about a more brutal form of persecution. Many were hoping to escape and hide before the tidal wave of Aliadin's power was at its height and greatest scope. This was what brought fear to the twenty-odd people who looked at Mark as a possible informer at the most and as a liability at the least.

As the people balked at riding in the same car with Mark, he felt the urge to run and get away. He did not notice the sympathetic gaze of Laura among the others. He got up as Rev. Casey was still trying to reassure the others, and with his jacket, walked to the door. Casey tried to stop him and talk to him, seeing his distress, but Mark just brushed past him and walked upstairs. He had the urge to go for a walk outside, but felt instead the stronger urge to sit in the chapel.

He sat down and started to pray audibly, pouring out his heart before God. Hot, wet tears ran down his cheeks. He was confused again. The world was moving too fast. He thought about his family and the change that had come at their death and how stupid and deliberately blind he had been to fall in with Uncle. He thought about his becoming entangled so easily in a strange web that made him an orphan, a runaway, and an outcast in a matter of hours. Feeling his hopelessness, he longed for his parents and sisters, but now for the first time he could clearly see that he loved and depended on Jesus alone. He confessed all his sins and hardness in wanting to live with Uncle and run his own life.

Like the lamb being singled out and pushed through one gate after another until it is in the right place, he saw that God had led him to this point. He felt so rejected, but he also now felt the unmistakable presence of Christ; feeling as though he could reach out and touch Him, hug Him, hold His hands; if he could only see Him. And oh how he wished he could do that for real. The reality of the room came back to him momentarily and he realized his life was not over and he must do something. But what? It was Christ's hand he wanted to hold and His face he wanted to see, His feet he wanted to fall before and be with forever. What else was there now? Why didn't He come back now and save him and those poor frightened people below him? He prayed for them and for Dr. Crawford. He now felt guilty that he had endangered them with his willful disobedience. He prayed that somehow they could be freed from the antichrist and fear. He continued to talk audibly in his prayer for almost an hour, shutting out all other things. He did not hear the doors below open and close and the cars in the back drive away.

In the corner of his eye he saw a person standing by the side door. Having been so intent in prayer and wanting to see Christ, he expected to see Reverend Casey, but instead he saw Laura. This startled him and he felt embarrassed, not knowing how long she had been there.

"What do you want? Don't you want to go with the others?" Mark said coldly.

"They just left," said Laura not sure of how to proceed. Mark looked away, irritatedly, toward the front.

"I thought you might want this," she said as she walked slowly toward him and placed the musty sleeping bag by him. She did not sit, but stood cautiously and meekly in the aisle.

Feeling that he should say something he asked, "Don't you have a family or something?"

"I did, they were missionaries . . . killed ten years ago in a plane crash." Anticipating further questions and not wanting the conversation to die, she continued, "I have lived with an aunt and uncle and my grandparents since then. I'm studying in college. I just decided that I would like to visit my uncle out west and this was the easiest and cheapest way to go."

"And the weirdest way to go," added Mark sarcastically.

She started to laugh, but ignored this comment and merely continued, "So here I am. I'm not resettling like the others downstairs."

Mark now noticed how beautiful she was and felt attracted to her but was wary and amazed that she should want to be with him at all. He then told her about himself and his family as briefly as she had. Then he said, "Aren't you frightened of me?"

"No, not at all. Should I be?" she said frankly.

"Hey you two! We got to get you out of here," said Rev. Casey, surprising them. He took the situation in quickly and was happy that Laura had put Mark at ease. He clapped his hands together and said, "Now, I have a plan."

Chapter 11

LAURA

hicago's Union station, restored yet again, stood surrealistically against the background of an other era because of the art objects and airport-like atmosphere. All the old smells and sights of earlier train travel were replaced by the new era. Uniformed hostesses welcomed the travelers. Engineers had finally found the status of the airline pilot and lowly bus driver; they wore uniforms. Real restaurants appeared, not just fast food. The old solid marble and heavy architecture had been hidden by panels, steel, and tile with colors unimaginable in such places before.

Sleek new trains, owned and run by private enterprise, made for fast, inexpensive travel and were finally safer than their past counterparts. America was awash in another wave of nostalgia, bringing back faint memories of nineteenth century capitalism and the impregnable Western mystique.

A new Pullman Company went into business making sleek new passenger cars.

Regular policemen and special police in their purple uniforms stood at various places looking into the crowds. Most of them were normally there, but now others had joined them. It was 6:30 in the morning and there seemed to be a great interest in a young man who was stopped at one end of the station. Many people gathered to take a look as he was frisked and marched away.

A young couple looked on, moving through a line toward the train platform (or embarkation bays as they were now called). Mark peered at Laura through his horn-rimmed glasses, smiling and looking relaxed. He felt the air conditioning blow on his head and felt his flat top hair cut with his hand. Ancient haircuts were in vogue again. He couldn't remember when he noticed his ears so much. He wore a cheap baggy suit and next to him stood Laura, looking pretty much as Mark had first seen her, except that she wore a maternity dress under her coat. She felt her well-formed abdomen and clutched Mark's arm in hers.

At the ticket counter a smiling hostess and a policeman looked at them and at the I.D. cards that Rev Casey had made. "Your double cabin is confirmed, Mr. Rickman." Mark and Laura flashed their wedding rings as he took the tickets and they walked toward the train.

Mark started to feel at ease, only to discover a uniformed man walking quickly after them. "Excuse me sir, you forgot this," the man said loudly. They were extremely relieved to see Laura's knit hat being handed to them. "Thank you," they said in unison.

They were shown to their sleeper cabin. Both plunked down as soon as they were alone in seats opposite each other by the window, and moved the recliners back. They both looked around at the compartment and then at each other and down at the rings on their fingers. Laura laughed uncontrollably. Mark was serious, but came to a smile slowly. Both said in their minds, "Now what do we do?" They sat silently looking out the window. Mark spotted a small camera in a corner of the room but found a small notice around it apologizing that the security system was out of order and with some relief discovered the camera was hollow. Still he turned it the other direction for his comfort.

The train moved out smoothly, almost unnoticed and with almost no sound. The old familiar clickety-clack was inaudible. Mark's eyes throbbed and they could hardly stay open, but he wanted to say something.

"Look, Laura, I . . . I want to thank you for . . ." Turning his head he was startled to see her eyes closed, mouth slightly opened and sleeping soundly. He resumed a careful silence, put his head back and knew no more.

He awoke groggy, his head throbbing, and fresh from a dream. He had been sitting with his parents and sisters having a discussion in a breezy, sunlit house. The windows in the house were wide open. A sultry breeze was blowing in and the rooms were filled with people coming and going. Joanne was trying to get a point across to the others in a somber discussion about her health.

He was disappointed on waking up and longed to be back inside the dream. For one thing he would then not have to do anything. Instead he awakened steadily to the disappointing reality that he was chilly despite a blanket having been placed delicately on him and the heat blowing through a vent near his head. He knew a cold was coming on by the way his throat felt.

Suddenly, he realized that he was alone. Questions flew through his mind. Where had she gone? Had they been found out? He went stiffly to the washroom. It was about the size of an airline toilet. He had liked the sleeper car and wondered what the suite rooms looked like.

His heart gave a leap as he heard the compartment door open with a bang. Cautiously, he looked out and saw Laura with a tray.

"What are you doing?" said Mark, as he closed the compartment door behind her.

"Bringing something for us to eat," she said. "I'm your wife, remember?"

"You're pretending to be my wife, remember? Besides, weren't you scared walking through the train?"

"No, because I'm not the one the police are looking for and we need something to eat or didn't you remember that?" said Laura snappishly.

"There is a steward service you know. You're supposed to be pregnant," retorted Mark. "Didn't anyone try to help you?"

"No, and never mind. We don't want any more attention than necessary, remember?"

They silently and hungrily ate the hot soup, sandwiches and hot cocoa. Laura then leaned across her tray and looked at Mark with a grin. They had yet to sit next to each other.

"I have a surprise for you," she said and then giggled. She held out a package of cupcakes."

"This is a surprise?" he asked cryptically.

She frowned playfully and smiled again. "Well it is our first anniversary."

"Come on, don't kid about that stuff! How long has it been, nine hours?"

"Twelve," she declared, "since Reverend Casey found these rings in his desk drawer."

Mark was impressed by Laura's easy-going manner and began to like her company. But he was still uncomfortable, especially when they got too close together, and wondered how long it would last.

Her blonde hair, parted to one side, looked soft and full as it came down to her shoulders in a slight disarray. She had a thin, carved face and delicate chin and nose. Her large and penetrating blue eyes added depth to her beauty, which Mark explored; they made him feel even more uncomfortable, knowing that most of the time they were on him. Mark was afraid that she really did not like him and was only playing with him for the time being, but he liked the company and hoped it would last.

Laura on the other hand had fallen in love with him back in the church sanctuary. Her parts in their conversations were a defense and a way of testing the waters. She already felt attached to him in one way, as a helper to throw off the police, and she was enjoying it. She instinctively, way deep down, knew they would be in this for a long time.

They finished their cup cakes and hot cocoa. "I'm glad we don't have to sleep here tonight," said Mark.

"You already have."

"You know, I mean . . . together."

Laura blushed and Mark changed the subject as he felt this had been a stupid thing to say.

He changed the subject. "Are we going to meet your uncle at the station?"

"No, I have to call him. I wrote him three months ago and he replied almost at once, but I have not heard from him since. I'm sure he'll be there as always. I've gone to be with him many times. He's a widower. I helped him with the house a few summers back. He used to farm, but he just rents the land out now; acres and acres as far as the eye can see he would say. His two sons decided to stop farming, get married, and move away. They still look in on him often."

They sat silently looking at their hands or glancing out the window. Not contented with the silence, both searched for things to talk about. They had another hour left before they reached their stop in North Dakota.

"You know, you talk in your sleep," said Laura.

"Yeah? How do you know?"

"I heard you. I woke up an hour or so before you."

"Yeah, and what did I say?"

"I couldn't quite make it out. You mumbled, but you were calling out to some one, I'm sure of that."

The sights outside took their attention away from themselves for a little while. They found a deck of cards in a drawer and played for the rest of the time and listened to their headsets.

A soft female voice came over the speaker and the headsets declaring, "Fargo, next stop, Fargo, Fargo, Fargo, North Dakota."

"We're early," chimed Laura excitedly. "Oh, I can't wait for you to meet him. He's such a wonderful and interesting old man. By the way, do you think I could take this off now?" she said, pointing to her belly and the dress. "My uncle is going to think it awfully strange and it will put you in an even worse light."

"Yeah, I guess so. I just hope that everyone that saw us, got off at the other stops like the conductor staff changes. We'll just have to take the chance that no one else really noticed us."

She pushed the small foam pillow down until it flopped out and onto the floor. They both laughed long and hard. She wanted very much to get out of that pregnancy dress and Mark stayed in the bathroom until she had changed back into her sweatshirt and jeans.

"I'm going to be glad to get rid of these glasses," he said as he held them in his hand and inadvertently put them in his pocket. Laura took off her ring in the bathroom and put it in her pocket. They both thought that once they got off the train they would not need the disguises.

Mark watched Laura go to the pay phone while he stayed close to the suitcases. The station was nearly empty as few people got off. It was early evening and the weather outside was gloomy as it had been in Chicago.

He decided to move the suitcases and keep closer to her. She was trying again, held the phone steady and gave him a worried look through the clear plastic door. She hung up again. He watched her slender hands as she studied her phone number again and tried once more. There was no dial tone. Instead a voice said that the number was out of use and the phone to which she was calling no longer available. She hung up and opened the door and stood frustrated with her head against it.

"I can't get him. I don't know what could be wrong."

She looked through the phone book, found his name and they both saw the same number. She called directory assistance and was told the number was discontinued. A concealed camera, smaller than a finger digit, watched the couple's every move and heard every word.

"I'm going to call a friend of his. Don't be alarmed, but he is a retired policeman, and an old friend of Uncle Bill's. He would know where he is. Don't worry, he won't know or care anything about you." She closed the door again and out of his hearing. Mark watched as she dialed and began to talk. Her face changed and her mouth curled down. Tears began streaming down her cheeks. She spent a few more minutes telling of her situation, and hung up.

She opened the door but couldn't talk immediately. Then, "He's been put in a home. He's got Alzheimer's. His son took him to Dallas." She grasped for a tissue, but could not find one in her pockets. Mark handed her his handkerchief and motioned to her to sit down.

"Why didn't one of the sons contact you?" he asked

"I often popped in on him from college and I have not talked to my aunt for awhile since I began to live with some other girls. I guess I should have."

She explained that this old friend, Mr. Travis, was going to pick them up.

After about a half an hour a stout, gray-headed old man walked in with a purposeful step. He put his arms around Laura and kissed her forehead and hung onto her coat sleeve.

"I'm sorry dear. I'm also sorry that someone didn't inform you or your aunt or grandparents. You can stay with us tonight or as long as you want. Who's your friend?"

"Oh, this is Todd Rickman, he's a friend from my church. We were coming out to help Uncle, but now I don't know."

"Let me see, you are the spitting image of someone I've seen," he said looking at Mark inquisitively. "Wait a minute, it's on the tip of my tongue. No, I guess not, I'll have to think."

"Perhaps, Bret Neitglow, the movie star. He does resemble him," said Laura who was afraid of the worst.

"That's probably it," Mr. Travis said, still looking at Mark as they walked.

They were ushered out in this perilous conversation and he drove them around town.

Happily, he changed the subject.

"You know the old town's not what it used to be. I don't know what's coming over the world. I want you to see something." He drove out into the country and in a few minutes they were approaching a huge bubble complex. "They're building them all over now. That one there will replace Fargo one day. They plan on building bigger and better ones so they can plant in the winter and summer." The closer they came the more they could see the superstructure of a vast dome which made it look even bigger than it was.

"See those buildings?" said Mr. Travis. "They're going to move everyone together in there. I've seen the plans at a city council meeting. They'll have a vast housing complex and recreational facilities. They say it will improve production while improving everyone's living conditions. Reminds me of something else in the past, but I can't put my finger on it. The word is on the tip of my tongue."

Like communism in the history books Mark thought.

"Who's paying for all this?" asked Laura.

"Well, the government and a large company are paying for this one. They call the new plan family-corporate ownership."

"Won't that make farming like factory work?" asked Mark.

"Capitalism with a communist organization, one news commentator branded it. They say this bubble will take care of one quarter of the state. They already have a few working down in Kansas and Nebraska. Won't be any small towns left at all by the time they're done. But haven't you read about this in the big city? Oh, but I forgot, dad and blast it, there are no newspapers anymore. Nobody knows anything anymore. Your uncle was dead set against it and he let everybody know it. Might be why he lost his mind. But people have been willing to accept it, as a lot of money has been offered to them for their land and future participation. Farmers who were going broke welcomed the idea, but many others still have pride in their own land, house, and lifestyle."

"What will happen to the ones who don't want to move in?" asked Laura.

"Don't have much choice. The companies have been buying up the land under some new law that's been passed for preserving, consolidating, and making more efficient the farm lands of America. At least that's what the black box says with their pretty language." Here they understood his derisive language was aimed at his car computer. "I'll bring you out again tomorrow, if you want. I've been a bad neighbor. You two must be starving." He turned the car around and headed back into the city.

At the Travis home they met the elderly Mrs. Thelma Travis and were forced to promise to stay at least two days. "It's been so long since this house had young people in it," said Thelma.

Embarrassment came when they were asked how they were together and what they planned to do. Having been entangled in one deception to get them out of Chicago and away from the police, it had not occurred to Mark or Laura that they would have to continue the hoax indefinitely without giving people suspicions or the wrong idea. They looked at each other. Laura began slipping her ring back on her finger and almost formed the word married but did not get it out in time. Mark won, saying how they had been recently engaged.

Mrs. Travis laughed and thought they made a cute couple. But when they were not looking at him, Mr. Travis looked at them suspiciously.

Chapter 12

OUTCAST WANDERERS

The next morning Laura and Mark, with a car loaned by Mrs. Travis, went out to her uncle's house and farm. They found a sign there stating it had been sold to the FarmFlo Corporation. They walked around for awhile looking at the farm. Then they went back into town and to the church that Uncle Bill had gone to and with which she was familiar. They met the pastor, who introduced himself as John Bradley and then they introduced themselves just as they had the night before. Bradley smiled warmly and bade them sit down. He offered them tea and some cookies. He was a mild man with large gray eyes, red cheeks, a big nose and a brown mustache that matched his hair. They looked at each other curiously for a moment. Then Laura and Rev. Bradley discussed Uncle Bill for some time, then about the farm and what would happen to it.

When there had been a sufficient pause Bradley looked at his folded hands and smiled childishly. Then almost as if he were talking to himself, he said, "How long were you planning to stay Mark Brogen?"

Mark and Laura sat up, their hearts each did a leap. Sweat formed on Mark's forehead almost instantly. "Ah . . . well . . . you know who we are, I mean, you know who I am?"

"Yes, I received a coded message from Rev. Casey saying you might turn up. How long were you planning to stay?"

"Ah . . . well . . . I, that is we . . . I really don't know what I'm doing."

"You'd better find out because you cannot stay here," said Bradley and at the same moment handed a wanted poster fresh from the internet. Mark was stunned to see his picture. It read at the bottom:

Runaway! Most important that he be found. He is mentally ill and could be dangerous. Reward $5,000. Phone nearest police station.

A sickening feeling came over him as he handed it to Laura who gave a short cry of disbelief. Mentally ill! Dangerous! A $5,000 reward! Once more he shook his head to think of being caught in ever-increasing difficulties.

"You must be careful," continued Bradley. "The flat top haircut has helped but make sure you wear some glasses. And the less you are out in public the better."

Mark took the glasses out of his pocket put them on and said, "Can you help me?"

"I'm sorry, I know nothing I can do except to give you some more money and put you back on the train. You can't stay here. In fact, people are coming soon to a meeting here. You should try to avoid as many people as is possible. All it takes is one person to recognize you and call. The police have become so much faster and more efficient these days. And it's the "purple police" as we call them who are the most dangerous.

Mark looked at Laura and said, "Why don't you stay here, you'd be safer than with me."

"No, we're a team. We have to stick together," protested Laura "Perhaps, Mark is right Laura," said Bradley. "If you're caught with him you could be in real danger. Anyway, you've already helped Mark in the best possible way in getting him away from Chicago unnoticed."

"No, I'll stick with him," she said, not looking at him and feeling embarrassed that she should have to admit her love for him in this way.

Mark was embarrassed and warmed all at the same time to hear her vote of loyalty; he did not know what to say. Bradley was also touched and told them how brave they were and that he would pray for their safety. He gave some money to Mark and they prayed together. They took the car for its oil change to complete their errand.

They walked back through town arm in arm, but as they approached the Travis house they saw two police cars in front. It was due to Laura's quick thinking that turned them around and prevented anyone seeing them from the house. They happened to be near a bus stop and a bus pulled up at that moment. She pulled Mark and they got on. As the bus went past the house they saw Mr. Travis talking to one of the policemen in the living room. They headed back to Rev. Bradley. Laura called him out of his meeting as Mark hid in the bathroom. Bradley let them into his house and had them hide in an old bomb shelter adjoining his basement and the basement of the church that had gone unused for nearly a century. It was musty and damp, but Bradley suspected that the police would be everywhere once they had any clue or suspicion that he was spotted. He closed the heavy door and suddenly they were in pitch dark and were warned to keep it dark, despite having given them flashlights and candles. A massive, oppressively heavy bookcase was dragged back over the entrance to where it had been. He sprinkled dust and sand back over the places that they had touched with their hands and so it continued to look undusted in the dark, badly lit basement.

No sooner was all this done when the police arrived, asking questions and looking around the house and church. They took a good look at the basement and even computer scanned it. The heavy lead door and room they were in prevented their detection. Bradley said he had not seen anyone of that description or talked to anyone else except those in the meeting that was still proceeding. The people at the meeting concurred.

Meanwhile in the bomb shelter, in the pitch darkness, the two orphans sat silently until they could not hold it any longer. The darkness made them hold hands. Mark's sore throat was developing and he fed himself the lozenges he was given. But he wanted to talk.

"Laura," whispered Mark, "I can't say thank you enough for what you've done." There was silence in the pitch dark. The two were blushing and were glad for the pitch black. He went on feeling the compulsion to tell her what was on his heart. "I have never known any girl well except for my sisters. I used to think there were no girls as smart as they were. I never had a girl friend in high school and I have never met any that I really liked since. Well, what I want to say is . . . you're great."

Mark breathed easy. He had wanted to say something like this for the last few hours. Laura had not made a sound all of this time and he felt as if he might be talking to himself. He could not see that Laura's eyes had become moist with tears by his words, nor could he know that she enjoyed it to the utmost.

It was more than six hours in the dark with only short, lighted breaks to find the oldest bathroom they had ever seen that still, thankfully, worked. However, Mark had broken the ice and they talked more freely about everything. He explained how with his sisters they would talk late into the night. He told her in greater detail how his family was, the house church, basketball, how he became a Christian, about his life with Uncle in the penthouse, going to college, how he met Dr. Crawford and what they had discussed before he met her.

Laura told of her missionary parents, how she had been born in Hong Kong and how they had died when she was only eight, how she really had never known them well. She felt she had come along as a mistake late in her parent's lives. She explained how she had a brother, but he was so much older that she never knew him as a brother and how he was a missionary in South America. She told him about life with her grandparents and aunt and uncle as the former were unable to take care of her any more.

She liked hearing how Mark and his sisters sat and talked in the dark; she in turn told him how she used to talk to herself in the dark when she was alone. One night, sitting on the back porch, she had the irresistible feeling that there was and always had been someone listening. She prayed for Christ to come into her life. Ever since that time she did not feel alone and knew it to be the presence of God. Later on she made a confession of faith at church but she knew she had already become a Christian on her own in the silence of the night. She had had a boyfriend but he went away to another college. She had gone to a city college with no particular interests, primarily because her grandparents could not afford anything more and they did not want her to live too far away from home.

It became a game to ask questions to each other and they enjoyed listening to each other's answers. Laura was hoping that Mark would sit closer to her and Mark was just thinking of doing this when the heavy door groaned and the light suddenly tormented their eyes. They staggered out and stretched their stiff muscles after sitting for so long.

Bradley told them of what happened and said that it would be far too dangerous for them to leave for a few days. They lived for almost two weeks in Rev. Bradley's basement, playing games, reading books, eating their meals, talking, pacing, and stretching. Bradley gave Mark cold medicine as his cold developed and lamented that even in this day and age no remedy could be found to cure the common cold. And though it was disconcerting to have to sleep in the same room, in different corners, they got used to it. By the end of the time both were restless and easily irritated.

Mrs. Sarah Bradley came back during this time from a distant church conference to discover them and she was brought up to date. After getting to know them she gave her opinion that Laura really should not be a part of this and formed a plan with her husband to save Laura from a life of misery and to ensure Mark would be safe. During the two weeks Bradley had been raising money among Christians he trusted and one of them, a car dealer, gave a used car, with the tax, title, and license all taken care of for Mark's plight. One evening as Laura was still planning to leave with Mark, Bradley brought Mark into his office while Mrs. Bradley entertained Laura and sent her for a hot bath.

"Now Mark, it would be best if you stayed to the back roads and headed for Canada or Montana or Idaho. I know of some Christian groups who have camps and homes out that way." He gave Mark a list of addresses in a code and then cleared his throat.

"You know that Laura has helped you an awful lot and I'm sure by this time she means something to you. Am I correct?"

"Yes sir."

"You have grown to like her, am I right?"

"Yes sir."

"Now this may be hard for you, but if you really like her, you should realize how impractical it is for you to stay together."

"Well, I don't know."

"If you really love her you'll sacrifice yourself for her. If you're caught there is no telling what will happen to her. And as long as you're running from place to place and hiding she won't have much of a life. Do you understand me?"

"Yes sir, I think I do." Mark listened and was sure Bradley was right. He figured something like this would happen eventually, and he resigned himself to this fate. But at the same time he was realizing that she was so much like him, orphaned and alone and he felt compatible with her. To top it off she liked him. She was pretty, warm, and her personality so disarming. She had filled a need. But wanting to do the right thing, he prayed with Bradley for God's will.

That night Mark drove off in the used station wagon having left a note for Laura. The Bradleys thought that it would be the best way. He drove away not thinking much of anything. His heart throbbed as the car traveled deserted streets. Then it began to tug at him and he missed his companion of the last three weeks. His mixed feelings and emotions eased away as he concentrated on driving. Fear of the police also made him drive with care. But this fear made him want to talk to someone and this only made him think of Laura again.

As he left the city and the car droned down the two-lane highway north, his heart grew heavier and heavier. "Did I do the right thing?" he asked himself over and over again. "What will she do when she reads the note? What if she sees Mr. Travis again? Will he do something to her? Will she hate me for leaving without saying goodbye?" These questions were vocalized to the dashboard and now he was feeling very lonely. Had he simply traveled with a group of people he didn't know or really care about, he would have been more comfortable in his aloneness.

He realized he had become used to being alone, having his own mind for company when he lived with Uncle. It was easy to go inside to self; self-pity, self-dependence, talking to one's self. But now he knew that was all wrong. Why had Laura entered his life if she was only to be left so easily? She had sacrificed for him. He knew she liked him, though he was still flattered that any girl should notice him, let alone come to his rescue and accompany him through the most hazardous time of his life.

He pointed his questions to God. He poured out his feelings as the fields and dark farms passed by and as the flat straight roads met his headlights and the dark vanished in the oncoming light. The more he talked the lonelier he became. Mark knew God's presence in his life, but there were times—and this was one of them—when his physical surroundings, the car, the darkness, the motor, all made him feel alone and cold, as if God were not there or He was purposely hiding.

He felt extremely tired as he drove almost two hours north. He had started out tired and now could not keep his eyes open and he turned off on a farm lane and parked near a thicket and a row of trees which hid him from the main road. His tiredness made him feel carefree and he was asleep as soon as his head fell on the seat.

Meanwhile, Laura had finished her bath and spent a wonderful night in a comfortable bed with only romantic thoughts in her head. She fully expected to be woken in the early morning hours and leave with Mark. When she awoke and saw sunlight through the curtains she jumped up and investigated the house. She found Reverend Bradley making breakfast and Mrs. Bradley just going out the back door to a ladies' meeting.

"Where's Mark?" she asked, not knowing that he was gone.

"Please, sit down my dear, I have something to tell you." These were all the words she needed to be suspicious. She sat stiffly, her face serious, eyes penetrating his head as it pivoted around while his hands worked on breakfast.

Then he looked at her and said, "Mark loves you very much, so much that he has left, leaving you free from the danger that surrounds him. He has left a note for you on the table."

"You mean he left? When?"

"Last night," he said as he put a plate of eggs and bacon down in front of her; but she ignored it. She found the note between the salt and pepper shakers. She read it, disbelieving that he did it.

Laura,

Please don't be angry. You've helped me so much that there is no way I can thank you. Rev. Bradley and I discussed the matter. My Uncle Ted is more dangerous than I ever dreamed. And though I like you very much and feel we could have gotten closer in normal circumstances, perhaps it is best if I leave. It was the Bradley's idea and they are probably right. You can be free and out of the danger. I don't know if I will ever be safe again.

Mark

P.S. I've never said this to a girl before. I love you.

The last three words broke her heart. Her eyes welled up with liquid. Tears ran down her cheeks and she sobbed over the plate. She pushed it away and went out of the room. Rev. Bradley did not follow and hoped she would calm down by herself.

For the rest of the morning she sat staring out the window. She had nowhere to go and nothing to do. The God-sent boy she had fallen in love with, and the thrill of going through dangers with him were taken away.

Reverend Bradley arranged for a train ticket to Milwaukee where she could get a bus back to her grandparent's house. As she thought about this she knew she would be more of a bother than helpful. Her aunt and uncle and her grandparents were hoping that she would become independent and find a nice young man. Though she had been a great help to them, they were more concerned for her future. She felt despair. She prayed about the blankness in her life, the uselessness of it. She cried to God, feeling her helplessness. The more she tried to think of Christ, the more her mind turned to Mark. He had said the magic words. Other thoughts crept in to help ease her mind and get used to the thought of never seeing Mark again. Besides she had only known him for three weeks. Besides, there was her old boy friend Burt. He promised her he would come home from college in the summer and spend some time.

However, remembering Mark back in the church, his praying and not knowing she was there, his face and those sincere brown eyes, and the "I love you" stayed with her as she gathered her coat for the trip to the train station. There could be nobody else like Mark and she would always remember it. She had only her coat now as everything she brought was left at the Travis home and she knew she could not go back there and face them.

The thought suddenly struck her that she was in as much danger as Mark, especially if she met people like the Travis's who had seen her with Mark. She felt proud of the thought that she would never tell about him and didn't care if she was caught—she was in love.

Submissively, she walked to the Bradley's car. He told Laura to get in and wait. He had forgotten to talk to the janitor who was in back of the parsonage and he wanted something done about the floor in the church basement. Laura sat gazing into space when an old dark blue station wagon came from the opposite direction and pulled up in a lurch on the other side of the street. She looked at it for a leisurely moment and then sat up, startled. It was Mark.

Her heart beat wildly. She looked back at the church, but there was no sign of Reverend Bradley. Mark waved his hand frantically for her to come quickly. She moved quickly and tried to control herself from wanting to hug him as soon as she got into the car. Mark sped off quickly and was out of sight when Rev. Bradley came out.

Unbeknownst to Mark, a patrol car had seen the blue Ford coming back to town. It had been reported leaving suspiciously the night before and an alert had been put on it. But his new development had the affect of discounting it and the look of the driver did not seem to be like the appearance of the poster or of any other outstanding cases. Just another farm boy the officers thought. Also, a camera smaller than a thumbnail and just as thin which had been placed on the ceiling of the car had fallen off. Not having the slightest notion of it, Mark had sat on it and it was lost between the seats.

"I couldn't do it," muttered Mark as Laura lay her head on the back seat and laughed for joy. "God help me Laura, I couldn't leave you and now we are going to need all of His help."

Laura looked playfully at him and said, "For a while I thought you were mentally ill." They both laughed hysterically.

"I am for coming back to pick you up," he said getting his breath. As soon as they were far enough out of town he stopped the car and they hugged tightly for a long time. Laura kissed Mark for the first time.

"Hey wait a minute," said Mark. "We seem to work everything backwards. First we are married, then we are engaged, and now we fall in love." They laughed long and hard and then grew quiet and simply enjoyed being in each other's presence.

Instead of going north to Canada they went west toward Montana. Laura brought up the idea because perhaps they would be looking for Mark harder at the border, which indeed they were. After three hours of driving Mark's eyes could not stay open any longer. He had not slept long the night before and he had awoken cold, headachy and feverish. He took all the cold medicine he had been given. The adventure of going back to rescue Laura had worn off and he was feeling sick and tired as his cold had refused to go away.

Laura took over the driving and this time Mark slept in the back seat. He fell into a dream of walking through fields; then he was riding a bicycle and some of his old friends from school rode with him. Then he was riding faster and they were chasing him. He did not panic, but instead he felt a peaceful longing to keep going though his bicycle went faster and the road got narrower and rough with water on each side. He was riding farther away from the dry land with the water on each side getting progressively deeper until it covered the road. But a voice was singing. It was a clear beautiful voice and he knew it to be somebody he knew intimately. It must be. It is. It's Jesus. He was coming to a great light. But there was nothing but water now and the song.

He woke up stiffly from the position he had been in. His neck was sore, his nose running. Laura was singing and he felt the desperate need to go to the washroom. She pulled over by the side of the road. Mark walked down a gentle embankment into the tall grass, bushes, and trees and out of sight. A police car came barreling down the road. Laura saw its flashing lights in her rear view mirror. Her heart skipped a beat. She held her breath and closed her eyes. But when she opened them it had sped past and turned at a distant corner. She let her breath out slowly and slumped down in the seat. Mark got back into the front with her and saw her strange behavior.

"Something wrong?" he said with a heavy nasal voice.

"Didn't you see the police car?"

"Yes, so?"

"Weren't you frightened?

"Yeah, I guess so, but I feel awful. I don't care about anything right now. Couldn't we stop and eat somewhere. I could use something hot. Aren't you hungry?"

"I've got these candy bars," she said holding them out and he looked at them disinterestedly.

"I was thinking along the lines of soup or something."

"Ok, but that means going near the highway. We really shouldn't, but I have got to go to the washroom too."

"Why don't you do it right here?"

"No! We'll go to the highway, but don't blame me if we're caught."

"If I don't get something for this cold, I'm not going to be alive to be caught."

They drove to the highway and traveled it for fifteen miles and discovered a twenty-four hour truck stop.

"Thank God," moaned Mark.

"Don't forget your glasses," advised Laura.

"Don't forget your ring," replied Mark.

They walked into the restaurant and sat in a booth. The only other customer in the whole place was a truck driver who sat at the counter. When they were finished they bought some aspirin at the counter. The truck driver observed Mark and Laura and they likewise looked at him as they walked to the register at the same time.

"Cool night out ain't it," said the gruff, stubble-chinned man. His smile revealed a missing tooth in front as he looked at Mark and studied Laura.

"Yeah, sure is," replied Mark. They noticed how the truck driver paid his bill. He pointed to his hand and lay it down on the counter. The waitress moved the wand over his hand as she would any item's bar code in the store. The register clicked and flashed the price and the paid up sign flashed. The cashier handed him his receipt.

The truck driver noticed Mark and Laura's observation and commented, "Best little thing they thought up yet." Mark knew that it was a very old idea and the technology was not new, but its time had come. He remembered Uncle Ted teaching him all this and the more sophisticated ways that were being implemented.

"Don't need to carry money anymore, and don't have to worry about being robbed. Then he looked at Laura and made a series of crude comments to Mark that had to do with horses, anatomy, and mating. They ignored him, got into the car and drove on into the night.

Mark and Laura were among the few people in the world to miss the important news of the day. They were not interested in the radio for much of their journey. The day was May 1. This was the day Aliadin officially proclaimed himself the Christ everyone had been waiting for. Playing on half-truths, Bible lore, superstitions, and the beliefs of all faiths, his prophet Arcane devised a number of miraculous happenings that everyone could see via computer, television, movie theatres and in a spectacular light show in the Middle East. The sky was used as a screen and it showed Aliadin coming for his people. It was called the Rapture.

The most significant of the miracles was the disarming of the world's nuclear arsenals where they existed in threatening nations. Tests were made which confirmed them;

hence the world was disarmed and at peace. The prophet Arcane, his constant companion, and number two power, claimed that Aliadin's recovery proved that he indeed was resurrected and alive—the Christ to Christians, the Messiah, to those Jews who would accept it, and Mohammed to Muslims. To any who might dispute this, the remaining nuclear weapons and a series of impressive miracles that were displayed would discipline all who did not fall into line. He really needed no threats. The majority of the world's population welcomed him. Finally there would be peace and order. Among his promises to the world was a plan to build the greatest temple of all time in Jerusalem on the temple mount where his throne would be. Historic Christians, Fundamentalists, and Jewish renegades were named as those groups who opposed or resisted him. These he blamed for the original terrorist killings of the president and the Congress and the attempt on his life. He pleaded with them to give up their resistance or he would be forced to retaliate.

Chapter 13

FALLING OFF THE WORLD

Where are we Laura? asked Mark as they drove back to the highway and then to the alternate routes. She showed him the map. He turned to the shoulder of the road, stopped, and studied it. They decided to try for one of Bradley's addresses and drove to Butte, Montana in the late night hours. They spent two more hours trying to find the place. The code was confusing. Finally, they succeeded and were taken in by a blurry-eyed woman with a night cap over her curlers and in a robe. They apologized for disturbing them. Brenda Moffatt gave them a snack and showed them to different couches once she heard Mark and Laura's story. They slept late the next day and were treated to a wonderful breakfast of pancakes and eggs.

They discovered they were among a large family; Mr. John Moffatt and three little Moffatts, Ted, Elizabeth and Jack, and a grandmother and grandfather. They also discovered Mr. Moffatt's reluctance to let Mark stay as they had little room to spare and because he demonstrated by another poster that they were concerned about having him there. They also related yesterday's news which did not bode well for historic Christians who would dispute Aliadin.

As Mark and Laura decided they would try the other addresses, John warned, "You're going to get the same response. I know these people. Either they are moving or they will have the same attitude. Not that we don't want to help, you understand, but we have many to think about and if we get caught with you we'll be in trouble too."

Mark and Laura glanced into each other's eyes as he said this and now they knew the frustration of being fugitives. To their credit, the Moffatts did donate money, food, some more sleeping bags, and old clothes. They left quickly and efficiently to the solitude of the open road and to each other's arms in despair. They prayed aloud. Laura opened her Bible that she had clung to throughout their journey in her shoulder bag, and read Psalm 37.

Traveling is fun when one has a destination, no matter how remote. But when one cannot go backward or forward it is not so enjoyable. Hesitantly, and on a much slower pace they drove into the mountains of northwestern Montana. They had money and food and so they felt safe. They had never been in any mountains before and so their attention was absorbed by their surroundings and breathing the fresh pine air. In a desire to lighten the seriousness of their predicament Mark related to Laura how Indians, explorers, and mountain men roamed these mountains. Laura pointed out that the Indians had also been hounded and wondered if they were the new Indians.

They were afraid to go to a motel, because surely with a reward that had now grown to $15,000 there would be a danger that anyone would turn them in. This was a wise choice because this kind of thing had already happened to people who only slightly resembled the poster picture. They spent a few nights at roadside parks where they walked and talked.

Eventually they drove the old blue station wagon into Idaho over a high pass that frightened them. A small town and valley appeared below but they did not see the road as it curved sharply around. The mountains now were more imposing and the trees thicker and taller. Snow gleamed on some of their tops in the lingering sunlight. Everywhere the evidence indicated that the spring weather had warmed considerably as the valleys were in thaw and the roads dry. They were glad because they knew that last pass would have been impossible in icy-snowy weather. Mark did not know where he was driving. The map had been thrown in the back seat, so they arbitrarily picked any road that looked interesting.

That night they parked in a deserted picnic area. Uncomfortable and still somewhat embarrassed to sleep so close to each other, Mark lay in the front seat with one leg over the seat and the other stretched as far as it would go. Laura lay in the back enjoying the full length of the station wagon. Laura offered to switch with him but he declined. Mark could not see Laura or out; he liked it better as the front seat was the perfect divider. He talked into the seat as Laura rested her head on her arm and talked back.

"Where we going?" asked Laura who cringed at her own question and was sorry she asked it as they had only said this to each other a hundred times.

"I don't know, a gas station, I guess. We need gas, we're really low, also somewhere for a good breakfast. Those apples and that candy just did not fill me up. You know Laura, I just don't know what to do . . . and I just can't shake this cold."

Laura stopped listening. As she looked out the back window she noticed that the headlights of a car went off at a distance down the road. Her alarm increased when two dark figures began walking in their direction.

"Mark," called Laura softly as they continued to progress near to their car. But Mark continued to talk.

"Mark!" she said louder, "there are people out here."

By the time Mark got up out of the seat to look, it coincided with a polite knock on the window. The figure motioned and yelled about wanting to talk.

Without thinking Mark opened the door to get out. The man moved his body to hold the door open with it.

"What you doin' out here?" asked one of the two guys, somewhere in their twenties.

"Ah . . . well, we were just camping, me and my . . ." Mark did not have to finish before the other guy noticed Laura.

"Well now, you lovin' it up out here, I see. I'll bet you have some weed and pills too. Let's see your stuff," said one.

"Come on out honey, and let's talk," said the other. Mark only now smelled the hot stale beer breath of the two men as they draped around him. Laura was not sure what to do when Mark said, "Stay in there, Laura!"

"That's not too friendly, boy. You gotta share and share alike. Come on out here honey."

"No!" said Mark, "Leave her alone, we're married."

The two men were not about to leave them alone.

"You wanna fight Mister? Come on!" said one, who kept Mark busy as the other took advantage of the open door and unlocked and opened the other door and dragged Laura out. Then both hovered around her and one forced her face up to his lips and kissed her. "Stop it!" she yelled and struggled to get out of his grasp.

Mark pulled one guy away and both took a few blows, but Mark got the worst of it. He was hit hard in the face near his left eye. He went down, his eyes watering and his head spinning.

The two men got Laura who was struggling furiously on the ground. They were about to get Laura's jeans open when Mark, recovered sufficiently and with adrenaline flowing, ran and kicked one man in the stomach as hard as he could as he was bent down. The other looked up long enough at Mark for Laura to free her one hand and scratch his face and poke him in the eye. Both men lay neutralized, but a third man appeared and quickly accosted Mark. Meanwhile, the man who was kicked in the stomach recovered enough to start beating Mark in the stomach while the other held him. Mark yelled to Laura to run, but she tried to fight and was pushed down an embankment into a distant gully where she rolled down among a labyrinth of bushes relatively unhurt. After Mark was sufficiently beaten up to the three men's satisfaction they threw him down that same incline of what was the final slope to the foot of a mountain. Bushes and small trees broke his fall and he rolled some fifty yards from the top. Laura lay still, face down, listening to the voices of the men in the still darkness.

"Wanna get the girl now?" asked one.

"Naw, she's probably one a them weak types," said the second.

"She's damaged goods now," said the third.

"Ya think we killed the fella?" asked the third.

"I don't know. Let's git. You drive ours and we'll take this one."

Eventually she heard both cars drive off into the night. An eerie silence followed, which included the wind in the trees and a far off sound of water. She began to call Mark's name. When she received no answer she began to cry. She continued to call out and began to rummage around in the dark carefully with a tiny flashlight the Moffatts had given her. There was only silence. When she had gone on like this for some time she despaired, sat down, and wept into her hands. Her head went up as she thought she heard a voice from some bushes below her down the slope. She called out and heard it again, then prayed as she went that he was not seriously hurt.

"I'm over here," he said painfully but louder. She walked, climbed, and slid down to find that he had fallen and rolled into a thick bush. His nose was bleeding, one eye was swollen, his jaw and abdomen hurt. His shirt sleeve was torn nearly off with his arm scratched to the elbow. His pants

were torn and his legs scraped. In addition, he felt a growing bruise on his thigh where he hit the ground. He had
only now recovered his breath.

"The car . . . is it still there?"

"No, they took it," she said, so happy to have found
him but not knowing what to do.

"Are you Ok? Did they hurt you?" moaned Mark softly.

"I'm Ok, some bruises and at least one cut."

Mark did not move and for a long while remained face
down, simply trying to assess all his hurts. Then ever so
slowly he turned over and worked himself out of the
clutches of the bush with Laura's help. He lay on his back
for an equally long time not saying anything. Then Laura
slowly helped him and they crawled down the rest of the
hill to a ravine and a creek and sat under a tree. Taking
account of themselves, they discovered that Laura had her
coat but little else. The car was gone and with it his coat, all
their clothes, sleeping bags, the remaining food and most
of the money which had been in Laura's shoulder bag. Besides this, Mark lost a shoe in the fall.

Stoically, Mark lay back against the tree using his remaining shirt sleeve to stop the bleeding from his nose.
Laura used the handkerchief that he had given her back in
the station, and she sat next to him dabbing his eyes and
the cuts on his face. He felt that in some way he had deserved this. Both thought that things could not get worse.
It began to rain. Rather than talk, Laura draped her coat
over the both of them, scrunched up to him as closely as
possible and they sat under the tree looking out into a dark
cold forest. They gradually fell asleep against each other.

In the morning, Mark awoke with Laura still sleeping, her head against his chest. Laura woke a few seconds later. As they struggled to rise, they were very stiff, cold, and wet. The rain had stopped and they looked at the morning sun on the trees and then they looked at each other. He groaned as he stood on his feet for the first time since the fight. He felt some old and new aches and cuts and shivered in the morning dampness.

"I thought God was on our side," he said cynically. She looked at him meekly and smiled. "You have one fantastic shiner," she said. His eye was swollen and half-closed. They went to the stream and he gingerly washed his face and arm in the icy cold water. Both dreamed of breakfast but nothing was said out loud.

"Do you think we can drink this water?" she asked.

"I don't know," he said, "a little won't hurt, but not too much."

They discovered that a pretty valley lay below them while they explored the woods around them and found Mark's other shoe and with it a path. It looked more appealing than the road that Mark refused to go back up to. Before they started walking anywhere he put his arm around her and prayed.

"Dear Lord, we don't know why all of this has happened. We don't know where we are and where we're going, or what we are doing, so please guide us today to some place safe. We are totally confused and rely on You completely. We thank You for our lives, our salvation, and bringing us together. If . . . if we have to die may we do it together. Please help us and may we accept whatever happens."

They walked down the path. It felt good to walk and the first part was easy as the path gradually wound down and around.

....

Chapter 14

DREAMS AND
HEALING

They were thirsty, hungry, tired and cold. Mark knew he had a fever and up to now somehow found the strength to continue, but his sickness was slowing him down and his breath was labored. He began coughing more often and felt burning pains in his chest. It was now about noon and the sun was bright and it had warmed considerably. A large collie-golden retriever mix began to follow them silently and then moved through the woods and trotted up the trail ahead of them. They encountered a hut and then saw a number of buildings through a cleared forest of pine trees. Then they saw a very large old house made of stone in a clearing and more open area and farther beyond two large barns. A series of smaller cottages were placed at regular intervals in a number of clearings. Nobody seemed to be around as they walked toward the house. They moved tentatively, observing everything and then looked at each other, noticing how dirty and disheveled each was. Both knew without talking that they were about to take another chance. They held hands and walked up to the large wooden porch and carefully went to the front door. The dog watched them approach from one side of the porch and began to bark. Only a screen door was between them and the darkened living room and the lighted and very active dining room. They saw a huge dining room table with at least 20 people around it. An older man was praying over an elaborate dinner. They waited and listened. Little children at the table fidgeted and babbled.

". . . and may we be of service to all who come through our doors and bless this most bountiful table. Amen." Heads straightened, dishes and utensils rattled, and one of the children looked up with small Oriental eyes, noticed Mark and Laura and squealed for her mom to look. She did and informed the older man who had prayed.

Suddenly, all eyes were upon them. Quickly an older woman in her late 50s with a warm face and smile came to the door. She was dressed in slacks and a camp shirt. At first she asked what they wanted, but when she opened the door and saw them closer she comprehended the problem. "Please come in. I'm sorry we didn't see you earlier. Oh, you look tired, and you're hurt. Come in, please. Are you hungry? My name is Naomi and you are?"

Mark thought about giving their false names but was not able to speak. "I'm Laura and this is Mark," said Laura, as they stood awkwardly before the large audience. A great many voices beckoned them to come and eat. A girl in her twenties came and introduced herself. "I'm Debby," she said and was then interrupted by Naomi who gave directions quickly. "Debby, be a dear and set two more places." People started moving around. Mark's sick and hurt body finally gave out in the activity and warmth of the house and he collapsed. Naomi barked out new orders and several of the guys helped Mark up to a room with Naomi and Laura behind. A Korean man soon followed.

Laura and the two men returned to the table soon afterward. Having been ordered to freshen up and go to dinner, Laura obeyed. She was too tired now to be worried about anything and simply accepted the new circumstances. Everyone there introduced themselves. There were the Turkoviches, Jim and Estelle, a tall Caucasian man and a short Mexican woman, Tom Dillard, a tall dashing figure of 28 and next to him Dick Bahnson, a shorter man about the same age with his arm in a cast. Next to him was Carol Myers, who was in her thirties. At the far end sat Peter and Ruth Yong and their children Paula and John. Next to them were the Kims—Dr. Lon Kim who eventually returned from upstairs—and his wife Tina and two children, Betty and Sam. Next to them was Immanuel Rodriguez, a young man Laura's age. Next were Kim and Anne Taylor and their infant son Timothy, followed by Jackie McCan and Debby Dratton. Next to them James Mitchel, a military man in his forties who wore army fatigues. Dr. Charles and Naomi Raymond formally introduced themselves when Naomi came back to the table. Naomi said, "I think you already met Pal, and I almost forgot to feed him too. Come on boy," she said to the dog.

A silence fell around the table as everyone still looked at Laura. She would have been more concerned for her appearance had she not been so tired. The children at the table broke the silence in comfortable expressions of delight or refusal to eat their required portion. Laura wondered if this was a dream as they ate mashed potatoes and gravy and roast beef and rolls and green beans and milk and salad. She ate heartily, regretting that Mark could not enjoy it. When her plate was nearly empty, Naomi automatically filled it again.

Dr. Kim finally reappeared and announced to all that the young man had pneumonia and a high fever. He had given him something to help him sleep. He asked Naomi if she would help monitor him periodically and to help clean him up and feed him later until he could get a medical report out of him so he knew how to treat him. Laura wanted to go to him immediately but Dr. Kim said no.

A few minutes later all the dishes were pushed aside and collected. Laura felt an automatic urge to assist but was told to stay seated. Pies came out and still the conversation held to food. But as the coffee and tea was being poured, Tom and Jackie opened the way for questions by asking what had happened to them. She was just about to speak when Naomi commandeered her and showed her around the house. She only asked questions that were important to her arranging them. Learning that they were not married, Laura was shown to her own bedroom and bathroom where she was soon enjoying a long, hot, steamy bath in the large old-fashioned tub. After being reassured that Mark was being well taken care of, she got into a wonderful double bed under all the blankets and was asleep as her head met the pillow.

Mark woke once that night and thought he was back in his old house in Rosedale until he bumped into a wall near the bathroom. When he discovered the difference, it startled him; then he felt his weakness and dizziness. James, who was asked to stay with him, awoke and instantly was up and helped Mark to the bathroom and then back to bed.

Given something that Dr. Kim had prescribed and another sleeping pill he knew no more.

Laura woke up early in the morning. She dressed quickly and tried to see Mark, only to be met by Dr. Kim who put his finger his lips. "Let him sleep," he whispered. She knew they would have to explain themselves and she wanted to learn more about these people.

She went down the ornate wooden stairs and found some of the young women doing housework. They all exchanged good mornings. Naomi saw her and beckoned her to eat breakfast, but she declined until things were explained. Naomi led her into the study where Charles and Tom were talking. Tom was asked to leave.

The house was enormous and the most impressive room was this study. Books lined the walls from floor to ceiling. A carved wooden desk sat in one corner on top of a thick carpet. On the mantle of the fireplace was an old family Bible. Next to it on either side were some flower vases with mountain flowers and cattails. A large painting that involved mountains, and a winding path led into a brilliant sunrise. There was a large translucent cross in the midst of it. It had an Oriental way about it. Later she discovered an array of compelling Christian paintings all through the house. The study had two old style windows with eight square panes, one facing the front and the porch, the other to the side and to the woods.

Over time she enjoyed exploring and looking at everything in this house. This library took up one fourth of the first floor and was the first thing one saw when coming in the front door to the left. To the right as one entered the front door was the living room with a thick but worn carpet of the type that Laura thought to be like her grandmother's. Old stuffed armchairs and couches lined the room with small tables and large lamps. Another fireplace was here and on its mantle and down by the sides were innumerable old Christian magazines. Carvings of African tribesmen, serene Chinese landscapes, and scroll paintings vied with Western art in gracing the walls and tables. Everything in the house had the unmistakable air of many people living together in community. The artificial was alien. A natural freedom took the place of the uninhibited, organized chaos that was interpreted as freedom in the world outside as Charles explained later in their conversations.

Laura sat rigidly in one of several large stuffed armchairs with a couple of small pillows at her back. Dr. Raymond, who made sure she called him Charles, had been sitting at his desk, but moved to a chair near her and Naomi took one opposite her.

"Now tell us who you are, how you came here, and how we can help you?" asked Charles. Before she started she had to ask who they were. She looked at them intently and asked, "Are you . . . are you . . . historic Christians?"

"Yes we are," affirmed Charles, smiling. "All of the people here are historic Christians. And I presume you are the same?"

She nodded her head happily and breathed a sigh of relief. With the air cleared, she did not hesitate to tell them everything. She felt these were special people and that God had answered their prayers. Laura told them of their whole adventure, beginning with how they met, who Mark was, how they left Fargo, had tried the Moffatts and had been traveling aimlessly thereafter. She described their being assaulted and their car stolen. After all of this she had to ask what day it was as they had lost track. They told her it was Sunday. She told them all about herself and then related all that Mark had told her about his family life long ago and how they had all died.

When she finished she waited for surprise or shock about Mark or for some sign that they knew about him already. "No, we never heard about Mark or you but we did receive a curious visit by the sheriff a few weeks ago. He took a look at everybody here and then left. He never did say specifically what he was looking for, but that it was his duty. You see, he is a historic Christian with us too. He rarely comes out here and pretty much leaves us alone," Charles said.

Once they heard the whole tale they made no conditions and were not even concerned about talking to Mark, but seemed to trust her and accept them both fully. "God obviously brought you here," said Charles. The feeling was very satisfying and she basked in the warmth of their company.

Laura asked about them in return. She learned that this was a Christian camp and that they had been the caretakers for the past twenty years. Before that they had been missionaries in Nigeria inside a leper colony for a decade. Naomi explained that the people Laura had met last night came to live in a Christian community as they anticipated the Anti-Christ. Some, like Immanuel and James, had been in the American military and anticipated the purges that were only now taking place. When all was said, Charles concluded, "You're a brave pair and we would like to invite you to stay with us indefinitely and join our fellowship."

Laura could not thank them enough. She was so excited she wanted to hug them. Naomi said, "And for now make yourselves at home and rest as long as you like. You come along with me and we can fix you a good breakfast. I'll make Mark something too. It's time that boy ate something."

Laura went into the kitchen with Naomi and was made to sit at a kitchen table. It was a large spacious kitchen with many windows looking over a patio and a large garden in the midst of a large clearing. Alongside was a solar garden, the same size as the open patch but enclosed in a clear paneled house. Immaculate pots and pans hung around and under the cabinets. The dishes used the day before were done and stacked on the counters. Naomi noticed Laura's observations of her kitchen and felt self conscious about the plates lying out. "No sense in putting them all away when they'll be used again in a little while."

Laura noticed over the next few days, weeks, and months that cooking was not a chore but an occupation which required all her aptitude and strength, but she did it all in such lighthearted humor. Something was cooking all the time, whether it was for the immediate meal or for one long contemplated and scheduled for another hour. There were also the ongoing projects of canning, jarring, and freezing things for future seasons. What awed Laura was that almost everything Naomi made was from scratch; even when

ingredients were missing she used an uncanny resourceful-
ness that made each meal a delight. And then she did it for
numbers unimagined when she took over the camp kitchen
and lodge in another part of the valley.

A toddler staggered into the kitchen and stared impla-
cably at Laura, who smiled and said hello. She got no apparent response.

"This is John Bartholomew Yong," said Naomi lifting
him up and holding him in her arms for a few moments
until he squirmed to be free. "His father and mother came
to us a year ago. His father is or was a physics professor
who was turned out. Charles invited him here and they
came and stayed. They're wonderful folks. Their grandparents came from Vietnam, but they're ethnic Chinese. Doesn't
he have beautiful eyes? Peter and Ruth have done wonders
for our garden. It was good before but it is even better since
they came. Just got green thumbs I guess. We're going to
plant as soon as it warms up more. Course it's been pretty
warm lately. You're lucky you came yesterday."

Naomi continued to talk as she moved about the kitchen
and the stove with spatula in hand. Laura listened atten-
tively, enjoying each word and the welcome homespun atmosphere. Naomi continued, "First few good days that we've
had. You don't know how much a miracle it is to have such
a garden in this area. We're so lucky to have fertile soil that's
not too rocky. It only took a month to get the rocks out of
that one. Thank God for the solar garden. We can grow
many things even in winter. By the way, even the house is
solar powered so we are self-sufficient. We used to get our
power from the hydro plants but praise Him again for the
new panels developed over the years. Even on the cloudi-

est days and in the dead of winter in a snowstorm they still pick up power from the sun. Don't ask me how. So we don't pay anything for power." Without missing a step or a word she expertly put breakfast before Laura. "What would you like to drink hon? We have orange juice, milk, tea . . ."

"Milk, please," said Laura who used this opportunity to get in a question. "Where are all the others?"

"They're all out gallivanting or in their cabins. Carol, Debbie, Jackie, and Charles and I stay in the house. The others live in the cabins along here. Sometimes we still get campers and guests so we have lots of other cabins through-out the valley and up along some of the mountain trails. And we keep a few rooms spare in the house just in case of drop-ins like yourselves."

"What do they do here?"

"They work around camp. But Tom, Dick, Debbie and Jackie still work outside. Deb and Jack are teachers and are off now. Carol was into law enforcement—a policewoman—but she quit and now attends the university farther away but comes back for weekends and summers. They all con-tribute to the living expenses and do work around camp to earn their keep. Oh, don't worry for yourselves, you two just rest for as long as it takes and don't worry about any-thing. All things in good time."

Ruth Yong came in the back door with a sun hat on and garden gloves. She said hello and introduced herself again briefly and took John who had been sitting on the floor playing with a wooden spoon and took him out of the room. Laura liked how easy it was to talk to Naomi. They talked about everything else over the late morning while they peeled potatoes and cut green beans and drank tea.

"Well, girl, it's time to raise your boyfriend back to life. He must be dying of hunger by now," said Naomi wryly. She picked up a full tray of food that included steaming hot soup in case he had to start slowly.

"Oh, could I go, it would be no trouble . . ."

Naomi looked at Laura and smiled as she handed her the tray and said, "You love Mark don't you?"

Laura blushed and nodded as she left the room. Naomi chuckled to herself.

Mark woke from the depth of uneasy and nightmarish dreams as Laura called to him. The room was cool and dark with the shades down. He had kicked off the blankets. She could see that he was feverish. His black eye was a dark blue patch, but he could open it now. He could not move easily but simply said, "Hi."

Laura put her hand on Mark's forehead and felt the fever. "Here, I brought you some food and soup. I'll get the medication," she said. He sat up and coughed for awhile. He was glad to see her as he drank the soup slowly and ate as much as he could. He tried to talk but found out how sore his throat was and how congested his chest was.

"Don't talk, it's all right. The Raymond's are really nice people—historic Christians. They said we could stay."

Mark's eyes widened and then he closed them for a few seconds and said, "Praise God," in a throaty attempt. Laura smiled and moved her hand to Mark's. He got the energy and said, "Thanks for doing all this with me . . . I love you."

Laura smiled a dream smile, squeezed his hand and kissed him on the cheek. "That's not how I used to be woken up you know," said Mark.

"I know. You used to wrestle your sister. Well, I want you to know that I can do that too. But I'm going to wait until you're better so I can beat you fair and square."

Mark laughed and coughed.

Naomi knocked and came in. "And how's this young man?" she said.

Wary of the new people, Mark did not know how to react. He slowly warmed up to Naomi as she mothered him in a mature fashion, not seeming to care that he was a total stranger to her. Naomi explained the earlier conversation with Laura and Charles and that he was accepted into their fellowship. Mark thanked her. She took his temperature and shook her head. He wanted to get up and get dressed and tried to, but found he was very weak. Dr. Kim entered in a timely fashion, refused him any activity, and prescribed bed rest for several weeks. Dr. Kim also changed the medication and gave him a shot in accordance with what he could glean from Mark's remarks of the night before. This put him down and out for the rest of that day. He remained in this in-and-out condition for almost two weeks.

The fever wavered over Mark and still ascended when the medication subsided. He coughed often and violently when his cold and cough medication wore off. Laura sat in a chair by the bed every day and would have stayed there every night had not Naomi forced her out and replaced her. Charles and Naomi were so concerned that when the fellowship met for Bible study, their prayer time was almost entirely for him. One night in the second week the fellowship prayed more intensely than usual downstairs. Meanwhile upstairs, Naomi and Laura sat with him, held his hands, and prayed for him with Dr. Kim looking on. Mark had waves of uneasy dreams when he did sleep. Thoughts of Mom and Dad, Joanne and Dianne came through his cob-webbed mind. Before the fever finally broke he had a nightmare.

He saw his parents and sisters beckoning to him. He walked through the streets and alleyways together. Everything was wet and bathed in a dreary yellow light. Joanne was kneeling and weeping before a sad full moon while she was chained around the neck to a robotic machine close behind her. Around her bodies without heads lay in dark masses along the streets, many still moving. Sickly uneasiness and terror all met at a crossroad. A man resembling Uncle Ted, but with a grotesque face approached and separated them. The face was like a waxen mask. Suddenly it was handsome, but cold and stern as if made of steel. He began to wield a large sharp blade and proceeded to cut their heads off. But before he could get to Dianne, Mark was so overwhelmed with emotion that he screamed in horror and began crying in horrific torrents. He was on his knees and pleading and whimpering into the folds of a skirt that he thought belonged to Jesus. He brought his face up to look into Christ's face, but it wasn't at all. It was a hideous face made partly of steel and what looked like putty. This figure wielded a scimitar and brought it down on him when he screamed and rolled violently. The fever broke.

He awoke, his pajamas and sheets wet in sweat. A soft lamp lit the room. Naomi was sponging his forehead and quietening him with a gentle, "Sssshhhhh, it's okay." Dr. Kim and Laura looked on. Charles arrived and Debbie and Jackie stood near the door looking in.

"What happened?" he said trying to sit up.

"Ssssshhhh, lay still. You just had a nightmare. I believe the fever has passed," said Naomi softly. But already feeling better, he had to sit up and blow his nose. He looked at Laura and raised his eyebrows quickly as if to signal, here I am. Dr. Kim began to check him out and found little congestion in his chest and that his temperature was indeed returning to normal. They all praised God almost in unison. Dr. Kim still prescribed more rest, but Mark could not sleep now. Charles and Naomi introduced themselves again and Charles and Mark talked for some time. He told them what happened in the nightmare.

"It's been over a year now since they died. So much has happened. My sisters used to have dreams like this once and in a while. They were great. I loved them and Mom and Dad so much." He looked into Laura's eyes as she sat on the bed next to him. "I felt so alone when they died, so lost. I'm sure glad you were there when I needed someone. I guess I should thank Jesus for that."

Everyone's eyes became moist and then he said, "I am so hungry, could I have something now?" Naomi squeezed his hand and chuckled, "You've said the magic words." Mark was allowed up to dress and he followed the others downstairs to what became a midnight snack for almost everyone.

The next day after a late breakfast and another check up, Dr. Kim declared him healed. His assorted cuts and bruises seemed to be better. Naomi gave him the very kind of vitamin his mother had always given him. "Now take these every day now," she said, giving him a small plastic bottle.

When Laura went out with the other gals and the house seemed empty, he found the study to be a safe haven and began to look at the many books. In the afternoon he took a long nap.

That evening he met all of the fellowship at dinner and talked with Charles at greater length. The fellowship easily accepted him and Laura. Naomi presented a special cake for dessert to celebrate their coming. After dinner all assembled for worship time a little earlier than usual because Charles wanted the entire group to hear Laura and Mark's testimonies and to celebrate the Lord's Supper.

Mark discovered that Charles was not only missionary and pastor but held a Ph.D. in church history. The latter fact drew him. As they talked Charles wondered at much in Mark's past. The name Wilshire interested him, but he could not remember where he had heard that name before. At the mention of Dr. Donald Crawford, Charles laughed and then became somber. Charles ruminated how he had known him as an underclassman and how they had followed each other's careers. "I hope you don't blame yourself for his being caught," he told Mark. "He was a fearless Christian and a great scholar; great books and solid teaching. He remained in that secular university world as a personal mission when the rest were retreating. Of course Fox, the president, of your university, still believed in the old fashioned liberal education and that helped keep him there. He knew he would die for the cause, if not for you then for someone else. He wanted to be in the front lines and die for Christ."

Peter Yong stopped Mark at his last name, when he was told about his sisters. He inquired about Dianne and then told about one of the last conferences he had attended in Chicago where a theorem was presented. "It was a small seminar session with students presenting their papers. A very young girl led it. She presented a paper called the Brogen theorem. Was that your sister?" he said.

"Yes, that would have been her," he said amazed.

"She presented it as a step toward world peace and safety. However, it became one of the key building blocks in Aliadin's nuclear neutralization demonstration. The theorem must have been taken after she died. I'm sorry for her loss."

Mark and Charles wondered in amazement at Dianne and at how small the world had become. Immanuel smiled at this but remained silent.

Laura then shared her story. It interested the Asian families to hear she had been the child of missionaries in China.

Some of the others shared. Immanuel, from Chicago, who had served in the army, James who had been a marine sergeant, and Tom who had been in the air force and trained as a dentist, all shared their testimonies. These had a common theme as they told of purges and in some cases pitched battles in the American and Western military forces to force out or eliminate the large numbers of Christians in their ranks. They shared how Christian armies were forming, especially in the south and southwest. Carol shared a similar testimony as she had been a police officer and been forced to resign. They were unanimous in their opinion that soon most of the country would be involved and feel the effects of all of this, including their valley. This brought a somber silence.

Charles called everyone to worship and they sang hymns and songs and had a wonderful Bible study and communion time. It all made Mark meditate on his old days at home and he became somber.

Afterward, when the house cleared and Mark found Charles alone in his study, he asked if they could talk. He had many questions and Charles decided he should have answers. They sat conversing about books for awhile, but then Mark started firing questions at Charles.

"What about the Rapture? Will it happen or is it just part of one great second coming of Christ, like Dianne thought? Why doesn't Christ come now? What is all this news on Aliadin that we missed? Why doesn't he just capture us and kill us and get it over with?" he asked.

Charles started to answer these questions at some length. Then he detected a change in Mark. He asked more questions that did not have obvious answers and they began to sound rhetorical.

"Why did God want to destroy my family? Why couldn't things just be normal? Why did my Mom and Dad, Joanne and Dianne have to die? Why did I not see who Uncle Ted was? Why did all those people along the way reject us? Why did God beat us up and make me sick? Why couldn't I have died with my family?"

With the last question Charles perceived that what was troubling Mark was not answers to these questions, but the need for forgiveness for the guilt and anger he felt in surviving his family's tragedy.

Charles broke in and with the last question, said, "God loves you so much. Jesus has been with you the whole way. Do you believe that? It's Ok. You can let it all go now."

Mark began to pray, talk, and cry at the same time. Charles put his arms around him and he hugged Charles all the harder and cried out, "I'm so sorry, Lord. I'm so sorry. Forgive me. I wanted to die with them. I did not want to live. I hated God. Please forgive me, Lord. I love You so much." The bitterness and the weight of the guilt came out and off as Charles whispered in his ear, "You are forgiven. Jesus loves you so much." He sobbed for some time and then became quiet. Then he held Mark's hands and looked into his eyes and said, "Your family is now safe in heaven and I am sure that your Dad as well as your heavenly Father are so proud of you. You had to come to us. I needed another son too. You see, I lost two sons. They died in missionary persecutions started by Aliadin around the world. You still have a purpose and a meaning down here. And until God decides when our end or the end of all things as we know them is, we must enjoy each moment and live each day in Christ better than we lived the last. It does not matter if Aliadin snaps us up. He is really more like a boa constrictor as he slowly brings his oppression our way. God will give us the grace to live. All the saints of history had the grace to live in the circumstances that were given to them, whether they lived a long time or for only a short time. We were called to live in this time, at the end of history, and we must do our part. Whether there still will be a separate rapture, I don't know. I would be glad, for one, if it took place right now. However, many believers in the nations and regions at the forefront of the great commission throughout the world have suffered the most severe tribulations long before this time and without the Rapture from the Lord.

A great tribulation would make no perceptible difference in their lives now. Our Lord said that all true Christians who are faithful to Him would be persecuted in one way or another. Perhaps God is judging America. And if He allows us to suffer throughout the entire Tribulation, however long this will be, we shall not abandon our Savior. The King will return and you and I will be with Him in that day."

Chapter 15

LIVING IN LOVE

Mark and Laura entered into the best times of their lives. Living in a closely knit Christian community was warm and full of home-made things. It was being given chores to do and errands to run. It was cleaning out a barn, making beds, brushing and taking care of horses, getting sore backs in the garden, fixing cabins, and helping campers. It was long hikes, learning to ride a horse, and then long rides in the woods, fields, and mountains around them. It was helping Charles to make and fix furniture in his shop, or it was helping Naomi can and freeze and cook from scratch. It was singing songs around a campfire or fireplace. It was long talks about God, life, man, and the world on the porch on summer nights or in the study when it was cold. It was helping Kim repair an engine. It was learning how to baby sit small children. It was getting tired and worn out from the mountain air and hard work. It was hot cocoa and oven fresh cookies around the kitchen table; it was laughing and learning to listen to others; it was occasional tears over irritations, things of the past or over being convicted by the Holy Spirit and the words of the Bible. It was prayer, confession, admonition, discipline, revival, and a healing of the heart.

Mark and Laura became part of a family again, but this time with many mothers and fathers, sisters, and brothers. Cut off from their native roots they were grafted into the life of a different one.

Mark had to get used to being treated like a little brother, especially by the older girls. He was now the youngest instead of the oldest. Tom, Kim, Jim, and Dick tried to treat him as an equal, but he kind of liked being called younger brother even by them. The Yongs and Kims at first seemed different, but only because he never knew what to say in their presence and he held them in something like awe. Of course Laura and Mark were most often found together and Charles and Naomi began wondering if they should take another step together.

Debby and Jackie were twenty-seven and twenty-eight respectively. They had been along with Tom and Dick who were the same age, in the same Christian organization, in the same university. The four of them were great friends and one had the feeling that the two girls were playing hard to get, but wanted the attention of the latter two. The latter two, though boyish around them, held aloof and seemed bent on life as bachelors.

Tom had been in the air force, studied dentistry, and had been a dental assistant in the service where he became a Christian. He went to college and decided to wait on God for life's goal. From college he drifted to the camp to work, having known Charles.

Dick had been in a near-fatal car wreck before college. A daredevil driver at one time, he came to Christ at the edge of death. His recovery had been a miracle, but he still retained a slight speech impediment and a need for certain drugs to ease pain that came and went. His most recent mishap was sustaining a dislocated shoulder in the middle of a touch football game.

Kim and Jim had been dropouts from college, gotten married, and worked at simple jobs. Kim, a lanky lad, was an outstanding gardener and mechanic and complimented the interests of the Yongs, Naomi, and Charles who had need of a camp mechanic. Anne had gone through college and came out with a degree in sociology. She had a very Irish face with wavy, thin brown hair, brown eyes and a golden voice. Kim and Anne had been married for over a year now.

Estelle was a very short, plump Mexican girl who grinned and peered through wire rim glasses. She was a study in contrast with her husband Jim, the tallest person in the camp at six foot, eleven. Jim had a slow somber personality which brought him into times of depression, but when he was happy he could joke and laugh like nobody else. In his pessimistic way he reminded Mark of Puddleglum from one of the Narnia tales.

Charles was a jack of all trades. Besides impressing Mark with his academic and missionary career, he was an expert carpenter and wood worker. His skin was tanned and weather beaten from outdoor work and his hands were calloused and hard. To Mark he always looked out of place and ordinary in old overalls and a heavy plaid shirt and baseball hat. Charles was only too pleased to have Mark follow him around; he listened to Mark and counseled and taught him about many things.

Naomi shared with Mark and Laura how once a quartet of Jehovah's Giros showed up at the camp and thought they had an old farmer to persuade. Charles played along but then started asking uncomfortable questions about their theology and founder until they realized they did not have an easy fish. Charles invited them in and the persuaders became the persuaded. One of the four called him up one day to explain that he had broken away from the cult and accepted Christ. Charles harbored the young man in the camp for many months until his old cohorts stopped pestering him. He was not happy with merely winning an argument; only if something important came of it.

Mark of course was confined to the camp, but he was so persistent around the study that Charles decided Mark deserved to finish his bachelor's degree and so he put him through a long reading program and even demanded papers and exams. They held class every day. Eventually, Laura, Kim, and Jim joined in. After several years of off and on again classes the graduates were finally awarded with bachelor's degrees from the Charles Raymond College in the Woods. Naomi and the girls arranged for a ceremony and party.

One night during their second month in the camp, Mark sat with Charles after worship as they usually did and he asked him more questions. Why were there no computers around the house? He said they did have them and did consult them occasionally, but they were not to be trusted or relied upon. He mistrusted the two-way nature that made the observer the observed. Mark also asked why this camp was not on Bradley's or Casey's lists when they set out from Chicago. Charles related how there were actually two Christian undergrounds bordering each other. Casey and Bradley were in a Christian underground that used computer technology to the maximum. They developed counter-computer measures to jam or destroy Aliadin's progress, even going on the offensive in destroying Aliadin's computer capabilities from time to time, creating viruses and the like. When interfered with correctly, the Christians could communicate with each other. However, the northwestern underground of which Charles and the camp were in were non-computer users and abandoned all or most use of them. Asked how they communicated, Charles said by messenger and by an old institution largely untouched and unmonitored so far and which Aliadin felt was beneath him, the post office. Thus they sent coded letters to each other.

Meanwhile, as Mark and Charles talked downstairs, Debby and Jackie sat with Laura in her bedroom and talked.

"You mean to tell me, that he never made a pass at you?" Debby asked.

"No, should he have? He's not like that," said Laura.

"Then he's a dream in this day and age," said Jackie.

"Tom and Dick have to be fought off every day," said Debbie.

"That's not so, I've seen you horsing around with them. You're in love too," said Laura.

"Listen to the new expert. Thanks," said Jackie.

"If we two ever finally got married, I'll eat all the hay in the barn," said Debbie.

Then Debbie and Jackie looked at Laura. "When is he going to ask you the question?" said Jackie.

"Yeah, has he ever asked you about marriage?" asked Debbie.

Laura smiled and said, "I don't know. I think he believes it's too soon and too impossible and too dangerous to do normal things. He's afraid of hurting me."

"Hurting you. You'll hurt if you two don't come together. You were made for each other, it's plain to see," said Debbie.

"Well, I don't know what I can do," said Laura "You may not, but we do," said Jackie.

"Oh, please don't ruin it," said Laura.

"Don't worry, sis, we will be subtle," chuckled Debbie.

From that time on the two found some way to bring the word marriage or the many allusions to it into the conversation whenever Mark was in listening range.

It was the day before Independence Day in July when Charles, Jackie, and Debby dragged Mark out of the library. They persuaded him to take a long trail ride up into the mountains to one of the lodges with the pretext of doing a little inspection and preparation work. At a beautiful little lake they ate a small lunch and talked. Charles was still interested in Mark's Uncle Ted and brought up the subject again.

"You don't know what he did for a living?" asked Charles.

"No, I don't," said Mark who was enjoying the mountains and the horses more than the conversation.

"I've heard that name before—somewhere. Wilshire . . ." said Charles.

"Well, because of his collections of gadgets, I always assumed it had to do with electronics or computers, but I don't really know," said Mark.

Charles began to think out loud. "There's something about all of this, but I need to think about all of the pieces. He obviously wields much power. But there is something else that name conjures up. If it's the right Wilshire, I want to say medical doctor. But, anyway, it's time to move on."

As they rode Charles taught Mark about the woods, about food that one could get if one needed it; some hardy fruit trees, mint leaves, berries, and nuts. Mark asked how the camp had acquired all the land. Charles related how they were in effect caretakers of the valley and the surrounding mountains as well. He said that in the normal times a number of activist environmentalists had become Christians in the camp and forced the government to keep undesirable companies from acquiring it and other lands like it. The camp was given the special privilege to keep and maintain the valley, offsetting the government's costs of overseeing it. The Evangelical Church League owned the camp and adjoining valley with a very large ranch that had also just been acquired. Harry Stewart, who became a Christian in the camp, wanted, after his father's death, to join his property to the camp. It doubled the size. Harry still lived in the house there and was a part of the fellowship. This was a tremendous victory toward self-sufficiency, because he raised cattle for meat and milk. Besides, God's humor was obvious as the camp now had Tom, Dick, and Harry.

Debby pointed out two mountain peaks close by each other to Mark as they rode. "They were called the bride and bridegroom in Indian lore, weren't they Charles?" she said, smiling at Jackie while Mark looked intently. Charles said, "Yes, they were. Some later called them the twins."

What Debby intended as a helpful hint, Mark heard both answers and settled on the second as he thought of his sisters. At the lodge, as they looked and worked, Jackie mentioned in Mark's hearing to Debby, "Wouldn't this be a perfect spot for a honeymoon?"

"Yeah, especially if our lunkheaded boyfriends would get the idea," Debby chided, with eyes glancing at Mark's back.

On the way back, Charles stopped them all and made them look at a buck and a doe coming out of the woods. "Looks like a husband and wife to me," said Jackie.

"Yeah, it sure does," said Debby and Charles. Mark said nothing.

In returning to camp in the late afternoon Mark discovered a surprise party in his honor. Picnic tables had been brought together and barbecues blazed. Everyone shouted, "Happy Birthday," and led him around to the back of one of the sheds. To his delight a basketball court with the posts, backboards and rims stood complete. However, the cement was still drying and the forms were still in place around the court. Everyone repeated their happy birthdays.

Kim said, "It isn't dry yet, but it's level. We should have some pretty hot games out here."

"Brogen, I want you one-on-one and I will beat your butt too," said James playfully as he pointed a trowel at him.

"Thanks . . . thanks a lot," said Mark to the fellowship. "I didn't have a birthday last year. Uncle didn't know and I forgot." He looked at Laura, "I forgot I had told you when it was." He meditated on being nineteen years old as Laura kissed him on the cheek.

Naomi chimed in, "Well, let's eat everybody. The other birthday boy has finally woken up from his nap. Sorry, but we had to squeeze yours and Timothy's birthday together. He'll be three tomorrow." She kissed Mark on the other cheek.

For the rest of the summer basketball was a nightly obsession for all the men. When they had enough, the volleyball net was rigged and the women joined in.

One morning, about a week later, Naomi was hanging up bedspreads to air out and freshly washed sheets to dry on clotheslines in the back yard between the house and the garden. Mark came along and sat on an old tree stump near her.

"I have something to ask you," he said.

Naomi stopped working, thinking something important was coming because he hardly ever asked her about anything except what was for supper. Charles got the hard stuff.

"Well, go ahead. Shoot," she said, putting her hands on her hips and cocking her head to one side.

"Do you think teenagers should get married?" he asked with all seriousness.

Naomi studied him for a moment and said, "In normal times, I'm sure your mother and father would have said absolutely no and made you finish college and have a job before they gave their permission. But these aren't normal times. And you've heard Charles say that we don't know how many tomorrows we have left."

"Well . . . ah . . . ah . . . well . . . ah . . ."

"Come on spit it out. I don't have all day."

"Well . . . ah, when you . . . and Charles, I mean when Charles asked you to . . . get, or I mean when he . . . proposed. What did he say? And how did you react?" said Mark looking at her in quick glances but looking predominantly at the ground, with a stick in his hand which he used to make grooves in the dirt.

Naomi began to chuckle, "Why Mark Brogen. What do you have in mind in that head of yours?"

"Well, I . . . now I'm just wondering . . . I don't know what . . . she'll say. But, I . . . well, I want to propose to her, but I'm scared."

"You mean propose to Laura? You've been with her every day for more than three months and you're scared? I shouldn't be saying this because it's nobody's business, but that girl has been talking my ear off about you since you came and you're frightened? Frightened of what? You were made for each other. Have you already forgotten what you went through to get here? She walked through hell for you when she didn't even know you. For land sakes, go to her.

You don't need any coaching from me or anyone else. She's been moping around here so much I'm surprised she hasn't asked you. Now you've decided to do it, do it! If you don't, I won't talk to you."

In the late afternoon, Mark was shooting baskets before dinner. He had been trying to get Laura out of the house all day, but she was working hard helping Naomi and Jackie can, bottle, freeze and cook. Even when Naomi and Jackie said it was Ok, Laura remained. Every once in awhile he would go in and needle her and ask her to come out. Naomi nodded to her and winked, "It's Ok go on out."

"Okay, I can play now," she said taking off her apron and coming out the back door. As they walked around the side of the house, he said, "Now it's too late. I don't feel like playing but, well, let's talk." He slipped his hand into hers as he had done many times before. She knew something was strange about this conversation because he was nervous when he usually felt relaxed and easy with her.

"Alright, let's talk," she said as they walked around the front porch. They sat down in the hanging porch swing. They swung for awhile but said nothing.

"Nice day isn't it, so warm and comfortable," said Mark.

Naomi saw them sit down as she walked through the house and then back to the kitchen. She met Charles there pouring a cup of tea with Jackie. "Land sakes, he's going to ask her!" she said. Charles looked up and said, "Who's going to ask who what?"

"Mark's proposing," she said and then chuckled. Jackie went out the back in order to tell anyone she saw and find Debby.

"Naomi Raymond. have you been meddling? Why, I should put you over my knee and . . . You say Mark is proposing to Laura?"

"Yeah, ain't it great?" she chuckled some more.

"It's about time," said Charles as he sipped his tea. "I know some others around here who are way overdue."

Naomi said wistfully, "Maybe this'll light a fire under them two buzzards."

Mark cleared his throat a few times and then sat for a moment and drummed his fingers on the armrest of the chair.

"Well? What do you want to talk about?" asked Laura.

Mark looked into her eyes and remembered the first few times he did so on the train and felt the same melting nervousness under her gaze. "Laura Simmons . . ." he said loudly, then he put his head on her shoulder and whispered in her ear, "Laura would you . . . marry me?" Then he raised his head and looked away at the barn. Laura closed her eyes, wanting to savor this moment. Mark thought she was stalling and he did not want to lose his momentum. "I mean, it's not like we've been together for a really long time but I think we've . . ."

"Yes, yes, yes, yes," she repeated in gleeful rapture, turning on him and smothering him with kisses. He pulled out a wooden ring he had fashioned in the workshop. She looked excitedly at it and put it on. It was hopelessly too big but it didn't matter. "It's beautiful. But wait a minute," she said.

Without warning she dashed away into the house with the screen door whizzing open and banging shut. Startled by the sudden movement, Pal, who had been lying nearby, rose and barked. She dashed up the stairs so fast that Charles and Naomi thought there was something wrong. There was a long misunderstood silence. Naomi took a few steps out of the kitchen toward the stairs. Suddenly Laura came bounding down the stairs, and the screen door whizzed open and banged shut. She landed on the swing with all her weight in one jolt making the chains groan and the wood creak. "Here," she said, "now we can really use these." She held out the rings that they had used to get away from Chicago. They laughed long and hard and hugged and kissed for a long time.

"Let's tell everybody," she said gleefully.

Debby and most of the fellowship with her were now coming for dinner and they congratulated the young couple as they passed by even before Laura could say anything. That night they announced their engagement anyway and asked Charles to perform the ceremony. He said yes, but it would have to be a marriage unto the Lord since they dared not approach the state for certificates. This made no difference to the engaged couple. "If God put us together who can separate us?" said Laura. They decided not to wait too long, and thus it would be a September wedding. Naomi did want some time to plan and have a truly grand celebration. Suddenly, Tom looked at Jackie and Debbie at Dick. Two days later it was announced around the dinner table that it would be a triple wedding. Laura reminded Debbie that she had some hay to eat.

Chapter 16

. . . .

THE LAST
WEDDING

Charles and Naomi prayed every day for the next month that nothing would interfere with the marriage ceremonies and celebrations they were planning. The news sent or told by messengers was not encouraging. Those in the camp that still came and went and did business with the outside world brought more evidence of the pressures to conform. A tattoo for the forehead was becoming a chic campus fashion statement, though not required yet. James told of armies of Christians forming in different parts of the country. One day a former Marine captain and a small entourage came to camp to recruit people. Immanuel, James, Tom, and Carol volunteered, but after some reflection, the captain ordered them to remain in the camp to train the others and more who would be sent to them. Shortly after this Immanuel disappeared and was never seen again in camp.

231

Despite all this Charles saw that the morale of the re-maining fellowship was resilient and affirming. Life went on with increasing vigor. The weather was absolutely at its best. Naomi and the women sewed and planned the wed-dings. In fact, they had the weddings put back two weeks in order to get things right. Charles commiserated with Tom, Dick and Mark on the porch soon after this and said, "Women, you can never figure them out. It's hurry up and then wait. They can't wait to marry, but then they'll make you wait to get the wedding right."

The hardest part about the day before the weddings was keeping Mark and Laura separated and not seeing each other. This had not happened in nearly six months. Mark was kept in his cabin or out in the woods. Laura was in the house sewing and preparing with Debby, Jackie, and Naomi. That night there was a lot of tossing and turning thinking and assessing. Laura prayed on her bed that Jesus would hold off a little longer—one more day.

The next day the bridal gown that had been Naomi's was ready for Laura. Jackie's and Debby's were their own creations with Naomi's strong suggestions. All the ladies in waiting had last minute fears and adjustments and ques-tions about everything from hair to shoes.

Mark, Tom, and Dick sat in the cabin and studied those archaic emblems of vanity—the cummerbunds. It was de-cided that they would make wonderful slingshots. Then came time to put them on and here Tom was very helpful, especially in tightening them on Mark and Dick. As they looked at themselves in their tuxedos, Mark commented, "What museum did these things come from?" Dick related that Mark's was Charles' original and the others came from a store in town that had closed a number of years before.

Kim escorted them to the house. The living room was arranged like a small church with couches and chairs acting as pews. Carol played hymns. Tears came to Mark's eyes as he thought how wonderful it could have been if his family could have been there. The weddings were truly homemade in the dresses, decorations, and food. They would not be married all at once, but in one marriage ceremony after another. Once Timothy stumbled up the steps and through the front door with Estelle leading him, everything began. Debbie and Dick were married first, followed by Tom and Jackie and then Mark and Laura. This order was made to accommodate the oldest first, and as Debbie wryly commented, before Dick could change his mind. Everyone had a part to play: Estelle, Ruth, Tina, Anne all played bridesmaids for each wedding ceremony. The children were ring bearers and flower girls. Carol played the piano and Anne sang for each ceremony. Peter Yong took the pictures. Jim, Kim, James, Dr. Kim and Harry were the groomsmen for each ceremony. Each wedding had two maids of honor and two best men. Tom and Mark were for Dick, Mark and Dick for Tom, Tom and Dick stood for Mark. Likewise each lady in waiting had two bridesmaids: Jackie and Laura for Debbie, Debbie and Laura for Jackie, and Debbie and Jackie for Laura. Each wedding ceremony was original to the desires of the couple. Tom played the guitar and sang with Jackie a number of songs and especially one about another place and time and seeing Jesus' face that had them all crying. Debby and Dick each restated their compelling and emotional testimonies and took communion.

Finally, Mark and Laura stood with Charles. Laura wore Naomi's wedding gown. She had a ring of wild flowers in her blonde hair. In order to symbolize their life with God and how He brought them together, Charles held one of Mark and Laura's hands throughout their vows and throughout a short sermon. Charles represented God who held them to Himself and together, no matter what might happen to them now or in the future. Then those same rings that were given to them in Casey's basement went onto their fingers once again. They took their vows and looked into each other's eyes with the mirth and excitement of children. Then with God's representative taking hold of their hands again they hugged each other with one arm and kissed.

After the ceremonies, they ate the celebration feast that included three unique wedding cakes. Peter and Ruth Yong, and Lon and Tina Kim contributed special Chinese-Christian moon cakes amongst the endless amount and variety of dishes prepared.

After the feast the newlyweds put on their roughest clothes, packed their few things and rode off. Each couple took a different path to a different cabin or lodge in a different corner of the valley for as long as they wished or until their provisions ran out. Mark rode Xerxes, the proud old racehorse and Laura reined Delilah, the dapple grey mare. Pal, who had taken to following Mark and Laura on their walks and rides since they came, followed and led them alternately. Tears came to Naomi's eyes as the different couples rode away. They did not get very far as night came on quickly. They stopped at one of the trail cabins on their way to the lodge beyond the lake that Mark had been taken to on his birthday. The cool fall air, the sound of water in the creek not far away, the rustle of dry leaves on the trees and on the ground made them even more comfortable as they started a fire and just enjoyed each other like they never could before. Pal began to bark at them and then turned and ran down the trail back home. They went into the cabin with their sleeping bags and closed the door.

The ride the next day up to the lodge was relaxing and beautiful. They had plenty of food and so they spent a week walking and riding, exploring, playing games, talking, studying the Bible together and praying. Pal appeared and disappeared. This all seemed too good to be true in their minds. They became vocally meditative together as they sat on the ridge and looked down at the valley below and the mountains beyond. The sun was setting in a spectacular sunset in a combination with the clouds.

"It's too bad we won't have a normal life, I mean, you know . . ." began Laura.

"You mean a house, a car, some kids, and a dog?" said Mark.

"Yes," said Laura, "especially lots of kids."

"Well, except for the car and the kids, we do have many houses and a dog," said Mark smiling.

"But it's not the same and what about in heaven or on a new earth. Will we have those things there?" she said, meditatively.

"I think we'll have those things and even more that we can't know about."

"But people aren't going to be married there," said Laura.

"That's heaven, but God is going to make a new world isn't He? Maybe we'll get to be married there, just like a renewed Adam and Eve."

"Yeah, I'd like that. We'd have our own garden and we'd be perfect. We wouldn't have to worry about anything. We'd be able to walk and talk with God like Adam did," said Laura.

"But it may not be like that . . . I don't know. No matter what, we will be together forever even if we're not married. Seems that people need an earth to live on and since God made everything, it seems hard not to think that He wouldn't make another. Maybe we will get to explore the universe and God will give us our own new world to start. Maybe everyone will start over like Adam and Eve, only this time there won't be a Satan to ruin things and we will love God so much that we would never think of living without Him," said Mark.

"Yes, and God will teach us and help us to build worlds which sinful man can't even dream of now. God will be our sun and everything. Then we could have lots of kids.

I couldn't say this before but I love children and working with them. I always dreamed of having a family," said Laura kissing him and laughing.

Mark looked into her face and he understood. He sighed long and looked at her solemnly and said, "Laura, I'm sorry we can't be normal here. About having a family . . . I don't think we can. Remember how Charles counseled us and Dr. Kim fixed us up and warned us not to deviate."

"We had more talks on . . . what did Naomi call it, the birds and the bees, than I bet anyone ever got," said Laura. "But in the Bible isn't it an honor and privilege that God bestows to have children?"

Mark took out the pocket Bible that Charles had given him and thumbed through it rapidly. He read Matthew

24:19–20. "This is one of the reasons I hesitated in asking you Laura." He brought his face close to hers and kissed her face as he held her, "I love you so much Laura. I wouldn't want to hurt you for anything in the world and I want to spend however much time we're given together. And I don't want you to have to suffer any more than is necessary when our time is up and we are put through new trials."

Laura gripped him tighter and kissed him for a long time. "Then we'd better get busy and love each other," she whispered in his ear.

It was not long before they were back at the lodge and the door closed for the night.

A week later, the newlywed couple came home to their own cabin a short distance from the house. It was only one room. The main house would still be the main area of living, but they made it as homey as possible. A table and chairs were brought in along with an old brass four-poster bed and a hearth rug. To go to the bathroom they still had to go to the house. Mark usually made a shorter trip to a camp facility late at night. They dug an old painting out of Charles' storeroom, a picture of Jesus on the road to Emmaus. It hung proudly over their bed. Mark made some rough bookshelves. They were home, but there were moments when it did not seem real that they were married.

Chapter 17

THE FELLOWSHIP'S HOUR

Through October and November, Mark and Laura saw Carol go back to university, and Debby and Jackie went to teach in the Christian Academy High School at the same time. Tom and Dick traveled back and forth to help at the camp. James, Jim, and Estelle and the others went off for long or short periods of time. Mark and Laura longed to get out too. For Mark, Charles said absolutely no. Laura was allowed to go to town from time to time with Charles and Naomi or the other families.

However, one weekday evening Mark heard on the radio how UCLA would play Washington State at Spokane. He remembered Jerome Gates and wondered if he had made it with that team. He pleaded with Charles and Naomi that he, and maybe Tom, Dick, and Laura could go to the game. Naomi said yes but left it up to Charles who eventually gave in. But he had to promise to have James go with them and to obey any order to retreat if he gave it. Jackie and

Laura drove out there and stood in line nearly all day to get tickets. This was Mark's only time to leave the camp.

As they walked through the crowds surrounded by their own secret service, Mark reminded Laura that this was their first date. Jerome Gates as a sophomore was the number one forward on the floor that night and he had grown an inch to six foot eight. He looked stronger and faster than Mark had ever seen. At the end of the game as the floor filled with students and fans, Mark and Company went down and he got Jerome's attention as he walked off the court. Jerome recognized Mark right off and shook his hand and gave him their old handshake. Mark noticed the seal on his hand and the Arabic letter on his forehead, which many of the students sported. They smiled at each other and Jerome looked puzzled at Mark's presence. "What you doin' here?"

Mark made up a story and while he talked he noticed how Jerome seemed changed. There was something different about the eyes. They seemed distant and a little sad.

"I'm going to school out here and am staying with some relatives," said Mark.

Jerome nodded and smiled warmly, almost coming out of his distance for an instant.

"How about you, you looked real good out there," said Mark.

"Yeah, I feel so good now too. Things are changing for the better, I think. Hey, you should get one of these." He showed him his hand with pride. But James, who was looking on, noticed the side of his neck as well. Mark smiled and nodded politely saying how nice it was.

"Where's your cross? You used to wear it at every game—said you'd never take it off," said Mark.

"It was hurting my neck, but I still have it."

Laura sidled up to Mark and put her hand in his. "Oh, hey, I want you to meet . . ."

"You ole sly devil, you finally corralled a gal."

"This is Laura," he said as they shook hands and Jerome whistled at Mark and said, "You lucky devil. Well I got to go. Look me up sometime down LA way."

Mark was displeased with this meeting. He expected more and did not expect what he saw in and on him. As he stood meditating on this, James whispered in his ear to go and gently pushed him in a direction away from the purple clad policemen who were approaching from the other direction across the floor.

On the way back to camp, Mark talked about Jerome and his thoughts about the tattoo and hand seal. James was more perturbed when he told Mark that he also had what the military community called "the collar." He had noticed the red bruise at the side of his neck that indicated a deep injection of a tiny microchip. It was impossible to get out without a major operation. It held all his information, he could be tracked via satellite if lost or kidnapped or even controlled to a certain extent. The technology was still improving.

"When you say controlled, how?" asked Mark.

"If he has undesirable thoughts he can receive a jolt of pain, or since the chip is often lodged in the brain stem it can even transmit suggestions to the brain, that is if and when they wanted to control him. And if he has the collar that means it is being administered much more widely. It means that Aliadin's desire for control will extend to every community until he controls everyone."

A year later, Tom and Dick were in town to shop and do a number of errands. They found that the stores refused their money. They were asked for their computer seals. Only begrudgingly did they accept the money.

On another day Ruth and Naomi took the kids to the dentist. The nurse told them that next time they would have to have a computer seal account.

Charles' Christian magazines stopped coming and the mail became far slower, more unreliable and even more expensive. Kim and Anne tried to go to church in town and discovered it locked and nobody in sight on a Sunday morning. Campers and camp programs stopped.

Paper and metal currency went out of circulation. In theory it did exist, but it was safely kept in the accounts of computers. The newer technology of eye and fingerprint scans for all businesses were making more progress.

Jackie and Debbie lost their jobs and could not exist without the seal. Carol could not go back to school. Peter Yong lost his job in town. Everyone thought the same question and knew the same answer. Why could they not accept the stamp? It was a practical and economic positive, but as Charles re-iterated, a good idea in a bad time. It was the antichrist's way of control. To get it, there was an indoctrination session where the question was asked, "Is Aliadin the Christ and do you believe in him with all your heart?"

Jim was tempted to get the stamp and discovered that this seemed to be such an innocuous question to answer when he sat before the bank officer. What if Aliadin was called the Christ just once? Was that selling one's soul? Could not one simply revoke it or get out of it at any time? Could a little white lie here really count in the spiritual warfare that few understood was going on?

However, in making this simple decision one was "urged" to attend a camp, conference, business retreat or whatever it was called from town to town and country to country for periods of time ranging from one week to several months. These affairs were intended to educate or re-educate individuals into Aliadin's ways and policies. If one had no particular religious beliefs or belonged to any non-Judeo-Christian religion, or if one had been a nominal churchgoer who believed good deeds was all that was necessary, then there were usually few problems. Aliadin's people did not pressure them but welcomed them.

However, there were other obligations, especially if one was a historic Christian, Jew, or revolutionary of some sort. They had to renounce all friends who did not have the stamp and then be brought instantly into a new peer group. Once one was accepted into this fellowship, one was free to work and live in the world's new society unharmed and unhindered. They were welcomed into life in the new United States of the World.

The fellowship never saw Jim again. Estelle did receive a phone call from Jim. He tried to get Estelle to come and renounce her old life. He tried to convince her that this other Christ was fictitious and His coming pure fantasy. Estelle hung up when she had had too much and the tears did not stop for many days. Charles tried to comfort her and told her that he could have been coerced to make this call and it did not necessarily mean he had truly changed. "If he is truly saved, Jesus will rescue him out of that," Charles reassured. The rest put their arms around her and tried to comfort her. Charles told the rest that they would have to face many difficulties and their perseverance would be tested.

Mark asked once again why Aliadin did not just attack and finish them off. Charles said that first of all he did not have to. His object was to make his victims miserable and to capitulate by slow, intense pressure. "Satan has done this behind the scenes throughout all of history and in every-day life."

As Jim left, others started coming to the camp. It started as a trickle, but soon it became a steady stream of historic Christians that included the Moffatts and Rev. Bradley and his wife. Some came who had gotten the stamp and who wanted to get rid of it. This kept Dr. Kim busy. Some who were fleeing had the collar and this posed a new danger for the camp as they could be tracked.

About this time a representative of the Christian under-ground from Chicago came; he providentially had a device which he gave them that deactivated the chips or blocked their use. When he heard the name Brogen in camp he made sure he took a good look at Mark and then moved on to the west coast. He told the fellowship that travel was nearly impossible now for historic Christians. He got through only by God's grace, and computer chicanery. Networks of concentration or "revival camps" as they were called had been set up around the country with reports of atrocities, interrogations, and a final solution.

A number of nominal townspeople and common citizens made up a third refugee group who simply knew what was happening was not right and they wanted the old American way back again.

This put more pressure on the camp to feed and house them. Charles and Naomi's foresight was now paying off with long stockpiled cellars of food; staples such a flour, sugar, yeast, honey, and meat, besides all that was canned, bottled, and frozen. Fortunately, many of these refugees had some resources in terms of houses, land, food, and farm products. Also, because Charles was well known to those in the community who did have the stamp, some agreed to a barter system. For example, a furniture salesman in town always liked Charles' work and arranged for food and needed equipment and clothes be exchanged for handcrafted furniture. This new turn kept everyone working and chipping in to the business.

Other sources of food included enlarging the gardens, utilizing those cattle and milk cows of Harry's, and the primitive methods of hunting and fishing. Years of environmentalist work on the northwest now paid off with a bountiful number of deer and all kinds of animals that had been forgotten about as food since the Indian and pioneer days of America. The men now labored in one or all of these categories; the women were left to the arts of gardening, preservation, and cooking.

God also gave the camp's valleys favorable weather and some of the best garden harvests in memory even when disasters of all sorts were reported in nearby regions. Charles pointed out to Mark that just as God protected the Israelites in the Egyptian captivity when Pharaoh felt his wrath right next door, he was doing it for them in the Tribulation.

All of this heightened the praise and worship. Charles preached a number of open air, open field messages that brought the nominal Christians and secular townspeople in their midst to their knees. The Holy Spirit sealed the revival when a cancer-ridden man who had been turned out of the hospital for noncompliance asked Charles for prayer and was healed before everyone. The prayer, the weeping, the broken hearts before God, the worship, and the leading of the unsaved to the Savior did not cease for several months. When they thought it had ended, two truckloads of renegade army soldiers came to camp and asked what was going on. Many repented of their past sins and many returned to the Savior as the others met Him for the first time. The fellowship went to work over these three years as never before, explaining the gospel and praying for all who desired it. Mark and Laura acknowledged to each other that this was the most gratifying time of their lives.

Mark understood now what it must have been like in the days of the first and second Great Awakenings. He felt like he was in a history book that was being written as he lived it.

18

A GIFT IN THE
MIDST OF WAR

The truckloads of renegade soldiers who were now Christian soldiers painted the white cross on their trucks and next to it the American flag and removed Aliadin's Arabic symbol and the USW flag. A week later a Christian corps commander came to camp with a large force and inducted the new soldiers into his army. He reported that a portion of his force would remain in the camp and train the other men as much as possible. A real civil war was being waged in eastern Montana and in and around the Rocky Mountains all the way to Colorado. How long it could be kept from here was hard to say. The northwest was one of many regions holding out. He reported that the Christian army in the southwest was on the attack, not on the defensive. Aliadin was being methodical and patient, but that they should be prepared for an attack at any time. With this news the camp and its assorted inhabitants went to work to prepare for defending it. Soon Christian Army soldiers were placed in the camp as a guard.

Resources at times were strained, patience and resolve were tested, and things went on in this fashion for another three years. This seemed impossible with the on-again off-again war that was still mostly rumor and not reality to those in the camp. Mark often asked Charles about when the Rapture would take place and if seven years had been taken up yet. Charles pointed out that it was almost six years since Aliadin had openly declared himself the Christ. But, it should be remembered that Aliadin's power had been felt and understood in the rest of the world for years before that.

One night at worship and Bible Study time with the fellowship, Charles began to ruminate. He said, "Seven in the Bible might not mean seven in our thinking. It is a godly number. Godly numbers there mean that He has it all planned out in His perfect will in a perfectly timely time. We often have the saying that timing is everything. In other words, I believe that God was telling Daniel and the other prophets that His timing is everything. Also, God does not count like we do. If He did, He wouldn't have told us that no one could know the time except Himself. That's why we should expect Him anytime."

Mark asked, "What about the three-and-a-half years predicted in Daniel?"

Charles answered, "Same principle. This is even better, because we know that the antichrist's time is short. Reverse the thinking. God will not leave us or forsake us for very long no matter what that means, whether it is symbolic or a real number."

Mark said, "What if He doesn't come back at all and we become another statistic for another time in history?"

Charles chided him. "All God's children were and are important in their time and all of them expected to see Him return. Time and space are not important to God. None are without significance in His eyes. Don't lose faith in God and the gospel. It will come to pass and sooner than you think. It is a lesson to us all to live for Him to the fullest in every moment."

Mark and Laura were given more time off to be together, as were all the married inhabitants. The long winter continued into March and April. Spring did not look like it would be coming soon. Around Easter time they rode their horses to the other valley and spent time at one of the new cabins built on Harry's property where Mark spent much time tending cattle.

As they rode they looked out into the frozen lake. The mantle of snow, the textures of white, and gray showed a changing beauty as the sun and clouds changed places. Then through the clouds came rays of sunlight bringing with them the clear piercing light that comes on clear cold days. The grays became green and the white became a brilliant fleece. A thousand paintings were mastered in the shifting light, revealing the works of the artist. Water caught in a moment of rushing changed to crystal, and the blowing drifting snow became the virgin's veil. The gray rock surfaces and peaks turned from black to grey, brown to gold.

Mark and Laura enjoyed the ride and each other. As they rode Mark studied Laura on horseback. They seemed so different now. Could it be six years since they first met? They both wore blue jeans and blue denim jackets with the white crosses and American flags emblazoned on the front and back. He had a rifle slung over his back as they rode their horses through the winter valley. He was riding into history again. This time he was at Valley Forge, only this time it was a revolution at the end of history. It dawned on him that their new war resembled the Civil War even more as freedom fought slavery once again.

On their second day at the far cabin Laura felt unusually sick and queer and Mark grew concerned. Mark went to Harry's house and informed the refugee families and a number of soldiers living and guarding that valley. It happened that Dr. Kim was there too. Laura was picked up by jeep with Dr. Kim and driven back to camp while Mark brought the horses back.

By the time Mark arrived at their cabin Dr. Kim had gone. Laura sat on the edge of the bed and he came and sat beside her. She looked whiter than usual. He looked into her eyes. Her eyes looked down.

"What's wrong? Are you sick? What did Dr. Kim say? Is it cancer or carbuncles?" he said at last to try to get a response.

Tears ran down her cheeks and she tried to look at him and smile but she couldn't talk and looked away.

"Please, Laura tell me what's wrong."

"I'm pregnant," she mumbled in a broken voice. "Please, don't hate me."

Stunned for a moment he digested this news, but he immediately put his arms around her and hugged her. Then he put his face into hers and began wiping her tears with his own cheeks.

"Oh, sweet Laura, I can only love you and forever and always, no matter what," he said.

This made her cry all the more. In moments between the waves of emotion she said, "It was an accident! I only did what Dr. Kim told me to do every time. He said it was not one-hundred percent perfect."

"Sssssshhhhhhhh. Don't talk. Besides, I think we're supposed to be happy about this aren't we?" Mark said as he began kissing her face. She nodded her head affirmatively, though the tears kept streaming.

"But . . . but it won't have a normal life and what if . . . . Remember the verse you read to me on our honeymoon? I'm already distressed."

"Laura, look at me."

She looked up into his face and he put his forehead against hers.

"This was no accident," he said.

"But it was . . . it is. This baby should never have been and not now," she said.

"You once told me that you thought you were an accident for your parents."

"It's true. I was in the way."

Now tears formed in Mark's eyes.

He whispered to her, "No. No. You were no accident," and he hugged her tightly and kissed her ear. Then he put his forehead against hers again and looked into her blue eyes and said, "God could not have made an angel as wonderful as you, to be there for me. You were no accident and neither is this baby and you know it. God is giving us a family, the kind of family we always really wanted. You and I must trust . . . really trust God now that He knows what He is doing. Even if the battle in this world should go against us, we must have the faith that nothing will separate us from God's intended plan for us. We will have a family and if not here, then in Heaven. If not there, then in a new world. This baby will live just like we will when Jesus comes back forever. We have to believe this no matter how hard it is right now."

"You sound just like Charles now," she whispered in his ear. Then she kissed him and they lay down together.

From that time on her disposition changed and she was back to her usually cheerful self even if her usual energy was now sapped more easily. Dr. Kim set new rules for her and suggested a new diet that had a decidedly Asian dimension to it.

Mark explained everything to Charles and so when the fellowship met for worship, Charles and Naomi did not lose a step in congratulating them and not letting anyone discourage Laura. Those with children looked on most sympathetically.

Living normally and positively was growing more difficult. More units of soldiers and their commanders came to live with them in the two valleys. Indeed the contrast could not have been greater than when tender Laura still looking normal and the Yong and Kim families walked through a camp with tanks, trucks, missile launchers, helicopters, and jeeps all taking up significant space on the camp's roads and in and around the camp compound.

Army tents could be seen all over the valley and in the mountains and on the ridges. Battle emplacements were created where military planners thought best. Old mines and caves were shored up and deepened. Helicopters clattered overhead often. Few planes could be seen in normal times. But one day several jets screamed low over the valley. They bore the white cross and American flag and within minutes were engaged in an air battle with several others that bore Aliadin's Arabic letter next to the United States of the World decals. The enemy planes were quickly destroyed; one high over the twin mountains; another fell and exploded in a large fireball into the mountain directly behind great house.

The reality of seeing the war in their back yard had a sobering effect on the fellowship. Mark asked one of the officers why they weren't being bombed all the time. He pointed to the corps of computer hackers who battled the enemy computer hackers in disturbing the coordinates, infecting jet computers, reversing missile assignments and on and on in an endless list of technological games that in effect neutralized much technology in the air and on the ground. This all made war more conventional. The jets he had seen were basically "winging it" when they fired their weapons.

Encouragingly, one day many of the troops were moved out. Charles understood from the commander of these units that they were about to join other Christian forces for what was termed the Battle for Washaho, the area still held by Christian forces. This area included western Montana and a large area of western Canada where Canadian Christians held out. But this Christian army was pressed hard in the southern part of the state and soon more of the army was in the valley. One evening, the generals and commanders all met in Charles and Naomi's dining room. The Spirit of the Lord was felt and Charles and Naomi held a feast and worship time with the members of the fellowship serving them. The tremendous singing was heard for a distance into the valley and soon the soldiers throughout the valley sang to the praise of God.

For the next week the battle raged and crept closer until on the day before Father's Day the very road and spot Mark and Laura tumbled into the valley was the scene of intense fighting. But the enemy was turned back.

Mark reluctantly left Laura for his daily chore of tending the cattle up the valley. She insisted he go and get fresh air and stop pacing in the cabin. He rode the same route he had done for years now, and with his rifle slung over his shoulder. He wondered if he would or could actually use it. He greeted, talked and joked with the many soldiers he had come to know. When he first met them they made fun of his name until some soldiers from Chicago explained that he was not just considered a fugitive but a terrorist as his name was brought up often in the news. His name had become a scapegoat name for the antichrist's leaders to blame for any criminal attacks, the kidnapping of important people or any public mischief that they chose to link him with. Thus, he now understood why they nicknamed him Robin Hood and when they saw Laura they called her Maid Marion. He laughed all this off, but as he thought about it he took some pride in knowing that in an unexpected way he had become famous.

He settled into a lunch with Tom and Jackie, Debbie and Dick, and Harry at the house that was once his. They ate, laughed and talked until a female soldier interrupted them and told them they were under attack. They had heard some thunder but had not thought about it. Once outside the house they saw jets and helicopters engaged in battle in the skies and soldiers streaming toward the battle in the next valley. The rifle was forgotten in the house as he mounted Xerxes and galloped toward camp. As he went he noticed the units surging with him and he did not realize it but he was an unintended participant in the attack. Actually, he was part of a reinforcement line to shore up the front line which was retreating. The main camp, house, barns and cabins were now in the middle of a battlefield and the Christian army did not want to fire into their own buildings as they were occupied by those who could not escape fast enough in this surprise attack. The antichrist's forces descended on the camp. White helicopters with the Arabic symbol and U.S.W. flag came down like locusts. Enemy soldiers were led by the purple police who directed this part of the assault instead of officers. This meant they were out to capture as well as kill.

Bullets whizzed and there were explosions near and far as Mark without hesitation galloped forward, thinking only of Laura and his object—their cabin. His movement had some effect on the Christian soldiers near him who surged forward in an attempt to protect him. They had already rescued Ruth Yong and her children, Dr. Kim and his family, Estelle and Anne and her children.

Mark saw Kim and Peter's bodies among the dead. Xerxes was shot and the horse crumpled beneath him. His forward motion flung him into a flip and he lay on his back for a moment. The soldiers and purple police were swarming into the house where they caught James, Charles, and Naomi. Before he could get up he saw Laura running toward him. A soldier and policeman ran after her. "Stop or we'll shoot," yelled the soldier in hot pursuit. She kept on running. Then Laura's and Mark's eyes met as she crashed through the brush as the soldier tripped her. They both tumbled and the soldier held her on the ground and she was struggling. Mark's adrenaline flowed. To the soldier who had his visor up, Mark came from nowhere as he kicked him in the face, knocking him back and unconscious. He knelt down and took Laura in his arms when the purple policeman arrived and gave several sharp blows to Mark's head. It was better that he did not see how Charles and Naomi and James were led out into the backyard. Each was made to kneel while one after another they were shot in the back of their heads. The house, the barns, the cabins and the bodies were burned.

The Christian army retreated and with it the remains of the fellowship.

Chapter 19

THOSE BOXCARS

Except for a few flashlights and an imitation lantern at one end, the long and large boxcar was dark. The people had enough room to sit down. Someone struck up *Amazing Grace*, and all the voices from dark corners came to life. Laura sang and prayed as she rocked to and fro. Near her lay Mark still and unconscious with his head in her lap. He had been out for so long she feared he was really hurt.

The cry of a baby came from somewhere to her left. She thought of her own and patted her stomach gently. She knew it was fine. More hymns were sung. Someone to her left began to pray out loud that in life or death they could glorify the one true and everlasting Savior.

Mark stirred and groaned. Then he cried out, "Laura, Laura!"

"Ssssshhhhhh," she held him closer and stopped rocking. "I'm right here, I'm Ok."

"What happened?" he asked dully. He tried to move, but his head felt like an anvil. Then he lay still and sent his hand into her hair feeling it and touching her face. "I love you." She bent down and kissed his face repeatedly.

The train rattled on endlessly. One end of the car was designated as a toilet and there were rustic chamber pots there for those who could wait no longer. The air became acrid and stuffy. During this confinement, friendships were struck automatically. The persecution seemed to harden nerves, drive away doubts, and bring resolution instead of panic. Each person was ready to meet Christ. They still hoped for His Rapture. But if death came first—let it come.

The train stopped at a makeshift station in the middle of a prairie. Nearby was an internment camp with its barbed wire fences and guard towers. Purple police and soldiers had all the inhabitants get out. After some inspection they were rearranged. When they saw Mark with a purple tag and understood his importance, he was led away with a number of others to another car. Others were taken to the camp. Still others and Laura with red tags remained with the train and were ordered to re-board. They were met by another large group from the camp who were parceled out to the cars. Laura found herself in new company.

The boxcar was much worse than before. Some had to stand for awhile in the cramped conditions. Laura squeezed into a corner. People began to pray around her out loud. Then she noticed a tall black man weeping in the shadows of the other corner. She squeezed to him.

"Excuse me, but is your name Jerome?" she said.

He looked at her vacantly. Then as if spitting out a wad of something, he said, "Please help me." He sobbed uncontrollably and hid his face in his hands. Then she touched him and tried to put her arms around him. He wrapped his huge arms and hands around her and both moved downward to their knees in an urge to sit. Then his head jerked up and he looked at her pensively.

"Who are you?" he asked. His eyes were sad and he was obviously deeply depressed. His hands shook.

"I'm Laura Brogen, Mark's wife. We met a long time ago. You were playing basketball in Spokane."

"Mark . . . Mark," he said as he thought for some time, not in loss of memory but as if that name were awakening him.

"Oh, please, you must help me. I have sinned," he whined. "I went with THEM! I have the seal on my hand and this blasted thing in my neck that doesn't let me sleep." He began to cry.

Laura took in the situation. Others overheard and looked down, praying for him. She said to him, "But you're Ok, you're repenting. Jesus loves you. He accepts you even now just as you are." She prayed for him for a long time, looking into his tired, watery eyes to see if there was any change.

"I have the seal of doom, I'm doomed," he said.

"No, no you're not. Jesus still loves you. You may have gone wrong, but you're repenting. You're sorry for that now. Jesus sees that. You're repenting. That's all God asks," said Laura.

Someone said behind her that he had been turned in for his neurotic behavior.

"Please, burn it off," said Jerome showing her the seal on the back of his hand. Someone else produced a small campfire lighter and said that they would do it.

"No, Mark must do it." Here he looked at Laura and said, "You are Mark's. You must do it. I have sinned against God and my brothers. Please!" He held his hand out to her.

After some hesitating Laura closed her eyes, said a short prayer, blew some breath out of her pursed lips and flicked the switch. Instantly the coil was red hot. Everyone in the train car turned to the corner and became dead silent at the scream. The smell of burnt flesh wafted over the car. Having to hold him somehow prevented her from getting sick.

A pastor and many others who could reach Jerome placed their hands on him and prayed that he might have the peace of Christ. He fell asleep after some simple first aid and did not awake for some time, even though his neck twitched now and again from the computer chip embedded in there.

The train came to a halt. The boxcar doors slid open and the occupants had to adjust their eyes to the brilliant morning sunlight. As Laura got up she could see in the morning light lines of people four abreast being loaded and unloaded onto boxcars and trucks. Soldiers quietly separated people, especially young women, from these lines and led them away.

With the crowd in her car slowly getting down and Jerome being led away with the other men it afforded Laura an opportunity to pause and to look over the crowd and look for Mark. It was a huge train yard. Several other trains had pulled in. There seemed to be an inspection of some selected groups. In the distance she could see a large viaduct that ran in an arc over the train yard. Then she was forced to get down and almost immediately looked into the eyes of Immanuel Rodriguez who was in the army uniform of the antichrist. They recognized each other easily, but said nothing to each other. She was immediately led to a truck with a number of other young women. They were driven in a line with other trucks to a concentration camp built in the midst of a large forest preserve that was surrounded by small lakes that used to be clay pits in the past. The women were led to a large open cell inside the prison. They prayed and talked briefly but for the most part were silent and frightened. Soldiers entered and leered at them and teased and made fun of them. An officer said something to them as he pointed at Laura and then he left. For two days they were cleaned up, fed, and inspected.

Mark almost did not recognize the C&O railroad yard in Rosedale as he was led off the train. He remembered what had happened here long ago when he thought he had seen something. At that time it was the beginning and kept secret so as not to alarm the townspeople. But now it was done in the open and became an everyday occurrence to terrorize everyone to obey the new laws. None of them wanted to end up here.

He looked through the crowd to see if he could see Laura but he could not. He was separated into a smaller group and as he expected, there was some activity among superiors when he had been identified. He was separated from the small group he had been in and made to stand alone.

He watched as the train doors were closed and the trains and trucks soon departed. For a long time he stood virtually alone with five armed guards around him.

Turning around he could see the screen of the restored outdoor theatre. A little farther was a water tower against the grayish sky in that direction which was the steel mill beyond. He also studied the old grain elevator with the rooster painted at its top which had been elevated to historic preservation status. The weather was hot and very humid. He had forgotten what day it was, but time ceased to have a meaning. When he was questioned about his age he had to think for a moment. "Twenty-four," he heard his voice say. Was he that old? What a life this had been. But now he was alone again. A large black limousine approached with a cloud of grey dust trailing behind it. It stopped only a few feet from him.

The blood rose in his face and a cold sweat formed on his palms as he saw Uncle rise out of the car.

"Well, it's been a devil of a long time, boy! What have you got to say for yourself?"

Mark stood silent.

"Come, my boy, all is forgiven. You had to get your wild oats out for awhile but now it's time for serious business."

"Like giving me to your friends for them to use?" Mark said.

Uncle ignored this and said, "Please get in, we have much to discuss."

He sat in the cool air conditioning and on the soft leather seats once again, listening to Uncle prattle on. "If you even now recant your silly pie-in-the-sky beliefs and accept our lord's terms, things might go more easily for you. You could live with me again. After all we are family."

Mark looked out the window. Then he looked back at Uncle and said, "Do you think I could live with you or accept your terms knowing you murdered my and your own family? Besides you and your precious lord have tortured and murdered the real Lord's people."

"I must confess things have gotten out of hand, all unnecessary. But we offered these people you speak of a good life and they refused. You are refusing now. Don't you want to live normally? Now come and choose again. I am offering you a last chance.

The lord in Jerusalem is very angry with you. And well, I should want to be truly repentant if I were you because he intends to meet you."

"Meet me? He's angry with me? Remember I'm just Mark Brogen—the average of the average."

"Oh, no you're not and I'm sure those so-called friends of yours along your journey often reminded you that you were no longer ordinary," said Uncle, having a good laugh.

"In fact, you're quite a celebrity of sorts, thanks to a little creativity from our media department." Here Uncle turned the limousine computer on and Mark watched a number of news bulletins that featured him.

He now understood why his soldier friends in camp called him Robin Hood. He was depicted as an infamous renegade and terrorist who seemed to be involved in leading numerous violent acts of aggression against Aliadin's innocent administration and people. The oldest report had him as the bomber of his own father's publishing firm. In the most recent he saw himself leading a charge on his horse against Aliadin's home defense force. Mark was stunned and speechless. Uncle enjoyed his reactions.

"So you see, in the official version it was you and not me who did the murdering of your family. You are making history, my boy . . ." he said. Uncle saw the rising anger and anticipated some violence. He aimed a small gun at Mark and pulled the trigger. A small dart hit him in the side of the neck as he turned his head away. Mark saw his hands swimming ahead of him as he tried to reach Uncle. As if he looked through the wrong end of a telescope, he saw Uncle getting smaller and then as if someone pulled a plug out of him, he knew no more.

"Oh, I so do enjoy these old toys of the past," laughed Uncle to himself.

Ordinary cement walls and tiled surfaces always seemed so innocent before. Now there was a stuffiness, a claustrophobic element that one might have only experienced in small sealed train or jet airplane compartments. One knows it is cool outside and the air fresh, but on the inside when the heat is too dry or the air conditioning malfunctions it can be uncomfortable and even terrifying. These long, low, milky white corridors with their many windows barred on the outside became the very essence of terror and imprisonment for hundreds of normal Christians, Jews, and assorted renegades who were now tabbed as mentally ill and dangerous. The windows made for the worst torment of all because all could see the innocent light of day, the green grass, the trees, and freedom. The building Mark was taken into was an ultra-modern one, part asylum, part laboratory, and part office.

A door to one room was opened. Mark was awakened and startled by the presence of two and then three people in white medical outfits who were gently waking him and telling him to walk. He looked down and his feet seemed to coalesce with the floor. He became dizzy as he was made to walk. All he wanted to do was lie down again and sleep, but they would not let him. They forced some liquid down his throat as he was propped between two orderlies. He drank more but choked and spluttered most of it.

Finally, he began to regain strength, and noticed for the first time that he had clean white bed clothes on. They were asking him to move and helping him to put on new clothes and suddenly he found himself well dressed.

He was led through those endless corridors. This was not in the city but in a distant suburb. He could tell by the trees and the remoteness that the building was only a few stories high and spread over acres. They led him into a room with a long conference table and many pieces and paintings in the sterile twenty-first century style. Many other people were there. He was seated at the table with six others; television cameras panned the group and the room as an announcer began his presentation.

The people at the table were told to sit quietly. Mark still found it hard to hear and comprehend what others were saying as his mind wandered. He heard the announcer talking and a camera pointing at him and panning all who sat at the table.

A commotion took place at the end of the table. One of the seven, a short, gritty looking man interrupted the announcer by getting up and yelling wildly that revolution would take care of them all. He was quickly held down and given a sedative. The camera covered all of this and the announcer got more excited in his reporting.

"That's right, next month at this time the great savior of our world will make an appearance here in Chicago. He will demonstrate once and for all his power to turn men to himself, even these seven lost souls: two revolutionaries, two Jews, and three Christians and change their minds about their heresies. So heretical adherents and renegades, stop resisting and come to your true lord."

The camera panned back over the people at the table. Another man in the middle broke out in a rage and said in a heavy accent, "Aliadin, I hate you! You will never take over my country." When a number of harsh expletives were screamed out the orderlies took care of him. This was broadcast to all corners of the world.

Chapter 20

···

METAMORPHOSIS

H e was alone in his room for several days when one night his door opened and the light from the corridor invaded the blackness of the room. A lean young woman appeared at the door and was silhouetted against the light. Mark called out, "Laura? Is it you, Laura?" When she entered, the camera in the corner of the room and several concealed cameras made it look like nobody was there and the microphones and sensors turned off immediately. She closed the door, put a patch over the eyehole, walked over and drew the curtains to the window and then turned on a lamp.

She wore a tailored all-black combat outfit with many zippered and concealed pockets that included a lightweight gun. Light body armor and a black T-shirt were underneath. This outfit included black socks, black running shoes and specially fitted black gloves that contoured exactly to her hands. She carried a black helmet with separate night vision goggles inside. Her face was gritty and she untied her golden brown hair from behind her head. It fell in a disheveled array around her shoulders, but it was characteristically parted down the middle.

The sharp beauty of her face and the emerald green eyes were remarkable. Tears streamed down her cheeks as she then stood silently by his bed. Mark was fully focused on her now and got off the bed but before he could take a step he was in a strong embrace. She buried her face into his shoulder. Her tears soaked the white night shirt with long sobs. She finally raised her head and looked into his face.

"Dianne? Am I dreaming? Am I dead too?" said Mark looking at her in awe.

She put her head into his shoulder again and cried some more. He forced her face up again so he could see the green eyes of his father, and the smooth cheeks, and the mouth wrinkled into an expression of extreme sadness. She was older, six years older and extraordinarily beautiful. She found it hard to speak and looked into his dull brown eyes still heavy with the sedative. She brought out a small container of something that she made him drink and as it burned down his throat it began to clear his head and waken him more than he had been in days. Suddenly the tears stopped and she said, "Can you walk? I've been in the underground here for the past six years and I can find you another safe place. I am dead and a non-person and so they've never known my identity since . . . since we parted. I know I owe you a lifetime of answers but they must wait."

A million questions went through his head but he addressed her now in a way she had never known him before. "I can't leave here now. Jesus has made it plain to me that I'm to stay here. If I'm to die for Him then it will happen here. Besides, you know probably better than I do, that if I am such a hunted person I would only ruin whatever good things you are doing. But I have so many questions. What happened way back then? Where did you go and why didn't you help me back in the beginning?"

She looked down at the glowing wrist computer that indicated a timer winding down. She pulled her hair back over one ear by old habit and Mark saw the round silver stud in one ear lobe. She gave vocal orders to her wrist computer and then turned off the lamp. Then she got on the bed and sat with her legs crossed and he did the same. She held his hands and cleared her throat. She prayed, "Oh, Lord please give us some time without any enemy interference, amen." They could still see each other because of the moon-light streaming in through a crack in the curtains.

"What's the ear ring for?" he asked.

She whispered, "It's a micro-computer to which I can hear its warnings and directions. I have one under a cap and filling in one tooth also, in case I lose or break this wrist computer. Among many things, they help control all the spy devices that would detect us on our missions. I can also hear and speak to our other operatives."

Mark smiled at all of this as she cleared her throat and related her story.

"That day at the fire Mom and Dad were busy talking with friends near the punch table. Joanne and I went to the bathroom. A woman began talking to us—interested in twins. We were in one of our silly moods. Joanne pretended to be me, so I pretended to be her. We had even switched I.D. badges. Then she began talking to Joanne exclusively. And as we left the bathroom, the lady asked Jo to come meet her husband. I tried to tag along, but a crowd got in my way and she was gone. Frantically, I searched and thought I saw her being hustled out into the alley. A demonstration of the new printing technology was going on where Mom and Dad and most of the people were. As I ran to catch up with her the explosion happened. I was blown out the door with some others across the street but unhurt. Fire and smoke poured out and more explosions took place. I tried to run but was dizzy and fainted. When I woke up I was in a limousine with a strange man and a number of other people."

"You mean Uncle?" asked Mark.

"No. Not Uncle Ted, but Ronald Darringen, a wealthy Christian who started the Christian underground here and made me a part of it, until he was arrested and killed and then . . . and then I became its . . . leader. I was trained with many others in police operations, special forces fighting and survival skills and military, government and world intelligence. I helped create programs and a computer network and warfare system. It was I who persuaded the underground to get you away from Uncle. Mark, I knew where you were and what you were doing almost all the time. Please forgive me for letting you believe that I was dead."

"Wow, maybe you shouldn't be here now."

"No, we need to have a long talk, especially if it is our last."

"Then you arranged for Dr. Crawford and Rev. Casey?" said Mark more surprised than angry.

"Yes, I planned that and Rev. Bradley in Fargo was also our man."

"You mean you knew what I was doing every step of the way?" Mark said smiling and shaking his head.

Dianne looked at him and smiled a bit for the first time. "Yes, except after you drove from Fargo. We lost all touch then . . . until our man went through your camp in Idaho. Then I knew where you were, but could do nothing for you."

"Did . . . did you know about Laura?"

"No. We never knew about her, that is, before that trip.

"She . . . she wasn't . . . part of your plan . . ."

"No, no except for what Rev. Casey did for you I never knew her, and we never intended for her to go with you."

"Did you know we were married?"

"No, but I'm glad for you big brother. I wish I could meet her. She must be something—to be able to tackle you." They laughed together. Then he told her everything that happened from that night at the Bradleys until now. "Please, find her and protect her . . . and she's pregnant."

"It will be my next priority," she said as she thought about this and smiled at him.

Mark still had questions upon questions and he went back to the day of the explosion.

"Wait a minute, your bag and watch were at the fire. What about your body?"

"My shoulder bag strap broke on the way and because my watch was irritating my wrist I took it off and put it in my bag, and you know, I gave it to Mom to hold. Lucky

Mom and Dad, they didn't know what hit them. They should have been in heaven the next second. As far as my body, I thought it would have been found out that I was missing, but I suppose there was a mistaken identity or they fabricated it somehow. Didn't you look at the bodies at the funeral home?"

"Di, how could I, I was sick just to think about it. Besides they said all of your remains were unrecognizable except through records.

"There was a girl by us that was our height and about our age, but . . ."

"What about Joanne who was mistaken for you? They told Mr. Danforth and me she was injured by the blast and fire. She wasn't kidnapped. What about her injuries?"

"Mark, they do things that make it all seem legitimate. Didn't you study her? If she had been in the blast she would have had burns. Did she have burn treatments?"

Mark now recalled that night and saw Joanne again as he had remembered it often over the years. "No, there were injuries to her body, but not burns. She had a broken arm and a cast on a leg and bruises on her face. But back then I didn't think about that. I was in shock.

"They beat her up because she would not cooperate or give them my kind of answers. But they obviously thought they still had me."

"But what about Uncle, I still really don't know about him."

Dianne looked at him queerly. "You mean you never knew that Uncle Ted is the head of a huge conglomerate that for the most part does research for Aliadin? They're into computer technology, medical research, and many other things. They arranged the explosion so that it would destroy the company, but capture me."

"This brings us back to her," Dianne said to him looking down. When she looked back at him there were more tears. She stammered, "There's something else about her and Uncle that I need to tell you." She licked her lips. Then a new tear came down her cheek and her chin trembled and she had a hard time starting. "Uncle Ted is a doctor and among other things he experiments on human . . . brains and hearts. This research center, which they call an asylum and hospital, is where they do it . . ." she swallowed again and her voice quavered, ". . . her brain and heart have been used."

Mark was puzzled and said, "But that doesn't really matter now does it? She's with . . ."

"No, you don't understand . . . she is not dead. She or a part of her . . . is still alive. She is one of Uncle's robots now."

"But how do you know she is—you haven't seen her."

"You forget, I'm a twin and I know she's alive, just as she told you or tried to tell you that I was alive at the hospital.

Mark once again went back to that night and orally recited Joanne's words once again, when she said, "Mark, run . . . far, di . . . far . . . don't let hat . . . man get . . . you." and then "Mom, Dad, die, with Jesus . . . but Di."

"If your name hadn't been Di it would have been easier," Mark said.

"But you still should have understood."

"But didn't she die there in the hospital? They told us she did."

"Mark they lie, and they lie very well. Didn't you notice the number of doctors attending her? There should have been only one."

"How do you know all this? You weren't there."

"That's because . . . I've talked to her many times since. She gave herself for me and has not stopped since that day. She has worked with me for the underground. And I might say that, whereever she is right now, I have let her listen to this conversation, so in a sense she is here." Here she tapped her wrist computer.

It took some time for Mark to digest all of this. While he was, Dianne lectured.

"Ordinary robots and computers in the past all failed to become more human. Scientists always wanted to create better, faster, more efficient brains or computers which would go beyond and do the impossible. That is, mankind wanted to create other living beings that would be ultra smart, but would have human characteristics and autonomy. They have tried to go two ways. One, make existing people more controllable or robotic—hence the collar and the newer technology to induce the brain and mind to do what that person wants or what others want that person to do, be, or think. The other way is to make highly efficient computers and computerized robots and combine them with the best computer ever made, the human brain. Uncle's scientists found a way to take a human brain and the heart and make it run a machine from the inside while keeping the personality alive and the organs functioning. Aliadin enjoys this research, but for him control and altering the mind to conform to his will is of the ultimate importance. So this is another part of their research. Whether they retain their human body or not they want to be able to manipulate the brain to believe what they want it to believe. Moreover, they try to make these part-human part-machine computers and robots obedient and safe. And for Aliadin, more importantly and his maker Satan, they try to make them become real believers in him and have no vestige of any belief in the real God of heaven and earth and His Christ. Fortunately, for us and those who have had to go through this, usually these attempts to alter the will in the mind end up doing one of three things: killing the victim, making him crazy, or simply failing, that is, if that will did not want to change. If they did want to change, they were successful. The person who wants this special lobotomy to forget his past or his conscience usually succeeds. The collar is and was only a temporary and limited answer. A victim who doesn't want it will also succeed; the will still has some autonomy though other things are controlled."

Joanne broke in and told Dianne through her ear computer that she was being monitored. Her wrist computer told her how long it had been operating. Dianne responded by sending signals from her wrist computer neutralizing it.

"And yes I have communicated and even depended on her. She wonderfully agreed to remain me and I even fed her information that could be leaked that made them continue to think so. She also told me all about what happened to her since that night in the hospital. And she is listening now to this conversation and in a sense is here with us." Here she pointed to her wrist computer and the screen read, "I am still Joanne and I am listening. I love you big brother."

"But where is she now?"

"I don't always know where she is, but it doesn't matter because she's a computerized robot now and I can communicate with her at anytime with another computer and she can communicate with me. Together we monitored you."

Mark still was digesting all this and then asked, "What about Uncle's personality computers and Vicki. Were they . . . ?"

"Yes, they were and are. We used the one you liked best to get to you and to make you leave, remember?

"That was your doing?"

"Yes. But Vicki is a rat. We tried to communicate with her, but she remained loyal. She nearly ruined it all. She's the one who alerted Uncle as soon as she sensed you were not there when you should have been. I hate to say this, but we watched you quite often in Uncle's apartment by using his security cameras." Here Dianne pointed to her wrist computer and he read Joanne's words, "I watched you every day when you lived with Uncle in Chicago, and went to the university and at the Danforth's on that Christmas holiday and many other places, and I prayed for you."

Mark closed his eyes and tears formed in them. He bowed his head and said, "Then both of you and God know how rotten I was back then. I confess that I liked that sinful life and didn't want to leave it. But God did not give up on me. I can't tell you how He has used all of this to make me love Him so much that . . . well . . . I would give anything for Him now."

Brother and sister embraced. She whispered in his ear, "See you in heaven," and then kissed him on the cheek and they hugged again. "God will help me get Laura and the baby and we will come to you when He returns."

Suddenly the lights went on and Uncle Ted in white medical clothes stood there with gun in hand. "Why, isn't this the family reunion? The dead do rise back to life. I was utterly astounded to hear your voice. If you, my dear, are the phantom that my colleagues in law enforcement have been trying to find all these years, then I'm afraid you have missed a step tonight. You may have done in the cameras and recording of it all, but these old twentieth century bugs do still work wonders for my hearing in this place." He found it in the lamp and showed them it and the earpiece. "I monitor this room whenever I'm here . . . in case unexpected visitors drop in. And you did."

Mark and Dianne said nothing, but she tried to lower her hands to one of her pockets and the concealed gun. "Huh, no dear, keep them raised. Please, give me the gun. And since our family is having a reunion of sorts tonight perhaps I can make it more complete. Let's go to the lab together. Uh, you first," he said, as he put her gun in his lab coat pocket.

They were led down several long halls to a large laboratory where a number of experiments were being done. It looked and smelled like a biology lab, but it also looked like a technology lab with many machines and computers. Three robots were standing around the lab, each three and a half feet tall. Dianne recognized them all by the letters and numbers on the sides of their robotic heads.

Uncle said, "Now I did not catch much of your conversation except a part of it; your lecture to Mark was remarkably accurate, but of course not complete. We are tapping into the brain to find the hidden strength and smarts there that have eluded us so far. And we can control these brains remarkably well, even those who resist. But we are not cutting up the brain, but leaving it whole and intact. Do you remember Vicki, Mark? These robots are not to torture people as your sister told you. Aliadin may have his idiosyncrasies and he may not be a real scientist, but he has allowed us to continue our work under his protection. We have had to add his agenda to ours, but it is only a minor inconvenience. Religion is ultimately a bunch of balderdash anyway, but our people can live with it. We believe that the brain and a heart of a real human protected in a suit of armor and with the efficiency of a computer can do almost anything, including go into outer space. Ultimately we will make the perfect man, and . . . woman. When they needed to they could think for themselves and yet be controlled too."

There was a knock on the door. A purple police inspector appeared. "Good evening inspector," Uncle said. As soon as Uncle turned his head and went to the door Dianne gave a wad of white stuff to one of the robots, whose robotic arm and hand extended and took it and it disappeared into the arm casing as it retracted.

Uncle returned accompanied by the inspector. They were introduced, "This is Inspector Holden and this is Mark, whom you've seen, and the young lady is Joanne whom you may have some interest in after we're done." Mark and Dianne both knew that he really had not heard much of their conversation, to Dianne's relief. The inspector went back and stood by the door.

"Now where was I? Oh yes, I was going to introduce you to these lovely ladies and one gentleman. This is Bob, but Bob's not feeling well today so I have him sedated so he can be fixed. This one is Susan." This computer spoke like Vicki and introduced herself via the same computerized voice and gave them more information about herself on her screen. "And this one is . . . Dianne."

Mark couldn't believe it and Uncle enjoyed his reaction and comments of disbelief. "She's been altered some since you last saw her and she cannot, I'm afraid, remember you two at all, nor can she do any violence."

The real Dianne stood amazed that Uncle really did not understand his own robots and what went on inside them. Nor had he comprehended the conversation she had just had with Mark. She was even more amazed by the act that these robots performed for their unsuspecting masters when they thought and communicated to her.

Uncle continued, "Introduce yourself Dianne, and show them what you're working on now." The robot did as the other one had and then on the screen showed a complicated physics problem that it was working on. The real Dianne nodded approvingly as one of the many special cameras that were the robot's eyes now looked past Uncle at her sister.

From the first minute they were caught the real Dianne had been forming a plan for them all to escape. She hoped that Joanne would feign a malfunctioning and would trigger a blackout and they could leave. The white stuff—the C-10 high explosive she gave her—was for a later mission.

But then the unexpected happened. Mark had been horrified from the minute Joanne introduced herself and Uncle enjoying that reaction decided to play with him. He put down the gun and removed the hood and front of the headpiece and asked her to open up another set of protective doors to reveal her brain and heart in a see-through container. They were bathed in her own blood, with all sorts of wires and tubes attached to the containers. The heart pulsated, and the brain moved with the surge.

Even to the hardened Dianne this was still shocking. But Mark fell to his knees and cried out in horror and put his hands over his face. The next moment he rose up in such anger not hesitating for a moment and with complete surprise to everyone and using every ounce of power he punched Uncle square in the face. He went reeling and crashing into a number of machines, falling to the floor, blinded momentarily. Mark went after Uncle for some more. The inspector at the door pressed his wrist computer for his guards and made for Mark but Dianne had him down and out in seconds. She turned to Joanne whose screen read, "Self destruct sequence set. Goodbye Mark and Dianne." A timer next to it read five minutes and it was counting down. Then Dianne noticed all the C-10 that she had given Joanne over time wound around her central power source, enough to take out a city block. Susan's computer board told her she and Bob had some too. "Please, Joanne I did not mean for this," she said, as she got Mark off of Uncle and somehow got him to understand what was happening. Joanne said in her computer voice and on the screen, "Go. Run. I will not let them catch you. I will not let you two become as I am. I serve Christ and you." They ran out the door and ran down the corridor, went through an emergency door that turned on every alarm and out onto the half mile of lawn and trees pursued, by a large force of police. Mark could not run long and tripped and fell down. Dianne ran like a shot and was not even aware that he was not with her until she turned at a distance and saw the guards intercepting him. He yelled, "Go, and don't forget Laura." When the guards turned to pursue her again she had disappeared.

Meanwhile, the guards picked Uncle up off the floor and he only opened his eyes to see, Joanne's screen read. "Christ Himself is in me," and to see the counter read 4, 3, 2, 1.

Outside they had just got Mark standing up and hand-cuffed when the explosion ripped through one end of the huge complex, throwing them all down.

Chapter 21

DARKNESS AND LIGHT

Meanwhile, Laura and her nineteen cellmates lived nearer to hell. One after another were separated out, led to another open cell for all to see across the way and then were interrogated, beaten, and raped and then shot through the head, and dragged out to a crematorium nearby. There was no hesitation on the part of the soldiers and they went through this procedure slowly and methodically. The on looking women screamed, cried, and prayed in the terror. With long intervals of inactivity, this went on for several days.

At one point, Laura watched another pregnant woman being beaten savagely in the stomach, destroying the child within. During this session Laura began to pray as loud as she could for the soldiers as well as the woman and her dying child. This rankled the participants so much that they had her removed to a distant isolation cell. As they led her through the dank, dimly lit halls they verbally threatened her and made her feel as though this was her turn. She trembled in their grip and in her mind pleaded to the Lord for help. They put her in a cell and then left her. It was totally barren of any furniture; all she could do was sit against a wall or lay on the concrete floor. She could still hear the occasional gunshot that ended another life.

She cried in despair as she anticipated being the next victim. "When will this end, Lord? When will I be able to rest," she moaned. She prayed for her baby for some time and then thought about Mark. Weariness so overcame her that she fell asleep.

She awoke with a start in what was now a totally dark cell. She felt like there was someone hovering over her and then felt hands grip her arms and lift her to her feet. A woman's voice whispered in her ear, "We're here to help you. Be quiet." She was led out between two completely invisible beings because of the total darkness. In a few momentary glimmerings of light created by things on their wrists, she could see they wore helmets, but she could not see their faces. A few more glimmerings of light and she was led around a number of dark human shapes on the floor she thought were the guards and some of the soldiers. She was led to a place where she had to climb down into what seemed to be a hole; other hands received her at the bottom. Then she heard a grating noise as a cover was moved over the hole above them. They made a lengthy walk in which they had to protect her head and lower her to a bending position in one place and then for awhile they told her to crawl through a confined space. At the other end, in the lesser darkness of night, she could see six figures leading a number of other women prisoners away in different directions. The two figures who led her had those black helmets and now she saw the black uniforms and gloves. Their eyes and faces were hidden behind night vision goggles. They led her around a number of obstacles and more bodies of dead soldiers and more black figures waiting and covering for them. They went around a small pond and through a densely wooded area to a waiting car on a dirt road. Once inside the two dark figures took their helmets off.

One was a man. It was Immanuel Rodriguez again. Before Laura could say anything, he said, "I know. I did run away from the camp in Idaho, not to join the antichrist but to come back to my home in Chicago. I rejoined the underground here. I still love Jesus Christ."

The other was a young woman who had her long hair tied back tightly behind her head. She wore a small round silver stud in her right ear lobe. She looked at her wrist computer and said, "Computer off" and then she introduced herself, "I'm Dianne . . . Dianne Brogen, one of Mark's sisters."

Laura shook her head and laughed through tears. "Aren't you . . . I mean weren't you . . ."

"Dead? No, only the world of the antichrist thinks so. I've seen Mark and explained everything. I'd do it for you too, but you've been through a lot."

"Thank you so much for getting me out of there. What about the others? Did you get them all out?" she said, still shaking and crying from the trauma and cold. Dianne put a blanket around her and then held her with one arm around her neck, one hand on one shoulder and the other hand holding Laura's other shoulder.

Dianne said, "We'll talk about all that later. We're trying our best. Let's get you safe and cleaned up. I bet you and that little babe inside that tummy are starving. Then we'll talk."

Immanuel headed into the city and downtown and into a parking garage between skyscrapers. Immanuel said good night, went into a washroom to change and disappeared into the night.

Dianne led Laura to an elevator that took them to the forty-third floor and to a studio apartment. The kitchen amenities included a small washer and drier. It was barren of any furniture except a kitchen table, two chairs, a bed and an old couch. Two small stuffed bears lay near a pillow. Dianne threw her helmet with the goggles and gloves onto the couch. "I'm afraid, I don't have much to offer," she said as she showed Laura the bathroom and gave her the one bath towel and washcloth and some pajamas. When she was done she was invited to sit at the kitchen table while Dianne found her one box of cereal, one bowl, and one spoon. She opened the refrigerator. It was empty except for a small container of milk and several apples. She placed these before Laura and told her to eat it all. Laura didn't disobey. Dianne found her backpack in the corner and took out several meal bars and lay them on the table. Laura ravaged them also. Both of them were so wired by the events of the last few days that they then sat and shared it all and to each other until they were exhausted.

As Dianne changed the bed and washed and dried her only sheets, Laura asked about the two little bears.

"Mr. Darringen brought these to me from Mom and Dad's funeral. He made sure I remained dead to everyone I ever knew to keep me safe. I couldn't even see Mark, until now. They are the only keepsakes I have from that time. When I look at them I see our house and family the way it all was. I see Joanne and I sitting on the step to the sidewalk that led to our front porch under that large old elm tree."

Laura enjoyed this and they were silent for awhile. Then she asked, "What about Mark? Can you still rescue him?"

"It's complicated. He is so important to the antichrist and such a symbol that he could not be rescued and hidden again without a sacrifice that is bigger than we can afford now. They are about to use him in a show-trial. More importantly, Jesus has told him that he must remain where he is. Besides, they have him so monitored now that my computer work won't neutralize it all. We would all be found out. I'm sorry Laura." Here she sat on the bed and held her hand and they prayed until the Lord gave them peace. Then she said softly, "I'm glad you're part of my family now."

"What about all those women in the prison, can you do something for them?"

Here Dianne lowered her head and then raised it and said, "Dina, Megan, Cheryl, Rhonda, Todd and Rose got the remainder of your compatriots tonight, but it's getting beyond us now. And you forgot about the men. They get tortured, raped, and shot too." Then Dianne's voice lowered and mumbled just audibly. "And you forgot about the children and the elderly. Besides regular prisons and these prison camps, there are slave camps and the experimental asylums. We try to make as many rescues as we can. The security force was successful as long as the prisoners were only a trickle. Our people have saved several hundred each month. We have been successful in hiding them in places such as this and even in giving them a life again. Some have even become performers in the theatres and clubs entertaining the very people who would have tortured them to death. It's getting harder to get our escapees to where historic Christians still are protected by our army in the south or in the northwest."

"However, in the last few years, our network has been depleted by injuries, defections and arrests; there are hundreds of prisoners almost every day who come through that one train yard alone. That prison camp serves as a vent for Aliadin's soldiers to blow off steam and keep them happy. There's one of these near every city in every part of the world now. Our only consolation is that the prisoner's time there is usually short and they get to go to our Savior sooner."

They slept that night and most of the next day. When Laura did wake up she found that Dianne had already been out and back again with clothes for Laura and food. Dianne was glad that Laura was still not visibly pregnant since it was summer; as those clothes were harder to come by, so she gave her the college girl look once again. Laura devoured her hamburger and salad and juice and most of Dianne's when she offered it to her. Dianne offered her a vitamin from a plastic bottle that looked familiar.

"Mark, took vitamins like this. Naomi gave them to him, but he said they were the same kind his mother gave him."

Dianne smiled, "Mom. I don't know how I get along without her."

Meanwhile, as Laura ate and talked, Dianne constantly worked at her computer.

"That babe of yours is hungry," said Dianne.

"Its mom is more hungry. How did you get this?" Laura asked.

"The network has army rations and clothes and furniture but sometimes fresh food like this is a trick. I use computer magic, Mr. Darringen's secret accounts and dead people's accounts. I only buy a few dollars of things at a time and since fast food and supermarkets are all self-serve and self-pay now, you just walk in and walk out. Everyone was supposed to have their own seal and it worked well, but the system is easily manipulated. That's why it got harder. Retinal scans and fingerprints came in for the most elementary needs over the last few years, but it isn't across the board. There is also a kind of invisible seal that can be placed permanently on one's forehead that contains all of one's vital information and accounts. For these places I make the computer eye malfunction for a brief moment as I pass using this ear computer or this hair clip computer or the wrist computer. I can also give the seal of someone else. And there are still some open doors."

"What about the underground? Who is it? Where is it? Aren't you supposed to have a central building or basement or something? I could never understand it when I used it to travel and when I met Mark. All I did was tell my pastor."

Dianne laughed. "You're looking at the Chicago underground. You are in the central command post. Most of it's up here." Dianne pointed to her head. "This lap top, a knapsack with some other tricks and these computers are it."

"But where's all the people, the resources. And Immanuel, what about him?"

"There never was a James Bond-like center with zillions of people working at computers in a huge underground facility. If there were we would have been found out long ago and destroyed. No, the famous Chicago underground is a lot of people spread out over the city living in their own homes or wherever they can. Word of mouth and the computer are our only common links. This is not the only place I can stay. There are a large number of other apartments and homes we could go to and stay. Mr. Darringen and his accountant Mr. Steinmetz owned quite a number of buildings, including this one that we fixed up with security and tricks of various kinds, but we've never had more than seven of our own people here at one time and usually never together in large numbers. There are stores and businesses that are secretly still run by Christians and Jews. The people and resources are so diffused that we cannot be destroyed easily. Only individuals are caught. All the members of the underground regularly meet in small groups in irregular ways and many places for fellowship, worship, and prayer."

"Also, in the tradition of local politics, the local police and aldermen who are still Roman Catholic have been a great help. They were made special beneficiaries to a number of Mr. Darringen's investment accounts, thanks to Mr.

Steinmetz. This means they serve as a buffer between our rescued and resettled refugees and the purple police, Aliadin's S.S. men. However, life is not perfect."

"Mr. Darringen was caught and killed four years ago and, Dr. Crawford whom you might remember also is dead. I really miss them. I miss so many people these days."

"How do you operate and how do you exist? Who makes decisions?" asked Laura.

"I do. Our weapon is what God has given us in here and up here." Here she pointed to her heart and head. "We were real good at being an underground railroad getting people out of the city. We were also great at helping the Christian armies to form and getting them classified information and tapping into and controlling military and secret satellites. Some of our programs are used to keep bombers and missiles from taking off or dropping off target and many other things. We did conventional spying with all those cameras I told you about last night. We can use our own or the enemy cameras for our own advantage or neutralize them. Unfortunately, Aliadin's hackers are mobile and can do the same to us. It keeps us on our toes."

"You say *we*. Are there others?"

"By we, I mean Jesus, Joanne when she was alive, me, and this computer. There are other hackers in our system and there are even more in those armies out there and many very resourceful people, but the ones around here all look to me or one of our gals or guys for training. When I joined Mr. Darringen I learned so quickly and began to make so many improvements that even before he was caught I was the brain behind the outfit. As I told you last night, I'm the one who got Mark to leave Uncle. God does keep me honest, however, as help comes from the most unexpected places. You were that help for Mark. I'm grateful."

Dianne got up from the table and the computer and began to freshen up, but continued to talk as she changed clothes to look like a very normal senior in college. However, Laura noticed her developed and hardened muscular arms, stomach, back, and legs now for the first time and also a number of healing bruises and two scars on the front and back of one thigh.

"Let's go out," said Dianne. Laura freshened up while Dianne got out a tiny jar of black make-up paint and a brush. "We might as well enjoy ourselves a little and go out in fashion. Dianne then painted on the left side of Laura's face, "Do Not Harm" and then on her right side, "My Anointed One," in Hebrew. She did the same in the mirror for herself.

Then Dianne and Laura did what young women of their age had done for over two hundred years to get over a difficult week. They went to the mall.

As they walked down the magnificent mile, toward the Grand Mall, Dianne explained that it was safe because merchants persuaded Aliadin's police that business would be hurt if they were prowling about and even got them to keep the security apparatus out. Only the economic kinds of cameras, sensors, and police operate here. However, just to be safe she activated her ear and hair clip computer that would detect and thwart any enemy intent in the computers, cameras, or hearing devices they may encounter.

Thus they shopped and shopped, but bought little and then sat and ate in the food court. As they sat there Laura became aware of how much they blended in. Almost every young person had letters painted on their cheeks. Most had at least the Arabic letters for Lord Aliadin. Others, however, sported obscure languages and with them the meanings. She looked at Dianne who sat eating her burritos and tapping on her computer in her university T-shirt and shorts.

"You've been here often, haven't you?" she said, sipping on her malt.

"I've had to in order to stay sane. If I stayed cooped up all the time, I'd go nuts. I also work out in one of our designated facilities or at one of the colleges.

"I've hung around the universities and studied and researched in the libraries. I still witness to students without telling much about myself. If I succeed I send them onto our operatives to disciple and train." She showed her a physics problem she was doing. "It's only a hobby now. There was a time that I fed problems and answers to Joanne here so she could impress those who inquired into her knowledge. With her we even solved some important problems dealing with satellites and then made it so they helped our forces."

Laura made the mistake of inquiring into Dianne's ideas about physics and science and then had to hang on in order to follow her. She did catch this much. ". . . The invisible really does affect the universe. Physics scientists over the centuries have discovered more and more particles and forces in the atom. The scientists before didn't believe they existed. The unbelieving scientist has been as much a part of this as the believers; together they have understood that the impossible can become possible and so atomic energy was discovered and put to work. The Uncertainty Principle back in the 1900's was simply an unbeliever's way of stating this. I, with some others, found that the atomic process could be halted and that was the paper that Aliadin's people stole and put to use. We know that with God all things are possible. And so many dimensions exist that God placed in the physical universe for us to find. This is all to say that science and Christianity really do fit together and indeed are necessary together to get the most complete understanding of the universe. Just the physics of Christ's Second Coming would lay this misunderstanding to rest. And I still communicate with other believing scientists in other countries."

"What about other underground groups in other countries. Are you ever in contact with them?" Laura asked, happy to find a way to get her on another subject.

"There is Simone in Paris and Erica in Frankfort who are still whole women like me. Then I have Elle, a Jewish Christian, who is now a robot who serves Aliadin and his administration and many other contacts. It's a sad fact that most of the leaders of these undergrounds are women. Women have more to lose in Aliadin's new world order. Because he treats us like dirt. All his minions treat us like dirt. All the men leaders, even his enemies like Mark get the publicity and at the least a show trial. Female leaders like me die our Savior's death. We've been crucified in obscurity at worst or become an experiment at best. The few good men are in our ranks and they are very dependable and effective in the rescue missions. But most Christian men these days are caught because they are lukewarm spiritually, or just are not good decision makers. Many are in sinful compromise with the world and thus are more vulnerable, more easily caught and killed. There are simply not enough real men and because of this we have failed many times. The whole underground operation has many days depended on me staying one step ahead of Aliadin's computer geeks and purple police and they do have some smart ones."

She shared for some time about Joanne. "Much of the information that I have about what goes on came from Joanne. If God has a prize for the most valiant performance during this time, she deserves it. She saved my bacon more than once. I did not mean for her to die like she did. She was supposed to plant the C-10 around that building when she was there, but apparently they did not keep her there. She used her computer arms that can go inside to fix their own insides behind the casing. In this case she kept the explosive inside, winding it around her middle. And I had given her a lot over time and apparently she gave it to others like Susan and Bob. They cannot, as Uncle said, go on the offensive and so apparently Joanne could only become aggressive in one way . . . activating her self—destruct mechanism. When she saw Mark and I were threatened she acted. I'm sorry she did it but I'm not sorry. I'm glad she finally escaped that tin can existence."

"Until you came, she was the only friend I could talk to at any time. The other gals and guys and I in our outfit do not get together often so we're not caught together. There was nobody that I could really talk to or unload on regularly for the last four years. Can you believe that—sisters getting along? I used to be so hardened and nasty to her in our old life. I guess even I can be nice to my sister after seeing her gutted and crammed into a space the size of a mayonnaise jar at the pleasure of perverted scientists. Left with only her mind, she became as intelligent and perceptive as I was. She did become me in that respect. We talked about everything. I love her so much."

"She even made up games with me to pass the time. In one of them we pretended we were both older and married and each had five kids. The only things we had to worry about were losing weight and getting the kids to their activities. When we stopped playing we realized we were still locked into this hellish comic book story. Satan and his clowns stole our lives and they will be made to pay."

"Well, it's time to move on."

At a musical instrument store Dianne sat at a piano, put her hands together, stretched them and cracked her knuckles and smiled at Laura. Before long she was drawing a crowd; the store manager was pleased and invited her back. Laura saw some cute things in one store and Dianne smiled at her choice. They looked at clothes for several hours. Dianne suggested getting some lightweight winter windbreakers since it would get cold soon. Laura asked where all her seasonal clothes were. Dianne related that she had very few personal clothes and that these things and the winter and rain uniforms were in various locations around the city where all those in the secret force came and went.

When the storeowner came out and saw Dianne, they embraced. She introduced Laura to Helga. "Helga is another mom in my life," she said.

"Are you Ok? Are you eating? Do you need anything?" Helga inquired. Dianne answered all these questions and told her what they needed. "No problem, take anything you need. Take her to Stan's for dinner. You need to eat better," she said, as she gave her a reservation card. "Don't make it so long next time," she said.

They had a long and big dinner at Stan's in one of his private dining rooms. Stan was another resource of the underground and Laura was impressed. Along the way home, Dianne saw an old fashioned cooking timer that she just had to have. It reminded her of Mom.

As Dianne and Laura lived together over the course of several months, they became the closest of friends. They followed Mark's trial news with interest. Aliadin had abandoned his plans to come to Chicago because of the terrorist bombing of his number one lab and the murder of his top scientist. Instead the trial that would include Mark would be in Jerusalem on a date yet to be determined.

Meanwhile, each night Dianne went off on rescue missions while Laura sat in the apartment and watched television on the laptop computer. She hoped to catch glimpses of Mark on any news program. During the day she accompanied Dianne on all her rounds and to the sector of the city for which she was responsible. They visited and prayed with many rescued and resettled families and groups in various houses and apartments. Then they went to a large facility that had at one time been a retirement home which now was an orphanage, a school and a social relief facility for the neighborhood. They joined a number of the activities and Dianne noticed how much Laura enjoyed being around the children. She seemed a natural at relating to them and in organizing and motivating them. Dianne learned that she had done this kind of volunteer work prior to meeting Mark. Dianne drew another crowd as she played the piano for everyone and Laura led the children in singing.

Laura noticed how a number of teenage and older boys had a healthy respect for Dianne. From several teachers she discovered that Dianne had won these gang leaders and members over to Christ and they now acted as allies in the war against the purple police and the antichrist. Instead of smuggling drugs and guns they now smuggled food and essential items in for the needy.

One day Dianne led Laura to the very same college that Laura had attended years earlier. They appeared to be about to attend a class as they approached a lecture room. Several male students with their backpacks sat on the floor outside the door and they did not seem to notice them but Dianne gave both playful kicks before entering. Laura soon discovered that she was in a large group meeting for the secret force and she had just seen the guards. However, it looked like any other college class with a great mix of races and nationalities and where the women decidedly outnumbered the men. They were all dressed so differently and with many expressions from rapt attention to others not seeming to pay attention. But she noted that all utilized small black laptop computers. They were of various ages but most were in their late teens or early twenties. Some were much older. Once she had Laura seated, Dianne went to talk to others. Laura recognized one older female professor as Dr. Evelyn Smith. She had been her favorite teacher when Laura was a student. When she saw Laura she came to sit by her. They hugged and were surprised by each other's presence. As they talked briefly, Evelyn realized that Laura was there as Dianne's guest and said, "You are the first outsider to witness one of these meetings. You should feel especially honored."

Dianne arose and methodically and succinctly went through procedures, methods, and plans for defense and rescue missions; the habits, strengths, weaknesses, and the psychological proclivities and policies of the purple police and all of Aliadin's armed forces. She presented Aliadin's local officials, officers, and spies and any and all information about them including their habits, hobbies, and personal lives. She reviewed new plans for team deployment in penetrating the enemy facilities, the use and procurement of various new weapons and explosives, sector assignments and national and world wide movements of Aliadin's forces. The overheads presented from her laptop computer presented everything from outlines to detailed, multi-dimensional maps, photos, drawings, and blueprints. She left time for discussion after each major section.

At one point she stopped the whole proceeding with a hand gesture as she heard her guards speak to her in her ear computer; the computerized voice gave detailed descriptions and identifications of the intruders. The overhead changed to an outline and photos on ancient Chinese bronze inscriptions and a well-dressed Chinese woman was up and in mid stride in her lecture. The intruders, a professor and several students entered briefly, realized their mistake, and left quickly. Dianne went back to where she left off.

As the meeting proceeded Evelyn whispered to Laura, "It's just like God to make an under-aged girl who technically never finished any part of her schooling the leader of a whole underground movement against the worst enemy of history. She started at the age of fifteen and here she is six years later, still a wonder. She has more brains, wisdom and courage than all the faculty combined. She has convinced everyone in this room and anybody she cares to meet that with Jesus Christ anything is possible."

Dianne finished with a short message without notes, a Bible, or a computer. She spoke on the war between the children of the light and the sons of darkness. She encouraged them though they must work in the dark now. The day was coming when there would be no more night. From Revelation 22:5 and going backward, she reviewed the Scriptures that concerned this theme. She dwelt on 1 John 1:1–5–7 and Philippians 2:14–16 for some time and then moved to Ephesians 4:17–24 and 1 Thessalonians 5:5, "You are all sons of the light and sons of the day. We do not belong to the night or the darkness, even though Aliadin twisted this and made us evil villains in his world." Then she utilized John 1:1–14 and Matthew 5: 13, "You are the light of the earth." She followed this with Prov-

erbs 4:18–19, Psalms 82:5, Psalms 46, and Psalms 27:1—
"The Lord is my light and my salvation. Whom shall I
fear?" She finished with Judges 5:31—"So may your enemies perish, O Lord! But may they who love you be like
the sun when it rises in its strength."

She prayed quoting and utilizing Ephesians 6:10–18
and encouraged them not to neglect their private and
small group times of prayer and Bible study. Then she
prayed Daniel's prayer for Jerusalem in Daniel 9:4–19
with such passion that all were in tears and in worship
as she finished with Revelation 22: 20–21, "Amen. Come
Lord Jesus. The grace of the Lord Jesus be with God's
people. Amen."

By design, the class dispersed quickly without much
lingering and talking. Evelyn took Dianne and Laura to
dinner to another of the underground's designated restaurants and they used a private room. Dianne introduced
Dr. Evelyn Jacobson to Laura by saying, "This is another
mom in my life whom I or this movement cannot do
without. She is grandmother to our underground."

Laura's mouth dropped open and then she said, "Back
when I went to college she, I mean you were my . . . and
I knew you were a Christian but . . . your name . . . I
thought it was Smith."

Evelyn smiled and said, "Yes, dear in those years I
looked to you like an ordinary economics professor. And
Smith was only my alias. But in addition, I worked for
Ronald Darringen and Jacob Steinmetz as I was the latter's
secretary for this underground movement. When Ronald
was killed I became the financial steward and planner
along with Jacob who no longer goes out in public. Only

I can see him. We hold the purse strings and procure the resources for running the secret force, and the entire underground movement's homes and hideouts. Jacob and I manage the funds and investments and have financial and military ties to the Jewish underground in New York and in Israel. I must say that without fluid capital—hard money floating around—it is easier to make everything work by computer. Aliadin actually made it easier for us. All our accounts can be hidden and used easily without anyone going to a bank or a store. The underground forces only have to pick up what they need when they need it."

Laura marveled at all this. Then she in return amazed Evelyn by recounting all her adventures with Mark until now. Evelyn shook her head and said, "Isn't it a wonder how God has used all of this to bring us together and in ways we would never have dreamed of only a few years ago. God has done miracles with all of us." Here she and Laura then looked at Dianne. Evelyn then asked Dianne, "Did everyone attend the meeting today?"

"Only one absent, and I will take care of him," she said as she gazed in thought beyond them at the far wall.

Evelyn said, "Dianne doesn't need to take attendance but can simply look over a familiar crowd and know who's not there. She would have made a great teacher. And further, I can tell you every young man in that room has had his heart broken as they know she has reserved herself for someone else."

Dianne blushed and continued to look down and then played with her food as she knew Evelyn was studying her. Evelyn said, "The real wonder in this room is this girl." Dianne became serious. Laura then shared with her what Evelyn had said about her at the meeting. Dianne smiled and said, "That's right, and I don't even have a driver's license." And they all laughed.

Then tears formed in Evelyn's eyes as she looked at them and she covered their hands with hers on the table. She waxed poetic and said, "The Lord has saved His best and most beautiful flowers, tender and delicate, to be last and sent them to confound hell's worst monsters. May the Lord bless you both and Mark even more."

Chapter 22

* *

ONE DAY WITH THE SECRET FORCE

Mark had been sequestered in his isolation cell for a month now. His inquisitors did not want to torture him because they knew Aliadin would want to do that himself before or after the trial so they deprived him of food and sleep to see if they could convert him to Lord Aliadin's gospel. But this simply served to bring Mark into the closest spiritual time with Jesus Christ in his life. He meditated on how Jesus must have felt during the forty days in the wilderness and how He overcame His temptations. He thought about Paul glorying in persecutions and difficulties. Before he had never understood or cared to understand about fasting in the Bible, but now he did. Isolation, hunger, and weakness made him depend so much on Christ that his worship of the Savior became continuous and ever deeper. He would sacrifice his life for Christ without any hesitation. Christ became so much more real and near him and in him. He found himself praying like he never had before. He prayed long and meditatively for Dianne, Laura, the baby, and that they were together.

Meanwhile, Dianne and Laura were at the neighborhood center playing with the orphans when an aide came and whispered in Dianne's ear for some time. She and Laura went toward the front entrance and reception desk where a small crowd had formed. Mrs. Dexter the receptionist was explaining to a distraught middle-aged Egyptian man that none of their volunteers was available to help him. This secretary was the center's first line of defense should Aliadin's forces come snooping around looking for Christians and Jews to arrest. She had perceived a threat in this man and alerted Dianne.

Dianne interrupted her, "Excuse me, but I'm a volunteer and free for the moment. How can we help you?"

The man blurted out, "My son is dying I have no where else to turn. I know that some of you here are Christians and I need one of them to come with me and pray that God would heal him. Please, know that this is not a trick, I swear."

Dianne calmed him by saying, "I'll find someone, can you give me a minute?"

She took Laura into a private room and said, "He's a purple police captain. I recognize him from our file catalog. Sometimes this is how they have gotten to our people. But he may be in earnest and if he is, God can and has used these opportunities. Would you be willing to come with me? It means we will probably be surrounded by the enemy and this could be the end of us or . . ."

Laura said, "Let's go. If you go, I go."

They prayed together and asked the Lord what to do. When they opened their eyes and looked at each other they smiled. "Let's go," they said in unison.

For awhile it did not seem like the right decision. The Egyptian man never changed his expression of distress and thanked them profusely for coming with him, but they were surrounded by purple police and made to sit separately between purple police officers in a van while the Egyptian man sat with the driver in the front. The danger was real, but Dianne had also activated her wrist and ear computers and alerted her peers to track and monitor their whereabouts as she went to the bathroom before they left. So there would be backup and a possible rescue if Dianne was alive to give the signal. She was glad that through the entire operation she was totally anonymous to them. The purple police, being the curious sorts they were, conversed with them. Dianne had told Laura that she would do all the talking if there was any to do and she actually answered some of their questions, but denied knowing anything about an underground movement as she was just a college student who volunteered her time at the center. From them she obtained some interesting information. They told her that they were stepping up their efforts to find the unidentified phantom leader of that insidious infidel underground movement, and that if she knew anything to tell them. As they talked among themselves they guessed that this leader must be a very shrewd and experienced man who was very strong. They warned the two girls to stay away from certain neighborhoods in the city for the next few days as they were setting up raids in order to capture this leader.

The van pulled up to one of the biggest hospitals in the city. Dianne and Laura were led into a beehive of purple police activity, as it seemed very important things were happening. At one point the Egyptian man was stopped by a fellow purple police captain who warned him about using witches to help his son; he leered menacingly at Dianne and Laura. The Egyptian man, in no mood to argue, led them on with many purple policemen accompanying or following. However, their group got smaller and smaller until they reached a remote corridor and suite where the Egyptian man's family met them and ushered them toward a room where the doctor was already shaking his head. The doctor took the family aside, but was still within the girls' hearing and reluctantly said that it was too late, the boy had died. But something inside Laura made her come over to the family and beg them to let them pray for the boy anyway. Dianne and Laura were led into the room and found more family about the bed wailing. They convinced them all to let them be alone in the room with the dead son.

Dianne asked Laura, "Have you done this before?"

"No, never. Have you?" she said.

Dianne said, "Sometimes one or more of us have prayed for the sick or hurt and they've been healed but never this."

They knelt down one on each side of the bed and held the boy's now-cold hands and began to pray the only way they knew.

Laura prayed, "Lord, please bring him back. Love him as you have loved us. Please. We know you brought us here for a reason. We know somehow you have come to the attention of this family and you need to deliver them. We are at your mercy. We only have words, but You have the power."

Dianne prayed, "Lord, we are in a tight spot. If You don't help this boy and us now, we're going to be cooked by our enemies. And even if we have to die, we ask You to let this boy live and be saved. Please, Lord we don't deserve life or anything from You, but now as Your children we beg for the crumbs from Your table. We beg for this boy's life and healing."

They both prayed silently and as they did they felt the warmth return and they took turns feeling his head and chest. The monitors now indicated normal activity returning. Suddenly, he opened his eyes and sat up and rubbed them. Dianne and Laura praised God excitedly through tears and laughter. He looked at them and said, "My name is Abdul, what are your names?" They introduced themselves and Laura explained to him that they were Christians asked by his father to come pray for him.

He looked at Laura and said, "A friendly man full of light touched me and said to go back and be His friend forever. Who was that man?"

Laura, through tearful eyes, said, "His name is Jesus Christ and He is Lord of the universe and all things and all people. A long time ago He died for all people and had the power to forgive us for not believing and loving Him and God His Father. He arose from the dead and now lives in heaven. When we really love Him and are sorry for all the bad things we have done, He becomes our friend forever and always stays with us. He is invisible to us now, but when He returns one day soon, we will all see Him and live with Him forever and we will never die."

The boy asked Laura, "Please, make me His friend." Laura told him, "Pray to Him. Talk to Him and ask Him to be your friend." Then Abdul prayed, "Jesus, forgive me of all the bad things I have done or thought and please come into my life and save me. I love You." Immediately, the boy laughed and said, "I feel Him right here," and he rubbed his chest with his hand. He gave Laura and Dianne hugs and both kissed him on the cheeks. As he got out of bed, the door to the room opened and the parents could not believe it and began to celebrate and rejoice. Then a number of purple police friends of the family came in and asked what happened as the boy and family all talked at once. Laura and Dianne felt the urge to leave, especially when the Egyptian father offered what he thought was the highest reward—dinners with the most eligible men in the purple police force. They both gracefully declined and communicated that no reward was necessary. He would have insisted on rewarding them had not more crowds of people arrived and diverted his attention. They slipped away.

As they walked Dianne said, "I don't think we want to be around when Abdul tells them how he was healed. If they hated our Lord when He was on earth for the miracles He did, some of those people in that room will go crazy with anger when they hear of Jesus."

"But I think the dad and the mom and sisters will come to the Lord, especially if they had enough faith in coming to get us and letting us pray for him," said Laura.

They walked the endless corridors back toward the front and found themselves in a lounge area that overlooked the main driveway and entrance. Here they saw Mark amongst a number of the political prisoners being escorted into the hospital.

"Why are they here?" asked Laura.

"It may be in preparation to send them to Jerusalem for the trials," said Dianne.

"Do you think there is any way I could see him?" Laura asked.

"Raising a boy from the dead may be the easiest miracle compared to doing that," said Dianne.

"Please, if there is any way. If God arranged for our coming here, might He not have also arranged for us to be together one last time?"

Dianne saw the pleading in Laura's eyes. She sighed, "Ok," and went to work on her wrist computer for some time and found a corner to talk to her computer network and the secret force members in the area. Finally, she put an arm around Laura's neck and brought her close and she prayed, "Lord, we have one more for You today. None of this will work without You. Let Laura and Mark have their time, amen." Then she looked into Laura's eyes, "All set."

Soon they met Todd Jones, a twenty-five-year old prodigy and doctor at the hospital and one of the medical officers for the secret force. He transformed them into nurses. Laura now remembered that this was one of the guards at Dianne's meeting and to see him up close she noted how handsome he was. She immediately wondered if he and Dianne had a closer relationship. They seemed to work so comfortably and playfully together that she wondered at Dianne's rather negative attitude to all men in past conversations. Together they located Mark's whereabouts and the diversion that Dianne had planned went into effect. The phantom infidel leader of that insidious underground movement was thought to be in a university hospital down the street.

The diversion was complete as only two purple policemen remained, but they too vacated the area as they reacted in horror to something that was around them and in Mark's room. They also found an unusually great assortment of baked goods in the cafeteria brought in by one of the best bakeries in town. They quickly ordered them as medical personnel to remain and sedate the prisoner and then they would be back in an hour. "No problem," Dianne, Laura, and Todd all said at once. They realized that an angel must be present and that the Lord had arranged this time.

When they entered, Mark was on the bed but not in it and still clothed. He and Laura were instantly together, their arms wrapped around each other tightly, kissing and weeping passionately. They remained in this embrace until they were both very quiet. When they felt out of place, Todd and Dianne began to make for the door but Mark looked up at them and asked what happened and how did they all get in here and why were they here. When Mark could pry Laura away for a minute he hugged Dianne and she explained everything up to the moment including how close she and Laura had become. He praised God and thanked Dianne for finding and taking care of her. He told them how he had prayed for them. Dianne then introduced Mark to Todd and told him that he was a real doctor and the highest-ranking man in the secret security force.

They all wondered about Mark and asked if he had been interrogated or tortured and he said not really. He seemed to be fine and did not know why he was here. Dianne related to him that he was here to be checked out before being shipped out to Jerusalem for his trial with Aliadin. She told him that the purple police often kept important prisoners in large public facilities such as this because of fear of the underground. She said, "Because we've blown up their prison areas and killed so many guards over the years, they often use the common people's facilities as a human shield."

Mark returned to Laura and felt her stomach and saw how it was getting bigger. He bent down and said, "I love you in there. It's your dad. Be good to your mom and your aunt Dianne."

Todd checked both of them out as they all related their stories and he declared both of them fit except that he noticed Mark was a little anemic and dehydrated. Dianne then produced the little tiny bottle and gave him swig of it. "What's in that anyway, Di. It really works," he said as it burned down his throat and he coughed, just as on that night in Uncle's laboratory.

"Let's just say it kept those forefathers you were so fond of reading about alive and kicking," she said. Todd produced a meal bar that he gladly ate with some juice.

Next she produced that little bottle of vitamins and gave him one.

"To Mom," Dianne and Mark said in unison as he swallowed it; everyone laughed together.

Mark told them how he was deprived of food and sleep for a number of weeks, but in recent days they had fed him and let him sleep again. At this news Laura, who had been as close to him as she could be all this time, fixed herself in Mark's arms and Mark looked at Dianne and said, "I can't tell you how good God has been to bring Laura into my life." Then he looked at Todd and Dianne and said, "You're not . . . ?"

"No, definitely not," said Dianne as she and Todd looked at each other. "No, we only work together," she added. Todd noticed how irritated Dianne's eyes looked when she looked at him.

Laura then pleaded with Dianne for some time alone with Mark. Dianne bowed to them and said, "Take as much time as you want. God will tell us when."

Todd and Dianne closed the room door and sat down on each side of it rather than sit in the lounge chairs in the carpeted suite around them. They were glad it was empty of other patients and so they were alone. Todd sat with his arms crossed and his legs stretched out and his head against the wall. Dianne sat with her legs and knees up so that she rested her arms on them and then rested her head on her arms.

She checked her wrist computer momentarily and whispered some orders and then shut her vocal part down, but left her ear computer on to keep her alerted as to anybody approaching in nearby corridors and elevators. A check was made on all cameras and hearing devices in the area to make sure they were all neutralized. She put her head down once again and rested it on her arms and closed her eyes.

Todd broke the silence, "Di, could I say something . . . personal?"

"What," came her muffled response.

He turned his head to look at her and took a deep breath. "I love you."

"Please Todd, don't go there. I can't do that," she said, not raising her head.

"But if I can't tell you now. Then when?"

She raised her head, but only looked ahead of her and said, "We can't go there. You know that. Besides, Mark and Laura have been together for six years now. They went through a lot and now they are paying the price. They must bear a harder cross being married and having a baby. Their sacrifices in being separated from each other mean more nails in the crosses they must bear. You can see it's more painful for both of them."

"Why can't we go there. We met six years ago too. We have gone through hell every night together for all these years. We have worked, fought, and sat in how many sewers together; 75 of us have remained pure and clean and single servants of Christ. How many nails are there in our crosses? One of mine is that I'm still human and I need to say it. I love you." He could see that she was affected.

"Don't do that," as a tear formed in her eye that she wiped away. "Make that 74. One of us, I believe, is a traitor who I am working on. And we have a mission . . ."

"To give aid and comfort and rescue and receive as many refugees as we can. We are soldiers," he said, knowing what her next words would be.

She began again, and said, "We don't have time . . . we have only . . ."

He broke in and said, "We have only today to live. We live only for the moment to serve and love Christ with all our heart, soul, mind, and strength and to die for Him or wait on His imminent return."

She began again and said, "Men and women in the force must remain single and give up . . ."

"We must give up and sacrifice · what lives we might normally have had in normal times for an abnormal life in the face of an abnormal enemy in an abnormal time," he said. "Dianne, you can keep reciting the secret force manual but the fact is, I love you. I've loved you for years now."

"But you know that marriage is forbidden, and my life is now for Christ only and you know because of what goes on in those prisons every day that I hate all *man* kind."

"Dianne, I didn't say anything about marriage, you did. And my life is for Christ only too and it has been, like yours, every day for all these years. And I know your all-men-are-trash lecture by heart."

"How did you learn that?"

"Through Joanne. She had a full text and she amended it whenever you had a particularly hard or bad day. I especially liked the part where we have devolved into soulless beasts and apes who think about nothing but what's between our legs."

Dianne said nothing, but looked away down the hall.

Todd continued, "She told me everything about you over the years."

"Everything?" she exclaimed, looking at him briefly and then away again.

"Well computers are thorough and she was your sister. She did tell me more than I wanted to know. And since Wayne made me your doctor after Leah and Lauren had so much to do, I guess I know a lot."

Dianne knocked her head on the wall—closed her eyes and held her hands to her head and grunted. "When I get to heaven and she has her head again I'm going to knock it off again. Can any secret be kept in this world? And remember when it's physical exam time—that's all it is."

He could see that she was embarrassed by all of this.

"So, my point is that I know you don't believe that about all of us. There are twenty-two of us who would give our lives up for Christ and you if you commanded it. And you would do the same for us. And when we stand down or have meetings together you fool around with us without any problem."

She put her head against the wall and closed her eyes. "Twenty-one of you now," she said. "And please note who the defectors have been since we began the service. All men. Four so far, and probably one more. And they are the reasons why we have had women killed, wounded, and probably how Deidra was caught. You'll remember Wayne insisted that the defectors had to be killed or our whole organization would be compromised. I had to eliminate three of them myself, along with any enemy officers they had talked to. These were the hardest things I've ever had to do. When the other one ran away and we couldn't find him we had to change all our codes as we did for the others. Commitment, does that mean anything to men? I stand committed to God to saving and rescuing His people and to the destruction of their persecutors as a soldier as long as it takes—as long as there is an antichrist. That is until I die or until Christ returns however long that may be, even if it means twenty, thirty, forty, fifty more years. Even if I have to become another Evelyn and train more. And who am I fighting Todd? Who's the enemy—evil, destructive MEN who God has given up on and who are doomed to destruction. The people we help in our neighborhood centers don't just come from the persecuted, but from Aliadin's wonderful new society where men don't have to worry about a law and now can wantonly abuse their wives, daughters, and children. But to our older volunteers in our neighborhood centers that is nothing new. They did that in the old days. They say that actually things are better in their neighborhoods in one sense since Aliadin began eliminating abusive, negligent, deadbeat fathers and uncles and brothers who were supposedly CHRISTIANS."

He turned his body now toward her, crossed his legs, folded his arms and studied her. He said, "Dianne, it still remains that the remainder of our men are solid and you talk with them and communicate with them regularly just as you do with every woman we have. You and I both know that they all have integrity and fidelity to Christ, each other, and to you. They are committed just like Wayne and Mr. Steinmetz. It also remains that I love you," and there was silence for a minute.

Then he continued, "You are so good and great at so many things. I am almost, but not quite your equal intellectually. You can beat me in chess. You can beat me to a pulp in a fight. You almost did in training camp, remember?" She smiled briefly at all these observations, so he knew she was listening. "From the time we found you on the beach I have been in love with you. After that it's like we grew up together. But I hid my feelings in my heart and submitted them to Christ. He allowed me the satisfaction of serving Him and you and just to be by your side has been enough." Here she grew more visibly meditative, but still did not look at him. Then he said, "You take so many chances that the more time has gone by I feel like if you ever got hurt, I wouldn't be able to be a normal doctor for you. I'd be blubbering all over."

"You'd better start blubbering because this might be my last day. You can see how much they are after me by just how much attention they're giving to our deception today. One of these days, they're finally going to catch on. Do you know that the average life span of an underground leader is six months to a year before getting caught? I hold the record because they think I'm a man. When they do catch me they'll tear me limb from limb. So, please don't torment yourself. Forget me," she said as tears formed in her eyes.

"I've been tormented for years now. So I'm going to say it while I can, "I love you."

She still would not look at him. Then she put her forehead on her arms again and looked down and she mumbled just audibly. "I've been tormented too. I love you."

Then she looked up and said, "And if you blab this about, I'll kill you."

Tears formed in his eyes.

Suddenly, she arose and then he did as she heard the warnings from her ear computer. Two purple police came down the hall, but once again they were repelled by whatever invisible threat that was visible to them. They barked orders to them to continue to guard the prisoner. They would be back in one more hour after Todd announced that a free lunch was arriving from one of the restaurants downtown.

They went down again and sat on the floor.

Todd said, "Dianne, let's just for a moment pretend that life was normal. Let's do the pretend game that you played with Joanne. Remember the game about being married and having five children each?"

"How do you know about that?" she exclaimed. She now looked at him for the first time.

"Di, we all played these kind of games all these years. Here we all are teenagers and young people who are very human but not allowed to be normal. Joanne could only play games and because she was a robot and computer she could play with many of us."

He could see her thinking about all this. "When you did play this game with Joanne, who did she set you up with in your pretend marriage?"

"You," she said, looking away and down the hall.

"And what was your response?"

"She told you that? Why that little rat!"

He smiled when he saw her smile as she thought of their pretend life and she looked at a distance. Then she put her head against the wall and closed her eyes.

"Now let's just pretend that we really love each other," he continued. "That when we first meet and I ask you out on our first date, your dad gives me the toughest, longest interview and lecture." She laughed. "Then we date and I court you for 6.9 years, at the end of which I take you to our favorite place on one of the highest sand dunes overlooking the lake and I say, "Dianne Brogen, would you marry me?" And you say.

"Yes," she said softly.

"I now ask your dad for your hand in marriage, with your mother listening from the kitchen and now he gives me an even longer lecture and interview." Dianne saw her mom and dad just that way and she had to wipe a tear away. He continued, "For our wedding we wear only the finest. I in my white tuxedo and I see you in the first dress I've ever seen you in." Dianne laughed. He continued, "And this dress has such a long train that it takes three little girls to help carry it. Our parents, Joanne, Mark, Laura, and my brothers are there." Here he paused, for emotion caught up to him. She knew how his parents and brothers died early to Aliadin. When he recovered, he continued, "Jonathan Edwards is our minister. Jesus is there and He silently holds our hands as we say our vows. Reverend Edwards says, 'Will you Todd Jones take Dianne Brogen to have and to hold from this day forward for better or worse in sickness and in health, to love, honor and cherish until death do us part.'"

"I say, 'I do.'"

"Then he says, 'Dianne Brogen, will you take Todd Jones to have and to hold from this day forward for better or worse, in sickness and in health, to love, honor, and obey until death do us part?'"

With her head still against the wall and her eyes closed, tears began to run freely down her cheeks and she licked her lips and said, "I do."

Todd smiled and enjoyed watching her and he continued, "We hug and are hugged by Pastor Edwards, and each one of our family and Jesus. Evelyn and Helga are there and they provide the multi-layered wedding cake."

Dianne broke in, "With two little figures of us on top."

Todd smiled and was glad she was enjoying this and he continued. "Jesus provides all the food and pop and we have a wonderful reception with everyone we know and love. Jesus provides all of the presents. It comes time for us to leave on our honeymoon and the limousine is all decorated. Jesus comes to us and hugs us and says, "Thank you for sacrificing your normal lives for Me and loving Me more than each other and yourselves. Thank you for remaining pure and clean and holy and for being My soldiers for such a time as this. Someday you will be given more than you can ever imagine." Then He sends us back to reality.

She opened her eyes and looked at him full into his face and those penetrating brown eyes and she reached her hand out and he extended his. Their fingers just touched and were about to come together when the door opened and they rose quickly.

Laura appeared, relaxed and smiling from ear to ear. Her face was redder and her cheeks more rosy than they had been. "You can come back in now. I'm sorry we took so long."

Dianne offered Mark one more chance for an escape. As soon as he said, "It's not His will," the spiritual atmosphere of peace and quiet changed and the purple police entered and ushered them out. Soon they watched from a distance and followed Mark as he was led out to an awaiting vehicle and he was gone.

They returned to the studio apartment in light spirits, praising God for such a remarkable day. That night they traded stories about Mark. Laura sat on the bed contented; Dianne sat at the table and worked on the computer for a long time and then showed some concern. She looked at the cooking timer and did not hesitate to begin to work on it with a small set of tools and some items from her backpack.

"What about a Bible? Don't you have one around here?"

"Don't need one. It's all up here," Dianne said, once again pointing to her head. "What would you like to hear?" She began reciting Genesis, but Laura interrupted and asked for John 15 and 16. Without hesitation she started with chapter 14 and recited 15–16 and 17 with passion, all the while working on the cooking timer. She went back to the computer for some time. Then she began sticking little boxes in the corners of the apartment and in the bathroom. "Don't be alarmed by this. These are just a precaution. My information tells me there is going to be trouble, but it is not likely to be here. But just in case." She tied her hair up in back, gathered up her black gloves, uniform, shoes, night goggles, and helmet and put them in the backpack. Leaving the computer on the table, Dianne put some more little plastic boxes in a hamburger bag. "I'll be back late," Dianne said. "There are some important things to do. I'll also bring back a snack. Please, by no means touch the cooking timer," ordered Dianne, as she carefully put it away in a cabinet.

It was nine P.M. when suddenly the door to the apartment opened and Immanuel appeared. He looked at Laura but did not smile or say hello; he looked around and fixed on the computer. "Where's Dianne?" he asked, as he walked over to the computer and opened it.

"She's out." Laura said. "I think you'd better wait for her before you use it."

"What do you know? Maybe I've done this a time or two and you don't know anything about our business," he said.

Something in his voice and manner was not right. He stopped and seemed to be listening to his tiny earpiece and a tiny transmitter-receiver on his collar. He reported back, "Don't do anything until I give the code words. She's not here, but she'll be back. We have bait. Let her find a way up." Laura walked over and put a hand on the computer and closed the case. A tug-o-war ensued. Immanuel pleaded that he knew what he was doing. Laura gripped harder until she won. Immanuel fell backward. She dashed it to pieces on the edge of the counter top in three tries. When Immanuel got back to her he slapped her in the face. He pushed her and threw her on the bed and told her not to move. Then the lights went out.

Dianne saw the unusual traffic and numerous double-parked police vehicles around the entrance to her building. She saw SWAT team trucks and purple police in great numbers. She ducked immediately into an alley, looked to her wrist computer and saw what was going on in the apartment. She tapped a signal and all power went out in the building. Even the emergency lights were useless. She put on the night-goggles and went in using a secret entrance. She ran up the stairs until she found soldiers in the upper stairs and then she altered her course and ran up a set of secret steps, but they too were filled with soldiers. Then she got out and studied her computer and found that a secret elevator was empty at the bottom. She activated the power only in that one shaft. It ascended the twenty remaining stories. She cautiously looked down her halls and no one was there. Just in case soldiers were hiding in the other apartments she had her computer lock them from the inside. They and the ascending soldiers were obviously waiting for a signal and had been interrupted by her. She knew from past encounters that she had six more minutes before they would counter her computer and get the power back.

She saw by her wrist computer where Laura and Immanuel were. Without hesitation she opened the door in the dark and swiftly kicked Immanuel between the legs with all her might. As he was crumpling to the floor in agony, within a split second, she kicked him again in the face breaking his jaw. His teeth severed part of his tongue and blood oozed out of his mouth. Swiftly she handcuffed his wrists behind him. She searched him and ripped his three different communicators and his wrist computer off and threw them in the toilet. His wrist and laptop computers had been made largely useless as she had sent a virus that had destroyed all vital information to them weeks earlier.

She handed Laura a small flashlight. "Quick, put the essentials in the knapsack," she said. She took the cooking timer out of the cabinet and wound it to five minutes and placed it on the table by a piece of paper. Little red lights flicked on from every corner of the apartment and by her wrist computer signals she knew the rest were turned on in all the other apartments on this empty floor and in many other places. Then she turned to the man lying on the floor and whispered, "Manny, you spineless liar. How could you live with yourself and God, giving us over to be captured and tortured. And for what? When your head comes to the front again may you truly repent this time." She shot him with one of Uncle's old sedation guns that she found in his pocket. Then she went to the bed and put the two little bears into the knapsack. With Laura's help they dragged Immanuel to the elevator she had ridden and they all went down twenty floors. Then it was sent to the bottom with only Immanuel still in it. The power went back on all through the building, but they were now below the soldiers and police who had been hiding on that floor and in the elevators and stairwells and who approached the apartment door now. They had waited patiently for Manny's signal, but now impatient they broke the door open. The cooking-timer rattled on the table and there was a note that read, "Sorry, you're cooked. See you at the judgment." Then there was a resonant *ding*. The explosion that followed could be seen and felt down the street and from a distance in any direction as it blew the entire floor out and destroyed an entire elevator shaft and a good portion of a sub-basement where numerous soldiers had hidden. Fire shot from a number of vents and not a few manhole covers blew off. The resulting fire destroyed even more as the building was evacuated.

They had braced for it. "Timing is everything," Dianne said. "Let's wait here," she said when they reached the fifth floor. She looked at her wrist computer. They waited and Dianne changed back into a college student again until the regular police and the fire department had arrived and took over. They joined the evacuation of the building and walked out the front door and down the street, mingling easily with the evacuating crowds and the even bigger crowds that gathered to watch.

Laura did not know what to say. She was so impressed with Dianne and her ability to adjust to every situation. "You've done this before," she said.

"Too many times," said Dianne. "The key is not to hesitate when action is needed. I'm sorry I left you like that but I had to relocate a few folks in another neighborhood as I didn't know exactly where the trouble would start. They faked me out this time. I won't leave you again."

"But I thought Immanuel was on our side."

"He should not be called Immanuel but only Manny. This was not the first time he's burned us."

"But you trusted him enough to rescue me?"

"Traitors are usually good for one freebie and Manny at least knew he owed me something in order to regain my trust. He succeeded."

"But, he could have simply turned you in at the prison?"

"No, that was not Manny's style. He worked for Uncle before his death and presumably is working for the next head scientist who would be Dr. Rafeis. They probably wanted to put my head on their research platter to replace Joanne's. By the way, thanks for destroying my computer. You saved us there."

They turned into an alley and then went into the back door of a small tavern. A graying, muscular man with a flat top haircut sat near the register watching his own television in the empty bar room and drinking a beer. "Wayne, I'm sorry but I need to blow through here," she said as she kissed him on the forehead. "Wayne Dombrowski, meet Laura, Mark's wife and my sister-in-law."

He turned to Laura and shook her hand, and said, "Pleased to meet ya. I'm glad you succeeded. I've tried to get Ms. Commando here to find a guy, but I think she has it out for men. She just sent another company of them to that hot place. Her only boyfriend is someone named Jesus."

"I had to deal with a traitor," Dianne said as she put instructions in code into Wayne's computer.

"Yeah, I know. Thanks to you my customers are down the street watching your show. His hands went to his head as if he had a headache. Then he said, "Di, how many times do I have to tell ya. You use way too much of that stuff. You only need a little. I should have flunked you in basic training. And this is the third time this month. You're lucky with God that that building was half empty to begin with. I think you hit a record tonight. They're saying 314 of their people are down and it may be more. That means your popularity is rising. They'll be after you more than ever now."

"I know. I may not be back this way again. Please, let Sidney and Steffan and the other hackers you see know they have to pick up the slack now and that I will give them the new codes by morning. Dina and Rhonda will be in charge and Todd with the men. I love ya. See you in that pearly place," she said. They turned to leave.

"Dianne," he said making her turn and look at him. "You are the best soldier I've ever seen. I'm proud to have served with you."

They saluted each other and she and Laura were gone.

Chapter 23

ORPHANS IN ACTION

They spent a week at another studio apartment on the north side. That first night, Dianne could not sleep, and in the early morning Laura awoke and began to vomit. She moaned about the baby. As she helped her Dianne complained about all the deceptions. "They have killed us. Sincere believers have been betrayed by mothers, fathers, uncles, aunts, cousins, fellow workers. Did you know Rev. Casey was turned in by one of his own elders, a guy named Bob. Mr. Darringen's own wife turned on him," she said as she cooled Laura's head with a wet cloth.

"Didn't his wife expose your operation more?" Laura asked.

"One of our men had to eliminate her." Dianne said. "It was a confused time for our outfit."

"And yet you trusted Manny again? Why?" Laura said, feeling better.

"I'm a sucker for second chances, like my Savior, I guess. And like I said, traitors want to establish a trust and so usually they're good for one mission, like yours. But when you need reliable people there is only one kind left."

On the second day Natalie, Bette, Rhonda, Kersten, and Dina came calling after Dianne sent coded messages to the entire secret force. Laura was very pleased to meet them. She understood that these were the officers for the female secret force units. They were of various ages. Natalie had a distinct Middle Eastern appearance with dark hair and dark brown eyes. She explained her Iranian-Indian background to a very interested Laura as she put down several pizza boxes on the kitchen table. Bette was Chinese and brought with her some moon cakes for all of them. Rhonda was a Sudanese whose coal black hair was braided most beautifully. These three were foreign students who had had some police or military experience and training, but were now caught between two worlds. They were not accepted back home. Nor did the new U.S.W. government accept them; so they joined the secret force at Dianne's invitation. Kersten, a blonde-haired blue-eyed soccer player, said she was simply from Minnesota. She brought the soda pop and ice. Dina, red haired and freckled and very fair skinned, brought several more pizzas. They carried black backpacks like Dianne's that had the same black police-army type pants and shirts and everything else neatly folded inside along with the helmet and night vision goggles.

They appeared to be five more college gals in a variety of college T-shirts and blue jeans but their muscles and leanness made them look like Dianne. Each had their wrist computers and laptops and various styles of earrings, but in only one ear lobe like Dianne. All prayed solemnly for each other for a long while and then it was party time. They jested and joked with each other. All raised their pop cans to Laura and the baby. They teased each other about who loved who with the few males in their numbers when they learned how wonderful Mark had been. They also poked fun at themselves, trying to come up with a fit name for their secret force. No decision was ever made about this.

"How about the *Grimy Grim Gals*," said Kersten.

"*Wild War Women*," said Rhonda.

"If we were all moms like Laura we could be *The Mad Moms of Mayhem*," said Natalie, "Or how about the *Ranis of Revenge*?" The pizza disappeared. Only Laura finished her moon cake. Bette left the rest for her when she saw she liked them.

All of a sudden it was all business and Dianne, Rhonda, Natalie, Bette, and Kersten prepared for the mission. Soon they were all in their black uniforms. Dina dressed also but was to stay and protect Laura. Dianne told her not to worry if she was not back even for several days. She would return. Before they left they had Laura pray for them as they all knelt down around her.

Dina sat on the bed with Laura for a long time and they talked about everything. Dina told Laura how she and Dianne had started out together at the very beginning of the secret force. This led Laura to make some observations and ask some questions that Dianne would not answer. Laura said, "I think that Dianne is like Superwoman. She seems to know everything and be able to do everything. I've even told her that and she just says she's a goofy girl with a super God."

Dina laughed, "What do you expect her to say. But I will tell you that she is the best leader our special unit could ever have. And she can do it all or will try. She has the same courage and heart for God that David must have had."

Laura asked about this special force and Dina related its history. "When the underground began to organize with Mr. Darringen, there was an idea to have a special, elite sort of force. Not for offensive campaigns or anything, but for defensive purposes only. Rescue missions of all those who were imprisoned and then to help resettle them somewhere in the area. However, we began performing missions to destroy their effectiveness or efficiency when Dianne became the leader. We have done the conventional bombing of key installations and also made computer warfare and havoc to keep them from finding the people we're helping. We carry guns, but only for defensive purposes, like policemen. Dianne made it so the computers and some well-placed bombs do the real work. However, when it comes to guns we know all about the enemy's weapons and can have a shoot out with the best of them. It is only a small force of 100, or it was. It only numbers seventy-four now. It has been depleted by some defections, like Manny and the rest have been killed or wounded. You've perhaps heard Dianne talk about Trisha and Susan. They were made into robots."

"But what about men? Except for Todd the other day, all I see is women," Laura said. "The Christian armies in the west were mostly men."

Dina laughed, "I'll wager that the only women you saw were in our former American army which has become the Christian Army. And that they were fighting for their lives because Aliadin's army is only men and very bad men; men that women should never have to be with. Aliadin did wonders for the crime rate, but many of those same criminals ended up in that army. Women are all we have here, or almost. It was embarrassing when we began and Wayne found that we had only about twenty men and the rest of the volunteers were women—girls like us. All this has given Dianne a very negative attitude toward men.

"Somehow, through God's grace and strength, we put in the work and became, if I don't say so myself, pretty effective. Wayne always remained skeptical until we started having success. We owe so much of it to Dianne's organization, her computer wizardry, and her instincts.

"But she is also such a fighter and has the uncanny ability to overcome the strength of a man in any fight she's in. She says it's like David having to fight Goliath almost every day. Wayne taught us all about many ways of fighting and since women are always weaker than men, we must use deception, speed, and skill. Di excelled beyond all of us. To look at her few would suspect she could be the leader of anything or could take on anything the enemy brings on.

"You don't realize just how many people Dianne and this force have helped. Sometimes I'm amazed. More amazing are the missions we undertake. Everything Wayne made us do or trained us for has come to pass. We've had to run, swim, climb everything including the insides and outsides of buildings downtown, tunnel under walls, run and wade through sewers, endure long hours waiting in confined spaces for the right timing. We have killed our share of the enemy, blown up, and thwarted much of his plans. The only thing we can't do is fly. We don't have any capes."

They both laughed. Then Dina resumed and said, "But this is only for starters. It's the evacuating or rescuing of as many prisoners as we can, and then arranging for hiding, feeding, and taking care of them that makes our work full time, as you have seen in living with Di. However, we do work in shifts and everyone gets some time off. We have many others in the network who actually do much of the placing and doctoring and whatever is needed. It is at night that we perform almost all of the missions. It is during the day that we police and make sure that they are not harassed or found out by the purple police. Each of us has a sector we patrol. We look in on as many as we can. We even have to become part of the law enforcement when we find crime happening in our areas. We usually incapacitate these and hand them over to the regular police. But to keep our security tight, justice often must be swift and uncompromising."

As Dina talked she began making security checks on her laptop.

Laura asked, "Do the members of the secret force ever socialize together? Is there any free time? The people in this force seem so young. What about supervision? Are there older people?"

"There's no dating. It's against the manual. Guys usually hang out with guys and gals hang out with gals. When there is a mix we meet for small group Bible study and prayer, but we only meet in small groups and rarely altogether for security reasons. There have been Christmas parties and summer picnics, but again they are rare. But communicating by computer is done all the time. During stand-down time before or after a mission, there is a lot of good-natured fun and jesting with each other. If there are serious needs we do get together for counsel or prayer. The force is organized so that there is an older designated 'mom' for every ten people. And growing females need a mom. Some of us like Dianne and myself who were only fifteen when we began had many growing problems and pains. Wayne had to be reminded of what we could and could not do physically each year of growth. Wayne has had to be drill sergeant and dad, a dad nobody wants to disobey. No other men have been available to be designated dads. Mr. Steinmetz has become our godfather.

"You also have to remember that all the members of this secret force are orphans, young people whose parents were killed. Some of our younger brothers and sisters had to be placed in the neighborhood centers that we look after. Also, since many of us were either finishing high school or college when our lives were disrupted, there have been provisions made for some continuing education by surviving Christian teachers and professors. When all the seminaries and Christian colleges were eliminated and their inhabitants killed, the few escaping seminary professors have also become mentors and teachers for us. Except for our few defectors we have been a remarkably consistent, holy orphan army before the Lord. Each one has a remarkable testimony and love for Christ. We're simply young people who have been given a tremendous amount of responsibility. The pressures are great. We've had to grow up fast. The Lord has been our strength."

Dina then sighed and said, "Then there's Joanne who as a computer did so much for the morale of our men and women. She gave her life for Dianne by pretending to have her mind. It's ironic that they took her for her brain. To the secret force she gave us her heart as she played games with us, prayed with each person, counseled and became a friend and pal. Since she was a computer she could do it with all of us at the same time if necessary. Dianne and our hackers could not have done without her spy work for us. We understood that these twins indeed were special."

Laura sat and thought about all of this as Dina worked and then asked, "How and when did Dianne become the leader of all this?"

"Did Dianne ever tell you how we made this rescue mission of a prisoner boat once way out in Lake Michigan?

"No, she didn't," said Laura.

"She probably won't tell you then. It was one of our first missions. It was also the night Mr. Darringen was arrested. It turned out to be a set up to catch us. His wife was in on this too. It's how Nikai and Jodi met their end. Dianne barely got away. She even took a bullet. It passed through her thigh. She somehow swam and floated for a night and a day and thought she was going to die. Miraculously she did not. As she tells it, she was at the end and gave herself up to God and then passed out. When she awoke she was on a beach in Michigan. Our own people somehow found her at the right time. Miraculously, she had no bullet wound at all. She had been healed. Only scars remain where it went in and where it came out. Praise God. From that time Dianne became the leader in every way."

"She has been so protective of us. On every mission she is the first one in and the last one out. If one of us is wounded she will not leave that person until they can be gotten out. The real hard thing for Dianne is to see any of us captured.

When Trisha and Susan were caught and we could do nothing for them Dianne took it personally. We did lose one other. That was Deidra. We were unaware that she had been captured until it was too late. When Dianne learned she had been burned to death like a witch she was beside herself. She's never forgiven herself for losing her."

Laura now was even more solemn and appreciative of Dianne.

"She will not tell you how much she has done for the people caught in those prisons and camps and laboratories," said Dina.

"Where is the secret force now and what are they doing?" asked Laura.

"You might call this week revenge week for all the raids they have done in the last few days. Dianne thinks that the enemy is really close on her heals now and she is going to distance herself from the rest of us after this week. We are going to continue on as we can. Most of the force is being deployed this week to . . . well . . . we can catch some of the news perhaps."

She turned to her laptop and as they lived together for the next two days they watched various news reports about explosions and fires at prisons and laboratories and army depots, and armories. When the news suddenly went off the air Dina said, "All communications, computers, and satellites were also targeted. In other words if Dianne is going out Dianne's taking as many with her as she can. This means a record rescue effort."

Three days later, Dianne reappeared looking like a college girl; she smiled and gave them the thumbs up as she came through the door.

Early the next morning, Dianne painted the Hebrew letters on the sides of their faces again, including Dina's, while they ate breakfast. She painted the letters on Laura's belly. Dianne told Dina that she and Rhonda were now in command and that she and Laura would stay in the Smith house in Ridgeland. Dina hugged Laura and Dianne and they left. They took the train to a suburb, to what Dianne called, "The Home Wood," a cemetery. She had been there many times in the last six years. They had to pass through Rosedale and to Dianne it might as well have been in the next galaxy. It had represented all that had been innocent and normal. Now nothing was innocent or normal.

Dianne carried a bag with food, primarily for Laura. Laura carried Dianne's backpack. As they walked Dianne pointed out a house they would stay in and then they walked a few more blocks. As they approached the cemetery, Dianne said to Laura, "It's a peculiar thing, but one of the best and safest places to be in the antichrist's regime is in a cemetery. I've been here often when I've needed to get away from things. And now that the heat is on it's great. His people and forces are for some reason mortally afraid of them. They cremate all their dead and even the bodies of their enemies."

They reached the cemetery gates and then began walking amongst the hills and graves. It was a beautiful fall day in early September. The fall was an unusually warm and dry one for this part of the country. Dianne sat down on one of the raised gravestones. Laura walked before her reading names out loud, "Brown, Ritter, Andrews, Hill, Johnson, Pranger, Unger, Brogen . . ."

Dianne said, "It's my great grandparents. There's more of us over on the other hill and Mom and Dad and Joanne and I are way down there." Here she pointed to another part of the cemetery with many large old trees but flatter terrain. They took their time walking down to this region, walking in the leaves. They sat down around her family's graves.

Dianne pulled out the two little bears and placed them on Mom's grave. She looked at the various headstones and said, "I love you all." This brought tears to Laura's eyes.

Then Dianne lay down on her own grave, and said, "What do you think? How do I look, alive or dead? I was baptized into Christ Jesus and baptized into His death. I was buried with Him through baptism into death in order that, just as Christ was raised from the dead through the glory of the Father, I too may live a new life. I died with Christ and died to the power of sin's rule over my life. It is not I who live but Christ who lives in me." Then she sat up slowly and rubbed her face and eyes with her hands, and said, "I'm so tired. Here I am twenty-one and I feel as though I've lived 100 years."

"When was the last time you really slept? You are going all the time," Laura said.

"Every minute counts in this business and there is so much to do that I cannot sleep. I wish I could sleep. In heaven I'm going to sleep until noon every day."

"I think we're all going to need a good rest," said Laura playing with the leaves as she lay on the grass. "You wonder why Christ doesn't come back or how we will survive another day. Through all of this, I just want to say you've been great. If there were super heroes you'd be one of them. Is there anything you can't do?"

"I can't cook!" she said and they both laughed. Then she became very solemn.

"The things over the last three-and-a-half years have become overwhelming. We have been able to help hundreds escape each year but the antichrist upped the ante by imprisoning and killing thousands more. I simply don't have the resources to save them all and it's very frustrating," Dianne said and she paused and reflected.

"Did you know I run the mile in seven minutes flat? Did you know that I have had to take on enemy marines a number of times and I won? I can't even remember how many rescues, special missions, and escapes I have made. Years ago, I actually dreamed of this kind of life. I looked forward to being a Christian for the end times. I wanted to do it all and be it all. I wanted to be Superwoman. I wanted to be independent of everyone: unemotional, efficient, and strong," she said.

Tears ran down Dianne's cheeks as she talked. "I've tried to be Superwoman and that has been my problem. In competing for Jesus I have competed with Him. I have wanted to do everything for Him, to please Him, to sacrifice for Him, to be accepted and acceptable to myself. I wanted to be perfect like Him and I wanted to save everyone."

Laura chimed in, "Charles would have said you were trying to overcompensate for the loss of your father and mother, and your sister and brother. Or perhaps competing with them."

Dianne nodded, "Yeah, I guess I have been doing that. I wanted to be perfect like Jesus more than anything." She mused, "Six years ago, when I first became the leader, an incident happened in one of our missions that turned me to where I could not get enough of Jesus. I couldn't love Him enough." Here she rubbed her thigh.

Laura said, "I know about that now. Dina told me."

"I floated and drifted in that water and I couldn't go on. I should have drowned. He came to me. He didn't say anything but only touched my heart and said He loved me. From that moment I started to see how selfish and hardened I had become. From the time they found me on the shore and we saw how He had healed me, I couldn't serve Him enough. I became aware of how many times He rescued me. My heart broke when He said that His love was made perfect in weakness. His love disarmed me and I could not stop worshiping Him. I love Him so much. I gave Him everything and submitted to His Lordship."

"From that time when I've been too tired physically, He has given me the strength to carry on. When I have come to the end mentally the ideas come from Him. When I have been depressed He gets me back up. When I am sad or in sorrow He has brought humor into my life. He has kept me from getting sick or hurt. When I have been exhausted and can't seem to do anymore, He has given me the strength to help or save one more life. I've seen so many miracles. His timing is perfect. Oh, how I love Him. My life has been incredible. He has kept my foot from the snare and has protected me from my enemies who are too strong for me. When I needed a mom and a grandma I had Helga and Evelyn. And when I was lonely and needed someone to talk to He sent you. And I've talked your ear off since you came."

Laura smiled and knelt and embraced her.

Dianne said, "He has even used my brother and sister to show me what sacrifice means. They sacrificed themselves for me. To me, you and they are the superheroes. Oh, how I love Jesus. He truly is my sword and shield, my ever-present strength in time of trouble. No, I am not Superwoman. I am just that goofy girl with a super God. The Master of the universe is master of this," she said as she pointed to her heart and her head.

"Now that the numbers are just too great, I've been awake many a night thinking and praying about all the men and women we cannot help. I realize we can't lose, but we cannot win. They are winning and winning big. We don't have the resources. The concentration camps, all the deaths are just too difficult for me now. I am so tired. We are in the Alamo with our backs to the wall."

They sat silently for some time and then lay down in the grass and both fell asleep for several hours. For a change Laura woke up before Dianne and she enjoyed the solitude and the beauty of the day. Dianne dreamed that she had her hands in her dad's and with her bare feet stood on his shoes as he walked her around the yard. She looked up into his eyes and then she thought it was Jesus because the hands that held hers and his bare feet on which she stood had nail holes. He was telling her how much he loved her as his face became brighter and brighter.

Dianne awoke with a start; the sun was in her eyes and she was all business again. She began digging near Joanne's headstone. Soon she was wiping the dirt off of a plastic bag that held another laptop computer. She unfolded it and started working on it with her tools.

"What day is it? It's Mark's trial day. Come on baby, work for me." Soon with a new independent power source put into it everything was fine.

Dianne and Laura decided to go back up the hill toward the center of the cemetery again and sit against and amidst the larger gravestones so as to have more shelter, privacy, and to have the advantage of the high ground if intruders came in. Laura was hungry again and she ate. Dianne discovered that they had missed the show trial. But Dianne, unperturbed, worked on the computer while they each spent the time talking and singing to the baby in Laura's womb.

Dianne contacted Elle, her robot contact in Aliadin's household. Then Dianne and Laura each took one of the ear receptors and fit them in their ears so they could hear everything including Elle's computer voice. They had been too late. The trial had been during their night and Israel's daytime. However, she did more than rebroadcast the trumped up version, but secretly kept the actual responses of Mark as well and the unedited version of the Anti-Christ's responses.

Mark and thirteen other political prisoners had been taken to Jerusalem for the show trial. Elle gave her own running commentary of all that had transpired over the last week and in the show trial itself.

The Emperor-Messiah was furious at the incident in his number one laboratory near Chicago and vowed to make Mark Brogen, the number one terrorist, pay unless he worshipped him before the world. Behind the scenes he was redoubling his efforts to locate and capture alive the unidentified assailant that acted with Mark. Here Elle gave a personal message to Dianne to hide because his top people were on her trail.

Dianne smiled at Laura, and said, "It's nice to know that I've finally got his attention, at least."

Then Elle showed the commercialized version with all the special effects. They saw the incredibly built temple, the size of five city blocks and six times bigger than St. Peters. Outside it stood Aliadin's monument, an image that was an exact replica of him. It rivaled the size of the Statue of Liberty and this immense figure could move and speak, especially at night in a holographic shape. All around it on show trial days and designated worship days were thousands of people bowing and worshiping. Inside the great dignitaries, the political and religious leaders of the world bowed and worshiped him. Here Elle explained to Dianne and Laura that Aliadin actually allowed all religions of the world to be retained as long as they worshiped and obeyed him. Only unrepentant Jews, historic Christians and political renegades were run down like dogs. His guard of honor and representatives of all his secret police and his generals were all there giving reverence. Raised somewhat higher was an area where a table and chairs were placed. This was where the prisoners sat for their public audience with the lord of the world. Finally, highest of all, was the throne of Aliadin and by him was his prophet Arcane. The prophet tapped his staff on the ground and lightening struck from heaven before and after the show trial, killing designated prisoners outside who had already been condemned to death. Aliadin was looking every bit the superman on this day. But Elle commented, "One could still tell that he had for the most part an artificial body because nobody ever looked like that outside a movie or cartoon." Both Laura and Dianne laughed at this comment and imagined her very Polish-Jewish accent in how she worded her comments, even though she could only speak with the computer voice.

Elle continued and showed how this show was broadcast on huge televisions and mile long TV screens around the Jerusalem temple and on similar screens in every city in the world. Every working computer, television, wrist computer, and movie theatre screen throughout the world showed this event. Even Somodromes and similar entertainment devices ceased and broadcast only this. Here Elle made a wry comment about how even escapist perverts cannot even escape their perverted king. Also, these events were especially broadcast inside labor and prison camps to destroy the morale of historic Christians and Jews.

Dianne told Laura that in the past when the antichrist had these events, his hackers went to work and the underground's computers had to be shut off or they would be infected with a virus if their programs detected obstructions. They had to reinvent their own firewall programs in order to fight this because the existing ones did not keep the antichrist's diseases out.

The prisoners on the stage sat silently, looking down at their hands or the table. This was preferable to looking up at Aliadin and Arcane. Each one in turn was made to stand and come alone to the center of a large pentagram circle. While they were doing so the person was introduced and their crimes read by one of a panel of judges who sat in a box to Aliadin's right. Then Aliadin asked them questions. After their guilt was clearly seen they each bowed down in the circle and kissed the ground, pleading the lord's mercy, vowing now to be devoted only to him. It became cloying when each buckled, whimpered, pleaded, and worshiped as they arrived in that circle in front of the grim faces of Aliadin and Arcane. Laura couldn't believe that each one did not fight this, or argue, or resist, even if it meant death. She was sure Mark would not give in like this. When it came Mark's turn one could see by his hesitancy and slowness that he was somewhat goaded to get up. Then he moved with alacrity. But one could see that he stopped before the circle. However, as the others did he fell into the circle and did not seem to kiss the circle so much as his mouth met the surface in his fall and then they heard him plead, whimper, confess his crimes, and worship the king and like the others he was dragged away afterward.

Laura could not believe it. But that voice, it wasn't Mark's at all. The only two souls in the world who would know that voice well knew it was not his. Laura and Dianne looked at each other. Elle anticipated their reaction and told them that that was the official version and not the real version. She would now play the real version for them.

It was not at all like the original. Almost all of the prisoners, knowing they were really condemned anyway, did put up a struggle and told the antichrist off. By the time they got to Mark they understood the reality. What really happened was this. Mark slowly got up and was goaded with an electric prod to get him going. When he got to the circle his real lips and voice said that he would not enter the circle. He would die first as it represented Satan's world kingdom and not that of the true Christ. The Prophet Arcane then went to work. He had the ability, a mixture of science, magic, and the demonic to invisibly punish, throw, or drag those at a distance. Mark, like the others, was staggered by this and the effect threw him down on his face into the circle, but then he got to his knees. Laura and Dianne heard his voice, but his message was not from this world. It was in perfect ancient Hebrew. It utilized the words of Jude 18–19; 1 John 2:18–23; 4:1–6 and was made more personal and from God's standpoint. It also rang with a personal condemnation, using the antichrist's original family name and did not address him as lord of anything.

Afterward, Elle accompanied Aliadin, so Dianne and Laura visually went with them. In his chambers for a private audience and private computer cameras of officials, he had the ten who had really affronted him beaten and tortured in front of him. Four he spared and said to take them to his private rooms. He would take his pleasure with them later. Elle told them this would be censored but everyone knows what will happen to them.

When he got around to Mark, he was most incensed and had him beaten savagely. Laura moved away in horror and tears, her hands went over her eyes and she got up and turned and walked a distance away. But just when it looked like that would be all for him, Aliadin changed his mind. "I want him to become a robot. Make him a robot!" he said to the scientists in his party. "Then he will grovel and serve me and renounce all other authorities. He can join Elle my faithful robot here. You are mine alone aren't you, Elle and faithful only to me."

Elle responded, "Yes sir, I can only serve you." He had Mark dragged over and held up before him and he said, "You will be my servant . . . and I will catch your sister. Oh, yes, I know by a certain robot informant that you have a sister and I know who she is now. I know her name and that she is the unknown leader of the Chicago underground." He listed the many things he would do to her when she was captured. "You will get to see it all as my loyal robot," concluded Aliadin.

Dianne inquired right away who the rat was. Elle said, "Not me, but Vicki has been brought to Aliadin recently and she knows a lot."

This was a new unexpected wrinkle. Dianne immediately wondered about how Vicki would have known. Dianne knew Aliadin was speaking to her. A bit of sweat formed on her forehead as she heard all his instructions.

"Now, there you see? Do it and do it tonight," Aliadin commanded. Dr. Rafeis who was among the scientists present would have said that it could not be done so quickly, but he dared not contradict him in his present mood. But he did ask one thing. "Sir, if I might have a word. It would be a big help if we could use another robot in the process. We have found it goes much smoother and faster."

Aliadin agreed, and said, "Take Elle with you. I know she will not fail and so you cannot fail. I want him to recant his God by tomorrow morning."

Elle promised continued coverage and that she would keep one of her links open to Dianne at all times in the next 24 hours. Dianne said that they would be watching the further developments and told Elle that if they succeeded with the procedure to take care of Mark. Elle promised she would do all she could.

As they watched all this Dianne noticed warnings in the corner of the screen and then looked at her wrist screen which said, "Gotcha. Come out or we'll come in." The noises of vehicles could be heard in the distance. A sizeable army and a number of purple police were surrounding the cemetery. She realized that they wanted her alive. Otherwise they could have simply invaded and killed them, but she knew there were more variables here and Aliadin's orders were being obeyed before her eyes.

Without hesitation she sent back a message saying that the cemetery was rigged and then played on their fears. She began reciting Job 19 out loud and to Laura and as a prayer to God. At the same time she sent scriptural warnings about Christ's Second Coming, the dead rising to life, God raising an army of angels, the destruction of God's enemies and scriptural epithets about what would happen to the enemies who defied the armies of the living God. Then she hit the *all* button for every computer in the entire Chicago area. When Dianne got to Job 19: 25, Laura worshiped God in tears and recited with Dianne verses 25 to 29. These verses were sent as a conclusion.

Chapter 24

GIVING IT ALL UP

Dianne then returned to pondering the antichrist's words aimed at her.

Aliadin's message had shaken her. Laura was asking her some questions, but she did not respond. Laura became silent and put a hand on Dianne's back.

"I need to be by myself for awhile," said Dianne. The wind picked up and the sky had many more cumulus clouds than before. The still-leafy trees dropped a few more leaves. Dianne staggered off around the cemetery and fell onto her own grave and spent several hours there though she had no conception of the time passing.

She began to weep and then wept hard and couldn't control herself. She prayed and moaned over and over, "Lord, I can't do it. I can't go on." She trembled. It was not what Aliadin said because she had heard these threats before. It was that she had been exposed. Her armor had been stripped from her. She had been invisible and now was visible to all. She tried to recall how she failed.

She had monitored, reprogrammed, or interfered with every camera and computer in every exposed place for nearly six years with her computer and wrist computer programs without fail. Then she remembered the scene before Joanne blew up the lab. Of course, Vicki, being the loyal and dedicated robot for her master was monitoring Uncle's whereabouts because it was late at night. Dianne remembered that she had forgotten, even though caught by Uncle to do in the cameras in that laboratory which she could have done easily. She forgot once. There was only one other time that she had exposed her identity and that was in that first year in the underground movement. It was in her efforts to get Mark out of Chicago that she had contacted Vicki anonymously, but in later attempts had Joanne identify herself to Vicki which left open the question of who she was. But apparently she had no use for that information until now.

This blow to her professional pride was harder than any physical blows could have been. She was now the hunted when for all this time she thought of herself as the hunter. She had always been able to elude the eye of the beast. Others had been vulnerable to that gaze, but as long as she was vigilant and faithful to the system she had devised, she was invisible, untouchable, uncatchable. She had taken great pride and encouragement from this. As long as the threats to her were only threats they could be ignored. Now there was a distinct probability that the threats would become reality. Now Satan and his antichrist had their full attention on her and she felt their heat.

Fear paralyzed her. She saw monstrous faces looking at her and chasing her. Despair seized her and her stomach ached from the accumulating pressure of the rapid play out of events. Horrible thoughts of the future invaded her mind of being captured and crucified with all the degradation and cruelty that would mean. It was all too much. She now understood what Jesus must have felt like in the garden before the crucifixion with the weight of the whole world and the underworld against Him; then allowing Himself to be put to that horrible death at their hands. And if all this troubled the Son of God in the garden, how could she go through this? She cried and cried now and felt so weakened she could hardly breathe. "I can't be like You, Lord. I am too weak. I can't go through that . . . I can't . . . I won't."

Then she saw Wayne Dombrowski in her mind standing over her. She remembered those early training sessions and exercises when she could cover most of the course only to fall short, crying with exhaustion and despair. He yelled at her then and he was yelling at her now. "Get your lazy chicken bones up. You can't live in the mall anymore. This is war. It's the ninth inning, the last quarter, the last mile. Are you gonna lie there and wallow around in self-pity and cry? Get up and fight until you have every ounce of life knocked out of you. You have to defeat the enemy spiritually, mentally, emotionally, and physically on the battlefield with everything you have. You did not choose this fight, Christ chose you . . . to be His marine for this time. If you are His you will get up and do the impossible and run the course and win."

With this she felt Christ's finger once again touch the deepest part of her heart. Now she was prostrate before the

Master of the universe and the waves of His love, grace, and mercy poured over her until she was shaking and crying in worship and thanksgiving for everything including her present situation. She understood that Christ's sacrifice was so much greater and worse for Him. Because He had to be separated from the Father in order to take her sin and the sin of the whole world onto Himself. Fear, despair, hopelessness, and self-pity dissipated in the deep humility before the Lord's love and power pouring through her being. And because she knew that the Lord knew that her pride had been her thorn in the flesh, she heard the apostle Paul speaking 2 Corinthians 12:1–10, which ended, "That is why, for Christ's sake, I delight in weaknesses, in insults, in hardships, in persecutions, in difficulties. For when I am weak, then I am strong."

She was reminded that her sister and brother had already painfully given themselves up for Christ and for her. Then it seemed like an angel stood over her and said, "Get up. You have work to do." She heard Laura singing praises to the Lord from up the hill. This was an added admonishment to Dianne, that if a pregnant mother who had lost everything could stand up to all this, then she could. The tears stopped and she wiped them away. She got up and walked back up the hill with renewed confidence. She was Dianne again.

Laura asked if everything was all right. Dianne responded, "Couldn't be better."

To pass the time as the operation was being prepared, Elle showed past footage of Aliadin in private. They saw the human side, or what was left of it. They discovered that he was really a combination of man and machine. However, Elle commented wryly, he was more like an animal. His head had been totally reconstructed and with it half his brain after the assassinations of him, the president and the much of the U.S. administration and Congress. He had ceased brain function and was clinically dead but was raised back to life by Arcane and the most expensive and complicated series of operations ever. Religiously, Arcane used the magic arts and sorcery of ancient times to bring his spirit and mind back. That was why in private Aliadin prayed to a series of demonic images. And why his own image was everywhere in his empire, including the immense Statue of Liberty-sized monument outside his temple. Scientifically, he was given one of the most intricate and complete body and head reconstructions of all time. He now had the strength and memory and ego power of 10 men, but still needed the guidance of his prophet in order to run things. Elle put it most succinctly in the end, "Satan runs the show, though all would deny it publicly."

They now watched Mark's operation. Elle did not cease her broadcast and Laura pleaded with Dianne to shut it off when the blood started pouring; she hid her eyes in her jacket sleeve. But Dianne left it on, only to look away when it got too much. She assumed that they were killing him and she wanted to know when he was dead. They prayed and cried together. Dianne had seen Joanne go through this and now to see Mark in this state was equally difficult.

Inside the operation, and inside Mark's being or what was left of him, he had a totally different perspective. There was no pain. He had no nervous system. He had no senses. There was only his heart and brain and what connected them and how he was still alive he couldn't say. But he was. Inside he was in the dark but he was conscious and he could still remember and see things in his memory. He was not alone. With him was a presence that held him as if he still had a body. The presence identified itself as the Lord's angel sent to protect him. Mark felt like this angel held him like a father might hold a young son as they lay in bed together. They were snuggled up tightly and while Mark seemed to be lying face outward, the angel lay right behind him with an arm securely around his middle.

Mark was not aware of the progress or problems of the operation, only that certain ideas entered his mind from time to time. Sometimes he felt like his mind was not very clear and he couldn't remember certain things. What was happening was that his heart was not beating at the tempo that they wanted and was not pumping enough blood into it. Once this was fixed he thought about everything. The scientist-surgeons hooked his brain up to various computer components and gadgetry; as they did they did not tamper with the brain as such. They did not try to cut anything off in order to change him like Dianne thought. Elle told her that when they did try that they found that the robot often was brain dead or ineffective in many areas.

Instead they used computer components and chips to augment and enhance the brain-power. Here Elle was used once the first plug-in unit was installed. She went inside

Mark's brain to become his tutor on how to function. Only they could communicate to each other, but she did broadcast what the scientists wanted to know and she broadcast what Dianne and Laura needed to know. She first asked him privately if he had his angel with him. And he said yes. Elle described this and all that Mark was feeling and told the girls that he was really out of harm's way. Dianne spoke the words of Isaiah 63:9, "In their distress he too was distressed and the angel of his presence saved them."

Then Dianne asked Elle to give Laura a lesson on these robots as they watched and heard her work on Mark. She actually lectured Mark as she communicated to Laura all of the following information. Like all the robots ever made, with a few exceptions, they were made out of Christians and Jews. For Aliadin it was punishment and servitude. For the scientist-surgeons it was making a better, more-efficient computer. They could do many things like go into outer space. Here Elle told how Joanne was the first of Uncle's line of robots to have made a trip to space station number five early in her time with a number of space workers. They named her R1D1=Robot 1, Dianne 1. Thereafter, they became used all the time in space missions. For those Christians who knew about these robots, they were to be pitied for being crucified in a new way and subject to a prison of being canned like a tuna for the rest of their lives. But for those Christian leaders of underground movements such as Dianne, they became the best-ever informants and spies because inside these robots they still were Christians and stronger ones than ever before.

To their new secular and antichrist worshiping owners they were only their servants, spiritless and soulless. These robots only said and did what their owners expected of them. In other words these robots became outstanding actors for their new owners. Meanwhile, because of their multiple connections to any computer in the world that knew any of their codes they could communicate and hold conversations and do things that their owners knew nothing about. They could be talking or serving their owner by giving certain information while at the same time telling a Christian underground worker all the details of their sordid lives and their plans. Dianne had used Elle's and Joanne's databases and their access to satellite imagery and their cameras and schematics for tunnels, and sewer networks, buildings, and prisons, military bases, missiles, tanks, planes and trains and weapons to use in her own wrist and lap top computers all the time. Elle could do this all the while she was under the watchful gaze of the antichrist and innocently doing his housework.

However, for the rest of the consuming world the robot computers that Uncle pioneered, nobody in that community knew the truth about them. When Uncle first brought back the old PC with its large housing, it caused a stir. Because in this time computers could be tiny, small or flat and none of them took up much space and yet were very powerful. However, Uncle's initial PC's, what he called his personality computers and the robots thereafter, were demonstrated to be a hundred times better than the others and had an intellectual and personal capacity that nobody else could match.

Elle began to get Mark to use his mind as it had never been used in conjunction with computer aids. As they completed his multi-tasking hookups and his vision cameras and his computerized hearing, she showed him that in his mind there were now many new movie screens and on them he could do many tasks. On one screen the scientists could type in or speak to the robot and he could communicate in words, pictures, mathematics, or by voice. The scientists turned a dial and his hearing was magnified. In his mind she showed him that he had numerous screens and could see behind him while he looked forward and to the sides. And on these screens he could communicate with two or more people at the same time through the computer links.

This operation went on and on, but Mark being a slow learner in normal life, was still a little slow in his robot life. Elle told them that this might take some practice. Most new robot minds needed lots of practice and so it was like exercising more than learning new things until he could communicate.

The last thing she did was discuss his role. He was to be a robot for the antichrist and he would have to act like it even though he was still Mark the Christian inside. Here Mark was informed by his angel who had been silent all this time that he had a special message for the antichrist and could not accept Elle's conditions. Elle's angel told her that she was not to tell about Mark's mission. It was his alone.

Chapter 25

DAVID AND HIS MIGHTY MEN

As it grew darker Dianne changed into her black uniform primarily to stay warm. Around nine at night they tired of watching the computer as the operation seemed like it would take a long time. Laura was getting hungry again and they had run out of food. All they had were a few crunch bars and a few bottles of water. Besides, Dianne was restless and she told Laura she was devising plans of escape and needed to do some scouting. Laura pleaded for her to find some food too. "For you my lady I will break through the line and get something from that convenience store down the street." Dianne took off her windbreaker and put it on Laura's legs and told her to keep warm. She took the night goggles, but not the helmet. She gave this to Laura in case they started shooting. She tied her hair up in back and put on the black gloves and put the black backpack on. Both of them still had their Hebrew letters painted on their faces. Laura noticing this told Dianne that she looked like something that might come from a graveyard. "I hope so," she said.

Before she left, Dianne dug a hole and told Laura to put the computer in there and cover it up if there was trouble, but not to break it this time. Off she went.

Deftly she moved and studied the whereabouts of the forces arrayed against them. There were trees and shrubbery and bushes on both sides of the high iron fence that bordered the cemetery on three sides to where all this ran to an even higher chain link fence that was the border between it and an immense limestone quarry. There no one could set up defenses or attack on the ground because just over that high fence was a drop of thousands of feet. Falling off that edge would be like falling off a skyscraper and it would be awhile before one hit the bottom. Centuries of digging limestone had made it like the Grand Canyon. Just on the other side of this high fence was a narrow rock ledge. In seconds, and without hesitation she climbed this fence and did an acrobatic move over its old rusty barbed wire at the top that would have awed and frightened any acrobat or gymnast. At one second in the move she was free of the fence altogether and her body over the pit but her momentum came back to the fence where her gloved hands caught the chain links. Her black shoes came back into contact and she climbed down smoothly to the rock ledge. She began walking along the rock ledge.

She noticed that her wrist computer was not operating any longer. She squatted down and played with it and shook it. It read, "Ceasing operations," and the green light remained on. It then listed the parts that would be required to fix it. She had none of them and knew she simply needed a new one. It still had enough power to let her empty it of anything important. She meditated on the fact that she had had this on her wrist without fail for four years. When she did take it off it was only for a short time and only inches from her. She bathed, showered, and swam with it but it remained with her and operating. She realized how dependent on it she had become. Now she took it off and threw it out into the quarry where she watched its green light fall for some time until it disappeared. She rubbed her wrist and whispered, "Christ is my strength." However, she did activate her tooth computer and so could still talk with the outside world. With her ear stud, she could still hear all that was going on in and with any of the computers in the area. She looked out into the quarry with the mist and fog that had formed in it. It reminded her of the abyss. She prayed that Christ would throw the antichrist and his prophet in there soon.

She got up and walked two hundred yards and then crawled for fifty more past tents and guards who were all positioned to look away from the quarry and into the cemetery. Then she deftly climbed back over the fence and swiftly moved into the woods behind the enemy lines.

She did not get far. Eight men intercepted her. Three were purple policemen with night goggles and pistols out with silencers on them. Five were regular soldiers with rifles not far behind. Her arms went up and she stopped. The three purple police were running toward her with one way out in front. He got within three feet of her. Swiftly and without hesitation Dianne reached out, took the gun from his hands and reversed it as she intercepted the lead policeman. She used his weight and momentum and her weight and legs to lift and flip him. As she fell backward, flipping him over and flipping over herself, she fired and killed him in mid-air. Before this dead man's back reached the ground she was on the ground and had killed the other two purple policemen. As she lay on the ground she would have immediately fired into the other five, but for the first time in these kind of encounters she broke her one cardinal rule, never to hesitate in action. But in that hesitation of a split second two of the soldiers were on their knees. The other three dropped their guns and one of them shouted out, "Jesus save us!"

"We want Jesus—please don't kill us!" they all began to plead.

"What?" she said.

"We want to surrender to you," said the sergeant on his knees. The other soldiers lay their guns down near her and backed away. "We want you to pray to your God to save us," said the sergeant again. One of the others said, "We want to pray to you too. You are the goddess that lives in the cemetery and takes revenge on us."

She got up and as with habit she looked at and touched her wrist where the wrist computer had been. When the soldiers saw her do this they all fell on their faces and begged her not to blow them up. It was just then that she realized all her actions against them had accumulated in their minds and they had made her a legend even when they thought she was a he. She realized that God had used all this to build up their fear of her. This kept them from further attacks.

She moved them deeper into the forest preserve where even more soldiers were assembling to see her and beg her to give them her God. This included a troop commander. She had him post a guard to keep the purple police from discovering them. She spent the next two hours telling them about the gospel of Christ and praying with each one. They insisted they be baptized also. So she poured a little water on each forehead from her bottle and prayed for each of the forty-three of them again.

It had never occurred to her just how superstitious they were or how many religious beliefs were rampant in the antichrist's army. Many of them were foreigners, but there still were some American soldiers; a few were there that night. She had to dispel all the mistaken notions that she was a god, an angel, or a demon. One soldier kept calling her Diana when she never told any of them her name and had to ask him why. He said that because she came out at night when the moon was out and she hunted all who threatened God's children and women. She was to him and many of these soldiers a reincarnation of the Roman goddess. She had them recant and pray forgiveness for all these superstitions as well as their crimes and sins against Jesus Christ and His people.

The late night convenience store clerk's eyes widened when he saw Dianne with her black army uniform, lettered face, and grim appearance. Few had ever seen the black uniforms in full light and close up and he noticed the embroidered crosses on one side and on her shoulders and the American flag embroidered on the other side all done in black silk. Next to her was the troop commander in the uniform of Aliadin's army with its Arabic symbols, medals and U.S.W. letters. They made for the oddest couple. On the counter lay some strange and unrelated food items and some girl's items, a roll of perfumed toilet tissues, and a pack of chewing gum. The clerk looked at them and their chosen items and simply thought, "Whatever." The troop commander happily let him scan his forehead. She lay down a Christian tract. And they walked out together into the night.

The clerk said to himself, "Now I have seen it all."

It was after midnight when Dianne returned to Laura, thinking how cold and hungry she should be and how she was going to apologize to her. But she stopped in her tracks. She realized there were soldiers sitting in the dark all around her and Laura. She rose immediately to greet Dianne putting her hands together and laughing. "They came from over there." She pointed down to where the other corner of the cemetery met the quarry.

One of the soldiers, a lieutenant said, "We are all believers in Jesus now. Please don't blow us up . . . and we've brought food."

Dianne saw the large Shopping City bags all around them. She handed Laura the small bag from the convenience store. She looked through it and said, "We have all this and more now. They both laughed and praised God. Laura said, "This reminds me of David when he sent his mighty men to get him a drink from the well near Bethlehem."

"And you're David and I'm the mighty man?" Dianne said with a hint of sarcasm. Laura nodded and smiled.

Dianne looked at her in an amused way with her hands on her hips, and said, "You're right and I'm sure that sitting with the Lord right now, David and his mighty men are saying to each other, 'So that's how two girls would do that.'" They laughed uncontrollably. When Laura recovered she said, "I'm sorry for making you go. God has set a table in the presence of our enemies."

Dianne said, "In more ways than one," and they recounted each other's stories. Dianne told her about the 43 soldiers who accepted the Lord and how they were to remain in their present positions and help them in their escape plans. Laura explained how these 17 soldiers had fearfully come up to her and begged for Jesus. They praised God for this turn of events.

They sat down and began to talk the situation over when Laura pleaded for a place to go to the washroom. They were not alone anymore. Dianne tried to get the lieutenant to help her open a barred tomb, but he declined. None of the new converts were quite over their old fears of the dead. So Dianne had to use a bit of C-10 she still had to blow it open. Laura asked if this was okay to use it this way. Dianne said, "We'll apologize at the resurrection," and they both laughed again.

They sat down again and talked the situation over with the lieutenant as Dianne dug the computer out of where Laura put it when the soldiers came up to her. Dianne had several plans. She did find a way out, but it would not be one for a pregnant lady to try. She explained, "But now with these soldiers 17 soldiers and their wire cutters they can go out wherever there is a weakness and where the 43 are and protect you as they go. I could stay here and draw the attention of the others and keep them busy while you get away."

Laura did not approve and did not want to separate from Dianne whether it meant life or death.

Dianne argued, "I'm the one they want and you are now the one they cannot identify. And as long as they don't have lights and we have this darkness as cover we need to use it."

Suddenly searchlights went on and began immediately panning the entire perimeter. Even the quarry side was now illuminated. The lieutenant told them, "These lights are late. They would have used them earlier, but someone sabotaged the power units."

Dianne exclaimed, "Thank God for the new converts. But these lights ruin our plans."

A battle erupted amongst the army around them. Something had gone wrong and the new converts had been found out somehow. She began to hear from her ear computer the orders of the contending commanders but she also received signals that indicated her own forces were in the area. She typed on the computer and opened her coded channels. "What's our status and what's happening?" She heard from Cheryl, that she, Megan and Todd were in the area. Dianne told them not to join the battle, but to back off. "I'm in the hot seat now and I can't see a way out. I'm fully exposed to Aliadin. Stay away and write me off. It's better to let me go and save yourselves to fight another day," Dianne said. She did not get an immediate response. Then Todd spoke, "We're going to try to find a way." Dianne responded, "No, don't do it. You'll be caught and killed with us. If God wants us to get out He will find a way but stay out and be patient." The battle went on for some time between the newly baptized soldiers and their counterparts. With some binoculars from the lieutenant they could see more purple police units and some of Aliadin's elite commandos arriving and putting an end to this coup. Some helicopters clattered overhead and landed in a distant field.

Now it felt more like the Alamo. The seventeen new Christian soldiers positioned themselves for a last stand.

Then there seemed to be a lull and Dianne watched what she missed for the hours she was gone and what Laura had seen. Mark was now functioning and could communicate. Elle directed Mark to Dianne's link and the screen in his mind that he could direct his thoughts to. Elle told him that his sister and Laura had watched all of his trial and his being beaten up and his transformation to a robot. They were watching now and she asked him if there was anything he wanted to say to them. He said to both of them that he was all right and thankful to Elle for helping him. He asked them not to feel sorry for him. He was not in pain. He did miss his body and with Elle looked forward to wrestling with Joanne when Jesus restored them. He told Dianne that he was grateful to her for all she had done for him and looked forward to the renewed triangle in heaven. He even recalled for her a number of their antics and family jokes that she remembered fondly.

He then addressed Laura and told her how he longed
to take their walks together again and he recalled many
of their most private and tender thoughts and encouraged her to be strong and trust Jesus. He addressed the
baby and told it to take care of Mom. He knew now what
being a baby in a womb must be like again. And like an
unborn child he had an angel holding him close to the
Lord's bosom. Mark quoted Matthew 18:10, "Their angels in heaven always see the face of my Father in
heaven." He also quoted Psalm 34: 7, "The angel of the
Lord encamps around those who fear him, and he deliv-
ers them." "Remember Mom. We will be a family again
and finally you can meet my parents and Joanne too.
Laura, I wish I could hold you close right now, feel your
hair and your face. I love you."

Dianne had to wipe the tears from her eyes and blow
her nose. Then she noticed the number of repeat hits
that the computer checker tabulated for that sequence.
She looked at Laura who was looking at her and she
smiled that winning meek smile at her. Then Dianne
moved and hugged her as both cried for a long time and
then she sat with her arm around her. Laura put her head
against Dianne's and she cried until she was too weary
to cry. It was in the early morning hours now and Laura
felt her morning sickness coming on and had to crawl to
the designated place. Dianne tended her until she could
sit and rest again. Dianne turned to the computer again
and Laura sat up hoping their contact with Mark would
be renewed. Dianne began to work on it and found her
connection to Elle blocked. Instead, the antichrist appeared on the screen and addressed Dianne by name and

when she tried a few things found that the computer was frozen there. Aliadin said, "You miserable witch. You will soon be wriggling before me. You will be captured by your next daylight. But as you wait, let me show you your brother now." Of course what was meant to be horror for them was already old news. He showed Mark the robot as he was now. "Now, Diana, goddess of the graveyard, or hell's human hag, watch your brother recant your childish religion."

Now Mark' mission went into action. Mark said, or more properly, the angel with him using Mark's computer voice recited from Ezekiel 28:2–10, 2 Thessalonians 1:8–9; 2: 3–4,8–12; Revelation 19: 11–16. Even the computer voice sounded more animated than it was meant or thought it could be and the message was in flawless ancient Hebrew.

Speechless for a moment, Aliadin became furious and he made sure Dianne and Laura watched him as he kicked and smashed Mark's robot body. Even when it seemed there could be no more life, his message board still read, "Your doom is assured." He made some loud orders to his generals and there was some activity as he continued to smash Mark's robot to bits and with it the last of his life. The bullets started flying, the helicopters began moving in, and men on the ground started moving in toward the hill they occupied. The seventeen soldiers began to fire at will and Dianne simply kept Laura down and by her as she fired over the tops of the grave stones that surrounded them at the enemy forms coming rapidly toward her, felling one per shot. As with all the other facets of her underground marine experience, Dianne had an extraordinary eye and now used the accumulated weapons given her by the saved soldiers. As she fired away, Cheryl and Megan reported to her that they were sorry but they could do nothing for her and were backing off and would stand by to see if they could mount a rescue if they were taken out of the cemetery. They both said in unison, "Todd is not with us and we don't know his whereabouts. We love you Di."

"I love you guys," she said. They were forced to fire at the helicopters and their searchlights. Soon smoke bombs were thrown and then thrown back by the defenders.

Inside Mark's world he really had it easy. His angel told him that he should not speak, but that the words would be given him to speak. So when the antichrist tested him he simply lay with his angel who now held him with both arms as if a dad was holding a sitting child in his lap. When the antichrist's anger rose, the angel moved to hugging him as a dad would hug a child with his face buried into his chest. The angel shielded him with his back. In the invisible realm Satan came to attack him as the antichrist moved to attack him in the visible world. The angel received the blows as Mark's robot body was smashed to bits. His heart and mind were also bruised and then smashed to pieces with the machinery and components. At the point of death it was like a door opened behind him and the angel moved him to the door. When Mark ceased to function on the outside and died on the inside, his spirit with the angel began to move out. Mark saw the room with the antichrist standing over his smashed remains and Elle his robot friend standing quietly by watching with the generals in his private throne room. He had a body again. Then he was moving upward with his arms extended. His angel held him around his middle. A familiar hand took hold of his right hand.

Chapter 26

THE ONLY LORD

The sun was just rising in the east on another unusually warm but what would normally be a beautiful fall day. The trees and gravestones that had been surrounded by so many beautiful days simply waited for another day.

Laura had been in a battle before and like the last she longed for it to be over, but now had no expectations either of surviving or escaping. She felt rather peaceful as she watched Dianne over her firing away. She simply prayed for a swift end.

Dianne wanted to go down fighting and did not mind taking as many with her as was possible. The ear computer told her of all the enemy instructions and she dreaded being captured, but she would submit to the Lord's will.

Neither she nor Laura knew that most of their Christian soldiers had been killed. They were surrounded by hundreds of men and a helicopter overhead illuminated them. Some of them held someone familiar out in front as a shield and she ceased firing. She had run out of ammunition anyway and clicked away as she moved around in a circle. An enemy commando came close to Laura with a knife and was about to stab her. In a few skillful moves Dianne drew his attention, made him drop the knife, and broke his neck in seconds. The purple police and elite commandos now stood around her with their weapons aimed at her from every direction. Todd stood in their grasp, his wrists handcuffed behind him. "I had to come. If you go I go. I love you," he said. Several soldiers grabbed hold of Dianne. It was too late to scold him for disobeying orders and so she said what was on her heart, "I love you so much," as tears ran down her cheeks. Then he yelled, "I'm the leader you're looking for."

"You lie like a devil," yelled the commander for Aliadin's personal force. "We know now that it is this witch!" He turned to Dianne and yelled in her face, "This she-devil will pay dearly and miserably for opposing our lord and killing his people."

He held up a two-way computer screen so Aliadin could see them and give them orders. Dianne struggled wildly between two soldiers when she saw how beaten up Todd was and kicked at an officer, striking him hard in the face. His nose bleeding, he retaliated and had her legs held down as he beat her in the stomach. They got Laura up and handcuffed her wrists behind her. Dianne fought and hated this moment. The commander in charge tired of her resistance asked Aliadin for his orders. "Break the witch leader's hands and feet so she will no longer resist or be able to fight or get away. But leave the rest of her for me."

She yelled, "Jesus Christ is Lord. He is my Savior in whom I trust."

"We curse your god who is the devil," yelled Aliadin. "I am the Messiah. I am God and there is no other."

All her being loathed her helplessness to the enemy even for a few minutes. The officers poured on the scorn and threats and spat into her face as they held one of her hands down on a flat gravestone. Todd pleaded with them that he was the dangerous one. Laura cried. A purple policeman produced a heavy iron pipe. He swung and brought it down on her hand. In one blow it shattered several bones in her hand. She cried out in agony. The pain was intense. All the soldiers around them grew quiet. Tears streamed from Todd and Laura's eyes, but through her pain Dianne cried out, "Thank You Jesus for allowing me to suffer for Your name."

The commander growing angrier slapped her face and told her to be quiet. Then they took both her shoes and socks off and put one of her feet on the gravestone. The same purple policeman readied the heavy iron bar. Just as he swung it she yelled, "I love Jesus." The bar cracked the bone leading to her big toe, but just to be sure it broke he swung it hard again. Dianne's intense cries once again brought dead silence. She experienced a momentary flashback to when she was six and Mom sat on the bed with Joanne and her, pulling the splinters from their feet as they had run barefoot into the unfinished room addition. Once again she refused to be quiet even though the smallest movement of her body brought sharp pain from her hand or foot and she trembled. She cried out, "Jesus Christ is Lord. He is my Lord. There is no other. Repent and go to heaven or reject Him and go to hell."

Her left hand was now put on the stone. The bar swung again and she cried out as two bones snapped in that hand. She yelled out, "I love my Lord Jesus Christ." In another flashback she was six years old again and she ran into her dad's arms as he lifted her off the ground hugging her and smothering her face with kisses.

Her left foot was now placed on the stone and instead of resisting and tensing up, she relaxed and said, "Lord, not my will, but Yours be done," as the bar shattered the bone that led to her big toe and she cried out again from the sharp pain. She yelled out, "Do not be afraid of those who kill the body, but cannot kill the soul. Rather be afraid of the one who can destroy both soul and body in hell."

Some soldiers in the crowd saw her bravery and suffering in another light and understood her words and they knelt around the captives and at a distance around the hill and their voices could be heard to mutter. "Jesus Christ is Lord. He is my Lord. There is no other."

Aliadin, his personal guard troops and the purple police officers grew increasingly angry and incensed and had all those shot who had acknowledged Dianne's words and now gave their allegiance to Jesus Christ. All the other soldiers around her were ordered to shout out the praises of Aliadin and that he was the only real God. They had Dianne's wrists handcuffed behind her which was a very painful exercise with her broken hands. More painfully they made her kneel. The commander yelled at her, "Can your God save your lover?" And he spat in her face.

Todd was made to kneel and with the iron pipe they methodically broke ribs in his back and side and a collarbone. While this was happening Todd cried out, "Jesus Christ is my Savior and Lord. There is no other." He haltingly prayed out loud for Laura and Dianne and then said, "Lord forgive these soldiers. They don't know what they're doing." When he could no longer talk and he began spitting up blood, Dianne cried out, "Here is a real gentleman who loves me and I love him. The rest of you are soulless beasts who can only hate, hurt, and kill."

Now their attention turned to Laura who was made to kneel. The officers around her told what all their men would do to her. She began to tremble as she did when she was in their prison. Dianne seeing this hoped to still save her somehow and she now spoke to reactivate her tooth computer. As quietly as possible she said, "Blue geese swim with the swan." This was her coded message to Cheryl and Megan to follow where Laura would be taken and rescue her. A soldier near her told the commander that the witch was making an incantation. She started to repeat the message but the commander realized what she was doing and slapped her face. He called for some pliers. Her mouth was then forced open and he saw the one capped tooth and pulled it out and with it the mini-computer. He also noticed the ear stud and took it out of her ear. He knew not to crush them because they would instantly send out a distress call with the smallest microscopic component that could not be crushed. Instead he opened his canteen and dropped them into the water. All communication thus stopped.

Now as they taunted and threatened Laura she could only pray. Dianne now knew true helplessness and as helpless as Christ on the cross. "Please, Lord," she prayed silently, "let them do their worst to me. I deserve it, Lord. I am given to You completely but rescue Laura. I pray for Your mercy to her here and now."

Instead of leading Laura away as they had threatened, Aliadin, who was becoming ever more angry with the situation as it was reported to him, commanded, "Let there be no hope of rescue for the devil's lover and this other garbage," meaning Laura, "Have them shot here and now. And bring the witch queen to me with all speed by tomorrow." Laura, trembling and in tears, began to pray, "Lord Jesus Christ come and save Your servants from these vile enemies of Yours. God, our Father, remember Your children and rescue us."

The purple police commander came behind Laura and Todd and yelled at Dianne, "Let's see your miserable devil god bring this dog back from the dead. We will give this cemetery two more of its own." Two of Aliadin's elite force moved close and drew their pistols and aimed them at Todd and Laura, when suddenly, the lights went out.

It was as if there never was a sun. The moon that was on the other horizon was of no help. There were no stars. Her computer that lay open on the ground was still in Dianne's view and she thought she saw the beginning of a mathematical formula with a post-script in ancient Hebrew. She praised God, as the computer popped and went off. Instantly, every computer everywhere went out, including the two-way screen that Aliadin was using. There was no power anywhere on earth. Even flashlights were useless. Thick lightening struck and the ground shook and every eye turned upward. A light was illuminating everything.

To the redeemed there came the sweetest, strongest, most beautiful trumpet music ever heard. To the lost loud, terrifying noises trumpeted doom.

The real Christ, Jesus Christ, could be seen coming on the clouds. The Alpha and the Omega, the Son of Man and Son of God, Israel's Redeemer and a thousand names went through the minds of His people as they looked on in the richest joy there ever could be. His face and hands and feet were as bright as many suns and His clothes so white people everywhere saw His coming. Even if they shut their eyes they saw Him coming. The blind, deaf, and dumb, those in comas and in their robot bodies could all see and hear Him. The sick, the diseased, the drugged, the drunk, those in their Somodromes all saw Him. They either hated and despised Him and attempted to flee or they loved Him and couldn't wait for the next part. The Christian armies and underground movements that had fought the antichrist's forces around the world changed places as they now came out of hiding; it was the antichrist's forces that headed for the caves and underground bunkers. There was no delay. Christ's angels pursued and slew them as they went. His lightening power struck many times now and the ground shook and many, but not all the graves and tombs cracked and opened. The resurrected stood all around the cemetery. Several stood in the midst of the prisoners, commanders, and soldiers. They were young and animated and alive and their bodies so real, but whole and different from when they died. The difference was as night is to day. The resurrected people waved and shouted to Christ and to each other.

The soldiers and purple police around Laura, Dianne and Todd were beside themselves and fled as fast as they could. But the lightening power of God that raised the dead killed the soldiers, police, and Aliadin's special forces as they ran. And it was a terrible death for their lives were sucked out from inside. Their eyes and tongues rotted in their sockets and their blood ran from every pour. Their skin and bones shriveled and imploded and their bodies fell and decayed quickly as small worms ate them. It was as if the breath God put in each of their bodies was revoked and sucked out and their spirits went to some dimension that could not be seen—a dimension without time, space, or light. The smell in the air around the damned was a foul odor of decay and death. But for the redeemed there was the most attractive fragrance ever experienced. To those enemies of Christ who were allowed to linger and run a little longer there was a grinding of teeth and many sighs of regret that were the beginnings of hell. For the redeemed, the revealed Truth was now satisfying to the extreme and to the core of their beings. Heaven had begun for them.

Those same strokes of lightning power brought healing to Laura, Dianne and Todd who suddenly found their broken and bruised bodies healthy and whole again as their handcuffs fell off. They were not just healed but transformed. Thus besides all the abuses by their captors being healed, old cavities and fillings, Dianne's bruises and scars, and Laura's flat feet were all fixed. They were beside themselves as they laughed, shouted, and danced. Another strike of God's power and a call from heaven and those who had died, but now lived rose to meet Christ in the air. The soldiers who had come to Jesus the night before and those who had just done so at the last minute in Dianne's witnessing to them in her suffering stood up and rose in great joy and waved at the three of them. Dianne saw her mother and father and they waved to her. She made a war whoop. Another curious thing was that Laura was no longer pregnant and she wondered about the baby. An angel nearby told them that it was safe and wanted in heaven and she would see it soon. The angel took an unseen bundle and flew toward Christ. Soon they too rose and were flying toward Christ. If they could have looked away from Christ they would have seen the cemetery, the quarry, Rosedale and the downtown farther away being destroyed from above and below. But the world had no significance anymore because the only thing that really mattered was to see Jesus Christ.

They saw more and more of their familiar friends and all the fellowship that had survived. Finally, this group was caught up with the dead who had risen first. And a tremendous worship and singing time was made stronger with more and more of the elect joining the crowd. Todd, Dianne, and Laura joined hands with Mark and Joanne and they did a jig together in the air. Mom and Dad, and Charles and Naomi joined them, and nothing really mattered but the most joyous worship and singing that was ever heard.

Mark and Laura had to pinch themselves to know if they were dreaming, but it was for real.

The first resurrection saints were joined by a remnant of Israel. These Jews had been oppressed and persecuted along with the Christians. They had accepted and recognized Jesus Christ as the Messiah and their Savior and Lord during the tribulation because of the witness and protection of Christians. Together and with all their angels they praised and worshiped Jesus Christ in the air and all around Him as He descended with them back to earth and his feet rested on the Mount of Olives. As the redeemed continued this worship, Christ, along with their angels, routed and destroyed the antichrist, his prophet, their armies and his images and palaces in the real physical world. He then bound and imprisoned Satan and his demonic host in the spiritual realm.

Jesus Christ looked on all His redeemed tribulation martyrs and saints and asked them to follow Him. He walked through the Golden Gate and sat on his throne on the temple mount cleared of all the idolatry of Aliadin's rule. Now His eternal kingdom came to rule and all those who were raised in this first resurrection were invited to join Him in the work of governing the earth. The Messiah, the Christ, who looked so bright and powerful before, now looked so human and He spent time loving and addressing them.

The happenings of that day, the feelings of the redeemed, and the total description of Christ's splendor and glory cannot be described in fallen earthly words. The events of that one day; the Rapture, His return, the victory over all His and their enemies and seeing His face were wonderful beyond all measure and would have satisfied any of His people, but this was only the beginning of the things He would do for them. For them the best part was spending time alone with Jesus.

Jesus spent time with all of His redeemed people in that first resurrection. This included all who had gone through the great Tribulation and all who had been persecuted by the antichrist's spirit in tribulations from the beginning of the church and the martyrs of all times. This included the apostles and many from the early church. This made for some interesting company if there was any waiting to be done. The second resurrection of the general dead of all time and the Great White Throne Judgment would not take place for a thousand years. And so He spent time with each individual and allowed all the time they wanted. How He did this no one could say, and nobody ever seemed to have to wait very long. It was one of the wondrous features of His being and power. Perhaps it was because in Christ's power there is no time. He also could meet them in what each believer knew as his or her secret place, that place where only Jesus and that person knew about. More impressive was that in these meetings Jesus treated every one of His people as if they were the only object of His attention and delight in the universe.

Chapter 27

HIS LOVING EMBRACE

Jesus seemed busy talking to many small groups with many questions on the temple mount and as He did so, He saw Joanne coming up the steps fighting through various crowds. Some of these wanted to talk to her. Even some of the apostles wanted to talk with her, but she fended them off. Finally her eyes met the Savior's and she ran up the remaining steps and across the pavement and she flew into the Lord's arms without any hesitation. She embraced Him with her arms and legs. "I couldn't wait any longer," she said having difficulty getting her breath. He knew she was still getting used to having a body again after six years without one. "I wondered when you would come," He said.

He immediately withdrew with her to her secret place. It was in her bedroom and they both sat on the bed much as the triangle, except much closer. They held hands and she looked in His eyes with tears flowing in love and adoration. He said, "I remember all your nights in here talking to Me. I loved how you shared everything down to the smallest things and details. I loved your poems, even the ones you hid from the eyes and ears of your friends and family. I loved your explanations and your faith and your singing to Me." He recalled to her mind her whole life and how He was so close to her all time. She couldn't say a word and was so overcome with emotion she got up and embraced Him so tightly and climbed and sat in His lap. Simultaneously, they said to each other, "Thank you for sacrificing yourself for me." This made her cry in love of Him even more. How could He compliment her like that? She added, "Thank You for wanting to spend time with me. I didn't think I was very important. I wasn't smart like Dianne or Mark. I used to wonder sometimes how the Master of the universe as Dianne would call You would have any interest in me? I was so silly all the time. My sister and brother were more . . ."

He cut her off. "You remained a child for Me. You used your heart. You loved Me. You loved your brother and sister and you sacrificed yourself for them. Dianne and so many people depended on you. You helped them save so many people and helped the secret force members in their difficult times. Thank you for being My servant in the most difficult time. Thank you for enduring that horrible prison of darkness and confinement for Me for those six years. It is your heart and your love for Me that make you Mine and very important. Even when you were imprisoned as a robot you remained a child at heart and I was with you and you know it. And when you sacrificed your life for Mark and Dianne, My mercy and grace were sufficient to bring you to Me. All your love, prayers, and devotion to Me matter. I want you and Elle to be My personal helpers and assistants from now on in the millennial kingdom. She cried and hung onto Him for as long as she could. When they both knew their time alone was ending, she whispered in His ear one more request. "That will have to wait until you're a little stronger. Remember what happened to Jacob."

Dianne had been avoiding it, but Jesus would not allow it. When she had risen to meet Him in the air she had rejoiced in Him and when their eyes met then she worshiped from afar. Now He sought her out. She wanted to fall on her face before Him, but He would not let her. He made her embrace Him and He put His forehead against hers and looked into those sharp green eyes that were now filling up with tears.

"You did not fail me," he said, knowing her thoughts.

She moaned, "I couldn't save the thousands and Deidra, and Trisha and Susan and . . ."

"It's all right. You can let it all out now." Jesus' eyes were in tears.

She began to cry hard and the sobs were truly heart cries. She could not speak. With her tremendous mind and memory and the desire for perfection that He put there, together they both saw all those difficult days of the Tribulation. First Jesus showed her persuading the triangle to keep secrets that concerned the whole family and concealing their early run-ins with Uncle Ted, but not telling her parents. Then she saw the explosion that killed her parents and her decision to be a part of the underground where she had to kill or be killed. She saw the first time she killed someone, the decisions, all the bombs and deaths and war she had to make in order to be a real soldier. She saw the agony of seeing some of her soldiers captured or killed and of having to kill her own defecting soldiers. They saw together all the horror of the antichrist's prisons and trains and the men and women and children she could not save pooled in blood or partly burned or in ashes. She saw the horrors done to Joanne and her explosive death, the torment of seeing Mark, but unable to do anything for him, all the frustrations, the constant danger, the untiring and unceasing work, the burden of being in command, and how everything depended on her decisions when her people were placed in danger by her . . . and the added frustrations of her own female desires for company and her secret love for Todd.

In broken language in between sobs and tears, she said, "I deserved that punishment in the end . . . and I should have been crucified. I so wanted to be . . . and do the right thing for You . . . but I couldn't and I didn't. In my taking the sword against my enemy, I became like them . . . wanting to judge and take revenge. In this . . . and in not telling Mom and Dad about Uncle at the beginning . . . I sinned against You and by the enemy's law and Yours I deserved to be crucified . . . but not with You—but as another thief beside You."

Jesus held her close for a long time as the sobs of the seven years of heartfelt frustration came out. He said to her, "I love you so much. Your faith in Me was incredible and what mistakes you made or you think you made, they were forgiven when I saw you from my cross at the other end of history. You did the job exactly as I called you out to perform. And you know how I loved you and you would have gladly been crucified for Me in the end, but I did not call you to suffer that." He had her place her now-perfect hands against and in His and her perfect feet on His. "I suffered that death for you on the cross so you, you, Dianne Brogen would not have go through that and also for that stubborn pride of yours. You did not have to prove anything to Me."

"But what about the apostles and your men and women in history and Deidra who did go through that?" Dianne moaned.

"What is that to you? That is none of your business. I did not call you to that. Don't ever compare yourself to anyone else ever again. I love you just as you are."

Dianne began weeping and He now held her close. And she embraced Him and she said, "Thank you. I love You so much. Thank You for saving me and letting me serve You."

He said, "In serving Me, I saw your love for Me. You used all your time, gifts, and talents for me. You used your head. Thank you for using all your physical strength for Me. Thank you for remaining pure and untouched for Me. In your love and obedience for Me, in all these ways, you did become My bride." This brought new tears of love and adoration and she worshiped Him.

Jesus took her to their secret place. They sat down on the step to the walkway that led to the front porch of the family home in Rosedale under a new and the most glorious elm tree ever seen. He went through her life moment by moment. In the midst of it He said to her, "Thank you for sacrificing your childhood for me. You grew way beyond your years." They laughed and cried together through all her days.

He even talked physics with her. He put His head against hers and together He showed and talked math with her until her head was spinning with more and more. She had to make Him stop because she could not keep up and eventually had to make Him stop altogether. She couldn't comprehend it all. She knew that this was just the introduction. It would take every day for a thousand years nonstop in her present state to show her the universe mathematically and that has an end because the present universe is finite. Then it would take every day, all day for eternity in earthly time to give her a small sampling of God's infinite nature. She worshiped the Master of the universe. He promised her when the time was right He would take her on a tour of the atom and show her how the universe began.

In the meantime, He asked her if she would be one of those in charge of His special force in His millennium army. She smiled, "I would love to," and asked, "Could Wayne and the rest of my force be with me?" He said, "It has already been done." Then he frowned at her and she immediately responded, "What is it Lord?"

"Isn't there someone you are forgetting? The someone you thought about many a day besides me and should be included in our plans?"

"But we're not supposed to . . . ."

"I never said you couldn't love someone here. You can love him more completely here in the new millennium than you could ever love someone in the old fallen carnal way," said Jesus.

Here he brought Todd out and before the Lord they hugged and kissed for the first time.

When Mark met with Jesus He automatically took him for a walk. But what a walk, through the hills of a beautiful country beyond description, with the sun shining, the birds singing, and the freshest air he had ever breathed. He told Mark He was with him on every one of his walks. Mark continually fell to his knees and hugged Him around His feet and worshiped Him for he loved Him so much. But Jesus kept making him rise and walk with Him. Mark thanked Him for his body again which he was still getting used to.

Then he stopped the Savior and asked, "Weren't You supposed to show me my whole life as I died?" The Savior smiled and said, "This is the right moment." Then Jesus embraced Mark and Mark returned the embrace and they remained this way for some time with their heads together. In that time, Mark's mind began replaying everything from the beginning of his life as a baby until the last moments. Wherever Mark paused, Jesus said, "I was there, with you." Mark tested this and remembered silly times and boring times in school, family fights, and quarrels. Every time Jesus said, "I was there."

"When I lied to Mom and Dad about my algebra?" he asked. When Jesus said, "I was there," he winced. When Mark stopped at the snowy night when he prayed for his family. Jesus said, "I was there." After the death of his family he saw himself on the bed crying and Mrs. Danforth rubbing his back and then at the funeral. Jesus wept and said, "I was there."

Then his mind went through the time he spent with Uncle and Mark pleaded with him to skip over this time but his mind went on viewing it anyway. "Please," Mark implored, "not there," as he recalled his ignoring God and his growing enjoyment of Uncle's enticements and pleasures and his sinful times in the Somodrome. He had stopped praying and reading his Bible. He did not walk with the Lord. He had ignored God's warnings even before meeting with Dr. Crawford. Mark cried now as he heard Jesus say, "I was there." Jesus, in tears, held him tighter and said, "I couldn't bear to see you like that. I missed our times together. But I was there. I love you so much. I saw you when I was on the cross at the other end of history and I forgave you."

Jesus showed him the holes in His hands and feet and Mark, trembling and weeping uncontrollably, fell to his knees and kissed those hands. Jesus made him stand and He placed those nail-scarred hands together on Mark's back and over his heart. Mark sobbed uncontrollably in love for the Savior and his whole being melted in His embrace.

"Thank You for loving me so much. I did not deserve it," Mark stammered.

When Mark recovered from this he wanted very much to have the examination continue. He enjoyed seeing his meeting Laura and all their adventures from the Lord's perspective and knowing that indeed He was with them through it all.

Jesus said, "Thank you for being pure and holy in your relationship with Laura until you were properly married. And thank you for listening to Me and obeying Me at the peril of your life and for all of your sacrifices for Me in the last days."

Jesus brought Joanne, Dianne and Mark together and they grinned at each other, held hands and sat down and renewed the triangle of knees and legs on top of a hill. They laughed and remembered all their old jokes and times together for some time. Then Jesus joined them and sat outside it for sometime telling them that He saw them in all their times together and heard all their prayers. They begged Him to stand in the middle of them and they worshiped Him as they held hands and raised them to Him and sang for Him. Then He showed them how their prayers and commitment to Him and the commitment to each other affected the lives of others. Soon Mom and Dad knelt and hugged them. When they stood, others came and stood around their triangle in increasing circles around them. Out came Laura, Jerome, Andy, the Danforths, Dudleys and the other house church families, Dr. Crawford, the fellowship, the secret force, countless soldiers and refugees both to the camp and to the neighborhood centers and the many saved, lost, and rescued including not a few enemy soldiers, and many people they had never met, but had been influenced by prayer or indirect influence through the others . . . because they were faithful.

The Savior brought Mark and Laura together once again and took them on a long walk through the hills.

But Laura had yet to have her time with Jesus and so Jesus asked to be excused and He and Laura went to her secret place. That place was on the screened back porch of her grandmother's house where she sat and prayed her heart out in the afternoons after high school, during college, and in the evenings. The older folks, including her aunt and uncle, sat on the screened front porch. When the Savior embraced Laura, she told Him, "I don't know how many times I wished I could have done this in those days. I wanted a father and a mother so much that I wanted You to be my father. I felt so useless and unwanted. Was I a mistake with my parents?"

Jesus said, "You were never a mistake, but called for my purpose and plan. You were wanted and you were too hard on your parents and grandparents and aunt and uncle. They're all here, you know, and you will meet them soon. They love you very much."

"Then what about Mark and I and the baby?" she asked. Jesus looked into her eyes and said, "I was there on that porch every night when you prayed for a marriage and a family. I saw how much you loved the children in the orphanage you worked in and in the nursery and Sunday school in church and how you so enjoyed baby sitting the children of the fellowship and being with the children in the neighborhood center with Dianne."

Laura enjoyed all this but was still troubled. "But aren't we in Your millennial kingdom and in heaven too? And so we're not married any more, right? How can we have children?" she asked. Christ smiled, "Oh, you of such little faith." He called Mark back and He joined hands with them and had them hold each other's hands just like Charles had and He smiled at them. He said, "What I have put together no one can separate. You will have the family you so desired. Your family will serve Me in the millennium, but you are all married to Me now."

"For you the old things have passed away and the new has come. I'm sure you have noticed that your love for Me and for each other is so much greater than it was in your old life and that it is growing. However, it is not sexual is it? You truly love each other and you love all your brothers and sisters, moms and dads now like you never did or could have in your fallen state. Your sexuality in your old life was meant to teach you the sheer pleasure in giving yourself over to one other in the most tender ways. To love each other there meant sacrificing one's self for the other. Marriage was meant to combine the highest physical and spiritual pleasure and joy that My man and woman could enjoy and know fulfillment. Love and marriage were supposed to remind you of My love for you and the close relationship that we were to have. Sin ruined that and many married couples who did not really know Me or My heart misunderstood and abused this gift, and consequently each other. You two enjoyed all this because you knew Me and really loved each other. Now you can begin to enjoy the new creation with Me."

"Lord, when you say Mark and I have a family, where is my baby and should we not have more children to properly call it a family?"

Jesus laughed and said, "I want to show you your children." Here the Savior became solemn and looked toward the hills. Mark and Laura looked in that direction. Soon they saw an angel carrying a baby and it was placed in Laura's arms. The angel said, "This is your baby, Mark and Laura. It's a boy." They rejoiced in it for some time, but then they saw more angels and children coming over the hills. Every child had an angel. Some angels carried their small children in their arms. Others led them gently. Others ran with bigger children. Soon they were coming from every direction. They were all healthy, whole, beautiful children and they kept coming and coming until all the hills and fields all around them were filled with babies, infants, and children of all sizes, shapes, ages, and races.

"What does it mean? Who are all these?" Laura asked the Lord.

"These children are like you, Laura and Mark. They knew what it was like to be orphaned. Your own baby here lost his father and was persecuted with you his mother.

"These children came to me during your short lifetime. There are many more. These are the unloved, the aborted, the kidnapped, the murdered, the abandoned, the orphaned, the abused, the battered, the maltreated, the deformed, and the handicapped children that the world did not want, who died before their time. This is your family. Enjoy them, love them, raise them and teach them all things with Me. They will be the leaders of their nations and peoples for me during the Millennium. In the Great White Throne Judgment they will stand with all the unwanted and abused of all time and by their presence will condemn those who refused to repent and who will-fully abused and destroyed them."

He had met with each one and wiped the tears from their eyes. After that the redeemed of that first resurrection had the best reunions, with Jesus addressing families and groups. Dianne's special unit met and rejoiced together with Jesus as He commended their bravery and valor in saving and rescuing so many. Deidra embraced Dianne the longest and spoke of her devotion to her and let her know that Christ gave her special grace and a miraculous entry into heaven out of that fire. Trisha and Susan also embraced Dianne and they renewed their friendship. Now the special force wore white and was clean and healed. They were now children of the light. Before they had worn black and had been forced to work in the darkness. Immanuel Rodriguez met Dianne and thanked her for letting him live and allow-ing him time to repent. Jesus met with all the Christian army forces and thanked them. He rejoiced with Charles and Naomi and the fellowship for their life and work to-gether and all they did in the last days. Dianne and Laura were introduced to Abdul, his family, and the enemy sol-diers who converted in their last hours. There were some awkward moments as when Dianne, Joanne, Laura, or Mark met one of the apostles and they did not know what to say. Jesus introduced Mark, Dianne, Laura and Joanne to a beau-tiful young lady whom they had never seen, but knew very well. "This is Elle and I believe you know her," he said. They all hugged in tears of joy and wonder. They thanked each other for the help each had been to the other. After-wards, many other gals and not a few guys were brought out so Dianne could see all the others who had been robots in her computer spying efforts. Becky had been the personality computer that Dianne had used to get to Mark. Both marveled and thanked her for her help.

When Dianne introduced Todd to Joanne he saw how beautiful and how identical to Dianne she looked. Joanne remarked, "It took you two long enough to take the hint in the marriage game. You hard-heads missed every cue that Wayne, Helga, Evelyn and not a few of your fellow soldiers gave." Dianne chased her sister and they tumbled into a wrestling match. Todd sighed, "Sisters, I never had any," as he looked at Mark and Laura and Jesus who were laughing. Mark shrugged his shoulders and said, "Sorry, but that's the way He made them."

One day Jesus took Mark by the hand and led him on what He called a living history lesson. As they walked Mark noticed that the rest of the first resurrection saints were trailing behind them and that they were walking into an even greater, more immense crowd. Jesus then stopped and asked individuals about their stories. Each one gave a unique testimony that was truly inspiring. Mark thought that if all these stories were turned into books there would be no end to their number, richness, or variety. Each one had a common theme: their faith, love, and devotion to Jesus Christ and their thanks to Him for all He had done for them. As Jesus spoke, Mark realized that He was paraphrasing and making Hebrews 11 more personal and He indicated that these were the martyrs of all of time on earth for Him. By the time He was done speaking and everyone in the two different crowds could stand it no longer, they began to praise and worship the Lamb that was slain for them. They thanked Him for saving them and answering their prayers in this worship. The songs that were sung were never heard before.

There came a day when Mark sat with Laura under a number of glorious trees in a large glade and looked out at the assembled gathering and picnic that was around him; he marveled at what he saw. Around him was Laura holding the baby with Joanne, Debbie, Jackie, Tom, Dick, Dianne, Todd, Elle, Dina and Jerome with many of the children crawling and sitting around their laps. They were all trying to persuade Laura to let them have a turn holding her baby. Mom and Dad sat with Charles and Naomi, Donald Crawford, Ronald Darringen and David and Lisa Simmons, Laura's parents, Wayne Dombrowski, Evelyn Jacobson, Helga Olsen, and Jacob Steinmitz—all laughing and talking. The rest of the camp fellowship gathered around, relating their stories while they sat and played with many of the orphans. Their angels stood behind them. In the middle was Jesus Christ, the Lord of the universe serving the food and drinks.

Later when it was game time, Jesus caught hold of Joanne's arm and she instinctively began to wrestle out of it. She succeeded and a childish glee came over her face. There was a renewed embrace and Jesus laughed as He and

Joanne rolled in the grass. The others sat under the trees and watched. The romp got wilder until Jesus stopped and let her regain her breath. Jesus began to run through the woods and Joanne was after Him and the others joined in a game of tag. When Joanne rested a moment against a tree, suddenly an arm reached around her and she was again on the ground tickling and wrestling with Jesus. She got out of that somehow and ran through the woods with Jesus and everyone else right behind and when Jesus caught her they fell and splashed together into a river. This river came from the direction of Jerusalem and the new temple. Jesus invited everyone to swim. The water was so clean and refreshing that whether you drank it or swam in it you were healed of every lingering problem or doubt.

After catching her breath, Joanne exclaimed, "You are the greatest!" as she looked into the loving eyes of Jesus Christ.

To order additional copies of

PAROUSIA

Have your credit card ready and call:

1-877-421-READ (7323)

or please visit our web site at
www.pleasantword.com

Also available at: www.amazon.com

Printed in the United States
70948LV00003B/44